Murder on Lexington Avenue

Also by Fiona Veitch Smith

The Poppy Denby Investigates Series

1. *A Front-Page Murder*
2. *Murder at the Old Vic Theatre*
3. *Murder on Lexington Avenue*
4. *Murder at Winterton Hall*
5. *Murder at the Art Gallery*
6. *Murder of an Oxford Scientist*

The Miss Clara Vale Mystery Series

1. *The Picture House Murders*
2. *The Pantomime Murders*
3. *The Pyramid Murders*

Murder on Lexington Avenue

Fiona Veitch Smith

embla books

First published in Great Britain in 2024 by

embla books

Bonnier Books UK Limited
4th Floor, Victoria House, Bloomsbury Square, London, WC1B 4DA
Owned by Bonnier Books
Sveavägen 56, Stockholm, Sweden

Originally published as *The Death Beat* by Lion Fiction in 2017.

A CIP catalogue record for this book is available from the British Library.

ISBN: 9781471417849

This book is typeset using Atomik ePublisher.

Printed and bound in Great Britain by Clays Ltd, Elcograf S.p.A.

Embla Books is an imprint of Bonnier Books UK.
www.bonnierbooks.co.uk

FSC www.fsc.org
MIX
Paper | Supporting responsible forestry
FSC® C018072

For Rodney and Megan. Always.

The New Colossus

By Emma Lazarus, 1883

Not like the brazen giant of Greek fame,
With conquering limbs astride from land to land;
Here at our sea-washed, sunset gates shall stand
A mighty woman with a torch, whose flame
Is the imprisoned lightning, and her name
Mother of Exiles. From her beacon-hand
Glows world-wide welcome; her mild eyes command
The air-bridged harbor that twin cities frame.

"Keep, ancient lands, your storied pomp!" cries she
With silent lips. "Give me your tired, your poor,
Your huddled masses yearning to breathe free,
The wretched refuse of your teeming shore.
Send these, the homeless, tempest-tost to me,
I lift my lamp beside the golden door!"

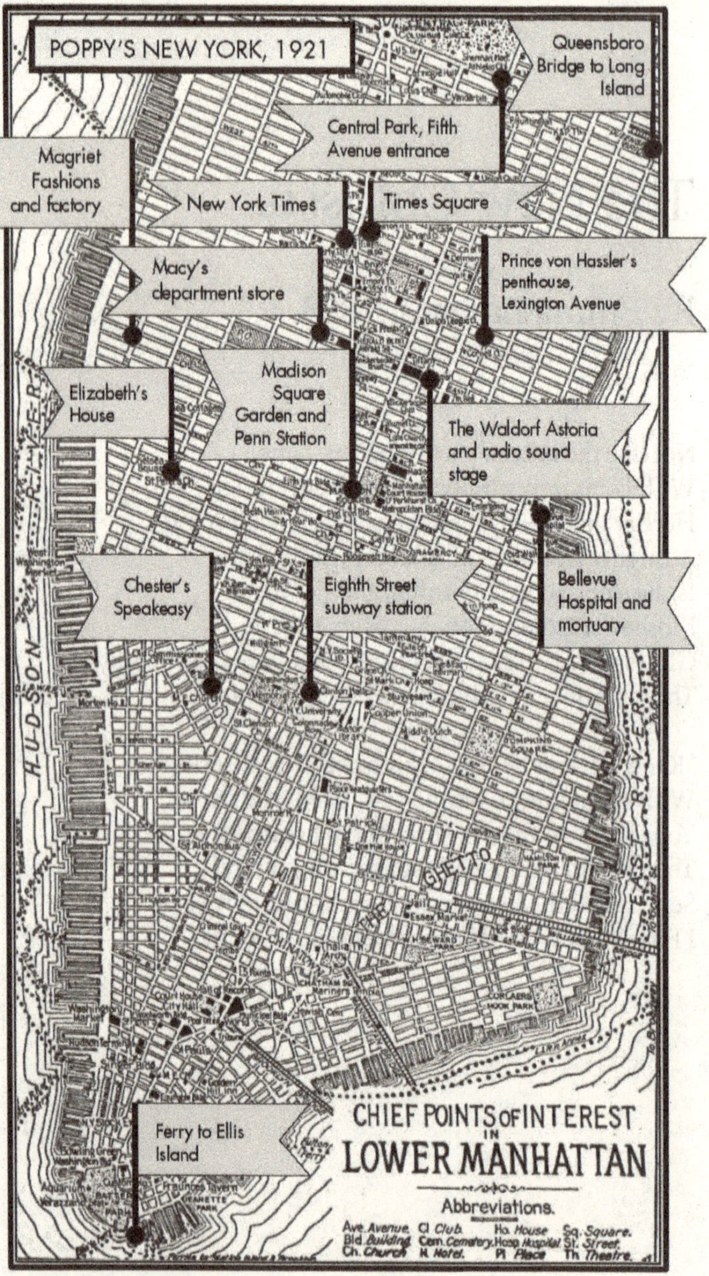

Courtesy of the University of Texas Libraries, The University of Texas at Austin.
From *The Automobile Blue Book*, 1920.

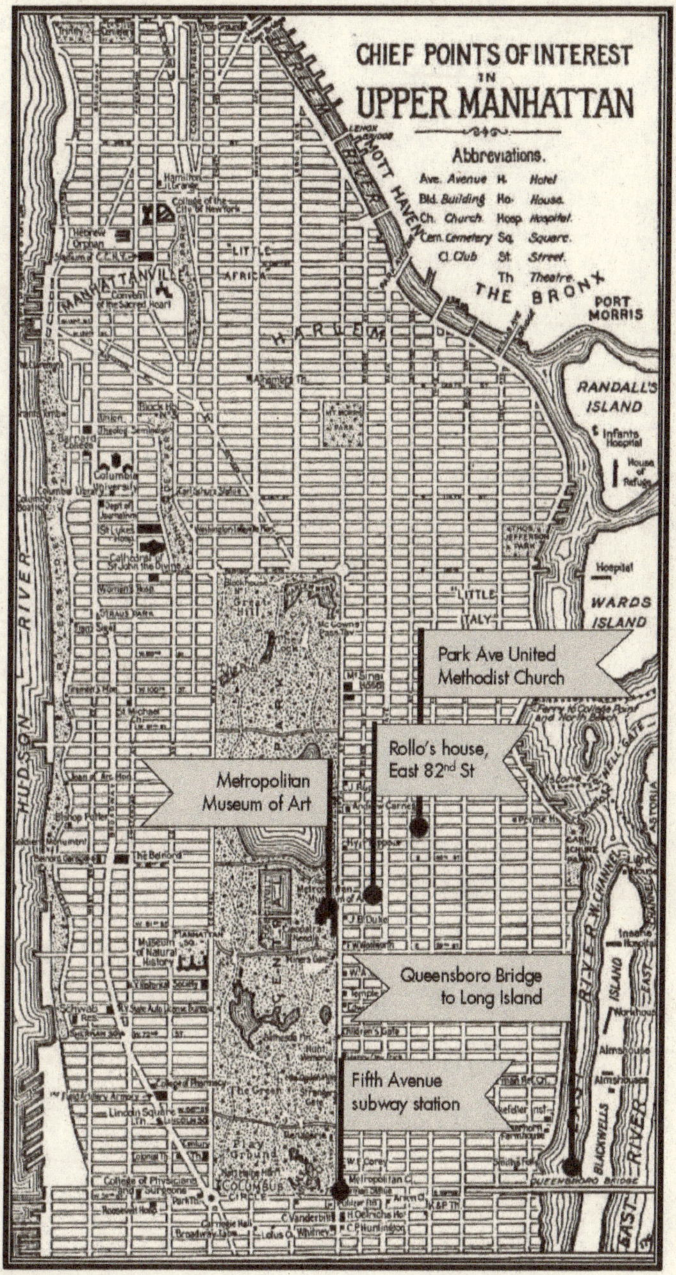

Courtesy of the University of Texas Libraries, The University of Texas at Austin.
From *The Automobile Blue Book*, 1920.

Chapter 1

The ferryman lit a cigarette and waited. He would get into trouble, no doubt, but he didn't care. It was cold, it was late, and the fog that mingled with the sewage fumes, cloying to the shore of the little island, would kill him long before any Lucky Strike. Besides, it wasn't his health his employer was concerned about but rather that the red tip would alert the harbour patrol that something was amiss.

And something was amiss; the ferryman was certain of that. Even though he tried not to think where his illicit cargo ended up when he dropped it on the big island after every trip, when he climbed into bed and placed his hands on his wife's pregnant belly, he feared that he knew. The child would kick against his hand. His wife would stir. And he would think of the jar in the kitchen cabinet that when full would pay for a ticket west. And then, reminded once again of why he was doing what he was doing, he would shelve his conscience again.

He heard the crunch of gravel that signalled footfall at the top of the stone steps. And then, one at a time, his "cargo" made their way down to the jetty and he helped them into his boat, their faces pale and fearful in the swirling fog.

Monday, 1 April 1921, London

The sun rose over London. And for the first time in a week the pea soup fog – known to locals as the London Peculiar – cowed in the face of its optimism. The sulphurous smog slinked its way back through the streets and alleys, past monuments and churches, over barrows and under motorcars until it slipped into the Thames like a wayward child returning to its mother. The face of Big Ben smiled over the city as the wheezing Londoners started their morning commute.

Poppy Denby got off the bus at the bottom of Fleet Street, intersecting with the stream of passengers emerging from Blackfriars tube station. A paperboy brandished a copy of *The Daily Globe* from his stand, declaring: "Thousands of miners stop work today – read all about it!" Poppy did not have to read all about it; she'd just seen it, first-hand. She shuddered to think what this was going to do to the country, but she didn't blame the miners one bit.

The misery she'd witnessed in the mines around Morpeth had not reached the capital, and commuters went about their daily routine as if a state of emergency had not just been called and the whole country was not about to grind to a halt.

Poppy passed St Bride's Church along with black-robed solicitors and barristers heading up to the Temple Inns of Court. As always, she gave a splash of colour to proceedings. Yes, there was bad news abroad; but there was always bad news. And despite what she'd just seen on her recent trip home, and fearing there was more to come, Poppy nonetheless felt a bubble of joy within her. It was spring and in its honour she wore a bright yellow daffodil in her lapel, offset, rather charmingly, by the sage green of her new suede coat.

She had purchased the coat at Harrods with her friend Delilah the previous day. Delilah, the daughter of a Maltese hotel magnate, had bought far more than a new coat, but Poppy had been pleased with her purchase. Oh, and of course the cloche hat she had bought to match. And the shoes . . . she felt a little guilty about the shoes. They were far more than she could really afford on her reporter's salary – even with the clothing allowance she received for being arts and entertainment editor – but nonetheless, she'd given in to Delilah's "Oh darling, aren't they just the cat's whiskers!" After all, the whole purpose of the shopping expedition had been to cheer up her poor old chum, so Poppy just didn't have the heart to say no.

The green Cuban heels clicked on the Fleet Street pavement. "Morning, Sarge!" she called out to the disabled war veteran selling carved wooden crosses outside the Empire Tea Rooms.

"Morning, Miss Denby!" he called up from his folded-up blanket that cushioned his bandaged stumps. His furry friend, a bulldog named Reginald, snuffled Poppy's hand as she reached down to give him a pat and toss some coins into his master's bowl. She would have stopped to chat with Sarge – no doubt he'd have some strong views on the miners' strike – but it was nearly half-past eight and Poppy wanted to get an early start.

"I'll see you later, Sarge!"

"You have a good day, Miss Denby!"

"I will!" She smiled and Sarge soaked in the sunshine.

It was Friday morning and she had to put the finishing touches to her copy for the Saturday morning edition. Poppy prepared herself to ascend the six marble steps into the offices of *The Daily Globe*. In the nine months since she'd been employed on the London tabloid the thrill of those six steps had not worn thin. She noticed a smudge on the brass straps around one of the marble globes that flanked them and took out a handkerchief to wipe it clean. She was proud of her newspaper and even more proud of the articles she had contributed to it – not least the two huge exposés that had set her up as one of the best up-and-coming investigative journalists on Fleet Street. But those sorts of stories were exhausting, and she was grateful that she'd had a few months of "ordinary" events to cover: gallery openings, book reviews, film premieres and celebrity interviews. It was a giddy world and she loved it.

She took in a lungful of spring air – hoping not to inhale too much pollution – and walked into the foyer.

Her heels clicked across the black and white marble floor on her way to the lift. En route her eye caught a new statuette in a marble alcove, carefully positioned to enhance the stylistic theme of the atrium. The concentric geometric frames gave the illusion of depth, and the mirrored back of the alcove reflected multiple versions of the brass Isis. *It* was *Isis, wasn't it?* Poppy leaned forward to look.

"Rollo brought it in this morning. A gift from Miss Reece-Lansdale, apparently." The explanation came from the direction of the reception desk.

"Morning, Mavis! You're back! Did you have a good holiday?"

"Morning, Poppy! I did, thank you. Mr Bradshaw and I took in the sea air in Brighton. How was your Easter break?"

Poppy took a surreptitious look at the black lacquer clock hands embedded directly on the white wall. Should she give Mavis the long story or the précis? Her Easter break, spent with her parents up north in Morpeth, had been ... *interesting*. She'd spent most of the time helping them with a soup kitchen for the families of miners at Ashington Colliery who were struggling to make ends meet on the pittance they were paid. It was in stark contrast to the high society life she was now living and had reminded her to count her blessings.

It was the first time she'd been home since arriving in London the previous summer, and her parents were itching to hear all about her new job ... and the new man in her life. But this did not go as well as she'd hoped. Poppy had been prepared for their concerns about the dangers she'd recently faced in her two big stories, but she had not been prepared for their objections to Daniel. She sighed inwardly ... *The précis, definitely the précis.*

"It was lovely to be home, Mavis. Nothing like home-cooked food, eh?"

Mavis looked at her shrewdly. "Well, isn't that lovely. You'll have to fill me in on it all over a nice cup of tea."

"I will!" declared Poppy, heading for the lift. "But I need to finish a story by deadline or Rollo will have my guts for garters!"

Mavis laughed. "Best you do that, Poppy. He's not in the best of moods ..."

"Thanks for the warning," Poppy offered as she opened the concertina gate and pressed the button for the fourth floor.

It had taken a while for Poppy to get used to her editor's mercurial moods, but she'd learned to stay out of his way as much as possible when he was in one of them and only offered sympathy if he asked for it. She'd also learned not to approach him before he'd had at least his second cup of coffee – which he should be having about now. Rollo was always the first to arrive and the last to leave the office, and Poppy respected his work ethic immensely. But his problem was that he played as hard as he worked, and he often came into the office without having been home. Poppy suspected that Rollo's foul moods were usually preceded by a night at his club. And her suspicions were usually correct.

As the lift stopped on the fourth floor she was met by a tearful

Vicky Thompson, the office assistant. "Oh, Miss Denby, I don't know what's happened," she blurted out, "but it's the worst I've ever seen him!" Vicky shook her head, sniffed back her tears and stepped into the lift. "If anyone wants to know where I am, I'll be helping Mr Molanov in the morgue."

Poppy nodded in sympathy and watched as the young woman pressed the button for the third floor archive, known in journalese as "the morgue".

It was heart-warming to see how well Vicky and the Russian archivist got on. Ivan was now training her to be his assistant – much to Rollo's chagrin. But the archivist didn't care. "Tell that Yankee he can get a doggy body anywhere."

"Dog's body," Poppy had gently corrected.

"He can have as many bodies as he likes! Mees Thompson is going to work for me."

There was no denying that Ivan needed an assistant, particularly now that he had a child at home and no longer spent his after-hours working, trying to keep his loneliness at bay. The bubble of joy rose again in Poppy's chest as she thought of the day Ivan had been reunited with his young daughter – and the role she had played in making it happen.

Yes, Poppy was in an optimistic mood and it would take a lot more than a grumpy editor, a country in industrial turmoil and disapproving parents to quench it. She pushed open the newsroom door and stepped into a haze of pipe smoke and coffee fumes. On her way to her desk she greeted three other journalists pounding away on their Remington typewriters, trying to meet deadline. Among them was the political editor, Ike Garfield, who had written the lead article on the miners' strike. He looked as if he hadn't slept a wink – and if she wasn't mistaken, he was wearing the same shirt, braces and bow-tie as he had the day before. "Morning, Ike. I hope you didn't spend the night here."

The West Indian man raised a tired eyebrow and grunted. *Oh dear,* thought Poppy, then put down her satchel at her desk and went to make them both a cup of tea. But as she opened the door to the small kitchenette she didn't see the diminutive frame of her editor coming out, carrying a hot brew. They cannoned into each other, splashing hot liquid over them both.

"Jake, Mary, and Jehoshaphat!" bellowed Rollo and released a string of New York expletives that would make a dock worker blush.

Poppy was tempted to swear herself when she saw the coffee stains on her new coat and shoes, but she refrained.

Rollo turned on her, his moon-shaped face ablaze. "What the –?"

Poppy put up her hand: "An accident, Rollo. It was an accident. We're equally to blame."

Rollo opened his mouth to speak, then closed it again. He scrunched up his eyes and took in a sharp breath, held it, and exhaled slowly. "Sorry, Miz Denby. Are you all right?"

Poppy's mouth was tight, braced for the fight she had thought was about to come. Then her face softened. "Nothing that won't come out in the wash." She took a dish cloth from the sink and mopped up the spilled coffee on the floor. Rollo stood over her, his short legs planted on either side of the brown pool. She thought for a moment he was going to offer to help, but instead he said: "I'll see you at the ed meeting at twelve. Can you make sure all the troops are there? I've got an important announcement to make."

Poppy looked up at her editor. The blood was slowly retreating from his face and his eyes . . . *Golly, are those tears welling?* But before she could examine him further, he took what was left of his coffee and left the room.

Poppy finished cleaning the floor, then examined the damage to her shoes and coat. Suede stained so easily; she did the best she could but soon decided a visit to the dry cleaners would be needed. She sighed, removed the dripping daffodil from her lapel and threw it in the bin.

Chapter 2

Poppy tapped her way through the morning on her typewriter, organising her thoughts about the play she had seen the previous evening – a controversial new show called *A Bill of Divorcement* – into a well-considered, balanced review. It was an "issue" play about a man returning to his family home after spending some years in a mental asylum only to discover that his wife had divorced him. Under the existing law, something like that could never happen, as women did not have the same rights as men to initiate divorce. But as Poppy and the playwright Miss Clemence Dane both knew, there was a bill working its way through parliament that would give women the same rights as men to sue for divorce.

If the bill was passed, her aunt's dear friend Grace Wilson – currently serving time in Holloway prison for perverting the course of justice – might finally be able to divorce the husband who had been refusing to initiate divorce proceedings for the past seven years.

Poppy wasn't sure how she felt about it. Raised in a Christian home, she believed that marriage should be for life. But having met Grace's estranged husband she doubted they would ever be happy together. And then there were the women she knew who suffered physical and emotional abuse from their husbands. Should they be compelled to stay married? And, in the case of the play, the wife who thought her husband might never return from an asylum. But what about the husband? It wasn't the poor man's fault that he'd become ill. And did he really deserve to be abandoned like that? Golly, it was a complicated issue. One thing she did know, though, was what was good for the goose should be good for the gander, and if men were able to sue for divorce then so should women.

She tried to keep her own views out of the piece and judge it on its artistic merits: good acting, good directing, a good script. And the fact that it gave the audience something to discuss and debate at the theatre bar afterwards was a bonus. Yes, she would give this one four stars out of five.

As she typed her final "ENDS" at the bottom of the copy there was a stir in the office as her fellow journos put down tea and coffee cups, scraped back chairs and shuffled their way to the editorial meeting room at the far end of the fourth floor. Poppy looked at her watch: *Crikey! Is it that time already?*

She strode across to the editorial in-box and placed her review on the pile waiting to be collected by one of the *Globe*'s two sub-editors. Then she went back to her desk and picked up her pencil and notebook. She left her sage coat on the back of the chair and straightened her chocolate-coloured skirt and custard-yellow blouse before joining the exodus to the noon-time meeting.

"You look almost edible," said a male voice from behind her. She turned to see the athletic frame of the *Globe* photographer Daniel Rokeby striding out of the stairwell.

Poppy felt a pleasurable glow in her cheeks. "Why, Mr Rokeby, you shouldn't say things like that. Tongues will soon be wagging."

"They can wag away," he grinned, and matched his step to hers. She resisted the temptation to put her arm through his. This was the office, after all.

"You up for a spot of lunch after the meeting?"

She shook her head, dislodging an unruly blonde curl from a finger wave. "Sorry, I said I'd meet Delilah. You know how glum she's been lately..."

Daniel gave a rueful smile, his grey eyes showing his disappointment. "We still on for tonight though?"

Poppy pushed the curl behind her ear. "Of course! I wouldn't miss it for the world!"

Daniel laughed and held open the meeting room door for her. "I hope you're looking forward to spending time with me and not Rudolph Valentino."

Poppy sidled past him and lowered her voice: "Can't a girl have both?"

Before Daniel could answer, there was a bellow from the front of the room: "Rokeby! Denby! Do your courting on your own time!"

The assembled journalists laughed, Poppy flushed and Daniel muttered: "What's got his goat?"

At the front of the room, standing only four and a half feet tall, was Rollo. Pacing up and down, his over-large hands bunched in fists, he looked only slightly calmer than he had in the kitchenette.

"Right, what have we got for above the fold?" he growled. "Ike?"

The West Indian journalist ran a hand over his stubble and sighed. "Threat of the Joint Trades Union walking out in sympathy with miners."

Rollo stopped pacing and glared at him. "What the hell has that got to do with London?"

Ike straightened up and glared back. "The whole damned city could grind to a halt if the transport union joins in!"

"Then say that!" yelled Rollo.

"I have!" replied Ike.

The newsroom took a collective intake of breath as the two journalistic heavyweights squared up to one another. "What's wrong with him?" whispered the sports reporter.

"Dunno," replied the finance editor.

After exchanging a few editorial punches Ike stood up and turned to walk out. "Copy's been filed," he grunted and headed for the door.

Rollo shouted after him: "Come back now!" Ike kept on walking. "Please . . ." Ike stopped. He turned around and crossed his arms over his chest, waiting for Rollo to continue.

Rollo ran his hand through his ginger hair and leaned his backside on a desk. "I'm sorry, Ike. You've done a great job in difficult circumstances. And I haven't made it any easier, I know."

Ike uncrossed his arms but remained standing.

Rollo cast his gaze across the assembled journalists, stunned into silence by his behaviour. "I'm sorry, everyone. But I've, well, I've just had some news . . ."

Poppy leaned forward. *Oh dear, what's happened?*

Rollo's usually robust complexion drained of blood. "And I'm afraid it affects all of you."

"Redundancies coming," someone muttered.

Oh no! Poppy steeled herself, expecting the worst. She felt tears well in her eyes.

Daniel reached out and took her hand. She squeezed it.

Rollo cleared his throat and continued. "I'm afraid you're going to be getting a new senior editor for a while."

Is he ill? Poppy assessed her mentor for signs of sickness. There was nothing she could see.

"Are you leaving, Rollo?" asked Ike, edging back to his seat. "Why?"

"Who's replacing you?" asked the financial editor, and the other journalists shushed him.

Rollo raised his hands. "No, that's all right. Harry's asking the right question. And so is Ike. I'd expect nothing less from this team." He surveyed the room and a look bordering on fatherly pride came over him. "You'll know that Archie Weinstein's been in town."

The associate editor of *The New York Times*. The assembled journalists nodded. Yes, they knew that. Rollo had been on edge since the day his fellow American paid him an unexpected visit last week. Rollo had done the appropriate back slapping and declaratory "why, what a top surprise, old sport" but Poppy and the rest of the *Globe* staff could see Rollo was far from pleased to see his old colleague from the home country.

"Well," said Rollo, clearing his throat. "The good news is that Archie was very impressed with our little rag. Very impressed indeed."

"And the bad news . . ." prompted Daniel.

"I'm getting to that, Danny Boy. The bad news is that he's looking at investing in a London newspaper. He wants to partner with someone this side of the pond."

"Well, that's not so bad, is it, Rollo?" asked Poppy. "You've been looking for some investment for a while, haven't you?"

Rollo looked at Poppy, his eyes pained. "I have, Miz Denby, I have. But not like this." He looked up at the rest of the staff. By now the printers, the accountants and even Mavis the receptionist had edged into the back of the small meeting room. Behind them Ivan Molanov the archivist filled the doorway, his broad shoulders blocking out all light from the hall. "Speet it out, Rollo. Tell us what you done."

Rollo let out a long breath, his chest visibly deflating with the effort. "He wanted a sixty per cent share."

Mutters of outrage rippled through the room. "I hope you told him where to shove it!" offered Harry.

Rollo's lips tightened into a smile. "I did, Harry, I did. And he was none too pleased. But then . . . well, last night we went to my club and –"

Dear God, don't let him say what I think he's going to say, thought Poppy, her eyes searching for Rollo's, willing him to look at her and tell her it was going to be all right.

"You lost it in a poker game," observed Ike flatly. There was no condemnation in his voice. It was just a statement of fact. Rollo shrugged.

The rest of the staff did not take it so calmly. The air went blue with expletives as Rollo stood, head bowed, unable to meet the vitriol of his friends and employees. Poppy had never seen him so cowed. Although a small man he normally had a giant presence and she willed him to rise to the challenge. Eventually he raised his shaggy head and then his hands and tried to calm the furore. The hubbub diminished but did not cease. "Let him speak!" growled Ivan and an uneasy silence settled in the room.

"Ike is partially right. But not entirely. Poker was involved, yes, but I did not *lose* the paper. Not yet, anyway. And if I have anything to do with it, I never will." His spine began to straighten. His shoulders relaxed, his chin raised.

Poppy nodded her approval. "Can you explain what did happen then?"

Rollo cleared his throat. "Indeed I can, Miz Denby. As I said, Weinstein wanted a sixty per cent share. I'd turned him down. But then, last night –"

"You gambled away our jobs!" spat out Harry. He was shushed by the rest of the staff.

"Let him finish," said Daniel and leaned forward, still holding Poppy's hand.

"Thanks, Danny Boy. If you all stop flapping your chops I'll tell you."

Harry grunted, folded his arms over his chest and leaned back in his chair.

"No Harry, I have not gambled away your jobs. Your jobs will be safe, no matter what happens. I did, however" – he raised his hands – "*unwisely* enter into a wager. Weinstein's nose was so out of joint when I turned down his offer that he announced in front of the whole club that if he was editor he could double the advertising revenue on our little rag within three months. I laughed at him and said he'd never get the chance. But then . . . well . . ."

Here it comes, thought Poppy and groaned inwardly. Rollo could never turn down a wager.

"Well, then someone suggested we play for it. If I won – and of course I almost never lose – Archie would go back to New York with his tail between his legs. But if Archie won . . . he would be given the chance to prove himself right."

"Meaning . . ." prompted Ike.

"Meaning," said Rollo, beginning to slump again, "he would take over here for three months."

"And you lost," said Harry, struggling to hide his disdain.

Rollo nodded glumly.

Poppy's heart reached out to him. "But it's not that bad. It's not permanent, is it?"

The editor shook his head. "No, it's only for three months. But . . . if Archie Weinstein succeeds in doubling the ad revenue in that time then I will have to accept his offer to buy sixty per cent of the paper. And if he has sixty per cent . . ." he shuddered. Poppy did too. If Weinstein owned two-thirds of the *Globe,* Rollo would no longer be in control. He might as well have lost the whole thing.

"But it's not a done deal, is it?" clarified Daniel, his tone encouraging. Poppy squeezed his hand gratefully. "You're a stonking businessman, Rollo – your poker habits aside – and if you haven't been able to double the ad revenue in three years, why should he be able to in three months?"

Rollo straightened up and grinned. Poppy chuckled. The Cheshire Cat was back.

"My thoughts exactly, Danny Boy. And I suppose it won't be the worst thing in the world going to New York . . ."

Poppy let go of Daniel's hand. "New York? Who's going to New York?"

Rollo shrugged apologetically. "I am. Weinstein said he doesn't want me around trying to scupper his deals. So we've agreed that while he's here I'll be in New York."

"And when's all this supposed to happen?" asked Ike.

"I'll be leaving next Saturday. So that's a week. Don't worry, I've got some ideas on how to minimise his chances of success. Ike, Poppy, I'd like to see you in my office after the ed meeting. But for now, we've got a paper to put to bed. So, what's going below the fold?"

Half an hour later the assembled journalists sloped back to their desks. Not much work was done as they gathered in groups discussing Rollo's mad-cap predicament and wondering what sort of boss Archie Weinstein would make. Poppy and Ike didn't join in, but, as requested, headed towards Rollo's office. Ike knocked and pushed open the door. Rollo was sitting at his desk, his red hair speckled with dust motes that had been dislodged from a stack of files perched on a filing cabinet behind him. He didn't bother flicking them away.

"Take a seat," he mumbled, his head bowed over a sheet of paper.

Ike pulled out a chair for Poppy, which she accepted with a small smile, then sat down beside her.

"Righto," said Rollo, putting his pen back in its holder, then taking a sheet of blotting paper and pressing it onto whatever he had been writing. After a moment he lifted the blotter, picked up the paper and blew on it before passing it over the desk to Ike.

"Here, team, are my initial ideas of how to keep the paper afloat while doing the minimum amount of work."

Poppy craned her neck to read the scrawl.

"I never thought I'd say it," Rollo continued, "but it's in our best interests *not* to get any scoops for the next three months. Do you think you can handle that, Ike?"

Ike grunted and continued reading the list. Eventually he looked up, shaking his head. "You're mad, Rollo, utterly mad, but . . ." he grinned, showing his large, square teeth, "I think we can do it. It's good timing actually – what with the miners' strike there's not going to be much else on the agenda. Even if there is a scoop it won't make it onto the front page – not with the country about to grind to a halt."

Rollo grinned back at his chief reporter. "That's the spirit!"

"But . . ." said Ike, his ink-stained finger pointing to the last item on the list, "what the deuce are you thinking by this – *get Poppy out of the picture*?"

"What?" said Poppy, grabbing the list from Ike, then tossing out a quick "sorry".

She too ran her finger down the list and stopped at number ten. It did indeed say *get Poppy out of the picture.* "What's that supposed to mean?" she challenged Rollo.

The editor shrugged and grinned sheepishly. "I'm afraid, Miz Denby, you are a liability."

She opened her mouth to speak but Rollo held up his hand to silence her. "Hold your horses. What I mean is that in the nine months you have worked here our advertising revenue has increased every time you've unearthed a big story. First the Dorchester scandal, then that Russian malarkey in the autumn. Things have been quiet for a while, but, as you know, I'm a betting man, and the odds are in favour of another big story sometime soon. With you out of the picture and Ike focused on the miners, we minimise our chances of unearthing it."

Poppy flushed slightly. It was a backhanded compliment. Yes, she did have a knack of exposing big stories but now, apparently, she was a liability. What was he planning on doing with her?

She cleared her throat. "So, are you sacking me, Rollo?"

Rollo's eyes widened to the size of saucers. "What gave you that idea? Of course not!"

"Then what are you planning?" asked Ike, taking the list out of Poppy's trembling hands.

"I'm planning on taking her with me. That is, if she'll come." He turned to Poppy, his eyes taking on the look of a pleading puppy. "I'm going to be working on the *Times* for three months. I've arranged for you to get a job there too. Will you, Poppy? Will you come with me to New York?"

Chapter 3

"So what are you going to do?" asked Delilah Marconi, cutting her cucumber and egg sandwich into squares.

Poppy sighed as she placed a tea strainer over her cup and poured herself a second helping of the golden brew. The Empire Tea Rooms were busy with lunchtime customers. Perhaps this was not the best place to discuss work. She looked around, checking to see if any journalists from the *Globe*'s rival paper *The Courier* were there: they weren't. Good. They'd no doubt find out soon enough, but she didn't want to be the leak.

"I really don't know," answered Poppy.

The dark-haired Maltese woman put down her knife and appraised her friend. "Well, I think it's a spiffing opportunity. You've never been to New York, have you?"

Poppy shook her head. Until last summer, she'd never been any further than Northumberland. Since then she'd been to London and Paris. But New York? New York was on the other side of the world . . .

"You'll love it. They call it 'The City That Never Sleeps'. There are theatres on every corner! And then there's Tin Pan Alley, and the moving picture studios . . ."

The young actress's face lit up as she recounted tales of her visits to New York with her wealthy father and influential great uncle, Guglielmo Marconi. "Uncle Elmo has been overseeing the launch of some radio stations there. And he said he can arrange an audition for me."

"Sounds like you're the one who should be going – not me," said Poppy.

"Well actually, I was planning on going over the summer, but I can always bring it forward a month or two . . ."

"What, you mean go at the same time as me and Rollo? *If* I go, that is . . ."

"Yes! Oh, won't that be the bee's knees? You and me strolling down Broadway together? And then we can go shopping on Fifth Avenue! And then there's Central Park, and the parties out on Long Island..."

Poppy held up her hand and repeated Rollo's phrase from this morning: "Hold your horses, old girl. I haven't said I'll go yet."

Delilah pouted, her mouth forming a shape some of the male arts and entertainment journalists in London claimed could rival Mary Pickford's. "What's stopping you?" she asked.

Poppy sighed and took a sip of her tea.

Delilah scowled. "It's Daniel, isn't it? You don't want to go because of him."

Poppy wanted to deny it but couldn't. Yes, it was because of Daniel. She hadn't yet had a chance to tell him of Rollo's offer – and had asked Ike and the editor to keep quiet until she did – but she already knew what his reaction would be. He would *not* be happy.

Delilah picked up her sandwich, holding it daintily between thumb and forefinger, and declared: "It's not as if you're married or anything." And then took a large bite and chewed.

Poppy chewed too, but not her food. Delilah was right. She and Daniel were not married. And although they had been stepping out for about six months, there had been no sign that he was ready to put a ring on her finger – or that she would accept.

The problem lay with his domestic situation. When she had first met him – on her very first day in London – there had been an instant attraction between them. Then, six weeks later she got a job on the same newspaper he worked on. The attraction continued to deepen to the point where he asked her out to dinner. But in the midst of her first big story for the paper, she had got the idea that he was not quite as available as she had been led to believe. At first she thought he was married, but then she discovered that he was in fact widowed, and the woman she thought was his wife was his sister, who had come to live with him to help look after his two young children.

Once that confusion had been laid aside, she and Daniel had started courting. However, it had taken them quite a few months before she was able to meet his children. His sister, Maggie, had considered it too soon after Daniel's wife's death to bring a "new woman into the home" – as she put it – and although they started courting in the summer it was November before she was able to meet little Arthur and Amy.

They were delightful children – six and four – with the eldest, Arthur, just having started school. Amy was still at home with her aunt Maggie. They took to Poppy instantly – much to Daniel's delight – but the same could not be said for Maggie. Maggie had lost her fiancé during the war, and now at thirty-two feared she was destined for a life of spinsterhood. Her brother's children were very much her surrogate babies and she was not going to give them up easily to anyone – certainly not to a twenty-two-year-old career woman who was likely to put her job before family.

During a particularly tense Sunday lunch Maggie had made her views known. Daniel defended Poppy, saying of course she would put the children first and would be prepared to leave her job if necessary. This had irked Poppy no end as he had not spoken to her about it first. Afterwards, when he drove her home, she told him she thought he had been out of line and that they had not yet even discussed the possibility of marriage, nor what she would do with her job if they did. He had apologised and said it was something they most definitely should discuss.

Yet, despite her protestations, Poppy knew she was just as much at fault as he. Perhaps more so. Every time he tried to raise the issue, Poppy would change the subject – much to his confusion. She had started to suspect Daniel's views on the role of women in the home were more on the traditional side during her second big story for the newspaper, when he had implied a woman should not be investigating things on her own. Yes, he had been worried about her safety – and that, in itself, was charming – but it suggested to Poppy that there may be problems down the line if she chose to continue with her career.

Delilah knew all about this. She and Poppy had sat up many a night in Delilah's flat, after an evening at Oscar's Jazz Club, discussing Poppy's options. Yes, they both admitted, Poppy and Daniel loved each other, but he'd made his views on marriage clear. And Poppy didn't know if she was ready for that. She was only twenty-two and had landed a plum job as a journalist on a London tabloid. Not many women had the opportunity she had to forge a career. Would she be prepared to give it up for marriage? Perhaps she might, one day. Or maybe she didn't have to – couldn't she do both? She wasn't really sure. But she did know she wasn't prepared to do so yet. Nor, however, was she prepared to give up on her romance. Oh, why had she met Daniel now and not a few years into the future? It was a cud she and Delilah had chewed until it was dry.

And now, here they were again, in the Empire Tea Rooms. "You know what, old girl? Men are just not worth it," declared Delilah as she lit a cigarette, sucked and then exhaled over the table.

Poppy wafted the smoke away from her tea cup. "Are we talking about Daniel or Adam?" she asked.

Delilah's nostrils flared. "I thought we weren't going to mention his name ever again."

Poppy gave Delilah an apologetic pat on her hand. "I'm sorry. How are you feeling about it all? That's why we were going to have lunch, anyway – not to talk about my problems."

Delilah gave a melodramatic sigh and tears welled in her eyes. She dabbed them delicately with a napkin. "How is one expected to feel when the love of one's life runs off with someone else?"

Poppy pursed her lips. She didn't mind helping soothe Delilah's wounded heart, but she wouldn't do it by perpetuating falsehoods. "He didn't run off with someone else, Delilah. He said yes to a job offer as the assistant to one of the world's greatest theatre directors."

"Well, it's the same thing," Delilah pouted. "He knew it would require travelling – spending months away from me at a time – but he chose Stanislavski over me."

Poppy made sympathetic noises and patted her friend's hand. Delilah was not used to being put aside and her pride was hurt. But Poppy knew it was more than that; her friend had truly fallen in love with the young actor. She felt desperately sorry for Delilah; however, if truth be told, it was actually Adam she sympathised with. Wasn't he too torn between love and career? Why, oh why, couldn't she have them both!

***

Poppy had just put the finishing touches to her lipstick when the doorbell rang. She heard the click of heels down the hall, signalling that her aunt's companion, Miss Gertrude King, was going to answer it. Poppy had been living with her father's paraplegic sister, a former suffragette and retired West End leading lady, since arriving in London the previous summer. The young reporter took a moment to appraise her reflection. She'd come a long way since she first stepped through the Chelsea townhouse door wearing a serviceable but dowdy beige suit. Tonight she was wearing a Jean-Charles Worth satin evening gown. It had been a gift from the designer – a friend of her aunt's – as thanks for a warm review she had given in the *Globe* of his latest collection. She had been reluctant to accept it at first, worried that it was tantamount to a bribe; however, when Aunt Dot pointed out the dress came after the review, not before, she had received the gown with thanks. She was a tad worried about what might happen when Worth's next collection came out. Would she be expected to gush about that too?

She smoothed down the pale pink calf-length satin gown and checked that the mother of pearl brooch was securely fastened to the sash at her hip. Then she leaned forward to make sure her bodice did not gape too much. The ribbon straps, strung with pearls, held her weight and she smiled as she thought of what Daniel would say when he saw her: it was a far cry from the flighty little flapper frocks she wore to Oscar's Jazz Club. As this was a film premiere – where Rudolph Valentino himself was going to attend – she thought the more sophisticated look was just what was called for.

She slipped her silk-stockinged feet into kid leather shoes with pearl-encrusted buttons and flicked a dusky pink-fringed shawl over her shoulders.

There was a knock on her door. "Mr Rokeby is here, Poppy," came the clipped tones of Miss King.

"I'll be right down," answered Poppy.

The babbling cinemagoers gushed out of the auditorium and waited for the appearance of the star: Rudolph Valentino. They didn't wait long. As they entered the foyer, Mr Valentino and his entourage were greeted by rapturous applause. The film, it seemed, was a hit with Londoners – as it had been in every city it was shown. The American-Italian heart-throb, in white coat and tails, flashed a dazzling smile and announced that if anyone would like to join him, he was heading down to Oscar's to celebrate. This was greeted by cheers and a round of "For he's a jolly good fellow" as the well-heeled audience – including leading socialites, politicians and show business celebrities – followed their new idol onto King's Road, where they were greeted by a phalanx of press photographers.

"I hope Max has got a good position," observed Daniel, standing on tiptoes to see over the crowd.

Poppy squeezed his forearm. "Seeing as you briefed him within an inch of his life, I'm sure he will," said Poppy and then pulled him out of the flow of traffic to stand next to a life-size poster of Sheik Ahmed and Lady Diana Mayo in a passionate embrace. Poppy felt a chill go down her spine and pointedly turned her back on the screen lovers. Unlike the rest of the audience, it seemed, Poppy had not enjoyed the film. She simply could not see how they could applaud the abduction of a woman, her subsequent rape – however tastefully it was presented – and the fact that she eventually falls in love with her repentant assailant. At the beginning of the film Lady Diana had been a strong, independent woman; by the end she was a willing victim in the name of romance. Poppy knew exactly what Aunt Dot and her suffragette friends would say about the film – and she agreed with them. She looked at the delighted expressions on the audience members' faces as they passed her by. And remembered too how Daniel had cheered and applauded with them during the standing ovation. She sighed. Perhaps she was reading too much into it, imposing her own situation onto the screen story; her own fear of being trapped by love.

"What's up?" asked Daniel, looking at her curiously. Poppy pulled her shawl tighter around her shoulders.

"Nothing. I just don't feel like going to Oscar's, if that's all right. It's supposed to be our night off but I think both of us will want to slip into work mode when we're there." She gestured towards Daniel's apprentice, who appeared to be holding his own. "Let Max deal with it."

Daniel nodded his agreement. They stood against the wall as the stream continued to flow by. "Do you want to call it a night then?" he asked, not trying to hide the disappointment in his voice.

"Of course not!" said Poppy. "In fact, quite the opposite. I want to spend time with *you*, not half of London."

Daniel grinned. "Now that's what a fella likes to hear. Should we go to The Queen's Head, then? They have a good supper menu and with word that the Sheik's heading to Oscar's we should easily get a table."

"The Queen's it is," agreed Poppy.

Twenty minutes later they were seated in the small restaurant of the public house, had ordered their food and were sharing a bottle of chardonnay.

"To us," said Daniel, raising his glass.

"To us," agreed Poppy and clinked his glass. *But what does "us" mean?* she wondered. She had been doing a lot of thinking in the afternoon after she'd left Delilah at the Empire Tea Rooms. And when she'd got home she had spoken to her aunt. She'd told her about Rollo's request for her to accompany him to New York. Without missing a beat Aunt Dot had declared, "But of course you should go with him! It's the chance of a lifetime!" Yes, it was the chance of a lifetime. And it was only for three months. If Daniel loved her as much as she thought he did, then he would understand that this was really important to her and would support her in her career; he would encourage her to go but eagerly wait for her return. Three months apart might even do them some good. What was it they said – absence makes the heart grow fonder?

"Penny for your thoughts," said Daniel, the quizzical look back on his face. "What's up with you tonight, Poppy? You don't seem yourself."

Poppy took a sip of her wine and then put down the glass. "Yes, I know; I'm sorry. It's just that I've got something to tell you. Something that came up today. Something to do with Rollo . . ."

Daniel's grey eyes narrowed. Did he suspect what it might be?

"He hasn't asked you to do anything underhanded, has he? To try to undermine the New York editor when he's here?"

Poppy smiled at the way Daniel's mind worked. Rollo was his friend and boss but he was under no illusions about the weaknesses in his character. "No, not that. But it's related." She then went on to tell him Rollo's plan to ensure Archie Weinstein would not manage to increase the *Globe*'s ad revenue, including his request that she accompany him to New York to make sure she didn't get any scoops while he was away.

Daniel's war-scarred hand tightened on the stem of the glass as she spoke. When she had finished he raised the glass to his lips and took a long sip, then put it down. His lips pursed and released and then he spoke. "I expected him to do something like this. Don't worry, I'll talk to him. It's wrong of him to make you do something you don't want to do."

Poppy's eyes opened in surprise. Something she didn't want to do? She hadn't yet told Daniel what she thought of the proposal, only what it contained. And he was assuming she wouldn't want to go? Why on earth did he assume that? How dare he assume that!

Poppy was just about to speak when the waiter arrived with their meals. They sat back and allowed the platters of steamed new potatoes and lamb chops to be placed on the table. Daniel rubbed his hands together and tucked in.

Poppy did not make any moves towards hers. He noticed and put down his cutlery. "Sorry, Poppy, were you going to say grace?"

Poppy's lips tightened. No, she hadn't been about to say grace, but perhaps she should have. Daniel was no longer a believer – having lost his faith during the war – but he had always respected her right to practise her religion. But that was not enough for her parents. On her recent trip home they had probed her about Daniel's beliefs and she had had to admit that he was an atheist. This had shocked her parents far more than the revelation that he was a widower with children. Poppy had listened to their lectures about being unevenly yoked with a pinch of salt. But perhaps they were right. Perhaps she and Daniel *were* unevenly yoked – religiously and in terms of her career and his family. And yet . . . and yet, she looked into his warm grey eyes and saw only love. How could that be wrong?

"Finished?" he asked.

"Yes," she said and picked up her knife and fork.

Daniel pierced a dollop of butter and rubbed it over his steamed potatoes. Poppy watched it melt into a pool on his plate.

No, she wasn't finished. She needed to tell him. She needed to tell him she was going to New York. And if he loved her, he'd understand – surely he'd understand. "Daniel, there's something I need to tell you . . ."

Chapter 4

Saturday, 6 April 1921, Southampton

Poppy and Rollo got out of the company Model T Ford at the Southampton harbour car park amidst a hubbub of travellers and their well-wishers. Ike, who had driven them there from London, hauled one trunk from the boot and unstrapped a second from the roof rack while Rollo summoned a porter. Poppy remembered the last time a gentleman had helped her with her trunk – it was Daniel, the first time she met him at King's Cross Station. Poppy bit her lip. Rollo had asked him to drive them down, but he had come up with some photographic emergency that could not be ignored. Rollo told him it could wait; Daniel said it could not. So Rollo asked Ike instead.

Poppy and Daniel had not made an official announcement about their break-up – it wasn't as if they'd been engaged – but it didn't take long for their friends and colleagues at the *Globe* to figure out that something was wrong. Rollo had tried to speak to Daniel about it but was given short shrift. Daniel clearly blamed the American editor for luring his girl away. But this just angered Poppy even further. "I was not *lured*," she told Mavis Bradshaw, when the receptionist bumped into her in the new ladies' water closet on the fourth floor. "Rollo invited me to join him and I was free to choose whether I would or not. It was *my* choice, not Rollo's, and Daniel should respect that." Then Poppy finished drying her hands and left the small room before Mavis had time to probe her further. It was a long week of sulking and whispered conversations and sympathetic looks. But finally it was over. And Poppy and Rollo were about to embark on the RMS *Olympic* for a five-day cruise to New York.

They would not be travelling alone. True to her word, Delilah had arranged for her trip to be brought forward so she could accompany Poppy as her chaperone. Poppy had snorted at the suggestion that the Bright Young Thing and flapper extraordinaire had the qualifications to be her moral guide, but she readily agreed. It would be fun to have Delilah in tow and Rollo had been delighted at the suggestion. "The more the merrier!" he declared. Unlike Daniel, Rollo's sweetheart, the admirable female solicitor Yasmin Reece-Lansdale, had wished him well and said she'd see him in three months – then turned her attention back to her latest legal brief. Poppy was in awe – and a little jealous – of how Yasmin so easily managed to balance her private and professional life. She couldn't imagine Yasmin lying awake at night agonising about what Rollo would think of this or that. Perhaps that's what came with age. Yasmin was in her late thirties, Poppy and Delilah their early twenties.

Ike had offered to give Delilah a lift too, but when they arrived at her apartment and saw the two giant trunks she intended to bring with her, he quickly ascertained there wouldn't be space. Rollo had offered to take the train so the ladies could have the motor to themselves. Delilah insisted there still wouldn't be room for all the luggage, but, being Delilah, she had another plan.

"The other plan" arrived in the form of a brand new yellow Rolls Royce pulling a trailer piled high with far more than two trunks.

"Good heavens! Is that who I think it is?" asked Rollo, grinning from ear to ear.

Poppy chuckled, her spirits suddenly lifted as first Delilah got out of the motor, followed by the female driver. The driver then opened the back door to reveal the plump form of Dot Denby in a fabulous fuchsia pink travelling coat and hat. "Poppy darling! I hope you don't mind, but when Delilah asked me for a lift in the new motor I thought I might as well come with you all the way to New York! So I got Gertrude here to telephone ahead and make some arrangements. She doubted we would be able to get tickets at such short notice, but" – she winked at Delilah, who giggled, while Miss King looked pained – "it turns out the captain is an old friend of mine!"

Poppy clapped her hands in delight. Oh, this was definitely going to be a *bon voyage*!

***

The RMS *Olympic* was the sister ship to the ill-fated *Titanic* which sunk in 1912 and the *Britannic*, which was sunk by a German mine in 1916. The sole survivor was going strong, surging back and forth from New York to Europe carrying immigrants and tourists between the Old and New Worlds. Poppy had never seen anything like it. Not even the Houses of Parliament seemed as vast. It had ten decks and could carry nearly 2,500 passengers. On the first-class deck there was a swimming pool, a Turkish bath, a gymnasium and even a tennis court! There were libraries, smoking rooms, games rooms and beauty spas. Compared with the only other ship Poppy had travelled on – a ferry between Dover and Calais the previous summer – this was like a small city. Delilah and Rollo looked perfectly at ease striding up the gangplank as if it were their second home. Aunt Dot, however, her wheelchair pushed by a porter with Miss King hovering at his shoulder, was surprisingly quiet.

Poppy matched her pace to the chair. "Are you all right, Aunt Dot?"

Her aunt looked up at her from under the brim of her fuchsia hat, her mouth uncharacteristically down-turned. "Oh Poppy, I was just thinking of poor Maud. All of that business with Elizabeth last year has brought her back to mind. And now here we are on a ship just like the one she died on."

Poppy took Aunt Dot's gloved hand and squeezed it. Her aunt was referring to her friend and fellow suffragette, Maud Dorchester, who had died on the *Titanic* nine years earlier. Her daughter, Elizabeth, had been central to Poppy's first big story for the *Globe* and now lived in New York. Aunt Dot must have been thinking the same thing as she said quietly: "I think I'll look Elizabeth up when I'm there. There are things we need to settle between us."

Poppy agreed that that was a good idea. And then, as quickly as Dot's cloud had descended, it lifted again. "Oh my, isn't this just splendid, Poppy?"

Poppy appraised the gleaming grey and white floating hotel. "It certainly is, Aunt Dot." She paused, looking the ship up and down. "As long as you're in first class, I should imagine."

"Actually, Miz Denby, the steerage passengers don't have it half bad either," said Rollo, drawing level with Dot's wheelchair. "I did a story about it when I was working on *The New York Times*." He went on to explain that compared with the rival *Mauretania*, the third-class facilities for steerage passengers were clean and decent. Instead of open dormitories, there were small cabins for up to ten people to house single-sex passengers or families. And they also had common rooms, dining rooms and well-designed bathrooms.

Although it didn't sound too bad, Poppy still felt guilty that she was travelling first class. If the *Globe* hadn't paid for her ticket she would have been with the line of less well-off passengers, shuffling their way up a lower gangplank at the stern of the ship. However, she was where she was, and she and her entourage were almost at the top of the gangplank. They were about to be greeted by a line of officers and stewards. One of them, her aunt announced – while primping her hair – was her "good friend Captain Gilbert Williams". But before they could hand over their tickets there was a commotion behind them.

A teenage girl, wearing an unfashionably long skirt and a blue headscarf tied under her chin, pushed her way to the front of the queue. She was stopped by a steward who asked for her ticket. She cocked her head from left to right and then answered in a foreign babble. The steward looked at her curiously, then asked for her ticket again. The young woman stared at him blankly and then pushed past him. He blocked her path. When she tried again he took hold of her arm – she screamed. The man, embarrassed, looked to his captain for help. "Take the young lady aside," said Captain Williams and nodded to some more of his men to help. But as the crew circled her, the girl kicked and yelled even more.

Poppy saw the terror on her face. "Please, let me help. She's scared, that's all." She leaned over the shoulder of one of the crew members and tried to catch the poor girl's eye. "It's all right," she said. "Calm down; they won't hurt you." But the girl continued screaming. Poppy was just about to push through the circle of men to try to take hold of the girl when someone else ran up the gangplank, puffing with exertion. It was another young woman, a few years older than the hysterical girl, with long dark hair tied back in a bun. Her eyes met

Poppy's briefly, then she turned her attention to calming the girl in the blue headscarf.

"Estie! Estie!" Then something in a language Poppy could not understand.

The younger girl stopped screaming and looked to the newcomer. She was panting, a line of drool running down her chin. "Mimi!" she said, then started to cry; great heaving sobs. The two stewards who held her arms looked confused. "Mimi" moved forward, speaking soothingly, and put both hands on either side of the younger girl's face. Estie's sobbing eased until it was a quiet sniff.

Then Mimi looked to the captain and said: "Let go she please. Sorry she not know. She baby."

Captain Williams nodded to his men. "Let the lady go." They did and Estie fell into Mimi's arms. Mimi, continuing her soothing monologue, turned around and led the young woman back down the gangplank. The well-to-do first-class passengers parted for them, some with disdain, some with pity.

"She'll be lucky if she gets off the island," said Rollo.

"The island?" asked Poppy, dragging her eyes away from the pitiful pair who were now turning towards the area on the dock where the third-class passengers gathered.

"Ellis Island," answered the American editor. "Immigration control. They've been known to turn away the feebleminded."

"Turn them away?" said Poppy. "Where to?"

Rollo shrugged. The queue was moving again.

"Sorry about that, ladies and gentlemen," said the captain. "A misunderstanding; nothing more." Then he turned his broad suntanned face to Poppy's group. "Welcome to the RMS *Olympic*, the most luxurious ocean liner in the world." The porter pushed Aunt Dot's chair onto the deck and Captain Williams' face lit up: "Miss Dorothy Denby! This is a rare pleasure indeed!"

Chapter 5

"Oh, isn't this just the bee's knees!" Delilah threw herself onto one of the twin beds in the cabin she was sharing with Poppy, her navy-blue silk culottes sliding across the white satin counterpane like a bobsleigh on ice. She giggled and pushed out her hands to steady herself.

"Are you sure you don't mind sharing with me?" asked Poppy, who knew Delilah had given up a more luxurious cabin – with double bed, sitting room and en-suite hot tub – to "room" with her chum, hence allowing Aunt Dot an upgrade. Poppy flopped onto the second bed, wriggling her shoulders to test the firmness of the mattress. *Nice, very nice.*

"Of course not! It's going to be such a jolly!"

"Well, thank you," said Poppy. "I don't think Aunt Dot would have survived for long in that pokey little cabin. I know it's the best Miss King could get at such short notice, but second class . . ." said Poppy, putting on an affected theatrical tone.

". . . I think not, darlings!" finished Delilah, sounding just like Aunt Dot. The two girls collapsed into fits of giggles.

Delilah rolled over onto her side, pulling up one leg and leaning her chin on her elbow. "So what do you want to do first? Tennis? Swimming?"

Poppy laughed. "Heavens, Delilah, we've barely left land!"

Delilah grinned, flashing her perfectly straight white teeth. "I know! But speaking from experience, if you don't make your mark on these cruises early, you'll never catch up."

Poppy screwed up her nose. "Make our mark? Whatever do you mean?"

Delilah swung her legs off the bed and sat up. "Watch and learn, old girl, watch and learn."

The dark-haired girl unstrapped one of her trunks and rummaged through a mountain of silks, satins and organzas. She pulled out three swimsuits with matching caps and held them up one at a time. "I assume you haven't brought one with you . . ."

Poppy's wide-eyed stare was all the confirmation Delilah needed. "So you can wear one of mine. Which do you want? The gold and green, the red, or the blue and white stripe?"

Poppy, who hadn't worn a swimsuit since she was ten years old – and even that had just been a pair of bloomers and a long-sleeved undershirt – tried to imagine herself in one of Delilah's flamboyant outfits with the very short shorts.

"Come on," said Delilah. "We'll be in New York before you've made up your mind. Should I choose?"

"No, it's all right. I'll have the blue and white horizontal stripes please," said Poppy, quickly assessing that out of the three on offer it would show the least amount of flesh.

"Good choice," said Delilah, tossing it to her. "Although you would look scrumptious in the poppy red!"

Delilah selected the exotic green with oriental-style gold flowers twirled across the bodice and down one leg.

Fifteen minutes later and the girls arrived at the pool wearing white towelling bathrobes over their suits. The indoor pool was heated, letting off warm steam. Half a dozen or so passengers had already laid claim to the deckchairs and benches around the poolside. Delilah paused in the doorway, striking a subtle but attractive pose, with her bathrobe open to reveal her beautiful bare legs, exposed from mid-thigh down, and waited. No one looked up. Poppy sensed the actress tense beside her. Delilah was not used to not being noticed. Poppy, though, was relieved. Frankly, she didn't know if she'd even have the courage to take off her robe; so the fewer people who noticed her, the better.

As the girls made their way to two available chairs and draped their towels over them, the other guests' collective gaze was riveted on a sleek, silver-clad swimmer, surging through the water like a dolphin, doing length after length. Poppy and Delilah sat down and were approached by a waiter asking for drink orders. Delilah requested a cocktail and Poppy a glass of freshly squeezed orange juice.

As the waiter retreated, the swimmer slowed and glided towards the pool steps. Then she – for by now Poppy had realised it was a woman – grasped the bars and pulled herself up. Gasps of admiration echoed off the tile walls. The swimmer stood at the top of the steps and slicked back her hair with both hands, allowing the other bathers to drink in her tanned skin and fantastically toned limbs.

"Good golly, it's Annette Kellerman!" observed Delilah. "No wonder no one was looking at us!"

"Who's Annette Kellerman?" asked Poppy, although the name rang a bell.

"*Who's Annette Kellerman?*" asked Delilah, laughing. "*What Women Want, Queen of the Sea* . . ."

Poppy bit her lip in mock contrition. "Oh, *that* Annette Kellerman!" The famous Australian synchronised swimmer and film star. The first woman to design and wear swimming shorts that revealed her knees – and who was arrested for it! The first woman to appear completely naked on film . . . Poppy felt herself starting to flush.

"She's a goddess," swooned Delilah.

"She is that," said an appreciative male voice with an American accent. Poppy and Delilah looked up to see a handsome young man with chestnut hair and ocean-blue eyes putting his towel on the bench beside them. "May I?" he asked.

"Indeed you may, sir," said Delilah, repositioning her legs to their best advantage.

The man was wearing a blue and white striped one-piece bathing suit; a masculine version of the one Poppy wore. The fabric stretched across his broad chest and thighs and it took all Poppy's willpower not to stare.

He reached out his hand first to Delilah, then Poppy. "Dr Toby Spencer, Long Island, New York. And this," he said, indicating a shorter but equally handsome man, "is my cousin, Mr Miles Spencer. In fact, he's directed Miss Kellerman in one of his pictures, haven't you, old sport?"

"I have indeed," said the darker-haired cousin, smiling warmly below his trim moustache. "But goddess that she is, she does not have a patch on these beautiful mermaids."

Delilah giggled and thrust out her hand. "Well, I'm very pleased to make your acquaintance, Mr Spencer. I'm Delilah Marconi and this is my good friend Poppy Denby. Poppy is a frightfully clever lady journalist and I'm –"

"A frightfully talented actress."

Delilah's eyes widened in delight. "You've seen me?"

"Indeed I have. I was in London last autumn and I managed to catch a few shows. You were sensational in *The Cherry Orchard*. Have you ever been on film?"

Delilah was now sitting up, her bathrobe fully open to reveal her petite figure. "I have not, Mr Spencer. But I'm hoping that might change."

At that point the waiter arrived with their drinks. Miles Spencer insisted that they be put on his tab and then ordered drinks for him and his cousin.

The afternoon passed with lots of laughter and good-humoured conversation. Miles and Delilah spoke mostly of the film business, but Poppy, as arts and entertainment editor at the *Globe*, was able to contribute her tuppence-worth.

"And what did you think of *The Sheik*?" asked Toby, who had told them that yes, he was indeed a "real" doctor and worked in a "real" hospital.

"Spectacular!" declared Delilah.

"Disturbing," said Poppy, before she could stop herself.

Delilah and Miles looked at her aghast; Toby tossed back his head and laughed.

"Ah, a feminist, I see."

Poppy tightened the belt of her bathrobe. "If by feminist you mean I don't think a woman should aspire to be forced to have intimate relations with a man and then still want to marry him, then yes, I'm a feminist."

Delilah, her forehead creased ever so slightly, laughed fetchingly. "Oh, do forgive my friend. As I said, she's frightfully clever and has very modern ideas."

Poppy's lips tightened. Was Delilah criticising her? She whose mother had died for the sake of women's suffrage?

But before Poppy could say anything, Toby Spencer interrupted, speaking to Delilah but looking fully and appreciatively at Poppy. "Oh, there's no need to apologise, Miz Marconi; I couldn't agree more. I would expect nothing less from a lady of Miz Denby's intellect and character."

If Toby's comments were meant to imply that Delilah was lacking in the intellect and character department, Poppy could not tell, but she was grateful that that seemed to be the end of it.

"Enough of this jaw-wagging. Let's swim!" declared Miles and, with a short run, he dived into the pool, splashing water over all of them. He surfaced and called out to them: "Who's joining me? It's divine!"

Delilah jumped up and headed for the steps. Miles swam over and reached out his hand to help her in.

"Are you coming, Miz Denby?" asked Toby.

Poppy smiled at him. "Not today. It's been a long time since I was last swimming. I would prefer my re-acquaintance with water to be slightly less public."

Toby nodded his understanding. "Do you mind if I do?"

"Of course not," said Poppy and watched as he joined his cousin and Delilah in the pool. Poppy laughed as, led by Miles, the three of them started a game of Marco Polo, splashing around like toddlers in a paddling pool. Soon other bathers joined in and shrieks of laughter filled the room. Toby participated with gusto, but whenever he was on the side of the pool closest to Poppy, he kept trying to catch her eye. The young journalist wasn't sure how to respond and wished she had a book with her so she could pretend she hadn't seen him – or his impressive physique.

Oh, he's good looking, thought Poppy appreciatively, *but not as good looking as Daniel.* Her heart clenched as she wondered what she would be doing if her former beau were here now. She sighed. *I'd probably be swimming.*

Chapter 6

The passengers were summoned to dinner by bugle call, which was the tradition on the *Olympic*. Poppy had taken a nap after her time at the pool, while Delilah had been out and about socialising. But by seven o'clock they were both bathed and dressed and ready to make their grand entrance into the first-class dining room, down the majestic oak staircase. Poppy wore the same pale pink Jean-Charles Worth she had worn the night she and Daniel broke up. She'd thought twice about it, but in the end decided it was the best frock she had in her trunk and she wouldn't let her emotions stop her from getting her money's worth – even if she hadn't paid for it!

Delilah wore a Madeleine Wallis leaf-green silk and chiffon sleeveless evening gown with a silver lamé sash and silver shoes. It was brand new, from the 1921 House of Paquin spring collection. She'd bought it on a shopping trip to Paris. Unlike Poppy, whose budget restricted her to the department stores of Oxford Street, Delilah frequently popped over to Gay Paree whenever one of her favourite designers was showing a new collection. Poppy had to admit that Delilah looked divine, and whatever the price tag, she could no doubt afford it.

The two exquisitely dressed women, one petite and brunette, the other taller, blonde and slightly fuller-figured, stood at the top of the staircase and drew the eyes of nearly everyone in the dining room below.

"Just smile and pretend you do this every day," whispered Delilah, who could feel Poppy tense beside her. Delilah squeezed Poppy's hand warmly, then linked arms with her friend and led her down the stairs. Poppy held her breath and prayed her Cuban heels would not get caught in her Vandyked hem.

At the bottom of the stairs they were greeted by Rollo, who inserted his squat body between them and linked arms. "Ladies, you both look swell," he declared, and steered them across the dance floor to the restaurant tables beyond. Already seated at a round table with a white damask table cloth were Aunt Dot and Miss King.

"Hello, you two! Delilah, darling, thank you again for giving up your suite for me. Gertrude and I have settled in very nicely, haven't we, Gertrude?" Gertrude King nodded solemnly. She was looking a little green about the gills, Poppy thought.

As Rollo pulled out a chair for her, next to the older woman, Poppy asked quietly: "Are you all right, Miss King?"

Miss King cleared her throat and replied: "As well as a landlubber can be, I suppose."

Poppy smiled at the dour woman's attempt at humour. Sea sickness was a horrible thing, she'd heard. Fortunately, Poppy had found her sea legs quickly and thought the gentle lilting of the ocean liner soothing rather than stomach-churning. On her previous sea voyage she had been more concerned about a possible attempt on her life than any queasiness, so she had wondered how she would get on in more benign circumstances.

Aunt Dot, a frequent traveller, looked in rude health, her blonde curls piled high on her head and held in place by her best tiara. She was extolling the virtues of her luxury cabin to Delilah and asking what it was like "slumming it" in the cheaper cabin.

"It's hardly a slum, Dot," said Delilah. "Just not quite as luxurious as yours. It's still first class. And of course," she added, grinning at Poppy, "I'm bunking with a first-class cabin mate."

Aunt Dot laughed. "What fun you girls are going to have!" And then, more wistfully, "What I'd give to be young, footloose and fancy free again."

"My dear Miz Denby, I'd take your age and beauty over these young flappers any day!" said Rollo, winking at Poppy and Delilah.

"You'd better watch out, Mr Rolandson, or I might just take you up on that," said Aunt Dot with a melodramatic flutter of her false eyelashes. "And it will be interesting to see if you can outrun a wheelchair," she added, and everyone at the table laughed.

Aunt Dot then went on to enquire after the health of Rollo's sweetheart, Yasmin Reece-Lansdale. The newly appointed barrister – one of the first women in the country to hold the position – was an old associate of Aunt Dot's from her days as a suffragette.

While Dot and Rollo were reminiscing, Poppy and Delilah took some menus from a hovering waiter and perused the culinary fayre. As Poppy was trying to decide between a soup or shellfish starter she heard a booming American voice call out: "Well, if it isn't Rollo Rolandson! How are you, old sport?"

Poppy looked up to see a tuxedoed gentleman of around sixty, sporting a salt and pepper moustache under an aquiline nose. His grey hair was slicked back and his sideburns were sharply trimmed. Poppy's heart started to race. The American man's patrician looks had for a moment reminded her of Lord Melvyn Dorchester, the man who had nearly cost her her life during her first assignment for *The Daily Globe*. However, the American's sparkling eyes were filled with good humour and he was pumping Rollo Rolandson's arm up and down with bonhomie.

"How many years has it been, old chap?"

"Too many!" declared Rollo, who braced his legs to absorb the impact as his interlocutor slapped him on the back with his spare hand.

"You will, of course, remember my wife."

The man let go of Rollo's hand and took the arm of a splendidly attired brunette lady in her mid-fifties and edged her towards the editor. She wore a navy-blue crêpe velvet evening gown, cut to disguise the spreading figure of middle age while accentuating her elegant neck and shoulders, as well as an exquisite diamond choker. She too carried herself with the bearing of an aristocrat, and although she did not wear a tiara like Aunt Dot, Poppy realised this was a woman born and bred to wealth. She reached out a gloved hand and allowed Rollo to take it. He did so, with some reluctance, Poppy thought.

"Good evening, Miz Spencer," said Rollo.

"Good evening, Mr Rolandson." The woman withdrew her hand as soon as introductions were over, turning her body away from the diminutive editor. *Hmmm,* thought Poppy, noting the body language, *there's some history there.*

"We-ell," said her husband in what Poppy was to learn was known as the Long Island drawl, "you ce-ertainly are the thorn among the roses." He nodded to the four ladies seated at the table.

Rollo preened like a rooster in a hen house. "That I am, Theo, that I am. Let me introduce you. Ladies, this is Theodore Spencer and his wife Amelia. *Senator* Spencer, I do believe he is now."

Theodore nodded his assent.

"Theodore is an old friend of my family from Long Island."

"Not that old, old sport!" laughed Theodore and bowed to the ladies. "Good evening, ladies."

Mrs Spencer politely inclined her head too.

Rollo continued: "May I introduce Miz Dorothy Denby and her companion, Miz Gertrude King, from London. Miz Denby is –"

"Heavens above! It's Dot Denby!" The previously subdued Amelia Spencer lit up like a Broadway stage. She stepped forward and thrust out her hand towards Aunt Dot. "I'm Amelia, Amelia Spencer. I'm sure – or at least I hope – Emmeline has told you all about me. I've been working with the sisters in New York to get the vote. And we finally have – glory hallelujah – we finally have!"

Aunt Dot's West End countenance lit up too. "Amelia Spencer! Well I never! Of course Emmeline has told me all about you. The Pankhursts hold you in the highest regard, and any friend of the Pankhursts is a friend of mine. How delightful to meet you!"

Poppy thought for a moment that the two women might embrace, but they didn't. Instead, Aunt Dot gestured to the other women at the table with a sweep of her plump white hand. "Let me finish Mr Rolandson's introductions. My companion, Gertrude King, my niece, Poppy Denby – a lady journalist, no less – and Delilah Marconi, who is practically a daughter to me. Delilah's mother was a sister too. I don't know if you heard of Gloria Marconi on your side of the pond . . ."

Amelia nodded solemnly. "We did indeed. She was mourned as a martyr to the cause. I'm sorry for the loss of your mother, m'dear," she said softly, "but she did not die in vain."

Delilah's large brown eyes grew wider and welled with tears. "Thank you," she said softly and lowered her head.

An awkward momentary silence ensued, but was soon broken by Theodore's loud and enthusiastic: "We-ell, we're delighted to meet y'all. Aren't we, m'dear?"

"We are," agreed his wife with what appeared to be genuine warmth. Whatever chill Poppy had detected earlier in relation to Rollo had thawed.

"May we join you?" asked Theodore, indicating the five empty seats at the table.

"Of course!" said Rollo and Aunt Dot in unison.

"Two more will be joining us in a moment, if you don't mind," said Amelia as her husband pulled out her seat for her. She looked over to the stairs, as if expecting the latecomers to arrive imminently, then smiled as two dashingly handsome young men approached from across the dance floor.

Poppy and Delilah sat up a little straighter as Miles and Toby Spencer joined the party. *Of course!* thought Poppy. *Spencer.*

"Ah! There you are, boys!" declared Theodore, and proceeded to make introductions around the table.

Chapter 7

Three courses later and the conversation had traversed from women's suffrage, to the British miners' strike, to the morality of curbing immigration into the United States, to the rights and wrongs of German war reparations, to the League of Nations and the possibility of world peace. Poppy was ready for a bit of fresh air. She looked longingly at the sliding doors that led out onto the deck and wondered when it would be polite to slip away.

Aunt Dot whispered something to Delilah who nodded enthusiastically, excused herself and scooted away across the dance floor towards the bandstand. Was she about to sing? Although Poppy loved hearing her friend doing a turn, it was not what she felt like tonight. She wanted to be alone for a while: to think, to breathe.

The last week had been a whirlwind of emotion from the time Rollo told them that the *Globe*'s future was on the line, to him inviting her to join him in New York to – and at this Poppy bit her lip – Daniel refusing to support her decision to go. Then there was all the packing and wrapping up at work: the filing and typing, the last-minute instructions to the man who was covering her beat, the telephone calls to her contacts introducing him and explaining the situation and . . . she simply had not had time to process it all.

The microphone yowled and the bandleader – a Jewish man with slicked-back black hair and a pencil moustache, holding a clarinet in one hand – announced: "Ladies and gentlemen, I hope you have enjoyed your first meal on board the *Olympic*. On behalf of the captain and crew I wish you a *bon voyage*. If we may make your stay any more comfortable please do not hesitate to ask. We are here at your service. And at this point, I would normally say, without further ado, let's start the dancing . . ." This was met by cheers and applause. The bandleader grinned but silenced the crowd with a "simmer-down" motion of his free hand. "However, before we do that" – he nodded to the young woman in the green dress beside him – "Miz Marconi here has informed me that tonight is an extra special night for . . ."

Delilah smiled, basking in the appreciative glances from the assembled guests. Poppy couldn't help but chuckle. *Anything to be the centre of attention. What "special night" is it for you, Delilah?*

". . . Miz Poppy Denby. Miz Denby, where are you?"

Poppy felt like a rod had been shoved up the back of her dress. *Good Lord, no . . .*

"She's here!" called Aunt Dot in a voice worthy of the Albert Hall.

All eyes were now on the young woman in the pale pink dress. The rod in her back crumpled and Poppy's shoulders slumped. She smiled self-consciously and nodded to left and right.

"Well, ladies and gentlemen," the bandleader continued, "I have it on good authority" – Delilah giggled beside him – "that today is Miz Denby's birthday."

Poppy expelled all the air from her lungs. Her birthday. It was. The 6th of April 1921. Today she was twenty-three years old. It wasn't as if she had forgotten, but with all the busyness she just hadn't given it much thought. And she wouldn't have minded if it had come and gone without notice. She was not in the mood for celebrations, but – as she took in the warm looks from her friends and family – she knew she just needed to pull herself together. It would be unkind of her to deny them the opportunity to do something for her. So she put her reclusive thoughts to one side, straightened her back and announced: "It is. Thank you."

The bandleader and Delilah shared the microphone and led the dining room in a round of "Happy Birthday", and as the applause came to an end, the bandleader declared: "And now, on with the dancing!" This was met by an appreciative cheer.

Aunt Dot beckoned Poppy over. Poppy obliged. The older woman reached into her embroidered blue satin evening bag and brought out a small parçel wrapped in pink tissue paper and tied together with a purple ribbon.

"Oh, Aunt Dot, you shouldn't have."

"Of course I should have! Who else am I going to shower gifts upon other than my beautiful niece?" She passed it to Poppy, who took it with a warm smile.

"Thank you."

"Open it!" said Aunt Dot with a look that reminded Poppy of a child on Christmas morning.

Poppy pulled at the ribbon and unfurled the tissue paper. Inside was a black leather box. She opened the hinged lid to reveal a string of pearls nesting in green velvet. She gasped. "Oh, Aunt Dot, the Prince of Wales's pearls!"

Aunt Dot giggled. "Yes! He gave them to me after my run as Juliet in Drury Lane in 1906." She turned to the rest of the guests at the table – Rollo, Miss King and the Spencers – and explained: "It may be hard to believe but this plump middle-aged woman, stuck in an invalid's chair, was once as lithe and beautiful as my lovely niece. And," she winked, "despite rumours to the contrary, the Prince of Wales and I were never more than friends. Nonetheless, he frequently gave me gifts. He bought these, he said, on a royal tour of Ceylon. One hundred and twenty-four of the purest pearls. Put them on, Poppy; let's see them on you."

Poppy untwined the string, lowered her head and slipped them on. They felt cold and heavy against her neck and chest.

"Stand up, my darling; let's see."

Obligingly Poppy stood and the pearls fell to her waist.

Aunt Dot clapped her hands in glee. "They were meant for you, darling. Meant for you."

Everyone at the table agreed.

Poppy bent down and kissed her aunt. As she stood she said: "You still are beautiful, Aunt Dot; and if the Prince of Wales was here now, he'd say the same."

"Hear, hear!" agreed the rest of the guests at the table.

"Hear, hear, indeed," said a bass voice. Poppy looked up to see Captain Williams approaching the table. He reached out his hand to Poppy, who took it. "Happy birthday, Miss Denby, and may you have many happy returns."

"Thank you, Captain Williams." Poppy did a little half-curtsy then felt foolish. Did one curtsy to ship captains? She wasn't sure.

The captain didn't seem to mind. "Well, Miss Denby, as it is your birthday I should ask for your hand to dance; however, if you will excuse me and my old hip, I should rather step aside for a younger man." He looked around the table and took in the eager faces of Toby and Miles Spencer. "I, instead, shall dance with your most beautiful aunt, Dorothy. I still remember the first time I danced with her at an Admiralty dinner back in . . . oh, when was it? Nineteen hundred and eight? She was the belle of the ball."

"Oh Gilbert, you flatterer! But you know I can't dance now."

"Nonsense," said Captain Williams. "Come, Miss King, I shall help you get the lady into her wheelchair and we shall spin around the floor like Romeo and Juliet at the masked ball."

A flutter of panic crossed Aunt Dot's face. Poppy reached out and took her aunt's hand. It was quivering. "Is that all right, Aunt Dot? Do you want to dance?"

"Of course I want to dance! But tonight is your night, Poppy, and I shan't spoil it by drawing attention away from you. Thank you for the kind offer, Gilbert, but perhaps we can dance here instead, using words instead of steps."

The captain nodded his assent. "My lady's wish is my command." Then he turned to Toby and Miles. "Now which of you gentlemen will be first to ask the birthday girl to dance?"

Toby was on his feet like a shot; he bowed with a flourish and reached out his hand: "Miz Denby, may I have the pleasure?"

Poppy looked into his sparkling blue eyes and said: "You certainly may."

An hour and a half later and Poppy had danced with at least half a dozen gentlemen. She was relieved that the music was finally slowing down and the guests were drifting into corners to smoke and enjoy their coffee. A number of older gentlemen had already retired to the smoking room to discuss things they thought ladies had no interest in, and some younger fellows took the opportunity to select partners for the more intimate waltz. Out of the corner of her eye she spotted Toby Spencer moving towards her. Nothing against him, but she would rather not.

At that moment a group of guests at the next table stood, providing a temporary barrier, and she used it to finally slip out through the sliding doors onto the deck. There were a few people already there, so she walked along until she found a quiet spot between two lifeboats and leaned on the rail.

Nine decks below her the Atlantic heaved and swelled. She allowed her breathing to match the rhythm of the ocean. It was still hard to believe that she was on this floating hotel, travelling to the other side of the world. It was something she and her brother Christopher had fantasised about as children, telling each other stories of what they would do and where they would go. Their attraction to boats and the potential they offered for adventure had begun when they visited the great *Mauretania* when it was being built at Wallsend in 1905. Poppy was seven and Christopher nine. Even when Poppy was carried high on her daddy's shoulders, she still felt like a speck of dust next to the giant liner.

"I'll go to India," said Christopher, who was reading Kipling at school, "and ride on elephants in the day and hunt tigers at night."

"And I'll go to London," said Poppy, "and have tea with the king and queen."

"You don't go to London on a ship," said Christopher. "Don't you know anything?"

The seven-year-old Poppy took offence at that and said she did. She knew lots and lots and lots. And going to India was just silly because – didn't he know? – tigers eat people at night. Everyone knew that.

Christopher declared that was utter poppycock and he would most definitely go.

Nine years later he *did* travel on a ship: across the English Channel to France. And then he travelled by train to Flanders. A year later he was buried under a sea of poppies, while thousands of miles away, nowhere near India, the *Mauritania*'s sister ship, the *Lusitania*, was sunk by a German torpedo.

Poppy sniffed back the tears that were beginning to well. *Oh Christopher, I miss you.* And not for the first time she thought: *Why did God choose to call him home?* Had all her prayers for her brother's safe return fallen on deaf ears?

Poppy's breathing was now out of sync with the ocean. She mustn't get herself worked up – she mustn't. It would do no one any good and it wouldn't bring Christopher back. And besides, raging against God was never a fair fight. He was God and – well – she wasn't.

She watched the waves again: the rise and fall, the fall and rise, and her breathing steadied once more. Being a fair-minded young woman, she decided to consider the other side. Weren't there times when God *had* listened?

The Lord giveth and the Lord taketh away . . .

A gaggle of tipsy guests spilled out of the dance hall and weaved their way down the deck. She leaned in closer to the bulwark, hoping no one would think of joining her. No one did. Once again she was alone. She breathed a sigh of relief.

"Poppy, are you all right?"

Poppy turned around and saw Rollo standing behind her.

She wiped at her cheeks with the back of her hands.

"Birthday girls shouldn't cry."

"S-sorry, Rollo; it's just that . . ."

Rollo pulled a large handkerchief from his pocket and passed it to her. "You don't have to explain. Your tears are your own, Miz Denby."

Poppy took the handkerchief with thanks and blew her nose with an indelicate snort, for which she apologised again.

"I fear, Miz Denby, that I am going to make you cry again."

"Why's that?" she asked.

"Because of this." He handed a small box to her, along with an envelope. "Poppy" was written in Daniel's familiar hand.

"He asked me to give this to you. He said that he had bought it before your . . . well, before the latest developments – and that he still wanted you to have it."

Rollo's brows furrowed and he put both hands into his trouser pockets and rocked back and forth on his heels. "I don't know what happened with you two, Poppy, but I hope when you go back to London after this little jaunt, you'll both come to your senses. Life is too short to let something as precious as love get away."

Then he laughed. "Don't tell anyone I said that. My reputation would be ruined."

Poppy smiled through her tears. "Thank you, Rollo, and mum's the word."

She held the box and envelope in her hand, stroking them with her thumb and looking pointedly at her editor.

"All rightee!" said Rollo, taking the hint. "I'll leave you to it." Then he turned on his heel and walked away.

When she was alone again, she opened the envelope and took out a single sheet of notepaper. It said:

Dearest Poppy,

Today is your birthday. I so wish we were spending it together. But circumstances have conspired for that not to happen. There is so much I want to say but don't think it is wise to do so. I do not want to say anything I will regret. I don't want to lose you Poppy, but we both know things cannot go on the way they are. I hope that in the following three months you will think of me, as I will most definitely think of you. I hope too that when you return you will feel differently about family and work and perhaps we can then figure out a way to be together.

Until then, with my deepest love and respect,

Daniel

Then she opened the box and nestled inside was a red enamel brooch in the shape of a poppy.

Chapter 8

As Poppy and her friends were dining and dancing nine decks above them, Miriam and Esther Yazierska, known as Mimi and Estie, were finishing off their meal of mince, dumplings and carrots. The sisters were seated at the end of a long wooden bench that could accommodate twelve people, running alongside a trestle table, with another bench on the opposite side. There were six tables in the dining hall, with no damask table cloths or silver candlesticks, although the wood was scrubbed clean. The steerage passengers, most of whom had sold everything they owned to purchase a ticket, were housed in simple but decent accommodation. There were no rats 'n' rags here. Nevertheless, it was a world away from the luxurious lifestyle of the rich and famous on the top deck of the liner.

As Mimi carried her and her sister's tin plates and cutlery back to the serving hatch, she knew that upstairs servants would be clearing up after the guests, who would not give them a second thought. She knew, because she once had been one of those servants. Not on a grand ship like this, but in a grand house, where people came on holiday when Yalta was a vacation resort for the rich and famous, and not just a collection point for refugees fleeing the Russian Civil War.

Although the war had officially ended six months earlier, the fallout from it had not. Millions of people who had fled the fighting or been driven out of their homes for being on the wrong side of the White/Red divide were struggling to find their place in the new Russia. Some hoped to return to their homes eventually; others, like Mimi and Estie, had no home to return to.

Mimi's parents, Jewish tailors who lived in Kiev, had been murdered in one of the many pogroms that swept Eastern Europe. Tsar Alexander II and later his son, the last tsar, Nicholas II – Mimi spat at the thought of his name – hated the Jews, blaming them for every woe that befell the Russian Empire. Mimi, then fourteen, had fortunately been out of the house with her ten-year-old sister when the hussars swept through the Jewish *schtetlech* settlements, burning everything in their path.

When the ash cooled there was nothing left of the family home and business, and no adults to look after them. Eventually, after wandering from town to town and village to village in search of the next Jewish settlement that might take them in, Mimi was told there might be work in Yalta, at the homes of the Russian aristocrats who spent their summers on the Black Sea. The rumour proved correct and, after a few false starts, Mimi eventually secured employment as a chambermaid – even though she had a good education and her parents thought she might become a teacher. Her sister was too feebleminded to work, so Mimi paid most of her earnings for the girl to board with a Jewish family in the town.

Life with the Pushtov family – who came and went every summer for the next four years – was not too onerous. Yes, Mimi was no longer able to go to school and finish her education, but the aristocratic family was not unkind, and the work was stable. Most of the household travelled back with the family to St Petersburg at the end of the season, but Mimi was one of the skeleton staff who remained each year to keep the house running. Work during that time was light and Mimi was able to spend more time with Estie.

Meanwhile, Mimi continued her studies in the hope of one day going to teacher training college. She sneaked into the Pushtov library in the evenings and borrowed books on everything from science to mathematics to world geography. She even started to teach herself a little English and French. It was in that library that two things happened that would change Mimi's life forever. The first was she found a book about America and the wonderful opportunities the New World offered. It was written in English and she needed a Russian/English dictionary to help her through it; but the pictures alone – of buildings as high as mountains, streets that were lit day and night, and people from all walks of life rubbing shoulders in a place called Times Square – cheering in the New Year – wooed her. It didn't take her long to start dreaming of America.

The second thing that was to change Mimi's life happened early in September 1917. The day after the family had packed up and left, Mimi finished her work airing the bedrooms and slipped into the library during her lunch break. She normally didn't go into the library during the day, as the senior servants did not approve of chambermaids "taking liberties", but on that day the butler had a business meeting with the estate manager, and the housekeeper was down with a cold.

Mimi closed the door behind her, checked that the gardener was not working outside any of the three windows that aired the ground-floor room, then reached for the familiar book on America. As was becoming her ritual, she held it to her nose and smelled the leather, imbibing a deep sense of satisfaction; then she kissed it and pressed it to her heart, hoping that one day she too would be transported to a new world.

But as she went to sit in her favourite leather winged armchair she dropped the book in shock. There, sporting an amused look and a riding coat, was a young gentleman. One leg, in silken breeches, was draped over an arm of the chair and the other was resting – *sans* stocking – on a pouffe.

"Can you get me some ice, girl?" he asked.

Mimi jumped from foot to foot as if she needed the lavatory, did a funny little bow, mumbled "yes sir" and scampered out of the room.

When she returned, she noticed that the gentleman had reached down and retrieved the book on America. Her heart skipped a beat. Oh no; she was in trouble now.

She stood holding the ice bucket, not knowing what to do.

The gentleman peered over the leather cover and nodded to his foot, resting on the pouffe. "I've sprained it. Riding over. Be a good girl and ice it for me."

Mimi looked around for a napkin or cloth to use. Nothing was available. The gentleman reached into his pocket and took out a handkerchief. He passed it to her. She opened it and noticed the initials "AP" – Anatoly Pushtov – embroidered in the corner; then packed it with ice.

Anatoly Pushtov was a cousin of the family who summered in the villa. In the three years since she'd been there she'd seen him no more than a couple of times. He was a handsome man in his early twenties, with wavy brown hair that flopped charmingly over his forehead. She had no idea what he did for a living – if indeed he did anything. She only knew that he was somehow related to her masters and had a right to stay in the house when he chose.

She knelt down, her hands shaking, and applied the cold compress to the visibly swollen ankle.

"Ahhhhh," said Anatoly. Then he added, "Thinking of going to America?"

She dropped the compress to the floor, bumping his ankle as she tried to catch it.

"Careful!"

"S-sorry, sir."

He lowered the book and took in the dark-haired young woman kneeling on the library floor.

"Sorry for hurting me, or sorry for stealing a book?"

Mimi smarted but tried to contain her tone. "I did not steal it, sir. I was just borrowing it. The family left yesterday –"

"Yesterday? By the deuce I thought it was next week! I was wondering why it was so quiet. Thought they were all out on the hunt."

Mimi reapplied the ice compress. Anatoly sighed again.

"What is your name, girl?"

Mimi swallowed slowly before answering. "Miriam Yazierska, sir, but people call me Mimi."

"Mi-mi," he replied, caressing each syllable with his lips. "Well, Mimi, are you telling me you can read this?" He held the book open before her. "In English?"

Mimi swallowed again. "Y-yes, sir. A little."

Anatoly smiled and his whole face lit up. "What a lovely surprise!"

Mimi flushed, but did not look up. She felt his brown eyes resting on her. Her chest rose and fell with the ticking of the library clock. How long was he going to keep her like this?

"Well, Mimi," said Anatoly eventually. "Leave that resting on my ankle and then pull up a chair."

Mimi looked up, uncertain what to do.

"Go on," he nodded, smiling at her kindly, "get yourself seated. I want to hear you read."

Mimi smiled to herself as she remembered that first day. Her English, it turned out, was not as good as she thought it was. But the young gentleman had been kind and helped her with her pronunciation. And then, of course, he offered to tutor her the next day, and the next . . . and while the rest of the staff wondered when he was going to leave, he sent a telegram to the family in St Petersburg, telling them he'd decided to stay on a few more weeks.

Soon the lessons in the library turned into walks in the garden – Anatoly leaning on a cane as his ankle healed – and, as that got better, walks further afield and down to the beach. It was an Indian summer and the sun shone on the backs of the two young people as he told her about all the wonderful places he'd visited, and she told him of her dreams of visiting the same places too. Top of both of their lists was America.

Towards the end of September they became lovers. She had been surprised at how long it had taken him to kiss her. But when he did, she was ready. She did not care about the disapproving looks from the rest of the servants; all she cared about was Anatoly, her prince, who would take her – and of course Estie – away to the New World, where chambermaids and aristocrats and Jews and Gentiles could marry. And then, as the clock would strike midnight, together they would watch the silver ball drop in Times Square.

However, as the shadows of September shortened, news arrived at the villa that Anatoly had been summoned to return to St Petersburg. The Bolsheviks were fomenting revolts all over the empire and the White Russians were gathering their forces to quench them.

Anatoly and Mimi sat together on the private beach on the Pushtov estate while the waves of the Black Sea caressed the shore. Their clothes lay scattered on the rocks and, as the evening turned chill, Anatoly pulled a picnic blanket over their bare bodies.

"Mimi, my love, I have to leave you for a while."

Mimi did not ask why. She already knew. She pressed her cheek against his chest and closed her eyes. She could hear his heart pounding against her ear. Then she felt him take her hand and slip something onto her finger.

She opened her eyes and saw a single pearl on a gold band.

She gasped in delight. "Is this . . . is this . . . ?"

He wrapped his arms around her and inhaled the scent of her hair. "It is a promise that I will return for you. When all of this Bolshevik nonsense is over. Will you wait for me, Mimi?"

"I will," she said. "And then we will go to America?"

He laughed. "Yes, and then we will go to America."

Chapter 9

Poppy woke the day after her emotional meltdown and stared with remorse at the black make-up streaks on her pillow. By the time she had washed her face and ordered coffee from room service for her and the still-sleeping Delilah, she had made up her mind to pull herself together and enjoy the rest of the cruise. She considered for a moment pinning on Daniel's brooch, but instead she packed it at the bottom of her trunk. Daniel would still be there when she got back to London. And she'd have three months in New York to think what to do about him. *Don't look a gift horse in the mouth*, she told herself. *It's not every day you get an all-expenses-paid trip on one of the most luxurious ocean liners in the world.*

The coffee arrived, she tipped the waiter and then she poured two cups. "Wake up, sleepy head!" she called to Delilah. "It's time to have fun in the sun!"

For the next four days – rain or shine – Poppy and her friends packed as much activity into their trip as possible. Days were spent at the pool or playing badminton. Poppy borrowed one of Delilah's tennis frocks – a Suzanne Lenglen inspired creation – and the two of them partnered up and played doubles with the Spencer boys. Unlike her three friends who were born into money, Poppy had never played the sports of the upper classes, but she was a strong woman, and what she lacked in skill she made up for in stamina.

Even Aunt Dot had a go at some of the deck games, and Poppy partnered her aunt in a game of shuffleboard. Aunt Dot was having a whale of a time on the cruise. Clearly she was in her social element – catching up with old friends and making new ones – and Poppy had not seen her this happy since before her dear friend Grace had been sent to prison. Poppy knew that her aunt still wept for her friend, and in unguarded moments a shadow might still pass over her face; but like her niece, Miss Denby Snr had made up her mind to wring as much joy out of the holiday as she could. She spent time talking books with a lady who told her she was a writer. Her name was Dorothy Leigh Sayers. Poppy had never heard of her, but Aunt Dot assured her that once she was published she was going to be the next Agatha Christie. Miss Sayers was going on a short holiday to New York.

Another new friend of Aunt Dot's was a Swiss gentleman whom Poppy had indeed heard of: Carl Gustav Jung. The large, physically imposing man with the fine moustache and round spectacles was the world-renowned psychiatrist – or, what was the name? Oh it was on the tip of Poppy's tongue . . . oh yes, the *psycho-analyst.* Jung had lived in London for a while and the *Globe* had a Jazz File on him. Most notable in it was his very public fall-out with the other leading psychiatrist of the day, Sigmund Freud. Jung was going to New York to present an academic paper on what he referred to as the different personality types. "Oh, it's fascinating!" declared Aunt Dot. "According to Carl I'm an extroverted, intuitive feeler! That man has such insight! He says I'm a rare combination."

"Not that rare," observed Miss King. "He didn't say *that* rare."

Aunt Dot bristled at the criticism. "Quite rare, he said. *Quite* rare. You can ask him yourself. Oh! There he is! Oh Carl! Carl! I'd like you to meet my niece . . ."

Fortunately for Poppy, who did not feel like being bogged down in a long conversation about something she only barely understood, she was saved by Rollo who was only too delighted to meet the famous "head doctor" and interview him for *The New York Times.* "Nothing wrong with getting a *head* start," he muttered to Poppy before offering to buy Dr Jung a drink.

Most evenings were spent with the Spencers; Aunt Dot and Amelia got on like a house on fire and Rollo and Theo enjoyed recounting their days of high jinx on Long Island. Rollo had never mentioned his family before but Poppy learned he had one older brother, a banker, who still lived on the island and who had inherited the estate when their father died. Their mother was still alive and living on the estate. Poppy thought she saw a cloud come over the editor's face when Theo mentioned her.

"So, old sport, when was the last time you saw the old bird?"

"It's been a while," said Rollo and took a swig of his whisky.

After dinner each evening Toby and Miles laid claim to Poppy and Delilah as their primary dance partners. The dancing started sedately, with waltzes and one-steps. But as the evening progressed and the older guests retired, the band leader loosened his bow tie, rolled up his shirt sleeves and led his fellow musicians in covers of the latest jazz numbers from Tin Pan Alley. Most of the songs were new to Poppy as they hadn't yet made it across the Atlantic and into Delilah's extensive gramophone collection. She'd heard one or two of them when she saw the Original Dixieland Jazz Band play at Oscar's the previous summer, but songs like "Margie", "Ain't We Got Fun", and "Mama! He's Making Eyes at Me" were new to her. But it was the raucous "Home Again Blues" that really shook the dance floor, and the guests called for encore after encore. Delilah, as usual, led the way, teaching everyone the latest dance steps – some of which Poppy was convinced she'd just made up on the spot.

It was after the fourth rendition of "Home Again Blues", as Poppy and Toby twirled around the dance floor, that she spotted Captain Williams, accompanied by a flustered steward, heading towards them.

"Sorry to interrupt your evening, Dr Spencer, but would you mind awfully coming with us? There's been an . . ." the captain cleared his throat and steadied his voice, ". . . a terrible accident."

Toby and Poppy came to a stop. Poppy felt Toby's arm stiffen at the small of her back. "Of course, Captain. Is the ship's doctor not available?"

"He's already in attendance. He asked me to get you. Apparently it's within your area of expertise."

"Righto!" Then to the steward: "Fetch my medical bag from my cabin, will you. It's on the floor in the wardrobe, on the right-hand side. There's a good man." He turned to Poppy. "My apologies, Miz Denby. Will you excuse me?"

"Of course!" said Poppy. But Poppy's curiosity was piqued. What kind of accident was it? Why couldn't the ship's doctor handle it on his own? What was Toby's "area of expertise"?

"Actually, I'll come with you," she said.

"I don't think that's a good idea, Miss Denby," said the captain sternly. "It's quite a distressing sight."

Poppy straightened her back and looked up at the captain. "I worked in a hospital during the war. There's very little I haven't seen, Captain Williams."

Toby appraised her for a moment then said emphatically: "Let her come, Captain. She may be able to help."

Captain Williams didn't look convinced, but there was no time to argue. He led them to the elevator at the back of the dance hall. "We're going to the engine room," he explained.

A few minutes later and they exited the lift on the lowest passenger deck, followed the captain through a door that said "crew only" and then descended a flight of metal steps. At the bottom of the steps the captain opened another door and they were hit by a wall of heat and the roar of engines. "Sorry for the noise!" the captain shouted.

Toby and Poppy followed the captain through the maze of metal and machinery. Poppy gagged on the smell of diesel and engine grease, but she swallowed her bile and braced herself for whatever sight she was about to see. As they rounded a bank of pistons, shunting up and down, they came across a group of men huddled on the floor.

"Keep pressure on it," said one of them as he stood to greet the newcomers, wiping bloodied hands on his trousers. He looked with disapproval at Poppy, but didn't comment.

Behind him, Poppy saw two other men leaning over the prostrate body of a third. The man on the floor was lying, torso outwards, with the lower part of his body trapped in the innards of a machine. At first, Poppy could not see exactly what had happened, but judging by the amount of blood, it looked serious. And then she caught a glimpse of a cavernous wound, exposed right down to the bone. Poppy gagged. For a second, she regretted her decision to come. But then the trapped man moaned. He must be in desperate pain. *We need to get him out of there!* She looked at Toby and the gravity of the situation was etched all over his face. No, she would not be leaving.

"Right leg caught in the gears," said the ship's doctor. "Can't get it out."

Toby nodded, took off his jacket and gave it to Poppy, then knelt down and examined the patient. He had a quick look at the trapped limb and checked the man's pulse. He looked up at the ship's doctor. "You thinking amputation?"

The older man nodded. "I can't see an alternative. Can you?"

Toby grunted and examined the trapped leg again. He shook his head. "Unfortunately not."

As the steward arrived with his medical case, Toby gave a further list of equipment he needed: freshly laundered sheets, pillows, carbolic soap, three buckets of boiling water, two empty buckets, a nail brush and a bottle of whisky. While he was waiting for it all to arrive, he checked with the ship's doctor regarding what pain medication had been administered, then opened his case and extracted a syringe and vial. "Morphine," he said to Poppy.

Although the man was unconscious Poppy was not sure how far under he really was as he twitched and moaned intermittently. Within a few minutes of the morphine being administered the patient's distress appeared to ease. Poppy was praying silently through the whole procedure and offered a word of thanks that the man's pain was subsiding.

The steward arrived with the items on Toby's inventory. He ordered the pillows to be positioned around the man like sandbags while he laid out one of the sheets and unpacked surgical instruments from his case: a saw, scalpels and clamps. He then thoroughly washed his hands with carbolic soap before dipping each of his instruments in hot water. They were then placed on a new clean sheet.

"You can administer the chloroform and ether now," he said to the ship's doctor, who held some gauze over the man's nose and mouth while Toby monitored the man's breathing and heart rate.

When the patient was suitably anaesthetised, Toby picked up a scalpel, looked up at Poppy and said gruffly, "Wish me luck."

"Have you done this sort of surgery before?" asked Poppy, worried but curious in equal measure.

"I have," said Toby, "but not under these conditions. I usually have the most modern conveniences of an operating theatre at my disposal. We're lucky that at least I have the basics with me," he said, nodding at his instruments.

The ship's doctor nodded grimly. "It is. And we're lucky Dr Spencer was on board. This sort of surgery is way out of my league."

Out of his league or not, the doctor ably assisted Toby over the next hour, clamping and suturing as the surgeon sawed through what was left of the crushed leg. Poppy was kept busy soaking bandages and dressings in iodine, something she had done during the war. The acrid smell masked the stench of blood and bodily emissions.

The captain stood by and watched. However, when the limb was severed – and what could be extracted from the gears of the machine placed in a bucket – he paled and swayed.

Toby noticed. "Give him some whisky, Poppy."

So that's what that's for, thought Poppy. She'd initially thought the alcohol was going to be given to the patient to further sedate him – or perhaps the surgeon to steady his nerves – but she was glad that such primitive methods were not needed.

Toby leaned back on his heels and wiped the sweat from his brow. The operation was over. The ship's doctor and his assistant gently edged the man away from the machine and onto a stretcher. He groaned and Toby administered another dose of morphine. Then he checked his vital signs again. Satisfied, he nodded to the other medics and told them to take him straight to the infirmary.

"I'll be up to check on him when he's settled."

Toby placed the last of his surgical implements into a bucket and instructed one of the crewmen to have them washed and sterilised in the ship's infirmary. Then he washed his hands and buckled his case shut. He turned to Poppy and smiled, wanly, his shirt front red with blood. "You were a tremendous help, Poppy. Thank you."

"I hardly did a thing!" objected Poppy.

"You remained calm, didn't faint, and passed me what I needed. I thought you were splendid."

Poppy flushed, pleased at the compliment, but as was her want, immediately deflected it. "Will he be all right, Toby? That poor man?"

Toby offered Poppy his arm and they followed the bucket-carrying crewman to the stairwell. "The sooner he gets into a proper hospital the better. Lucky for him we're docking in New York tomorrow. I don't think he would have survived a longer trip."

"But will he survive *this*?" Poppy pressed.

A cloud came over Toby's face. "We've done the best we can under the circumstances. Still . . . I honestly don't know."

Chapter 10

The lady stood silhouetted against the sunset, as if her copper torch radiated the sun itself. The passengers of the *Olympic* crammed onto the decks of the luxury liner as she edged her way into New York harbour, trying to get the best view possible of their entry into the New World. As the Statue of Liberty was spotted, a roar reverberated through the ship, starting with the steerage passengers and ending with Poppy and her friends on the first-class deck.

Then Aunt Dot's theatrical voice rang out:

"Not like the brazen giant of Greek fame,
With conquering limbs astride from land to land;
Here at our sea-washed, sunset gates shall stand
A mighty woman with a torch, whose flame
Is the imprisoned lightning, and her name
Mother of Exiles. From her beacon-hand
Glows world-wide welcome; her mild eyes command
The air-bridged harbor that twin cities frame."

Her recitation of the first stanza of the famous poem was rewarded by a round of applause. She soaked it up with pride. Poppy squeezed her aunt's shoulder and sighed. What lay before them in this new city? What adventures might they have? She listened again to a second roar from steerage, this time not echoed by the upper-class decks. For them, she reminded herself, this was more than a three-month jaunt. It was to be the start of an entirely new life.

Rollo, standing next to Poppy, seemed to be thinking the same thing, as he muttered under his breath:

"Give me your tired, your poor,

Your huddled masses yearning to breathe free,
The wretched refuse of your teeming shore.
Send these, the homeless, tempest-tost to me,
I lift my lamp beside the golden door!"

"Good luck to the poor beggars," he grumbled.

"Yes indeed," said Poppy. "Good luck to them."

Rollo grunted at this, then turned on his heel and walked away, his shoulders hunched and his head bowed.

What's up with him? wondered Poppy. But before she could ponder her editor's strange demeanour further, a glass of champagne was thrust into her hand, and she raised it along with Aunt Dot, Miss King, the Spencers and Delilah.

"To the Lady Liberty!" cried Delilah.

"To Liberty!" they all replied.

The sun had set by the time the *Olympic* berthed on the south-west tip of Manhattan Island, which projected like an index finger into Hudson Bay. To the west was the squat digit of New Jersey, and to the east the Brooklyn thumb. But whatever their eventual destination, all passengers had to disembark in Manhattan. As it was nearly seven o'clock by the time the liner docked, the passengers needed to wait until morning for the customs officials to arrive. It was a minor annoyance, as most of the passengers were expecting to get off straightaway, but nothing could change the working hours of the United States Department of Immigration.

The next morning, the first- and second-class guests were requested to gather in their respective dining rooms, where they were treated to a buffet breakfast while they awaited processing by the US Immigration Service. The well-to-do passengers were afforded the honour of the immigration officials coming to them, while the third-class passengers had to alight from the ship, board a ferry and be taken to Ellis Island. Poppy wondered what happened on the famous island, and had been disappointed to hear that she would not be going.

"Not unless they find a problem with you or your papers," said

Theodore Spencer, between puffs on his cigar. "And I doubt, Miz Denby, anyone will find a problem with you." He winked at his son who, to Poppy's mild annoyance, seemed to have taken a proprietorial air towards her since their adventure in the engine room.

Which reminded her: "Will that poor sailor . . . what was his name . . . ?"

"Seaman Jones," offered Toby.

"Has he got off the ship all right?"

Toby straightened his day suit jacket and brushed a stray hair from his trousers. "He has. They let him off last night – as a special case. I helped them get him to the ambulance. I'll check in on him tomorrow. They're taking him to my hospital. I got the captain to telegraph ahead and have given instructions to my team."

"What actually happened there?" asked Delilah.

"We're not really sure," said Toby. "The man was a steward in third class. He also worked as a registration clerk, I believe. He wasn't a mechanic, so there was no need for him to be in the engine room. The captain will no doubt have some questions for him when – if – he wakes up . . . before the return journey to Southampton."

There was a flurry of activity as the team from the US Department of Immigration arrived to set up shop. The passengers were split into two groups: those with US citizenship and those without. Rollo and the Spencers were in one group, Poppy, Aunt Dot, Delilah and Miss King in the other. Alongside them were also Carl Jung and the writer Dorothy Leigh Sayers.

The passengers were called forward, one at a time, as they appeared on the ship's manifest – which was filled in by registration clerks upon their embarkation in Southampton. There were the usual details about age, gender, height, hair and eye colour, marital status, place of birth and purpose of visit to the United States. In addition one had to declare whether or not one had $50 upon one's person. Poppy did not, but Rollo had told her to just say yes, as he would provide her with the cash as an advance on her salary for the next three months. More puzzling, though, were the questions about whether or not she was a polygamist or an anarchist, and whether she intended to overthrow the government of the United

States by violent means. *Golly,* thought Poppy, *if I were any of those things, would I tell them?*

There were further questions about physical and mental health, and then one that affected both Aunt Dot and Rollo: "Whether or not deformed or crippled – the nature, length and cause."

When it came to Aunt Dot's turn, she answered "no" – with a giggle – to the questions about polygamy, anarchy and the violent overthrow of the United States government. However, when it came to the question about the reason for her being in a wheelchair, she began to wax lyrical about her activities as a suffragette in 1910 that led to clashes with the police, resulting in her paralysis. It was a story she was used to telling and she did it with aplomb, becoming more enthused as she realised people all over the dining room had stopped whatever they were doing to listen to her. When she was finished, she received a round of applause, and a "hear, hear!" from Amelia Spencer.

When the applause subsided, the immigration official, a gentleman in a brown suit who had placed his bowler hat on top of a small pile of manila folders, stopped writing and looked up at Aunt Dot.

"Correct me if I'm wrong, Miz Denby, but did you not say you are NOT an anarchist and have NO intention of taking part in any action to overthrow the government of the United States?"

"I have no need to correct you, sir; that is what I said."

The man slowly screwed the lid back on his fountain pen and positioned it under the name Dorothy Denby on the ship's manifest. Then he placed his hands on either side of his ink blotter and leaned across the table, looking directly into the eyes of his interviewee. "It concerns me, Miz Denby, that you have participated in violent actions of civil disobedience, have willingly clashed with law enforcement officers and have attempted to undermine your own government. Why then should I not think it possible you may try to do the same thing here?"

Aunt Dot shook her blonde curls in disbelief. "Good heavens, man, what *are* you saying?"

The man grunted but did not answer. Instead he removed his bowler hat from the pile of files, then extracted one. He opened it on the table before him to reveal a dossier of newspaper clippings and official memoranda. From where Poppy was standing, it seemed to be a record of Aunt Dot's career as a social activist.

But before he could interrogate her further, Theodore and Amelia Spencer arrived and stood on either side of Aunt Dot.

"Is there a problem here?" asked Theo.

The official looked up and recognised the Long Island senator. "No, Senator Spencer. I am just ensuring that no communists or anarchists threaten our country."

"But Miz Denby here is neither a communist nor an anarchist."

The man cleared his throat and ran two fingers along the inside of his collar.

"She is a self-confessed socialist," said the man.

"That is hardly the same thing!" said Theo. "Miz Denby and my wife here have both proudly pursued the right of women to vote. That hardly makes them political undesirables, does it?"

The man continued trying to loosen his collar. He looked from Amelia to Aunt Dot. He was in a fix, thought Poppy: it was one thing to call a foreign national an anarchist, but another to say that of an American citizen and wife of a United States senator.

"Er, no sir," said the man eventually, and stamped Aunt Dot's certificate of entry to the United States.

She took it with a humph and a flounce. "Thank you, Theodore and Amelia. If you don't mind – and if you've finished here yourselves – I would appreciate it if you accompanied me back to my cabin. I don't want to get tossed overboard by any over-enthusiastic immigration official." She glowered at the official, who looked suitably embarrassed.

"I'll meet you on the pier, dear," she said to Poppy and then left the dining room, clutching her papers, accompanied by Miss King and the Spencers.

The immigration official let out a deep sigh, unscrewed his pen and checked the next name on the manifest. He visibly tensed. "Denby," he said, as if announcing his own death warrant. "Miz *Poppy* Denby."

However, to both Poppy and the official's relief the interview was short and uneventful. Rollo had finished his interview too; as had the Spencer boys. Miles and Toby bid their farewells and asked if they might drop in on the ladies for a visit.

"Of course!" said Delilah. Poppy, however, did not want to encourage Toby any further. He clearly felt there was something to be pursued; she was suitably cautious. Oh yes, he was attractive, and she enjoyed his company, but it was a little too soon after Daniel. She didn't want to get swept up into a holiday romance when things had not been properly settled at home. Nonetheless, she had no good reason to turn down a friendly visit, so she politely agreed.

After the Spencers had left, Delilah was called for her interview. Rollo took a seat beside Poppy and pulled out his pocket watch. It was ten o'clock, local time. "Let's hope this doesn't take too long," he said.

"It shouldn't," said Poppy. "How did yours go? Probably just a formality for people born here, I imagine."

Rollo gave a mirthless laugh. "Imagine being a dwarf."

"Why should that matter?" asked Poppy.

Rollo crossed his short legs at the ankles and Poppy noted that they stuck over the edge of the chair like a child's. She wondered, not for the first time, what it would be like to have a child-sized body in an adult world.

"Did you see that question on the manifest about being crippled or deformed? The one that got your aunt into such trouble?"

"Yes," said Poppy. "But it wasn't the fact that she was crippled that got her into trouble. It was the story she told about how it happened."

Rollo grunted in agreement. "It was, yes, but if she had been born crippled or had ended up that way through illness it would have been very different."

"Why?" asked Poppy.

"Have you heard of eugenics?"

"No."

"It's a scientific theory that a population can be purified and strengthened by stopping the weaker members from breeding."

"Weaker members?" asked Poppy.

"Yes, such as dwarfs and people with other inherited illnesses and infirmities. As well as the insane and feebleminded. My country is trying to filter them out before they come here."

"But surely they can't turn you away from your own country!"

"They can't, no," agreed Rollo. "But if I were not an American citizen, and I was intending to live here permanently, like those poor beggars in steerage, they very well might."

Rollo nodded to Dr Jung as he was leaving the dining room. "I'll call on you next week, doctor."

"I look forward to it, Mr Rolandson."

"I'm going to ask Jung his opinion on it. About whether mental infirmity can be inherited."

Poppy looked over to Delilah. "Well, at least she won't have to worry about that. Delilah's as fit as a fiddle, body and mind." But Delilah's body language was tense and she was leaning over the desk and whispering furiously to the official. The official was red in the face and looking even more embarrassed than before.

"Oh dear, what's going on there?"

"Let's go see," said Rollo and jumped off his chair.

He and Poppy sauntered over to the desk. "Is everything all right here?" asked Rollo. "Miz Marconi is staying with me for three months and she has sufficient money to sustain her. There shouldn't be a problem."

If Rollo expected his intervention to have the same impact as Senator Spencer's, he was wrong. The official looked down on him with contempt.

"And who are you?"

Rollo straightened his shoulders and replied: "Rollo Rolandson, editor of *The Daily Globe*, London; temporary editor for *The New York Times*. Citizen of the United States. What is the problem here?"

The official pushed a dossier across the desk. It contained newspaper clippings featuring Delilah at various theatre openings, galas and parties on the arms of different gentlemen. Among them Poppy spotted her most recent beau, Adam Lane, and a previous suitor, Alfie Dorchester.

Delilah looked near to tears. Poppy reached out and took her hand.

"He is suggesting I am – I am some kind of – *p-prostitute*," whispered Delilah, then looked over her shoulder to see if anyone else was listening. They weren't.

"Not a prostitute, miz. But we are concerned that your behaviour has not been of the highest moral standard. We believe you are guilty of moral turpitude," he said, and flushed beetroot.

"Moral what?" asked Poppy.

"Turpitude," said Rollo. "It's another one of my country's immigration criteria. We don't want any naughty people corrupting the locals. Where did you get all this?" he asked the official. "It isn't usual to have dossiers at first interviews like this. But you've had one for Miz Denby Snr and Miz Marconi here. It looks like you were prepared for this. Were you?"

The official pulled Delilah's file back to him and slapped it shut. "We were sent information in advance, yes."

"By whom?" asked Rollo.

"A concerned citizen."

Rollo snorted. "A concerned citizen with access to London newspapers. Some of those clippings were from my paper, the *Globe*, which isn't available here. Someone has gone to a lot of trouble –"

"Excuse me, gentlemen," interrupted Poppy. "Do we really have to get into this? Miss Marconi and I are travelling with my aunt, Miss Dorothy Denby, and as you have already heard, she is a personal friend of Senator Spencer. Perhaps we can call him back to discuss Miss Marconi's case too . . ."

The official paled and cleared his throat. "Erm, no. I don't think that will be necessary. Welcome to the United States, Miz Marconi." He stamped her entry permit and passed it to her.

Rollo glared at the official as Delilah gathered her things. "You have not heard the last of this," he growled. And then to Poppy and Delilah: "Welcome to America, ladies." He hooked his arms on either side.

Poppy and Delilah slipped theirs through, relieved that the awkward interview with the immigration official appeared to be over.

"Let me show you the town."

Chapter 11

Mimi and Estie Yazierska shuffled along with the other third-class passengers, carrying their worldly belongings in carpet bags. Mimi took in what she could of the New York skyline in the morning light: there wasn't much to see. Beyond the harbour was a lovely park, she'd been told. But all she could see from her vantage point were hulking cranes standing guard like giant sentinels, blocking the rest of Manhattan from Battery Park. But she knew that beyond them would be buildings that reached to the clouds and a giant clock that marked in the New Year and where she would find Anatoly waiting for her – every day at twelve noon – for as long as it took her to come to him.

This was the promise they had made to each other the day he left to join the army fighting against the Bolsheviks. He had told her to wait for him in Yalta for as long as she could, but if the war turned against the White Russians, and it looked as if her life might be in danger, she should buy a ticket to New York and meet him there. He had left her enough money to pay for a second-class ticket each for her and her sister.

She'd waited two long years. By the time the Red Russians took over Yalta in 1919, the money was worthless. The wealthy homes all around her were looted – if not by the Bolshevik soldiers then by the people of the town or the staff of the villas themselves. Most of them – like her – had not been paid for months. Mimi brought Estie from her home in the town after the people she was staying with packed up their belongings and left on the first boat they could get. Mimi found Estie eating what was left of the kitchen scraps.

Back at the villa, with the few servants who had not yet fled, they had enough food for a few weeks – but it wouldn't go far. Half the city was already under Bolshevik control and – if the sound of shellfire and mortars was anything to go by – it wouldn't be long until they too were overrun. But Mimi did not want to leave without Anatoly. Each day she woke thinking, *Today he will come*, but each night, spent huddled in the cellar with the door to the rest of the house barred, she fell asleep fearing he never would.

Some of the homes in the Black Sea resort were occupied by aristocrats in exile. Mimi had heard that only a few miles away from the Pushtov estate Empress Maria Federovna, Mother of Tsar Nicholas II, was holing up. Mimi knew a maid at the royal villa who told her the British were going to rescue them. They were going to send a warship to the harbour and they would all be saved.

But Anatoly still had not come. That night, as Estie slept beside her, she prayed to God: *What must I do? Do I wait for him and perhaps die for him? Or do I save Estie and leave on the warship?* She waited for an answer, but, like the time she prayed when her parents died – that the God of her ancestors would bring them back to her – there was no reply. *Why, God, do you not speak?* She resisted the urge to spit. Instead she wrapped her right hand around her left ring finger and felt the pearl press into her palm. She had waited long enough. Even if Anatoly was trying to get to her, he would not be able to get through the Bolshevik lines. In fact, she was risking his life by waiting here. Better she make her way to New York like they had agreed. And the first step was to go on the British warship.

The next day she woke early, packed as many of the valuable household goods as she could carry and, with a still-drowsy Estie in tow, headed for the harbour. True enough, there was the British warship – the *Marlborough* – along with some smaller vessels flying the flags of other nations. Mimi recognised the French and Greek among them.

She joined the throng of people crammed onto the pier clutching the hands of children and the leads of pets. The royals, it seemed, were already on board, and Mimi spotted some of them strolling on the decks and watching their subjects below. A regal old lady in a fur coat and a large hat – possibly the empress – was speaking earnestly with the British captain, who was gesticulating to the crowd. Mimi could not hear what was said above the hullaballoo of the refugees but she could guess: "We cannot fit them on board, madam."

"But you must, Captain; they will die here if we leave them."

Or perhaps it was the other way round: "Let us leave immediately, sir. Before the Bolsheviks arrive."

"But what about all these people, madam – what will become of them?"

Did the royals care about them at all as they, safe on the ark of rescue, looked down on them from their haven?

Mimi wasn't sure, but more people were being crammed onto the boat and she, and the now fully awake but confused Estie, continued pushing forward.

"I'm hungry, Mimi. I want to go to the kitchen for breakfast."

"There will be food on the boat," said Mimi, hoping she was right.

Estie's eyes widened in excitement. "Are we going on the boat? On the water?"

"We are," said Mimi. "We are going to see Anatoly."

"Toley!" shouted Estie, pushing forward with all her strength – to the aggravation of the other refugees waiting their turn.

Mimi tried to calm her, but it was too late. The girl pushed and shoved and, before Mimi knew it, was at the front of the crowd, launching herself at the British sailors, who tried to push her back.

The men, holding rifles across their chests, muscled her back. Estie tried to get around them, shouting "Toley, Toley!" but she could not get past. And then one of the officers on board shouted to the guards. They held up their weapons and pointed at the crowd. "We're full!" they said, or that's what Mimi thought they said with her newly acquired English. Mimi reached Estie and pulled her back.

"Toley's not there, Estie."

The younger girl, her hair pulled back under a blue scarf, looked at her sister wide-eyed. "No Toley?"

"No Toley," said Mimi and took her sister's hand. The sailors started pulling up the gangplank. The crowd surged forward. Some warning shots were fired into the air.

Mimi and the rest of the crowd scattered and then regrouped and tried their luck with the other vessels in the harbour.

By the time Mimi and Estie reached the front of the queue, the

French ship too was full. But the Greek ship still had room. People were not so keen to go on the Greek ship. As it was only going to Athens, it would not take them that far. No one wanted to claim asylum in Greece, with the country decimated through war with Turkey. No, they all wanted to reach Western Europe – or even America – where it was truly safe. But Athens was better than Yalta, and, as far as Mimi could remember from the map in the Pushtov library, a little closer to New York.

Two years later, after making their way from port to port, bartering and selling, begging and pleading, Mimi and her sister were finally on the border of the Promised Land.

And so they walked across the gangplank onto the ferry that would take them to the third-class immigration station on Ellis Island. As happened with each new boat they boarded, Mimi had to assure Estie that "Toley" was not on board, but they were getting closer to him. Mimi found a seat for them on a wooden bench, beside a family of six who had started their journey in Sicily. The mother, holding a sleeping baby to her breast with one hand and trying to stop twin toddlers bickering with the other, looked exhausted. Mimi smiled at the woman. The woman nodded back, then, taking in Estie who was singing a song to herself, her eyebrows furrowed. She said something which Mimi did not understand. Then she pointed and twirled her finger at her temple in the universal gesture indicating madness.

Mimi bristled. Estie was not mad; she just had a young mind. The man at the port in England had said that as long as she paid extra money – a fine, he called it, for the feebleminded – they would be allowed into the United States. So Mimi had handed over the last of her money. She had seen the man on board the ship, so she knew he was here in New York. She had taken note of his name, so if there were any queries at the immigration station she would tell them that he had told her they could come.

Mimi looked over the rail of the ferry and saw the rich ladies and gentlemen climbing into motorcars and horse-drawn traps. She noticed the young blonde woman who had tried to help Estie on the first day. She had kind eyes, Mimi remembered. And there she was with her friends: the young dark-haired woman with the boyish haircut, the short man, the old lady in the wheelchair and her silent companion. They were laughing and chattering as they watched their trunks being lashed to the back of a small cortege of yellow motorcars. A pang of jealousy shot through Mimi's chest. Their journey was over; hers was not.

She clutched her right hand around her left ring finger and felt the pearl press into her palm. Then, as the ferry pulled away from Battery Bay towards Ellis Island, she closed her eyes and conjured up an image of a smiling Anatoly, lying on the beach at Yalta, his clothes piled beside hers. "I'm coming, my love," she whispered. "Please wait for me."

Chapter 12

What was called Ellis Island, in the singular, was in fact made up of three interconnected islands, with much of the geo-structure man-made. The ferry docked in the small harbour created by the islands on three sides. Mimi, Estie and the rest of the passengers were ushered off the boat and into a large, imposing double-storey entrance hall. They were instructed to leave their luggage on the ground floor and then go upstairs to another hall. Once there they joined a queue that snaked its way through a maze of channels demarcated by railings. It was efficient and organised, and despite the babel of voices around her, everyone seemed to understand the direction they needed to go in.

They were funnelled through a channel edged on either side by men and women in white tunics who had clipboards and were making notes. Occasionally they would mark one of the passengers with chalk on their clothing. Mimi wondered what the chalk marks meant and became increasingly worried when Estie, too, was selected to be chalked. The younger woman touched the chalk mark with her fingers and then tasted it. She grimaced and stuck out her tongue.

By the time they got to the front Mimi was hungry, thirsty and sick with worry. She had seen two chalked people taken away, their family members crying out after them. She held Estie's hand tightly. Estie was also hungry and thirsty and had been saying so, loudly, for the last five minutes. Mimi prayed to God that her sister would not have an emotional outburst before they got through the immigration control.

All the passengers had been given name tags including their manifest number when they were still on board the *Olympic*, so as the sisters stood in front of the processing desk, the clerk was able to see their name, their nationality and whether or not they required the services of a translator. He ran his finger down the list and then called out: "Russian!"

Mimi and Estie's mother tongue was actually Yiddish, but Mimi was fluent in Russian. Estie less so, but rather than requesting an additional Yiddish translator, Mimi said she would translate whenever necessary.

Via the translator, Mimi was asked the same questions that were on the manifest while the clerk checked to see that her answers corresponded with those given in Southampton. Then he frowned. "What did you say was the name and address of the person you will be staying with?"

"Anatoly Pushtov," said Mimi. "One Times Square."

"Toley! Toley!" said Estie, her head flicking from left to right, looking for the man.

"Shhh, Estie."

The clerk scowled at Estie over his half-moon spectacles, then turned his attention back to the older Yazierska sister.

"Are you sure of that address?"

Mimi thought for a moment, then nodded. Yes, that's what Anatoly had said. One Times Square.

"Well, Miz, I think you are mistaken. One Times Square is the address of a newspaper building, not a private residence."

A newspaper? Mimi did not know what to say. "I – I – I'm sorry, that's the address he gave me."

"And who is this man?"

Mimi flexed the fingers on her left hand to show the clerk her ring. "He is my fiancé."

"Your fiancé." The man made a note. "And do you have any letter of invitation from your fiancé that I can see?"

"A letter? No, I do not have a letter. He told me this in person. The last time we were together."

"Hmm," said the man and made another note.

"Estie need pee-pee!" said Estie and started doing a little dance.

Mimi bit her lip. "I'm sorry, sir, but my sister needs to use the toilet; is there somewhere she can go?"

The man looked at the younger woman and nodded. "I was coming to that. She is chalked with an X. We will need to examine her further."

"Pee-pee! Pee-pee!"

"Can she use the lavatory there?" asked Mimi.

"She can," said the clerk. "You, however, will need to stay here until we sort out this business with your fiancé's address."

He motioned for a guard to escort Estie. The man took hold of her shoulder; the girl screamed and pulled away from him.

"She cannot go on her own, sir!" said Mimi. "Can we finish our conversation later?"

The man let out a long breath and checked his notes. "I have a lot of people to deal with today, Miz; you will have to go to the back of the queue again . . ."

"I will," said Mimi, who noticed a little puddle forming around her sister's shoes. She grabbed Estie's arm and followed the guard out of the hall. As the door closed behind them she heard someone shout in English: "Janitor!"

"But the man said she could come!"

A man and a woman sat on the opposite side of a table to Mimi and Estie and the Russian translator. Estie was drawing pictures on the back of a sheet of paper – the very sheet of paper that she had failed to read. It was a literacy test, and no one, including Mimi, was surprised she had failed. Estie had never been to school. Did one need to have been to school to come to the United States? No one had told her that. But it wasn't just Estie's lack of literacy that was the problem. Her interrogators came to the conclusion that the "X" chalk mark on Estie's shoulder was indeed correct. The Jewish Ukrainian girl was most definitely feebleminded, possibly even a moron.

"She will have to go back to Southampton," said the man and stamped a sheet of paper with the word "Denied".

"Southampton?" said Mimi, desperately trying to get her head around what was happening, wondering if something had been lost in translation. She tried again, explaining to the translator: "Southampton is where the man was who said Estie could come. And then he was on the ship. I saw him there. He said if we pay a fine she will be able to come. He said simple people had to pay more money. But he didn't say they couldn't come."

The translator repeated her comments in English.

"And what man is this?" asked the male official as his female assistant took notes.

Mimi listened to the translator and replied, "Jow-ness," hoping she had pronounced the unfamiliar name correctly.

The man behind the desk looked puzzled. "Jowness?" he asked, looking for confirmation from the translator. "Who is Jowness?"

"He – he – was the registration clerk on the *Olympic*," Mimi replied in Russian, reaching across the table and poking a finger at the copy of the manifest. "He was the man who wrote that." The man listened to the translation, then turned to his colleague and whispered something. She whispered something back.

"I'm sorry, Miz Yazierska. But there is no way we can let your sister into the United States. She will have to go home. You, on the other hand, are free to join the queue again in the registration hall." He cocked his head towards the door.

Mimi listened to the translation then swallowed hard. She looked at her sister, who was much calmer now that she had been to the toilet. The girl was drawing a childish picture and humming a little tune.

"Please, sir," whispered Mimi in English, trying to hold back the tears. "Please ask for Mr Jowness."

The man's face softened. "I'm sorry, Miz, I cannot do that. Whatever this Mr Jowness told you was incorrect. I shall pass on the information to the captain of the *Olympic* – and if one of his crew was taking bribes he must deal with it – but it does not change the fact that your sister cannot enter the United States. It's up to you whether you stay or go."

Tears streamed down Mimi's face as the translator repeated the words in Russian. Estie stopped drawing and looked at her sister, then reached out her hand and touched a damp cheek. "Mimi sad? Why Mimi sad?"

"I'm sorry, Miz," said the man again, clearing his throat. "Rules are rules."

But rules apparently weren't rules for everyone. That night, after Mimi, Estie and a few other undesirables were fed and given a place to sleep, someone came to visit. It was the female assistant of the man who had declared Estie feebleminded. She gently shook Mimi awake and whispered to her: "If you want to come to America, come now. You understand?"

Mimi looked around her, confused. Had she understood properly? Her English was not very fluent. "We go America?" she asked. "Mind change?"

"Yes," said the woman and put her finger to her lips. "But secret, yes? Just you and your sister. Not the others."

"Why not others?" asked Mimi, aware of a large Polish woman beside her, mumbling in her sleep.

"Secret," repeated the woman.

Mimi sat up, careful not to disturb Estie, who was lying beside her, sucking her thumb. "Me and sister? Not just me?"

The woman nodded. "Yes, you and your sister. Are you coming? If you are, you must come now. There is no other time."

Mimi thought for a moment. There was something funny going on. But she wasn't sure what. However, if it really meant they were going to America, and the chance of seeing Anatoly again . . . She made up her mind. "Yes," she said. "We come."

The ferryman lit a cigarette and waited. He heard the crunch of gravel that signalled footfall at the top of the stone steps. A woman in a black coat and two young women, their faces pale and fearful in the swirling fog, approached him. Two more immigrants who had been turned away from the front door; two more who would get in through the back.

As the girls sat huddled under a blanket in the bow of the rowing boat the woman in the black coat handed over some money to the ferryman. He weighed it in his hand then pocketed it.

"Their names are Mimi and Estie. The younger one's a moron but the older one won't come without her. Take them to the usual place."

"Aye, aye, ma'am," said the ferryman and pushed his vessel away from the shore.

Chapter 13

Friday, 12 April 1921, New York

Poppy, Delilah and Rollo climbed into the back of a bright yellow taxi cab. Aunt Dot was already safely ensconced in another cab from the same company, with her wheelchair squashed into the back seat beside her, and Miss King in the front seat next to the driver. Poppy thought it strange that the steering wheel appeared to be on the wrong side of the vehicle and was even more alarmed when they headed out of Battery Park and onto the main road called Broadway on the *wrong* side of the road. She mentioned as much to her companions and they broke into fits of giggles but failed to tell her why their lives were not in imminent danger.

Both Rollo and Delilah were in buoyant moods, having left their worries at the immigration desk. And both tried to outdo the other, pointing out to Poppy this or that landmark on their ride through lower Manhattan. On their right, apparently, was the Financial District, and as they passed the intersection to Wall Street Rollo told her that his brother Frederick – known as Freddy – worked there.

"I think I've met your brother. The last time I was here with Uncle Elmo," said Delilah. "It was at one of those outrageous Long Island parties – we all jumped into a champagne fountain!"

"That sounds like Freddy," said Rollo with a grin. "When he's not in champagne fountains, he works just down there at the New York Stock Exchange."

Poppy was a little puzzled. Champagne fountains? Wasn't alcohol banned in New York? She asked her friends and was again met with a giggle from Delilah and a snort of derision from Rollo. "The sale of it, yes, and the production of new liquor. But at these sorts of parties they don't sell it – not officially anyway – and it comes from the host's private stock. Thank all that's mighty the Drys haven't managed to stop people drinking in the privacy of their own homes . . . yet," he growled.

"Oh look, Poppy, over there, on the left – that's the Woolworth Building!" chirruped Delilah.

The yellow cab had stopped at the intersection of Broadway and Barclay, and Poppy looked to where Delilah was pointing. She gasped. Towering above them was the tallest building she had ever seen. It was designed like a Gothic cathedral, but towered far, far higher than any European church steeple. She opened the window and looked out, craning her neck as far back as she could, and still she couldn't see the top.

"They call it a skyscraper," Delilah informed her. "Because, I suppose, it scrapes the sky!"

Rollo chuckled. "Superbly deduced, Miz Marconi."

Despite his teasing tone, Rollo too appeared impressed. "I rode the elevator to the very top when President Wilson opened it in 1913. I covered it for *The New York Times*. Sixty storeys up! You can see right across to Montauk, Long Island, on a clear day. If I'd had a telescope I bet I could have seen my family's house."

This was the second mention Rollo had made of his family this morning. Poppy noted that whatever tension she'd detected the other evening when he was speaking to Theo Spencer had gone. She wondered whether she'd get to meet Rollo's family – his mother and his brother. She hoped so. She was intrigued to find out more about her mentor and what made him tick.

The cab pulled off again and proceeded north on Broadway. They passed the City Hall on their right, whose white marble façade and Georgian architecture reminded Poppy of something from the Avenue des Champs-Élysées. Gothic on one side of the street, French Renaissance on the other: Poppy was struck by the hodgepodge of Old World styles – all of them bigger and more impressive than anything she'd seen before. And in between were spanking new buildings in the latest style. Poppy's neck was beginning to ache from trying to take it all in.

Rollo looked at her, his blue eyes twinkling. "Don't worry, Miz Denby, there'll be plenty of time for sightseeing."

But Poppy couldn't keep her eyes off it all: block after block. At Madison Square Park, the cab forked onto Fifth Avenue and a few blocks after that Delilah squeaked: "There's the Waldorf Astoria! That's where they're going to be recording my radio show – I did tell you, didn't I, that the director saw me in London and said I didn't need to audition?"

Poppy said that she had.

"Isn't the radio station out of town?" asked Rollo.

"Yes, in Schenectady," answered the effervescent actress. "But they've also got a studio in the hotel!"

"Golly!" said Poppy. "A real radio show. How exciting for you. I'd love to see how they go about it. Do you think I might be able to sit in on one of the recordings? And, Rollo, do you think the *Times* might be interested in an article on it?"

"They might be," he said. "I'm not really sure of the set-up there at the moment. We'll find out who's who and what's what on Monday. But it's always wise to have something in the bank just in case you're asked for a story idea. Just like you did the first day we met. Do you remember?"

Poppy did. And ironically, it was a story that involved Delilah too.

"I was very impressed that you weren't waiting around to be told what to do. Editors like go-getters, Poppy." Rollo smiled at his protégé. Poppy smiled back.

"Thanks, Rollo. As long as that's all right with the people at the radio station, Delilah."

"I don't know why it wouldn't be," answered the young actress. "They'd be fools to turn down free publicity – but, like Rollo, I'll have to wait and see what's what on Monday. I'll let you know."

"Thank you," said Poppy, then looked over her shoulder to see if Aunt Dot and Miss King's yellow cab was still behind them. It was.

Poppy pursed her lips as she thought about her aunt. She hadn't voiced her concerns yet to anyone, but she was a tad worried about Dot.

Dot, being Dot, was as effusive and jolly as ever. But on the voyage over Poppy had watched her aunt when the older woman thought no one was looking, and a pall of sadness came over her. Poppy wasn't surprised; there was a lot for her to be concerned about. Primarily, of course, there was Grace – Dot's long-term companion, who was now in prison for perverting the course of justice. Dot and Grace cared deeply for one another, and Poppy knew that Dot's heart was breaking not being able to see her. There was talk that Grace might have her two-year sentence commuted – and Rollo's sweetheart, the solicitor Yasmin Reece-Lansdale, was working on it – but for now the former bookkeeper and suffragette remained in Holloway prison.

Then there was Elizabeth Dorchester – the woman who had been at the centre of Poppy's first big story. Elizabeth had stayed briefly with Aunt Dot when she was finally released from the mental asylum she had been kept in for seven years, but during the short stay the two women had not had a chance to talk through all the bad blood and misunderstanding that had developed between them over the years. Dot carried a lot of guilt for being unaware of Elizabeth's suffering for so many years, and for the inadvertent role she had played in it. Dot needed to make things right between them, but, Poppy knew, she feared Elizabeth would spurn her efforts at reconciliation.

Poppy feared the same. Elizabeth's sudden departure to New York had been heralded by barely more than a scrawled note left on the kitchen table of Aunt Dot's Chelsea townhouse. Elizabeth, no doubt, had wanted to distance herself from the people and places associated with her confinement. And that, Poppy suspected, included her former friend Dot Denby.

If Poppy had had a chance to discuss all this with Dot before her eccentric relative arrived unannounced at Southampton harbour, then the young journalist would have tried to dissuade her aunt from travelling all the way to New York only to be hurt again. But Dot was a grown woman who could make her own decisions. And Poppy had to respect that. Nonetheless, she worried about her and would try her utmost to help ease the tension between the former friends. After all, Elizabeth owed Poppy her life.

Poppy reined in her thoughts and turned her attention back to her companions in the cab.

"When do you start recording?" Rollo was asking.

"Next week sometime. We'll have a few days of rehearsals first, starting on Monday," answered Delilah.

"Good-o! That will give us the weekend to settle in. Then Monday we can all travel downtown together. Will you be able to get to the Astoria on your own, Delilah? It's on a different line to the *Times*."

"Easy as pie," said Delilah, and then confirmed with the native New Yorker the route she would need to take.

"Will we be passing the newspaper building soon?" asked Poppy.

"No. That's on West 43rd Street," answered Rollo. "If we'd stayed on Broadway we would have passed it, but that would have taken us to the wrong side of the park. On Monday we'll catch the subway. That's like the Underground," he added for Poppy's benefit. "It's far quicker – and cheaper – than travelling by cab."

Poppy sighed. She hated the Underground in London. She disliked being in tunnels and the stifling hot air – she far preferred travelling by bus; on the open-air top deck, if possible. Here she saw trams running down the middle of the road. That would be a much better option! She'd raise it with Rollo over the weekend. For now, she took in the rest of the journey through central Manhattan, with New Yorkers out and about in the April morning sunshine, waiting at crossings or buying wares from hawkers' barrows. Poppy was pleased to see that in this most modern of cities, with offices stacked in layers, ordinary folk could still buy and sell on street corners, and horse-drawn trolley cars were not yet extinct.

Half an hour later, with the beautiful Central Park on their left, the cab turned into 82nd Street and pulled up to a five-storey townhouse. This would be their home for the next three months. "Welcome to Chez Rolandson," said Rollo, and winced as the driver slapped him with the fare.

Chapter 14

Saturday, 13 April 1921

Oh, what a spiffing weekend this is turning out to be! thought Poppy as she stepped out of the bathroom she shared with Delilah and opened her wardrobe to decide what to wear. Tonight she, Rollo and Delilah were going to a speakeasy, which, according to her friends, was a bit like Oscar's Jazz Club, only its location was supposedly a secret. It was all very intriguing, and Poppy, of course, could never resist a mystery. That, on top of the fun-filled day they'd already had, was making New York a giddyingly exciting place to be.

On Friday, the five of them had settled into their new lodgings – a townhouse owned by Rollo's family and made available to them for the full duration of their stay. With five storeys, it had more than enough room for them all. Of course, Aunt Dot insisted that she couldn't possibly impose, as her decision to come to New York had been so last-minute, and if Mr Rolandson would only point her in the direction of the nearest hotel . . . Rollo, naturally, had pooh-poohed this and said he had the perfect set of rooms for her on the first floor, with a balcony overlooking a small walled garden, and a stair-lift to help her up and down the stairs.

Rollo had had the lift installed the last time he was in New York as his dwarfish legs made ascending and descending most difficult. Back home in London he lived in a penthouse on a single floor, and of course at work – at the *Globe* office – he had a lift to ride. As Poppy had come to realise, with both an aunt and a boss with handicaps, the world was not built for such as them. So Aunt Dot and Miss King settled in on the first floor, with connecting rooms and a shared bathroom, and Poppy and Delilah took the matching suite on the floor above. Rollo's room was on the third floor, along with his private study and bathroom. The top floor housed Freddy (who, to Poppy's disappointment, was away for a few weeks on business), and other members of the Rolandson family if they chose to visit or stay over in town. The ground floor held the reception rooms, and below ground was the kitchen and staff accommodation. There was a butler, a cook and two maids who lived in the house, whether or not any of the family were in residence. Rollo commented on the expense of it all – seeing as Freddy was hardly there and his mother only rarely visited – but then added that seeing as the family money was no longer his, he had no say in it.

The money was no longer his? Poppy wondered what he meant but didn't probe any further. Rollo, despite his ebullient personality, was a private man and wouldn't appreciate her sticking her nose into his business uninvited.

On arriving at the townhouse, everyone was tired from their journey so they decided to stay in to eat and then have an early night. Delilah looked disappointed, but said she would delay painting the town red until Poppy had the energy to accompany her. "But don't take too long, old girl; I'm not getting any younger!" Poppy had laughed and said she promised to make up for it the next day.

Poppy hummed to herself as she flicked through her wardrobe, remembering the events of the day so far. The morning had dawned bright and lovely. Despite all the traffic in New York, somehow it didn't have half as much smog as London. During a vast breakfast of eggs, bacon and some odd-looking but delicious ring-shaped pastries, which Rollo called "bagels", the household had discussed their plans for the day. It was agreed that they would start with a visit to the Metropolitan Museum of Art, which was only a short walk away on the edge of Central Park, and that they would follow that, if the weather held, with a ride around the park in a horse-drawn carriage.

"And then," said Rollo, "we'll top it off with a visit to my favourite café, which makes the most devilish cheesecake."

Cheesecake? Bagels? Poppy feared her girth would be spreading on this trip to New York, then had stared in horror as Rollo slapped some bacon onto his bagel and drenched the whole lot with maple syrup. *Would it be rude to ask just for a slice of toast tomorrow morning?* she had wondered.

But as the day turned out, she indulged in everything New York had to offer, from bagels, to museums, to carriage rides, to cheesecake. And yes, Rollo was right: it was devilish.

Poppy sighed at the memory of it all, then pulled in her tummy as far as she could. Sometimes she wished corsets were back in fashion. Her fuller figure didn't look half as good in the latest shift frocks as the waif-like Delilah's.

There was a knock on the door. Delilah stuck her head round. "What are you wearing, old bean?"

Poppy turned around, hands on hips, wearing just a pair of camiknickers and one of those new-fangled bandeau brassieres that supposedly flattened the breasts to boyish proportions. Her tummy might not be strapped in, but her bosoms certainly were! Golly, how was a girl supposed to breathe in these things?

Delilah didn't need a bandeau; Delilah didn't need anything to make her look more beautiful. Poppy gasped when she saw what her friend was wearing. "By Jove! Isn't that what you had on the first night I met you at Oscar's?"

Delilah twirled around. "This old thing? Oh fiddlesticks, I think you might be right! Should I change?"

"No!" said Poppy. "You look – well – you look simply heavenly."

Poppy remembered the first time she had seen the young actress: when she had just come off the dance floor after swooning from her first ever glass of champagne. Back then, Poppy had thought Delilah looked like Cleopatra reborn into the twentieth century; she thought the same again now.

Delilah had just trimmed her sleek black bob so the fringe – or "bangs", as the Americans called it – brushed the top of her shapely, dark brows. Her Mediterranean olive skin perfectly accented her coal-dark eyes, further emphasised by thick lines of charcoal. She was wearing the shortest sleeveless dress Poppy – back in the summer of 1920 – had ever seen. A shimmering gold number, covered in tassels from neck to hem, which stopped a good two inches above the knee. She wore a long string of pearls, knotted halfway at waist level, and matching "slave bangles" on each bicep. On her right forearm she wore another bangle, styled like a snake, winding its way up from her wrist.

"Not too much?" asked Delilah with a mischievous smile.

Poppy threw back her head and laughed. "Oh Delilah, you're always too much. But that's what I love about you." And then she turned back to her wardrobe. "But actually, if you're wearing that, why don't I wear this?"

She pulled out a dress and held it up for her friend's approval. It was a sheer red satin shift with a Vandyked hem that would brush the top of her knees and reveal lines of tantalising flesh between the fingers of fabric. The red satin was overlaid with navy blue lace and cobalt blue beads appliquéd in abstract swirls.

"And that's the dress you wore the night I met Charlie Chaplin!" squealed Delilah and clapped with delight. "And of course you must wear the red satin shoes with the Cuban heels and that gorgeous little evening bag with the tassels, and the red satin headband with the feather brooch!"

"Of course!" said Poppy and did a little dance on the spot.

Oh yes, this is going to be a marvellous night!

Chapter 15

Rollo – dapper in top hat and tails – escorted the ladies to the trolley car stop at the corner of Fifth Avenue and 82nd Street. They would have a short ride down the east side of the park and then go underground at the Fifth Avenue subway station. From there they would go "downtown" – as Rollo termed it – riding the subway all the way under Broadway. This would be the route they would take to work on Monday too. Poppy followed the journey on the map Rollo had given her. The line went first west one stop to the 57th Street Station then turned south. Tonight they would be getting off at the Eighth Street Station. "After that," said Rollo, tapping his nose, "it's a secret."

"Oh, do tell us!" said Delilah, pulling her gold lamé wrap closer around her shoulders to keep out the evening chill.

"If I did that, Miz Marconi, I'd have to kill you," chuckled the editor as a horse-drawn trolley car pulled up. He grabbed the handrail and with a heave hoisted himself on. He paid the driver a couple of "bits" – what that was, Poppy wasn't sure as she had not yet got her head around American money – and then grunted his disapproval that there were no seats available. Poppy and Delilah could easily reach the straps provided for standing passengers; Rollo could not. He braced his backside against the partition near the door and muttered something about speaking to Freddy about a motor.

Fortunately the drive was brief and they alighted at the south end of the park.

Saturday night in Manhattan was as busy as the West End of London. *But oh my, the lights! There must be enough electricity surging through these few square miles to light the whole of the city of Newcastle upon Tyne,* thought Poppy. Theatres and restaurants, products and services, were all vying to have the biggest, brightest illuminations.

Ever-ready safety razors were being touted for $1.50. Coca-Cola – not a drink Poppy had yet tried – claimed it would give her "life". The Ziegfeld Follies high-kicked alongside Macy's department store and Lucky Star cigarettes lit up with style. Poppy's eyes were beginning to hurt and she was grateful to go underground at the Fifth Avenue subway station – despite her aversion to confined spaces. Actually, she was pleasantly surprised. New York's subterranean rail network was better lit and ventilated than its older London counterpart, and Poppy didn't feel nearly as claustrophobic as she did back home. As she sat down between Rollo and Delilah, in a carriage filled with New Yorkers ready to hit the town, she breathed a sigh of relief. Seven stops later, with the streets of Manhattan pulsing above, they alighted at Eighth Street Station, the nearest commuter stop to Greenwich Village. "We'll get a cab from here," announced Rollo. "It's only a few blocks away."

The cab wound its way through streets filled with residential buildings and small businesses, closed for the night. The glitz of uptown was toned down here and the only lights were the intermittent street lamps. The cab stopped and they got out in an ordinary street in an ordinary neighbourhood.

Where on earth are we going? thought Poppy, who imagined they would be painting the town red under the lights of Broadway.

The cab pulled off, leaving them alone with a flickering street light under attack from midges and moths. "Where to now, Rollo?" asked Delilah, her voice seemingly amplified by the concrete pavement slabs. Rollo put his finger to his lips to shush her. Delilah giggled and mouthed "sorry". The editor cocked his head and indicated that they should follow him. He walked a few paces, then turned right into an alleyway. They passed some bins and skips – or what Poppy had heard referred to as "dumpsters" in New York – and then found themselves in an open courtyard, hemmed on three sides by residential buildings. A flick of a curtain from an upstairs window and the glow of a cigarette tip suggested they were being watched.

Then there was a mutter of voices behind them. They turned round to see a bevy of well-dressed New Yorkers. The two groups stared at one another for a moment until one of the gents, wearing a swallowtail coat and white bowtie, whispered: "You first."

He and his party stepped back into the shadows as Rollo led the ladies across the courtyard to a nondescript blue door. Rollo rapped a little rhythm with his silver-tipped cane. A small trap slipped back and Rollo pushed through a calling card on top of a wadge of dollar bills. Moments later the door opened just enough to let Rollo, Delilah and Poppy through.

A large man in a pinstripe suit led them down a narrow, dimly lit corridor and then pushed open a door to reveal the sights, sounds, smells and sweat of a small jazz club packed with patrons clearly intent on having a good time. This was Chester's, opened only recently by the socialist Chester Wainwright, in the premises of a former blacksmith's workshop. The purpose of the club was to flout prohibition and provide a safe place for New Yorkers to drink and dance. Alcohol was not actually sold here, but the hefty entrance fee covered the bar bill and if anyone was deemed to have drunk more than their share they were asked to make a donation to "charity". If they declined, they simply would not be let back in. And for the bright young people of New York society that would be a fate worse than death.

First entrance to the club was by invitation only and had to be approved by Chester Wainwright himself. Rollo, it seemed, was a personal friend of the host and had secured an invitation only a few hours earlier.

Poppy, Delilah and Rollo stood at the entrance and took it all in. Crammed in the corner on a small stage, a negro jazz band jostled one another for space. The two trombonists were on high stools in the very back corner, with the rest of the brass and woodwind section seated on low benches below them. As Poppy watched, a clarinettist rose up to stretch his back and nearly lost his head when the trombonist extended his slide; he was saved only by the flugel player who pulled him down in time.

In front of the bandstand, thrusting out onto the dance floor, was another platform hosting three high-kicking dancers with sequinned thigh-high leotards and feather headdresses.

"They're moonlighting from Ziegfeld," Delilah observed with authority. Poppy didn't know enough to contradict her.

On the dance floor itself, five or six couples jiggled and jaggled, cheered on by friends and patrons around small tables squeezed into every available space. People were even sitting on the bar, and Poppy noticed a particularly leggy brunette wearing a scarlet boa surrounded by a bevy of male admirers.

Delilah squeaked. "It's Theda Bara! She played Cleopatra!" She was just about to head over to see the screen siren when a booming voice, emanating from a short, rotund man wearing a purple velvet dinner jacket, called out: "Rolandson! You yellow-livered hack – glad you could make it!"

"Chester! You old dog, flouting the law again, I see!" The editor and the squat proprietor shook hands vigorously.

Introductions were made, hands kissed, and the Rolandson party was ushered over to a reserved table; but not before a canoodling couple were evicted and told to do an "86".

"What's an '86'?" asked Poppy.

"It's the code we use for a police raid," explained Chester as he pulled out a chair for Poppy.

"There's a raid?" asked Delilah, her eyes wide, her bobbed head flicking from side to side.

Chester chuckled. "No. But those two are so many sheets to the wind they won't know that. They've drunk way beyond their share. Let them think there's a raid and save my bouncers the trouble."

"But why an '86'?" asked Poppy.

Chester cocked his head towards a door to the left of the bar. "This is 86 Bedford Street. That's the entrance there. The cops, when they raid, always come through the courtyard entrance – the one you did – so it gives the guys and gals time to get out the number 86 door." He opened his hands wide and grinned. "It works every time."

"But," continued Poppy, still curious, "how do you know they'll always come through that door?"

Chester curled back his top lip to reveal a pair of buck teeth and chortled. "You need to brief your reporter a bit better than this,

Rollo." Then he winked at Delilah, who already appeared to know the answer.

"Because, Miz Denby, that's what we've agreed with them!"

Before Poppy could ask any more, he called over a waiter and put in an order for a bottle of champagne, without asking if that was what everybody wanted.

"Sorry ladies," he explained, "we're limited with what we have. But it's a good bottle of bubbly."

Poppy smiled. She liked bubbly. And she liked Chester Wainwright. And whatever questions she had about this speakeasy – like why it was called a speakeasy – could wait. For now, she, Delilah and Rollo were going to have as much fun as they could. And the thought that at any minute they might have to "do an 86" made it all the more exciting.

An hour later and Delilah had already established herself as *the* girl to dance with. She had even joined the illicit Ziegfeld chorus line for a few numbers. Poppy had done a couple of turns on the dance floor, one with a surprisingly nimble Rollo, but now was content to sit and watch. She needed to use the powder room. She surveyed the club and assessed where she thought the facilities might be housed then excused herself to Rollo – who was enjoying a fat Cuban cigar – and skirted the dance floor. Just as she was passing the door to the courtyard entrance it opened, and a new group of guests was escorted in by the surly doorman.

"Miz Denby!" said one of them.

It was Miles Spencer. Behind him was his cousin, Toby, who grinned and raised his top hat. "Well hello, Poppy! I was hoping to see you again, but didn't expect it to be so soon! Are you here with anyone?"

Poppy nodded towards her table. "Rollo and Delilah," she said. "Good evening, gentlemen."

The group were passing their coats and hats to a concierge. There were six of them: four men and two women. Introductions were made. The ladies were Trixie and Jemima Adams, sisters, and the other two gents, Richard Wainwright – nephew of Chester – and Count Otto von Riesling from Liechtenstein. Poppy shook hands with each in turn until she came to the count. The man was a step or two behind the others, making a fuss of unbuttoning his overcoat.

"Otto, old man, shake a leg," said Toby. "This is the lovely lady I was telling you about. The one from the *Olympic* who was such a trooper with that poor fella in the engine room. Poppy, this is Count Otto von Riesling."

Poppy prepared to greet the final member of the party, a welcoming smile on her face. But as he turned towards her, having finally offloaded his coat to the concierge, she felt a wave of nausea flush over her. The music dimmed and Toby's voice took on a distant air as she stood facing a man in his thirties with jet black hair and moustache, and piercing blue eyes.

"Poppy, this is Otto von Riesling," Toby said again, and waited for the two to shake hands.

The count stood up very straight, his eyes, she was convinced, flashing recognition. He put out his hand. "A pleasure to meet you, Miss Polly Denny," he said in a German accent.

The nausea had now subsided and it was replaced with a surge of red-hot anger. "It's Denby. Poppy Denby. As you well know, Viscount Dorchester."

She snubbed his hand, pointed a finger at his chest and turned to the rest of the Spencer party. "This man is *not* Count Otto von Whoever-he-says-he-is; his name is Alfie Dorchester. Viscount Alfie – Alfred – Dorchester. Son of Lord Melvyn Dorchester of Windsor, and a fugitive from British justice."

Anger flashed again in the blue eyes, and his lips – under what must have been a dyed moustache – tightened into a thin line.

"I have no idea what you are talking about," said the count. "Wainwright, I suggest you ask your uncle to vet his guests more carefully. Either this young woman has had too much to drink or she's just escaped from an asylum."

Toby, Miles and the other three guests looked bemused. Poppy's hands were now on her hips, her voice raised. "And you would know all about that, wouldn't you, Dorchester, seeing as you kept your poor sister locked in one for seven years!"

"Good Lord, Poppy. What are you saying?" asked Toby.

"I'm saying, Dr Spencer, that this friend of yours has you duped. How long have you known him?"

"I – I – don't know," answered Toby, looking intently at his European companion. "How long is it, von Riesling? Four or five months?"

The count turned his back on Poppy and addressed his companions. "It does not matter. You do not have to answer this woman's questions. Wainwright, call your uncle."

Wainwright junior looked flummoxed. His eyes flitted from his friend to Poppy and then across to the bar where the rotund figure of his uncle could be seen talking to other guests.

"Yes, Mr Wainwright, that's an excellent idea. Call your uncle. I'm sure he'd want to know that you've brought an attempted murderer into his club," said Poppy, positioning herself between the count and the door, in case he tried to escape.

"Attempted murderer?" asked Wainwright, his voice high. "I'm sure you are mistaken, Miz Denby. A case of mistaken identity."

"No, Mr Wainwright; it is not! This man is Alfie Dorchester. He tried to murder me – twice; and Delilah; and a woman called Grace Wilson, *and* his own sister, once. Along with his father, who is now in prison. But this man . . ." She turned to point at the count again.

He was no longer there but was grabbing his coat and hat from the concierge.

"Where do you think you're going?" screamed Poppy just as the club music came to an end. All eyes flashed towards her, including Delilah's and Rollo's. She shouted over to them: "It's Alfie Dorchester!"

Rollo and Delilah jostled for a view. But they were too far away to see the dark-haired count properly. Poppy tried to hail them but then the count stepped right in front of her, so close she could smell his sweat.

"Get out of my way, madam. I will not stand here and be accused of such an outrage," he said. Although he retained his accent, Poppy was sure she could hear the clipped English tones of her nemesis underneath.

"I will not get out of your way. I'll – " But her voice was silenced as he roughly pushed her aside and threw open the door.

"Steady on, old sport," said Toby. But before he could intervene, the count was gone and a voice bellowed across the club: "Eighty-six, eighty-six!" All hell broke loose.

Poppy ran towards the courtyard entrance to catch up with the count, but she was blocked by the large doorman. "It's a raid, Miz. They'll be here in a few minutes. Go that way."

He pointed to the stampede of revellers heading for a door to the left of the bar. She could not see Delilah and Rollo in the throng.

"Come on, Poppy, let's go," said Toby, who was still at her arm. His tone was no more than civil; cold even. *He's probably upset by the scene I made,* thought Poppy. *Well, bully for him!*

She was going to say "Thanks, I'll make my own way" but an ungentlemanly shove by the doorman pushed her in the direction of the exodus, and she was caught up in the flood, Toby close behind her. As she passed the bar she noted the drinks cabinet revolving on some mechanism and being replaced by a shelf of tea caddies. Waiters were clearing bottles and glasses off tables with military precision, then passing the crates to a man in a hatch on the floor – in the place where the piano had been a few minutes earlier. The piano would roll back when the hatch closed. It, in turn, would lead to an underground cellar and perhaps even a secret tunnel like the one at Oscar's Jazz Club in London.

Poppy's journalistic mind took all of this in as she was pulled and pushed towards the exit. A woman tripped on her heel and fell. A friend pulled her up and dragged her along as she cried: "My shoe! They're Ferragamos!"

Poppy wondered what the police officer who found it would think. Would he search for her like the prince for Cinderella – and slap a pair of bracelets on her instead of a ring?

Poppy was pushed through the Bedford Street door onto a residential street. Incredibly, taxis were waiting for some of the guests – *pre-ordered*? Other guests knocked on doors and were hauled inside – *pre-arranged*? The rest, like Poppy, ran as quickly as they could while the caterwaul of police sirens filled the night. Toby Spencer called to her from a cab. She pretended not to hear and ran on. A surge of anger shot through her. What relationship did Toby have with Alfie? What game were they playing with her?

She joined a giggling crowd of flappers and fops who'd clearly done this before, and navigated the maze of alleys and streets through Greenwich Village. Toby was left far behind. And only the Lord knew where Alfie Dorchester was. But she would find out. By Jove she would find out.

She allowed herself to be carried along with the throng until finally she was reunited with Rollo and Delilah at the entrance to the Eighth Street subway. Together they descended the steps into the station, holding themselves like naughty school children as they passed a pair of police officers and tried not to laugh. They only had a few moments to wait until the uptown train pulled in, and, with a group sigh, they climbed on and found a place to sit.

The carriage was half full of refugees from Chester's, the atmosphere electric. Rollo and Delilah joined in with a round of "Mama! He's Making Eyes at Me"; Poppy remained silent.

As the song came to an end, Delilah looked at Poppy apologetically. "Sorry, Popsicle; I got carried away. I know you were getting upset before the raid. You thought you'd seen someone who looked like Alfie Dorchester. That must have been quite a shock."

Poppy's brows came together in a scowl. "*Not* just someone who looked like him, Delilah – it was Alfie Dorchester *himself*. The real McCoy, as they say here in America."

"How sure are you that it was Alfie?" asked Rollo, his face suddenly serious. "From what I could see the fella had black hair. Alfie's blond."

"It was dyed," said Poppy. "A good job, but it was dyed. It was him; I'd know those eyes any day." She took a deep breath, trying to calm herself. "We'll report it to the police – as soon as we're off the subway."

Rollo shook his head and lowered his voice. "And tell them what? So far you are the only person who thinks it's him. His friends know him as . . . whatever he called himself –"

"Count Otto von Riesling."

"So it will be a matter of his and their word against yours. And unless you have some evidence other than you thought you recognised someone you last saw a year ago, who according to all sources is still in Monte Carlo, and now he turns up at an illegal speakeasy that you can't actually admit you were at – unless you want to get yourself,

Chester and the whole damned lot of us arrested – you haven't got a hope in hell of anyone taking you seriously."

"But it *was* him." Poppy's voice caught with unshed tears.

Rollo cleared his throat and nodded. "I believe you, Poppy. But going to the police at this stage is not an option. We'll need more proof. And where we're both going on Monday morning will be the best place to get it."

Chapter 16

Friday, 12 April 1921, off Ellis Island

Mimi and Estie huddled in the prow of the rowing boat – Estie because she had been told it was a game of hide and seek and Mimi because the ferryman had warned her that the police would put her in prison if she didn't. Although her English was not very good, she knew enough to understand that what they were doing was illegal and there would be severe consequences if they were caught.

When they reached land they were ushered into a wagon and hidden under sackcloth while the ferryman strapped in his old nag. She was kept in the backyard of a coopery – for a small monthly fee – while her master was at work. The cooper chose not to mention the ferryman's unusual cargo he occasionally brought back from Ellis Island, just as the ferryman chose not to mention the smell of cheap liquor coming from some of the cooper's barrels.

Unlike Poppy and her friends, the sisters did not travel in a bright yellow taxi up Broadway, oohing and ahhing at skyscrapers in the mid-morning sun. Instead, they traversed the cobbled back roads beside the great Hudson River, winding through the poorly lit docklands of the lower west side.

Through the Meatpacking District and up past the Hudson Docks, Mimi could hear women's voices calling out to the ferryman: "A dime a time." She'd been through enough docks on her journey west from Yalta to visualise the scene: poorly dressed women, their faces painted, offering all they had for all they could get.

There had been times when she thought she would end up doing the same, but somehow she had managed to avoid it. She had judiciously rationed out the valuables stolen from the villa and, when they ran out, washed dishes and cleaned tavern latrines. Estie helped her without complaint, happy to be thought important enough to be given a job to do.

Although Mimi worried for a minute that she and Estie might be headed towards a similar fate, she reminded herself that the lady at Ellis Island had told her there would be decent work to do. She hadn't said exactly what it was – or if she had, Mimi hadn't understood the English words – but she had understood enough to know that she and Estie must work for some time (months, years?) in payment for their entry into the so-called "Land of the Free". So she would work – but only until she found Anatoly. And then he would pay the people so she could leave . . . and they could get married . . . and they could live happily ever after . . .

"A dime a time!" croaked a whore.

"You dumb Dora," answered the ferryman.

Monday, 15 April 1921, Manhattan

Poppy, Rollo and Delilah were on the subway heading to Times Square. It was just past eight o'clock on Monday morning and the train was full of office workers and schoolchildren. The snappier dressers in their pinstripes and derbies were uniformly hidden behind the financial pages of the *Times*; the flat caps and baggies shared the sports pages between them. Poppy could see that someone called "The Babe" was declaring that the Yankees were on track to win the World Series. Rollo explained that the headline was referring to baseball – similar to English rounders, but people actually paid to watch it – and no other countries were playing: the "World" was just America.

Teenage girls in pinafores and straw boaters giggled at a young lad sporting an enormous pimple on the end of his nose while he looked out of the window in embarrassment. Poppy glared at the girls; they lowered their eyes in shame.

Rollo was reading the inside pages of the *Times*. He chuckled and pointed a stubby finger at an article halfway down column three: "Wets escape raid on Village speakeasy – Drys cry police pay off".

"We made it into the papers, ladies. Fame at last, eh?"

Delilah giggled. Poppy smiled wryly: not quite the way she wanted to get into the news. But, she had to admit, the night had been fun – at least until her shock encounter with the fake count.

After getting home safely on Saturday, the three of them had chewed over their options regarding Alfie Dorchester and decided that Rollo was right: nothing could, or should, be done until Monday. They also decided to keep it a secret from Aunt Dot and Miss King, as Poppy's aunt was already emotionally fragile, and news that the man who attempted to kill her loved ones was loose on the streets of New York might be too much for her. So Poppy spent the rest of the weekend pretending everything was all right.

On Sunday, she accompanied her aunt to the nearby Park Avenue Methodist Church – pointed out to them by Rollo. Between singing Wesley hymns, she wondered what the folk would think if they knew she had spent the previous evening running from the police and drinking, illegally, at a scandalous speakeasy. She knew what her parents would think.

Why was she there? She had got out of the habit of going to church in London. She told herself it was because she was often working, but the truth was, she didn't really know how her new life would be judged by the congregation. What did it mean to be a good Christian? Did her new love for clothes and music and going to the theatre and dancing in jazz clubs now disqualify her? She didn't know. She just didn't know.

The train pulled into Times Square Station. Poppy stood up, gathered her satchel and prayed for help on her first day on the job. Yes, she still prayed. Despite her unease in church, faith was still part of her life. And boy, did she need that now. Apart from the pressure of trying to find evidence that a Liechtensteinian count was actually the British aristocrat and fugitive Alfie Dorchester, there was the small matter of fitting into an entirely new newspaper in an entirely new city on the other side of the world.

Thank heavens she had Rollo with her. He would know what to do. He would be able to direct her, help her, advise her. She would have reached out and held his hand – like a child needing affirmation from an adult – but it wasn't the appropriate thing to do.

Up the subway steps and onto Broadway, she and Rollo bid goodbye to Delilah. Delilah's session started at ten o'clock, so she had plenty of time. She said she would take in the square and jump back on the subway to 34th Street Station, then walk down to the Astoria via Macy's, where she would buy a new hat to match her lilac and white frock. Her "old" hat had not been in a proper hat box and had got squashed in the trunk on the way over. "That's what I get for last-minute packing!" she confessed.

Poppy gave her friend a cuddle, wished her happy hat hunting and told her to break a leg. "Does one still break a leg on the wireless?" she wondered.

Delilah giggled. "I don't know! But I'll soon find out." Then she skipped off to window-shop around the square.

"Righto," said Rollo, as Delilah turned a corner. "To work we go." He led Poppy south and then west along 43rd Street, explaining as they walked that One Times Square no longer housed the editorial offices, although it was still owned by the paper.

"Don't be overwhelmed when you see the building," he warned. "It's eighteen storeys high and the editorial department alone is spread over six floors."

Golly, thought Poppy. *The* Globe *is only four floors – the entire building.* If she was already nervous, then this made it ten times worse.

As if reading her mind, Rollo stopped at a pedestrian crossing and turned to her: "Don't worry, a newspaper's still a newspaper. You'll fit right in." Then, as a gap cleared in the traffic, they crossed the road.

Five minutes later they arrived at the imposing edifice of 229 West 43rd Street. En route Rollo told her that the entire company employed eighteen hundred people, had a daily readership of just under half a million and an editorial staff of around two hundred. The *Globe* had only ten. Back home in London Poppy was called the "arts and entertainment editor" – implying that she had an entire department under her, but in reality she was a staff of one. At *The New York Times* they had separate editors for book reviews, music, drama, society and art, with a staff of twenty working under them. Poppy would be one of the staff. Rollo would be working as a sub-editor, housed on another floor, but he said he would get her settled in before he started work.

They entered the building and signed in at a formal reception desk. Poppy was disappointed to see it was not manned by a motherly Mavis Bradshaw clone, but a dour-looking gent in a grey suit. The foyer was buzzing with staff arriving for the day shift and bleary-eyed workers knocking off from the night. "All the news that's fit to print" – the company's motto – required round-the-clock attention.

Rollo and Poppy caught the lift – or "elevator", as the Americans called it – to the sixteenth floor. Poppy had never been so high in the sky. She wondered if she would feel dizzy if she looked out of a window. But before she could check herself for vertigo, Rollo ushered her through an enormous newsroom abuzz with typewriters and the sound of telegraph tickers. In London, if Poppy or any of the *Globe* staff needed to send or receive a telegram they had to walk to the nearest post office on Fleet Street. Here they had their own system installed. "They were one of Marconi's first customers," Rollo informed her. "Delilah's Uncle Elmo," he added, as if she didn't know.

Some newspapermen looked up from their desks as the young blonde woman and the dwarf passed. A few of them raised their eyebrows appreciatively; one or two greeted Rollo by name. They asked to be introduced to the "dame", but Rollo brushed them off with a laugh and a promise of a catch-up later. "This is Miz Denby, one of London's finest young journalists. But I want to introduce her to Judson first."

Judson Quinn, Rollo had told her, was one of the two associate editors who ran the paper under the editor-in-chief, Charles R. Miller. Miller was currently visiting the Washington office while the other associate, Archie Weinstein, was in London trying to buy the *Globe*.

Rollo knocked on a door at the end of the newsroom. "Enter!" came the reply.

He opened the door and stepped aside to usher Poppy in. She walked into an office that was far tidier than Rollo's back in London. The walls were graced with framed front pages of the *Times*, showcasing the greatest journalistic scoops of the last thirty-five years. Along one wall was a bank of filing cabinets, and another two were decked with floor-to-ceiling bookcases, the spines smartly aligned like soldiers on a parade ground. In the alcove of a bay window – sporting a dizzying view of Midtown Manhattan – was a large desk, covered with ordered stacks of files, photographs and galley proofs.

A sparsely built man with thinning grey hair got up from his chair. Poppy noticed a slight weakness in his left side and arm, while his face drooped slightly on one side. *A stroke?* Poppy wondered. But behind his wire-rimmed spectacles, Judson Quinn's brown eyes were as sharp as tacks. "Well, if it ain't Rollo the Rogue Rolandson!" He reached out his right hand. "And this must be Miz Daredevil Denby."

Rollo laughed and Poppy flushed as she took Quinn's hand. "I don't know what Mr Rolandson has been telling you, Mr Quinn, but I'm sure it's all a gross exaggeration."

"That you single-handedly put a corrupt lord behind bars, embarrassed Marie Curie, saved the life of Constantin Stanislavski and fought off the entire security detail of the Russian Embassy?" His eyes twinkled. "Surely none of that is an exaggeration, Miz Denby."

"Let's just say a bit of journalistic licence has been applied," observed Poppy.

Judson Quinn gave a lopsided grin and turned his attention to Rollo. "You've grown!" he said. Poppy winced at his insensitivity. But Rollo just laughed and patted his belly.

"London food ain't as bad as they said it would be," he quipped in a fake cockney accent.

"Jellied eels, quick as yer please, guv!" countered Quinn in an even worse rendition of an East End lilt. And the two men doubled up in mirth. Poppy couldn't help smiling at the two old chums. She had always been under the impression Rollo had left *The New York Times* with bad blood. If he had, it certainly wasn't with Judson Quinn.

Eventually the two men straightened up and turned to Poppy. "I'm sorry, Miz Denby, it's just been a while since I've seen your editor. We were cubs together – did he tell you?"

"He didn't," she said. Rollo shrugged.

"But," said Quinn, taking a step back, "unfortunately our friendship has to stop at the office door; as I'm sure Rollo understands."

Quinn looked over his spectacles at his old chum. Rollo shifted slightly from one foot to the other and nodded. *Ah*, thought Poppy, *there is something hanging over them.*

"Rollo can tell you about it himself, but just to say my senior, Mr Miller, and my colleague, Mr Weinstein, are not quite as fond of old Rolandson as I am. And, although I'm in charge when they're not here, they have made it clear that I am not to give either of you cushy jobs for the next three months."

"Cushy jobs? What the hell do they think we want? Walnut-lined offices?" asked Rollo. His voice was jocular but there was an edge to it.

It was Quinn's turn to shift from foot to foot. But with his weak left side it ended up as more of a lurch. Poppy almost reached out a hand to steady him, but he regained his balance without her help.

"You know what I mean, Rollo. Nothing 'career furthering'. You've just got to be kept busy, that's all, until it's time for you to go back to London. So you're going downstairs to copy tasting and Miz Denby here will go on the Death Beat."

Rollo rocked back on his heels and crossed his arms. "Suppose it could be worse."

There was a knock on the door and a bald man with a flush-red face popped his head around.

"Ah, Saunders, just in time," said Quinn.

"*Saunders?*" Rollo said in disbelief, then he turned towards his old friend. "Oh, Judson. Why didn't you tell me?" Rollo's voice was cut with disappointment.

Quinn avoided his eyes and went back to his desk. He sat down and absently started straightening a pile of papers.

"I'm sorry, Rollo. A personal request from Weinstein."

Rollo strode over to the desk and placed both hands on it, leaning in towards the associate editor. "And you didn't have the tackle to stand up to him?"

Quinn slumped to one side and with an obvious effort straightened himself again. Poppy reached out a restraining hand and placed it on Rollo's arm. She didn't understand why he was so upset, but clearly Quinn's health was not able to withstand much more.

"Rollo . . ."

Rollo's muscles relaxed under her touch. "Sorry, Poppy. Quinn. Don't worry; I'd be delighted to work with Saunders."

He turned around to face the bald man still standing in the doorway, sporting a self-satisfied smirk. His voice was flat as he said: "Miz Denby, may I introduce Paul Saunders."

Saunders reached out his hand. Poppy took it, nervously. It was limp and clammy. The obligatory shake over, she started to withdraw; then, suddenly, his grip tightened and his eyes narrowed. "Good day, Miz Denby. I believe you know my cousin, Lionel. Lionel Saunders. Oh, he's told me *sooooo* much about you."

Chapter 17

Friday, 19 April 1921, Manhattan

It had been a long, hard week working on the "Death Beat" – journalistic slang for the obituary column. Poppy was tasked with scouring the daily police reports of deaths in the city to see if anyone notable had died overnight. If they had, she had to access their files – similar in set-up to the Jazz Files they had at the *Globe* – and write up an obituary. Prominent celebrities, business leaders and civil luminaries who were known to be ill or infirm already had pre-written obits that just needed to be updated on their actual death. Anyone seventy years or older automatically had one written. Poppy spent most of the week writing up draft obits for people due to turn seventy in 1921, from a list provided by Paul Saunders.

Saunders, although physically nothing like his British cousin, was every bit like him in spirit and he set about making her life as miserable as he could, with snide remarks and a refusal to answer even the most legitimate of questions. "If you're such a hot-shot reporter, missy, find out for yourself," he answered when she asked where the ladies' rest room was.

Rollo was convinced that Paul Saunders was the source of the Department of Immigration's files on Dot and Delilah, and that Lionel was Paul's source in London.

Lionel had been working at the *Globe* when Poppy first joined the paper in June 1920. They had immediately got off on the wrong foot and he had gone out of his way to undermine her at every opportunity. But soon the undermining turned more sinister and it became clear that Saunders was acting on behalf of some very dangerous people. Once the case was closed there was insufficient evidence to link the former arts and entertainment editor to any crimes, but Poppy, Rollo and the rest of the staff at the *Globe* believed him to be involved. Rollo fired him and gave Poppy his job. But Lionel still had lots of influential contacts on the London social scene and he soon got a job at the *Globe*'s rival, *The London Courier*. Since then he had tried to scoop Poppy on every story. And now, here he was by proxy, trying to make her life as miserable as possible in New York.

But Poppy refused to let Paul and Lionel Saunders win. Instead, she set about looking on the bright side of her time on the Death Beat. So, although Rollo muttered and moaned about his humiliating comedown from editor-in-chief to a mere copy taster, Poppy realised she was darned lucky to be working on a paper as famous as *The New York Times*, in any capacity.

The work itself, although tainted by Saunders' spiteful comments and obstreperous behaviour, was fairly interesting. Poppy enjoyed research, and although she would have preferred not to be tied to her desk – with the whole of New York to explore – she relished finding out about the lives of the rich and famous. There were some extraordinary people living in the city, many of them world-famous, and here she was having a little glimpse into their fascinating lives.

One of them was Melvil Dewey, the director of the New York State Library, and the man who had invented the Dewey Classification system. Even in London they used it! It was thanks to Mr Dewey that Poppy was able to find her way around her library so easily – which helped immensely when she needed to do some quick research for a story she was working on. Mr Dewey would be turning seventy in December and she set about writing a glowing obituary from the information she found on file. As she finished, she hoped it wouldn't be needed anytime soon.

It was just before lunch. Poppy had not yet had the latest crime report for the night before. It should have arrived first thing in the morning and Poppy suspected Saunders had deliberately kept it from her. He'd done it before – two days earlier – and she had got into trouble with the departmental editor for filing late copy. She had seen Saunders smirking at his desk. She had decided, then, to take the moral high ground and not publicly accuse him, knowing there was no evidence to back her up. Wednesday and Thursday passed without incident and she began to wonder if she had misread the man. But now that it had happened a second time, she knew her initial suspicions were correct. She would speak to Rollo about it at lunch. Perhaps he could have a word with Mr Quinn on her behalf.

She looked over to Saunders' desk and noted that the bald head was not bent over the blotting pad as usual. And, she further noted, his hat was not on the hat stand either. *Hmmm, dare I?*

The Lord helps those who help themselves, she thought, and then giggled to herself. Poppy was sure snooping around a colleague's desk was *not* what her mother meant when she used the maxim, but that's exactly what she was going to do.

There were two other journalists in the room. One was typing furiously, trying to meet deadline; the other had his back turned, talking loudly on the telephone while standing looking out of the window, cigarette in hand. It was now or never. Poppy got up quickly and went over to Saunders' desk. She skimmed through the pile of papers in the in-tray: nothing there. She checked each bit of copy on the desk: again, nothing. Then she turned her attention to the two drawers. The first was filled with stationery: ink bottles, blotters and red pencils, along with a half-jack of Johnnie Walker whisky and a pack of Lucky Strikes. The second drawer, however, was full of files, and right on top was a single sheet of paper entitled "New York City Crime Report, Thursday 18th April 1921".

Poppy's heart skipped a beat. So he *had* kept it from her! After a quick glance to see if anyone was watching, she removed the sheet of paper. She intended to gloss over it to see if there was anything of note, then replace it. She would ask Rollo to spread the word that Saunders had been seen putting the report in his drawer. Rollo still had friends on the paper and a word in the right ear would be all that was needed for the rumour to get around. Then, hopefully, it would reach Mr Quinn's ear – or the ear of the departmental editor – and they would challenge Saunders on it and perhaps ask him to open his drawer. It was all unpleasantly underhanded – and Poppy didn't feel comfortable doing it – but after being on the paper only five days she knew her word alone would not be enough.

She skimmed the report – yes, there had been a notable death. At least she assumed it was notable because it was located in a posh area of town called Lexington Avenue. When she started on the Death Beat Rollo had given her a run-down of areas she was to concentrate on, where she was likely to find the residences of the rich and famous. If she wasn't sure, she was to ask him. This, of course, should have been Saunders' job – to guide her through the who's who of New York society – but he had made it crystal clear that he would rather jump off the Brooklyn Bridge than help the woman who had almost ruined his cousin's career.

Poppy turned her attention to the report. The body of an eighty-three-year-old gentleman had been found in his penthouse apartment on Lexington Avenue: Prince Hans von Hassler of Liechtenstein. The circumstances of his death were described as "suspicious but as yet unexplained". *Liechtenstein?* The hairs on the back of her neck quivered.

Alfie Dorchester – that's where his alias came from too. Surely that can't be a coincidence . . .

All thoughts of framing Paul Saunders were driven from her mind and replaced with an image of Alfie posing as Count Otto von Riesling from Liechtenstein. *How many aristocrats from a tiny Alpine principality can there possibly be in New York City?* She didn't know, but she was jolly well going to find out. She folded the page and was just about to shut the drawer when she noticed the top-most file – a Death Beat file labelled "Prince Hans von Hassler".

She scooped the file from the drawer and slotted it under her arm. *Two can play at this game,* she thought, and plucked her hat and coat from the stand.

"This fella was in his eighties," said Rollo between mouthfuls of bagel filled with roast beef and pickle. "I saw the report this morning. Passed it on to a crime reporter. The old boy's housekeeper found him collapsed in the bathroom. He'd hit his head and there was a lot of blood. She reckons he was attacked, but there's no evidence of a break-in and the geezer could just have hit his head when he fell. We'll see what comes of it."

He took another bite of his bagel and swilled it down with coffee as thick and black as crude oil.

"Geezer?" asked Poppy. She chuckled. So Rollo hadn't quite left London behind.

They were sitting in a diner just off Times Square. As Rollo demolished his lunch and ordered seconds, she nibbled at her own bagel – with a more modest filling of cheese and tomato – and read through the information on the dead man in the Death Beat file.

Prince Hans von Hassler had lived in New York for twenty years, having come to America as a younger man to make his fortune in the Mount Baker Gold Rush of 1896. And make his fortune he did, founding and owning a very lucrative mine. But the harsh conditions of the northwest did not suit the cultured European and, as soon as he could, he put a manager in charge and "retired" to a penthouse on Lexington Avenue, where he had lived ever since.

Von Hassler, who lived off earnings from the family estate in Liechtenstein – of which he was the sole heir – as well as his gold mine, was wealthy enough to be ranked in the top echelons of New York society. Although becoming quite the recluse in more recent years, he was a generous benefactor of the arts and community projects.

"Oh look!" said Poppy, picking up a photograph. "Here he is with Amelia Spencer. The caption says it was taken in May 1910 at a gala dinner for the Eugenics Society. Is this the same eugenics thing you were telling me about on the ship?"

Rollo banged down his coffee cup and took the photograph from Poppy. He flicked it over, read the caption and gave it back to her. "Yes." His voice was cold.

"Golly," said Poppy, "surely that doesn't mean – "

"Amelia Spencer is a supporter of eugenics?" he said bitterly. "I'm afraid that's exactly what it means, Miz Denby."

Poppy looked at her editor, noting the furrowed brows and tensed neck. "Ah, so that's why you don't like her."

Rollo whipped his head up to look at her. "Who said I didn't like her?"

"You could have frozen haddock when the two of you met on the *Olympic*. I just didn't know why." Poppy picked up the picture again and looked at the beautiful Long Island woman – who would then have been in her mid-forties – and the elderly prince, still tall and upright, despite his seventy-odd years.

"But I thought she was a socialist," offered Poppy.

Rollo stirred a spoonful of sugar into his coffee. "No, not a socialist. Far from it. But she did campaign for women's suffrage and as such rubbed shoulders with lots of socialists like your aunt and the Pankhursts."

"So where does eugenics fit into it?"

"Amelia believes in sterilisation for the poor and weaker members of society – particularly for negroes, but poor whites get the treatment too. As you know, many women's advocates also believe in birth control – but perhaps for different reasons."

"Like Mary Stopes," offered Poppy. "Isn't there some controversy about her?"

"Yes, there is. Abortions are the real hot potato. But that aside, she wants to give women options, not just purify the population like the eugenicists. Amelia, I think, supports it for both reasons. She and my mother are good friends."

Poppy frowned. "Your mother?"

"Yes. That's how I first met Mrs Spencer – they travel in the same social circles, although Amelia is a good fifteen years younger than the mater. Both of them were founding members of the New York Eugenics Society, which," he cocked a thumb at the photograph, "von Hassler seemed to have been financing."

Poppy nearly choked on her own coffee. "Your mother believes in eugenics! B-b-but how can she? With your – your –"

"With me being a dwarf?" finished Rollo. He inhaled and exhaled slowly, clearly trying to keep his temper under control. "It's because I'm a dwarf that she got involved. She never forgave me for not being the perfect son. She said she didn't want other people to repeat the . . . *mistake* she'd made."

Rollo looked out of the window at the lunchtime passers-by. It was starting to rain and umbrellas jostled for space on the sidewalk. Poppy didn't know what to say. If it was anyone else she would have taken their hand and squeezed it and said she was so very sorry. But it was Rollo, and he didn't do well with public displays of sympathy.

Instead she said very quietly: "That's dreadful. Just dreadful."

He nodded. "It is. But, I can't complain too much. I'm white and wealthy and well educated. And despite what the old girl thought, my father and brother loved me just the same." He grinned, trying to whip up the old Cheshire Cat. "I'm not the only fella in the world with a mother who didn't care for him, Miz Denby."

Poppy smiled at him, playing along with his attempt to bring levity to the conversation. "So, von Hassler was a eugenicist too."

Rollo shrugged. "Nothing illegal about it. So was half of New York society at the time – half of them probably still are. What else does it say about him?"

Poppy turned the page and read on. "Aha!" she said, pointing to the second paragraph down. "Seems like he was also a business partner of Theo Spencer. Some kind of textile business."

Rollo nodded. "Yes. Theo's got his fingers in lots of pies. Doesn't surprise me. He and my old man were partners in a couple of ventures too. Nice fella, Theo, for an industrialist."

Poppy agreed that he was – despite his wife's dubious beliefs.

Rollo hailed the waitress for the bill. As he was counting out the coins he said: "Look, Poppy, I know you think it's too much of a coincidence that the fella you thought was Alfie Dorchester is posing as someone from Liechtenstein – and then this old geezer up and dies – but really, European aristocrats are more common than you might think in these parts. So perhaps we should start looking into other . . ."

But Poppy wasn't listening to him. She was completely engrossed in reading the third paragraph down:

Prince von Hassler never married. His sole heir is the son of his now deceased sister. Name: Count Otto von Riesling, resident of the Principality of Monte Carlo.

Poppy looked up, her face pale, her hands shaking.

"What is it, Poppy?"

"Oh my, Rollo, oh my. I think we've just struck gold."

Chapter 18

The good thing about being a nobody on *The New York Times* was that no one expected Poppy to work beyond her contracted hours. At home in London she worked as many hours as she needed – day or night – to get the job done. But here in the salt mines of New York – when all the work she was officially allocated could be done in the office – she was a simple nine-to-five girl. So after having lunch with Rollo she went back to the office and put in the required time until knock-off at five.

She was relieved to see that Paul Saunders had not returned to the office during her lunch hour and a quick question to one of the other journalists revealed that he was out following a story. No one knew when he would be back.

Perfect. She could write the obituary for the prince without having to explain how she'd found the file. Then she could start doing some real work: tracking down Alfie Dorchester. At four o'clock she checked her watch and calculated that it would now be nine o'clock at night in London. Hmmm, should she send a telegram now and wait for it to be delivered tomorrow or just send it tomorrow? If she sent it tomorrow morning, it would be afternoon in England and precious hours would have been lost. No, she'd send it now.

She wasn't sure if she was allowed to use the telegram machine or not. It was operated by a young man in his early twenties who, whenever he was not sending or receiving telegrams on behalf of the newsroom staff, was usually propped up on one elbow catching forty winks. He sat bolt upright with a snort when Poppy spoke to him.

"Frank, isn't it?"

Frank looked sheepish. "It is. I wasn't sleeping, ma'am, I swear."

Poppy smiled. "I'm sure you weren't. Can you send a telegram for me, please?"

Frank looked around, trying to catch the eye of someone more senior. "Well, I'm not really sure if I can. Are you on my list?"

"List?"

"Of staff members who can send telegrams." He reached into his desk drawer and pulled out a dog-eared list of names.

"What's the name, ma'am?"

"Denby, Poppy Denby. But . . ." Poppy opened her blue eyes as wide as she could. "I'm probably not on the list yet, although Mr Quinn said I would be soon. So if you don't mind . . ."

The young man picked at some dirt under one of his fingernails. "Well, I don't really know, ma'am. I really shouldn't."

Poppy took a step closer and leaned on the desk. "Oh, I'm sure you won't get into trouble. It's not as if you've been napping on the job or anything . . ." She smiled with as much charm as she could muster.

The young man's eyes flitted to left and right and then down to the list. "You sure Mr Quinn said you'd be on it soon?"

"Abso-posi-tootly," said Poppy, using a word she'd overheard some New York flappers using at Chester's.

He nodded. "All right then. But just this once. Until Mr Quinn gets it sorted."

"Of course," smiled Poppy. "Just this once."

Poppy gave the text of the telegram to the operator. It was addressed to Marjorie Reynolds of the Home Office, London. But as it would be arriving after office hours in England, Poppy had given Marjorie's home address, rather than her office.

Marjorie was a friend of Aunt Dot's, one of the first female MPs and a minister at the Home Office. She also had ties to the Secret Service and she and Poppy had worked together on a case the previous autumn involving international espionage. If Marjorie couldn't help her, Poppy thought, no one could.

The telegram read: "Marjorie STOP Poppy here STOP Need to find Count Otto von Riesling last seen Monte Carlo STOP Where is he now STOP Ties to Dorchester STOP Urgent STOP Reply to Rollo NY address STOP."

After the young man tapped the final "STOP" Poppy thanked him and promised that she would sort it all out with Mr Quinn as soon as she could, then left him to resume his nap.

It was now half past four. Thirty minutes to kill until home time – although Poppy had no intention of going home. Saunders still had not returned so she slipped the file on von Hassler back into his drawer. One of the other journalists saw her do it and raised an eyebrow.

Poppy smiled and explained: "Something I borrowed." The hack, approaching the end of a twelve-hour shift, shrugged, yawned and turned his attention back to his typewriter.

Poppy breathed a sigh of relief. So not everyone in the office had been briefed to keep her in line. Or if they had, they didn't care to. Good. And they probably wouldn't mind if she used the telephone. If asked why, she would say it was to fill in some gaps on the obit she was working on – which was, of course, entirely true . . .

She grasped the phone by the neck, picked up the handset and spoke into the mouthpiece: "Bellevue Hospital please. Orthopaedic department. Dr Toby Spencer."

Following Rollo's directions, Poppy got off the subway at 23rd Street then jumped on a trolley car heading to the East River, and Bellevue Hospital. Rollo in the meantime said he was going to drop in on an old pal in the New York Police Department to find out what he could about the von Hassler investigation. The two of them agreed to meet later that evening at the Waldorf Astoria to join a live audience for the radio broadcast Delilah was involved in. "Make sure Dr Love doesn't waylay you," advised Rollo with a wink.

Poppy had pooh-poohed the suggestion and waved goodbye to her grinning editor. But, Poppy suspected, Rollo was not entirely wrong. On the ship she definitely had the impression that Toby Spencer was romantically interested in her. All that might have changed since their encounter at Chester's Speakeasy, when the young doctor had seemed less than convinced by her accusations about the fake count. So Poppy was not sure how she would be received when she got to the hospital.

She needn't have worried. As soon as she arrived at the reception desk she was met by a smiling nurse who announced that Dr Spencer was waiting for her, and ushered her into his office.

He was seated behind a desk piled high with files, in front of a wall lined with what Poppy assumed were x-ray plates. She had seen something similar when she went to Marie Curie's Radium Institute in Paris the previous year: shadowy white shapes on a black background. As she stepped through the door she passed a skeleton – suspended from a frame – jauntily sporting a trilby hat. As soon as he spotted her, Toby jumped up and strode across the floor. Gone was the dashing tuxedoed socialite from the speakeasy, and in his place was a professional young doctor in a white coat. But the auburn hair – slicked down with Brillantine – and the sea-blue eyes remained the same. So did the smile.

"Miz Denby! You made it!"

"Of course I did, Dr Spencer. It's just a short journey on the subway."

He grinned, making him look younger than his thirty years. "Indeed it is, but it seems an eternity since I last saw you."

"You flatter me, Dr Spencer."

"Toby, please, after all we've been through together . . ."

The nurse, who was still standing in the doorway, raised a quizzical eyebrow.

Poppy flushed. "We have only met a few times, Dr Spencer, and . . ."

Toby raised his hands in mock surrender. "Of course. Forgive me for giving the wrong impression to Nurse Forbes. I meant when you helped me with the emergency surgery on the ship. Nurse Forbes, this is the young woman who so ably assisted me with Seaman Jones, who, no doubt, is the reason you are here . . ."

Seaman Jones, thought Poppy. Of course! The injured sailor had been brought to this very hospital. How convenient for her. "Indeed it is. I was wondering how he is?" she quickly offered.

A slight smile played at the corner of Toby's mouth. "I shall take you to him shortly." Then he turned to the nurse. "Nurse Forbes, will you ready the patient for a visit?"

The nurse said she would and retreated from the room.

As the door closed Toby leaned his backside on his desk and

folded his arms. Then he frowned. "I suspect, Miz Denby, from your reaction, you did not come to see Seaman Jones after all."

Poppy cleared her throat to speak, but before she could he grinned and said in an exaggerated Long Island drawl: "And that, I can tell you, pleases me no end, no end at all."

"It does?" asked Poppy, surprised.

"Indeed it does. After the other night at Chester's I thought you and I . . . well . . . I didn't think it went very well. Do you?"

Poppy shifted her satchel from one shoulder to another, alerting Toby to an ungentlemanly oversight. "By Jove, I'm sorry!" Then he jumped up and pulled out a chair. "Please, take a seat. May I take your bag? It looks heavy."

"Full of files," said Poppy, and sat in the chair as Toby placed the satchel at her feet.

Toby sat opposite her and crossed his legs, showing a pair of red and blue checked golfing socks under his smart work trousers. "Well, I –" they both started at the same time and laughed. "Ladies first," said Toby and leaned forward to hear what she had to say.

Poppy wasn't sure how to proceed. She was here in an investigative capacity but she did not want to put him on edge, thinking he was being interrogated. Neither, though, was she comfortable playing along with the idea he seemed to have that she might be open to progressing their relationship along less formal lines.

Seaman Jones was an option . . .

But before she could decide which tack to take, Toby chipped in: "Look, Poppy, I'm sorry about the other night. You were very obviously upset when you thought von Riesling looked like that bounder who assaulted you. Cousin Miles filled me in on the whole story after the fact. Apparently it was all over the papers – even here. I must have missed it. I'm sorry."

He cleared his throat and re-crossed his legs in the other direction.

What exactly is he sorry for? wondered Poppy. That he hadn't known or that he hadn't believed her? It was her turn to clear her throat.

"Well, thank you, Dr Spencer – Toby. But there's no need to apologise. I don't expect everyone to know everything. Particularly something that happened in another country. But – and you might not like what I'm going to say – your friend doesn't just look like Alfie Dorchester – "

Toby raised his hand and interjected. "Oh, he's not my *friend*; merely an acquaintance."

"Oh?"

"Yes. His uncle and my father have some shared business dealings. I only met von Riesling a few months ago."

Poppy twirled the strap of her satchel around her forefinger. "Does he live in New York?"

"I think he intends to settle here, yes. He lived in Monte Carlo before this. Moved here because his uncle was becoming increasingly infirm. He's an old fella – well into his eighties – and Otto is his only heir."

Toby was speaking in the present tense. So, he didn't know the "old fella" was dead then.

"Was – is – Otto staying with his uncle? In the same apartment?"

Poppy tried to keep her voice nonchalant. She decided that as long as Toby was giving her the information she came for it would be counterproductive to antagonise him with further accusations that his so-called acquaintance was in fact her assailant, Alfie Dorchester.

Toby picked a hair from his trousers and flicked it into a waste paper basket. "I'm not sure, to be honest. I never had dealings with him at home. We would just sometimes bump into one another when we were out – Chester's, Club Deluxe, places like that. I first met him at a Christmas party at my parents' place, out on Long Island."

"Ah, I see," said Poppy. "I assume he was with his uncle then?"

"No," said Toby. "Old von Hassler is a bit of a recluse. No one has seen him outside his apartment in years. But Otto introduced himself to us. He said he'd come on his uncle's behalf. The old duffer had been invited – as a business courtesy – but no one had really expected him to come."

"And no one was surprised that someone claiming to be his nephew arrived in his stead?"

Toby cocked his head to the right, his Brilliantined hair staying primly in place. "No, why should we? We all knew he had a nephew. Just hadn't met him, that's all. Look, Poppy, I'm not sure what all this is about but –"

There was a knock on the door. The nurse entered. "Seaman Jones is ready to see you now, doctor."

Toby looked at Poppy curiously. "Do you want to see Seaman Jones or is there something else you would like to know?" His tone was similar to what it had been that night at Chester's.

Be careful, Poppy . . .

"Of course I'd like to see Seaman Jones." She stood up and picked up her satchel.

Toby stood too, looking relieved.

"How is he, by the way?" she asked, allowing Toby to take the satchel from her.

"Better than expected," said Toby, as he led her to the door. He ushered her down the corridor and explained his patient's medical condition as they walked.

Seaman Jones had been taken straight into surgery when he arrived at the hospital so Toby's team could "clean up" what he had done in the makeshift operating theatre on the *Olympic*. Then he had been placed in a private room – paid for by the Carter Shipping Company – and monitored day and night for signs of septicaemia setting in. So far it hadn't, and yesterday, for the first time, Jones had regained consciousness and was starting to take small amounts of food and water.

"He's doing as well as we could hope, all things considered," said Toby, as he pushed open the door to the private room, "but he's not quite out of the woods yet."

Lying in a sea of white sheets was Seaman Jones. The bedding over his legs was draped over a frame, so it would not touch his tender stump and would give easy access to the medical staff. Poppy had seen similar contraptions at the military hospital she had worked at during the war.

The man's eyes were closed but they opened as Poppy and Toby approached.

"How are you feeling today, Seaman Jones?" asked Toby as he

cast an expert eye over the patient and took his wrist in hand to feel his pulse.

With considerable effort the injured sailor composed himself to answer: "On the mend, I hope, doctor."

"I think you're making good progress," said Toby in a tone of voice that Poppy suspected he used when he was being non-committal but wanting to provide encouragement. *He's a good doctor and a decent chap,* Poppy decided, and wondered why she was so averse to any romantic overtures from him.

Because it's too soon after Daniel. She looked at Toby's hands as he lifted the sheet and examined the stump underneath. The skin was smooth and unscarred, so unlike Daniel's. But both men were strong, she could tell that. And gentle. *Is it really too soon?*

Poppy pulled herself out of her romantic reverie as Seaman Jones's eyes turned to her.

"Hello," she said. "I'm Poppy Denby. You probably won't remember, but I was with Dr Spencer when he operated on you on the ship."

There was no recognition in the man's eyes.

"Yes," interjected Toby, "the lady was a godsend. And she has come to see how you are doing. Isn't that kind?"

Jones's bloodshot eyes narrowed. "You from Carter? I told that last'n I'd done nothing wrong. Nothing others haven't done afore me."

Toby's and Poppy's eyes met over the bed. They were equally puzzled.

"I'm not from the shipping company," said Poppy soothingly. "And I'm sure they only have your best interests at heart. They were probably just trying to find out what happened. What did happen?" Poppy ventured.

The man's eyes flitted from left to right. "Nothing wrong . . . others done the same . . ."

Poppy leaned in towards the man. "What have you done, Seaman Jones? What have others done too?"

But Seaman Jones was no longer listening. His eyes rolled back and his limbs jerked uncontrollably.

"He's having a seizure," announced Toby and proceeded to apply first aid, removing the patient's pillow and lowering his head so it was level with his body.

"Nurse, pad the leg." The nurse flipped back the sheets to reveal a metal arch and proceeded to stuff pillows into it to protect the stump of the amputated limb from bashing against it as the man's limbs flailed.

Poppy stepped back to allow the medical staff to do their work. She had seen patients in the military hospital having fits, but had never quite got used to the shock of seeing a body in the full throes of convulsions.

Eventually the convulsions eased. The seizure had almost run its course. Toby felt the man's pulse. "I need to do some tests. Excuse me, Poppy, but perhaps we can meet again in less distracting circumstances. I'll telephone you at Rollo's, if I may. There's a party – "

"Doctor!"

Seaman Jones began to wheeze, his face turning beetroot. Poppy withdrew from the room.

Chapter 19

Friday, 19 April 1921, the Garment District, Manhattan

Mimi looked to the dirty barred windows. It appeared to be a sunny afternoon in New York City. She wondered what it would be like to sit on the grass in Central Park, holding a parasol with one hand and an ice cream cone with the other – just like the photograph in the book on America she and Anatoly used to read.

Anatoly . . . she'd been in the city of her dreams for seven days now and she was no closer to finding him. She must find a way to get to Times Square. But how? And if she did get there, would he really be there waiting for her?

In the seven days she had lain awake in the garment factory dormitory, Estie tucked in beside her, she had begun to ponder whether her dreams could ever become a reality. Yes, they were what had kept her going the last two years, moving from port to port, trying to earn enough to keep her and her sister alive. She had told the story of her fiancé-who-was-waiting-for-her-in-New-York so many times that she had come to believe it herself. But was he really waiting for her beyond these damp factory walls? Had he even made it out of Russia alive? On her travels she had seen the detritus of the once-great Russian Empire. The women and children wearing little more than rags. The aristocrats commandeering carts piled high with the remnants of their wealth. The injured and dying soldiers . . .

She had to face it: the chances of Anatoly having made it to America were slim at best. And if he had, how would they find one another? The man on Ellis Island had told her One Times Square was the office of a newspaper. How could he wait for her at a newspaper? They had been fools. Young, romantic fools.

And yet, here she was. Against all odds. And Estie, safe and well beside her. Estie had also been given work. She was expected to sweep up the threads and scraps that fell to the sewing room floor – a job the young girl was immensely proud to do. For now, anyway. It wouldn't take long, Mimi knew, until Estie got bored and wanted to play another game. And she, Mimi, was already tired of sewing zips day after day after day . . .

Yes, their current circumstances were not quite what she'd dreamed of, but at least they were here – in America – where, with or without Anatoly, she could start a new life . . . eventually. Despite her occasional romantic delusions, Mimi was no fool. She was well aware that her back-door entry to the United States had strings attached – and that they weren't legal. The woman on Ellis Island had told her she would have to work for two years to pay for her entry; but after that she and Estie would be free to start a new life. Mimi had agreed to it – what choice did she have? – without knowing what the work would entail, still thinking she'd be able to contact Anatoly and that he would be able to buy her freedom.

She'd held on to that thought all the way through Manhattan in the back of the ferryman's cart, twirling the pearl ring on her finger. She had whispered it to Estie when the younger girl started fretting. She had continued to believe it when she was handed over to the manager of the garment factory and told she would be making clothes for American ladies. It was good work, tailoring – it's what her parents had done back in the Ukraine. She would enjoy doing that until she could find a way to meet with Anatoly . . .

But things were not that simple. Yesterday she had been taken aside by one of the other girls. Her name was Katerina – Kat for short – and like Mimi was from the Ukraine. Kat was in the second year of her two-year service and had been given the job of dormitory supervisor. It was Kat who gave Mimi and Estie clean sheets and towels and showed them to the communal bathroom they would share with twelve other illegal women.

It was Kat who explained that the doors to the factory were

locked – for their own safety – to keep the immigration officials and the police out. "If they find us, they will send us home," she warned, her green eyes communicating the fear all the immigrants shared.

And it was Kat who showed them the exercise yard where they were allowed to sit, walk or eat their lunch for an hour every day.

Kat also arranged for Estie's and Mimi's photographs to be taken – for the factory files. And that, it seemed, was where things started to go wrong.

Kat called Mimi aside during the exercise hour. "You are a very pretty girl, Mimi."

"Thank you."

Kat looked at her curiously, her eyes narrowing. "The Boss Man wants to see you."

"The Boss Man?" Mimi looked up at the window of the factory manager's office.

Kat shook her head. "Not him. The real boss man. The one who pays Slick."

Slick, Mimi had learned, was the nickname for the factory manager, whom they only saw at the beginning and end of shift. He spoke English and used Kat and an Italian girl called Lucia as his interpreters. Slick never smiled.

"No, Slick is not the boss," confirmed Kat.

"Then who is?" asked Mimi.

"I cannot tell you his name. If the police come – or the Immigration . . ." Kat made a cross in the air to ward off any bad luck, "you might tell them."

"But *you* know," said Mimi.

Kat stood up straight, her cheeks flushed with pride. She was a beautiful girl with blonde hair and green eyes.

"Yes, I know," said Kat, "because I am special. He only tells the special ones – but only after he has tested them for many months."

Kat reached out a finger and pulled a lock of hair from under the edge of Mimi's head scarf. Then she lowered her voice and said: "He has seen your photograph and he thinks you might be special too." She twirled the lock around her finger and pulled.

"Ow! Let go!"

Kat pulled again. Mimi reached up and grabbed Kat's wrist. The supervisor's eyes narrowed again, but then she laughed and released the lock. "You think that hurts? That is nothing."

Mimi let go of Kat's wrist and they stood toe to toe in the exercise yard, while the other women chattered around them. Estie was playing a game of hop-scotch.

Kat looked over at her and kept her eyes on the simple-minded sister as she spoke. "The Boss Man wants to see you. He has other work for you. Special work."

Mimi's stomach clenched. She had been in enough ports and taverns in the last two years to know what this "special work" might entail.

"And if I refuse?"

Kat grinned, still keeping her eyes on Estie. "Then someone might just be put out on the street . . . alone. You are the one who has signed the contract, not her. The boss does not need her. But because he is such a kind man, he has allowed her to stay. And now you must show your gratitude."

Mimi's fists clenched. She was itching to give the other woman a good punch in the face.

"Mimi! Mimi! Come play!" called Estie.

Kat turned to the older sister and smiled. For the first time Mimi noticed one of her teeth was gold. That did not come cheap. The "Boss" had invested in her.

Mimi swallowed and forced a smile onto her face. "I'm coming, Estie!"

As she moved to join her sister, Kat grabbed her wrist and squeezed, her thumb digging into the tendons. "Tomorrow night. At the end of the day shift. I will take you to him. Be ready," she hissed.

Mimi wrenched her wrist free and with a pounding heart went to join her sister.

Slick, a whippet of a man in a beige overall coat, unlocked the door to the work room and rang a bell. Fourteen machines stopped. Fourteen women let out a tired sigh and started tidying their work stations for the night-shift that would be arriving as soon as they had gone.

Mimi lifted the foot of her machine and checked that both top and bottom threads were neatly pulled through. Then she loosened the flywheel to deactivate the mechanism and covered her machine with a dust cloth.

She stood up and joined the queue of women shuffling towards the door. At the door each worker had to lift up her skirt to show she had not hidden any items underneath it. Slick checked each woman, his face impassive. If he was enjoying the view he didn't show it. It was humiliating, but as with everything else in the factory, the women had no choice but to comply.

Mimi waited her turn. She looked out of the window and onto the street below. Women from other factories – legal ones – were coming to the end of their shift and spilling out from buildings throughout the New York Garment District, laughing and gossiping as they headed home to their families. Mimi envied their freedom and blinked back tears. *Pull yourself together,* she told herself. *Crying will not help you and it will not help Estie.* She sniffed and shuffled forward. On the street below, a middle-aged woman with a long auburn plait sticking out from under a black felt hat stopped to talk to a group of garment workers. She gave them each a small parcel from a basket she carried.

"That's the Angel of Chelsea," said a voice behind her in Russian. It was one of the other women who had been there a few months.

"Why do they call her that?" asked Mimi.

"Because she lives in Chelsea – which they say is not far away – and she helps them."

Helps them with what? wondered Mimi.

Suddenly the Angel looked up and caught Mimi's eye. The two women held each other's gaze for a few moments until the queue shuffled forward and Mimi moved out of the Angel's sight.

Chapter 20

Friday, 19 April 1921, Midtown Manhattan

It was almost seven o'clock when Poppy arrived at the Waldorf Astoria Hotel on the corner of Fifth Avenue and 34th Street. The WGY radio station, housed out in Schenectady, New York, had a satellite studio for the "in-town" stars who didn't have the time or inclination to travel out to the more far-flung headquarters. Poppy and Rollo had been invited to join the live audience for the experimental broadcast. She doubted her office wear – the same sage green coat over the honey skirt and blouse with the brown trim she had worn back in London – would meet the expected dress code. But she didn't have time to squeeze in a trip back to Rollo's to get changed *and* fit in her meeting with Toby. She hoped the doorman would not get shirty about it.

There was Rollo, pacing near the entrance to the hotel cloakroom. He had already checked in his coat and hat, and Poppy was thankful to see he too had not had time to change. His chequered bowtie and braces were also not appropriate dress for an evening do. He looked relieved when he saw her. "Thought you'd never get here, Miz Denby. They're about to start."

Poppy passed her coat and hat to the concierge, who raised a disapproving eyebrow at the second guest that evening who was underdressed for the Astoria. A dollar bill, tucked into his top pocket by Rollo, silenced him.

Rollo took Poppy's arm and led her down the hall to one of the ground floor reception rooms that had been converted into a makeshift studio. Inside was a select audience of around thirty people, all dressed up to the nines as if going to a "proper" theatre performance. Eyebrows were raised and tongues tutted as Poppy and Rollo made their apologies and shimmied along a row to their two allocated seats in the middle, right next to Miss King, who was without her employer. "Where's Aunt Dot?" whispered Poppy. But before the older woman could answer, a tuxedoed gentleman stepped onto the stage and announced that the broadcast was about to begin and could there be silence, please.

In the middle of the stage was a single ring-mounted carbon microphone surrounded by a circle of chairs. Behind the chairs was a prop table full of all sorts of paraphernalia, from a clapboard to a gravel tray with two pairs of shoes – a man's and a woman's. Delilah had already explained to her how the sound effects were made and Poppy was very excited to see it all in action.

Stage left was another table laden with machinery essential for the broadcast. Poppy had no idea how all the dials and knobs worked, but she assumed the two gentlemen wearing odd-looking devices over their ears did.

"Ladies and gentlemen, welcome to the live broadcast of *The Wolf* by Eugene Walter, brought to you by WGY radio. We're trying something brand new here, folks – broadcasting a play through sound only – so listeners can tune in with their wirelesses without having to leave their parlours." He grinned and raised his hands to indicate the studio audience. "We're not sure if it will work properly but we've got some folks primed at home and ready to give us a bell as soon as they hear it. If someone comes in from the lobby, don't be alarmed. It's not the Germans invading; it's just a fella who will give us the thumbs up or thumbs down."

The audience chuckled appreciatively. Poppy joined in, although she raised an inner eyebrow at the idea that the Germans would have made it all the way to America – three years after the war was over.

She was grateful, however, to hear that the play was not a fanciful rewriting of German/American history, but a drama set in the Canadian woods. It was an adaptation of a play that had originally been staged at the Lyric Theatre on Broadway in 1908. It was about a man called Jules who goes to look for his half-sister – a woman who is part French Canadian and part Indian – only to discover that she has been seduced by a man called McDonald, has had a child by him, and is then driven into the woods where she and her child are attacked and killed by wolves. Meanwhile, Jules falls in love with a young woman called Hilda, whom McDonald (aka the Wolf) also sets out to seduce. The resultant melodrama, of Jules trying to find the killer of his sister and save the virtue of his love, made for a gripping if far-fetched play. Poppy was pleased that in this play, unlike *The Sheik*, the rapist got his just deserts.

The biggest surprise though – when the cast, including Delilah, came out and gathered around the microphone – was the announcement that Miss May Leigh Rose, who was scheduled to play the sister, had come down with a bout of laryngitis. There was a collective groan from the audience. The compère raised his hands to quieten them. "But not to worry, ladies and gentlemen. The delightful Delilah Marconi, all the way from London, England" – he indicated Delilah, who took a little bow and received a round of applause – "let it slip that a legend of the West End stage, and someone who has previously trod the boards on Broadway, is right here in New York." A titter went around the audience as they turned to one another asking who it might be.

"Good for you, Dot," mumbled Rollo. Miss King could not keep the smile off her face when Poppy looked to her for confirmation.

"Ladies and gentlemen, may I introduce to you the legendary Miss Dorothy Denby!" A cheer went up from the audience as Dot wheeled herself in from the wings. One of the male actors greeted her with a kiss to the hand. Her face was aglow. Poppy had never seen her look so beautiful, or so happy. She felt the tears welling up.

"Oh, Aunt Dot," she sniffed. Rollo passed her a handkerchief.

The forty-five-minute play was a sensation – both in the studio and, apparently, in broadcast. The thumbs-up came fifteen minutes into the performance that the signal was being received around the greater New York area. And then, after the show, over soft drinks in the Astoria bar, it was reported that when Delilah – playing Hilda – had screamed (while purportedly being attacked by the dastardly McDonald) a police officer had run into a home in New Jersey, believing a woman was really in peril.

Cheers went up all around. Then someone whispered to someone who whispered to someone else that perhaps they should decamp to Chester's Speakeasy to "stiffen up" their drinks. However, Aunt Dot said it would be too tricky for her to get there in her wheelchair. Rollo instead offered to host an impromptu shindig at his house on 86th Street. Everyone thought this was a splendid idea.

"Oh dear," said Delilah. "I'm not sure what to do," she confided to Poppy and Dot as they were all waiting for cabs. "Miles Spencer popped in before the show and asked if I would accompany him to a party on Long Island this evening. He wants me to meet some producers there. Apparently they're casting soon for a moving picture that he thinks I'd be just perfect for."

"That's wonderful, darling! But what's the problem?" asked Dot.

"I want to help you celebrate your return to the stage, Dot," said the younger woman.

Dot smiled and took Delilah's hand. "You have already helped me, my dear, by suggesting me for the part. You go with Miles."

Miss King cleared her throat.

"Yes, Gertrude?" Aunt Dot looked up at her companion.

"Do you think it's appropriate that Miss Marconi goes on her own to this party?"

"Oh, but I won't be alone!" chipped in Delilah. "I'll be with Miles."

"Yes, but it might not be considered appropriate, considering the questions you were subjected to by that immigration officer . . ."

Delilah was just about to pooh-pooh Miss King's advice, when Rollo stepped in. "Delilah, I think Miss King is right. The Department of Immigration have already got a bee in their bonnet about you, so perhaps you shouldn't give them any more ammunition."

Delilah looked crestfallen. "But this is my chance to meet those producers."

Rollo shrugged. "It's up to you, but I think you might be stoking a fire here . . ."

"What if I go with her?" suggested Poppy. "If we go together surely that will be all right. Won't it?"

Rollo and Miss King looked at each other. Miss King's mouth tightened into a straight line.

"Well, I think that's a splendid idea!" said Dot. "You two youngsters go to the party and we'll all go to Rollo's. Where is it at, Delilah?"

"Miles said they're using Senator and Mrs Spencer's holiday house for the evening."

Aunt Dot looked smug. "Well, there you go. A senator's house. My niece as a chaperone. What could be more respectable than that?"

Miss King let out a deep sigh and raised her hands. "I give up."

Delilah clapped hers. "Fantabuloso!" Her smile widened even further when Miles Spencer, dressed in a tuxedo and top hat, walked into the Astoria lobby.

"I heard you on the wireless!" he declared. "Incredible! It'll just be a matter of time now until they figure out how to put sound with pictures too. Then we'll have talkies we can watch!"

"Oh, I hope not," whispered Aunt Dot to Poppy. "Then I'll be out of a job again."

"I'm sure there'll be room for both of them, Aunt Dot. And after what I heard tonight, you'll be in work for a long time yet. Do you think they'll be doing it in England too?"

Aunt Dot nodded enthusiastically. "Delilah says they will. Her Uncle Elmo has some plans. I'm just not sure when that will be . . . perhaps I should stay here in New York!"

"Perhaps you should," said Poppy, but wondered whether her aunt would feel the same in the cold light of day. She would have to leave all her friends in London, and Grace would be getting out of prison sometime too . . .

"Are you ready, Poppy?"

It was Delilah, with Miles standing beside her.

"We'll just pop up to Rollo's to pick up some glad rags, then we'll be off. Miles said he would be delighted to have you with us. And . . ." she winked, "Toby is going to be there too."

"Oh!" said Poppy, and, despite her best efforts, blushed.

Chapter 21

An hour later and Poppy, Delilah and Miles were zipping over the Queensboro Bridge to Long Island in the film director's swanky new 1921 Lincoln Model L. It made the Globe's Model T staff motor look like a child's push-car. Poppy felt like a princess in the back of the luxury vehicle and was glad Delilah had insisted they stop off at Rollo's to change clothes.

Poppy was wearing her pale pink Charles Worth gown – with the Prince of Wales's pearls – and Delilah, a new red flapper frock she'd bought earlier in the day at Macy's, as well as a black feather boa. It had a matching red and black ostrich feather headband. It was just as well Delilah was short in stature, Poppy thought, or the feathers would have bent against the roof of the Lincoln.

Below them the bobbing lights of the boats and barges of the East River illuminated their journey over the wrought iron cantilever construction. The span of the river was interrupted, briefly, by a sliver of land known as Blackwell's Island. According to Miles it had once been the home of a lunatic asylum. Poppy squinted through the dark, trying to make out the shape of the buildings below her. It reminded her for a moment of Willow Park Asylum in Battersea, where she had first met Elizabeth Dorchester, the sister of Alfie.

Poppy shivered at the renewed thought of Alfie Dorchester on the loose in New York City. She wondered how Rollo had got on at the police station and if he had found out anything more about the dead Liechtensteinian prince. They hadn't had time to swap notes after the radio broadcast, as Rollo was too busy instructing his butler as to which liquor to bring up from the cellar for the party. It would have to wait until tomorrow.

The powerful motorcar made short shrift of the distance between the Queensboro Bridge and Lake Ronkonkoma – where the Spencer house was situated – along the Long Island Motor Parkway. "In my old motor it would take around two hours to do the fifty miles," Miles explained as he geared up to overtake a slower moving vehicle, "but this baby has a top speed of seventy!"

"Isn't there a speed limit on the road?" asked Poppy, her fingers clawing into the leather of the back seat.

"Oh yes," he replied. "It's around fifty-five on the open road, but at this time of night, no one's checking!"

Delilah threw back her head and laughed. Poppy took hold of the strap over the passenger door and prayed.

The Lincoln delivered its passengers to their destination just after ten o'clock, joining a long line of motor vehicles already parked on the driveway and extending to the grass verge for a good fifty yards or so in each direction.

Light, laughter and music spilled from the elegant three-storey building. Poppy had never seen such a large and beautiful house made of wood and wondered how durable it would be during one of Long Island's famed hurricanes. But Miles assured her it had lasted thirty years so far and was stronger than it appeared. The wide porch roof was held up by red cedar pillars, each a complete trunk of felled tree, and the walls were made of three layers of two-inch-thick planks. To the right of the house Poppy could just make out the outline of a tennis court, and to the left was a line of stables and garages. Poppy sniffed. Yes, under the dominant scent of pine and spruce was a faint smell of horse manure. These horses would be for recreation only, of that Poppy was sure.

A pristine lawn sloped down to the road, beyond which was a line of maple trees, and beyond that, Miles told her, was a private beach, jetty and boat house. He would show the girls the sights in the morning, he promised.

"The morning?" asked Poppy.

"Oh yes," he answered, helping first Poppy then Delilah out of the Lincoln. "The party has just begun!"

As the threesome climbed the wide steps to the house, Poppy noticed two men in earnest conversation. One, his face illuminated by the porch light, was Toby; the other's face was in shadow under his top hat, but by his body language he did not seem very happy. He turned on his heel and stormed past them, making a beeline for a Bentley on the drive below. He climbed in, revved up the motor and drove off at speed.

"What's got his knickers in a twist?" asked Delilah of Toby as they stepped onto the porch. The young doctor ran a hand through his hair and sighed.

"I was trying to get him to stay and talk to you. To clear up this confusion once and for all. But he'd have none of it. He said he was insulted and had no need to defend himself."

"He being . . ." probed Delilah.

Toby looked at her in surprise. "Didn't you see?"

"No," said Poppy, but she was beginning to suspect.

"Otto von Riesling. When Miles telephoned ahead to tell me you were coming to the party with Delilah, I thought it would be a good opportunity to get you to sort it all out. It's obviously a case of mistaken identity."

Or stolen identity, thought Poppy.

"I didn't know he was going to be here," offered Miles, half apologetically.

"Neither did I," said Toby. "You know what he's like though . . . got a nose for where the latest action is . . . heard through the grapevine . . . arrived around nine with a car-load of girls . . ."

Just like Alfie, thought Poppy grimly.

"How are the girls going to get home now?" asked Delilah.

"Oh, I'm sure lifts can be arranged. Or they can stay over. There's plenty of room," said Toby. "Anyway," he said, changing his tone and turning to Poppy, "I'm delighted you've come. I didn't have a chance to invite you at the hospital – Seaman Jones has stabilised, by the way – then I rang Rollo's, but the butler told me you were out . . ."

"At my radio broadcast!" said Delilah as she stepped over the threshold uninvited, clearly anxious to get into the party, and seemingly not sharing Poppy's suspicions about the identity of the man who had just left.

"I know. We all listened in!" said Toby. "The early birds anyway..." But Delilah was already gone, with Miles scampering after her.

Toby laughed. Poppy, angry that she had missed a chance to confront Alfie again, and that no one – including Delilah – was taking her seriously, did not.

Toby frowned. "I'm sorry, Poppy; I tried."

"Where is he staying?" she asked, looking in the direction the Bentley had gone.

"I don't know," said Toby with a shrug. "There's a good crop of hotels around the lake, or he could be staying with friends..."

Poppy pursed her lips and folded her arms. Toby sighed. "Look, Poppy, there's nothing we can do now. Your best bet is to contact his uncle..."

"I can't," said Poppy. "He's dead."

"He's what?" Toby looked genuinely shocked. "Where? When?"

"It will be in the evening edition. Or perhaps the morning. He died last night. He was found in his penthouse. How is unclear."

"Well I never! Von Riesling never said a word! I would have offered my condolences. No wonder he was so out of sorts..."

It was Poppy's turn to laugh, but there was no humour in it. "And yet here he was with his glad rags on, ready to kick up his heels."

Toby frowned at her. "Perhaps it just hasn't sunk in properly yet."

He just doesn't believe me. Poppy shook her head. There was no point flogging a dead horse. And there was nothing she could do now anyway... not until she had heard from Marjorie in London about her enquiries in Monte Carlo, or Rollo's findings at the police station. On top of that, she was in the middle of nowhere with no independent transport. And Delilah didn't seem interested in anything other than the party.

"Yes, Toby, you're right. Perhaps that's all it is."

He cocked his head to the side. "Does that mean you're coming in?"

Poppy smiled up at him, resolving to make the best of it... for now. "Well, I didn't put this old sack on for nothing!" she said, doing her best impersonation of Aunt Dot.

Toby smiled, relieved. He offered her his arm and led her into the house.

* * *

Poppy thought Toby a little old to be having a party while his parents were away so was relieved to hear that The Lodge – as the twelve-bedroomed dwelling was quaintly referred to – was a holiday home shared by the whole extended Spencer family. Senator and Mrs Spencer had a residence in Washington D.C. when Theodore's political work called for it, and their main residence in Riverhead, the county seat of Suffolk County, Long Island, just under an hour's drive east. They only spent their vacation time at The Lodge and so Toby and Miles – and a gang of other cousins – were free to use it for weekend getaways and parties whenever they wanted to. *Ah,* thought Poppy, *the privilege of wealth. Aunt Dot's and Delilah's London lifestyle has* nothing *on this.* The whole of the ground floor was filled with partygoers. The entrance hall – bisected by a sweeping cedarwood staircase – was the main dance area. To the left of it was a bar, manned by two gents in white jackets and black ties, and to the right a six-piece jazz band. Poppy was slightly disappointed to see there was no champagne fountain. When she mentioned this to Toby he laughed and declared: "We couldn't afford it! You wouldn't believe the price of champagne on the black market since prohibition."

Ah yes, the black market. Poppy wondered what Senator Spencer thought of the borderline criminal activity taking place in his holiday home . . . But no one else appeared to be giving it a second thought, as flappers and fops, dandies and debutantes, and an assortment of fashionable New Yorkers danced and frolicked to the latest tunes. Poppy accepted a glass of champagne from Toby just before he was collared by a gaggle of guests wanting to hear all about his recent vacation to the "Old World". He raised his glass apologetically to Poppy. She raised hers in return and smiled. "Don't worry," she shouted to make herself heard over the band. "I'll just have a mosey around."

Before Toby felt he should extricate himself from his guests, she slipped away to reconnoitre the ground floor of the house. A series of rooms led off from the hall: a living room, dining room, bustling kitchen and what looked like a trophy room. Poppy shuddered at the dead animals on the walls, but smiled as she contemplated the large glass-fronted cabinet filled with photographs, cups and shields celebrating the achievements of various Spencer family members. There was canoeing, tennis, debating and librarianship. *Librarianship?* More seriously were photographs of Senator Spencer with a who's who of world leaders, from Theodore Roosevelt to David Lloyd George. And Mrs Spencer was not to be outdone either. There was Amelia with Marie Curie. And again with Emmeline Pankhurst and – a photograph she had seen before – Prince Hans von Hassler of Liechtenstein at the opening of the Eugenics Society of New York. *Yes, tomorrow I'll follow this up. In fact I might give Rollo a ring now to make sure we can connect . . .*

Poppy looked for a telephone and couldn't find one. She enquired of a couple of guests, smoking and chatting on a cluster of leather armchairs, and was directed to the library, which, apparently, was vaguely *that way.*

That way was back through the entrance-cum-dance hall, past the band and kitchen and to a room off the dining room. A long leather sofa lay in front of the door. She thought for a moment this could mean Toby and Miles wanted to keep people out. She considered going back and asking Toby's permission, but he had not been in the hall as she passed through and she was no longer sure where he was. *Surely he won't mind. I'll explain when I see him,* she thought.

She slipped behind the sofa, pushed open the door and, as directed, entered the library. And there on a desk near the window was the telephone she needed. However, the room was not empty. Seated, erect and silent, were four young women, all stunning in their fashionable dresses.

"Oh hello," said Poppy. "I've come to use the telephone. Sorry to interrupt. Do you mind?"

None of the girls said anything. But four pairs of eyes followed the young journalist as she made her way towards the window.

"Don't mind me," said Poppy. "Do carry on."

Silence.

This was getting awkward. "All right; I'll be as quick as I can." She picked up the receiver and dialled for the operator. She gave Rollo's number and waited to be connected.

After a few moments, Rollo's booming voice came down the line. "Hallo? Who's there?"

"It's Poppy." She raised her voice to be heard over the raucous sound of laughter and music from Rollo's end of the line. "You sound like you're having a fabulous party!"

"We are!" shouted Rollo back. "How are things there?"

Poppy looked at the four silent young women, then thought of Count Otto von Riesling, aka Alfie Dorchester, who had left the house in such a hurry. "Interesting," said Poppy. "Listen, Rollo, there's been a . . . development. Can't say too much now, but just wanted to make sure we can meet up tomorrow. I need to hear what you found out this afternoon."

"Righto!" said Rollo. "Over there, behind the ice bucket!"

"What's that?"

"Not you, Poppy, sorry. It's a little mad here. Can we talk tomorrow? When will you get back?"

"I'm not sure. That's up to Miles. But as soon as I can. Will you be in?"

"That's it! Pour me a glass, will ya? What's that, Poppy?"

"Will – you – be – in?"

"Yes!" shouted Rollo in reply. "And if not, I'll leave word where you can find me. Have fun!"

"You too!" shouted Poppy and then Rollo hung up. Poppy looked at the four women and smiled. "Sorry about that. Seems like everyone's having a party. I'm Poppy. Poppy Denby? Are you enjoying yourselves?"

Silence.

Then the door opened. Four pairs of eyes looked towards it. Four flushed, merrily drunk gents spilled into the room. "Luv-er-ly!" said the first one as he eyed the seated women. "Can I go first?"

"First come, first served!" said the second gent – an older man with mutton chop sideburns and a red wine stain down the front of his shirt.

"Ahem! I'm sorry to interrupt," said Poppy. "Just using the phone."

The four men flicked their heads towards the window.

"Who are you?" asked the mutton-chopped fellow.

"I'm – I'm –"

"Pow-pee Den-bee," said one of the girls, a brunette with a shock of recently bobbed curls, only partially tamed by a pearl hairband. Poppy looked at her curiously. There was something familiar about her.

"She talk tel-phone," said the girl in a Russian-sounding accent.

"Er – yes, I was just using the phone. Sorry to interrupt – I didn't realise this was a – er – private party . . ."

"The more the merrier, honey!" replied one of the younger men, who strode over and put an arm around her.

Poppy immediately pulled away. "I beg your pardon, sir! But you are being too familiar!"

The man laughed and moved in again. Poppy stepped aside, putting the telephone table between her and the man's obviously nefarious intentions. She looked to the young women for help.

Silence.

But then one of them spoke. The curly haired brunette. "She not us."

The man whipped around. "She not what?"

But before the girl – or Poppy – could answer, the door opened again and Miles and Delilah stood there. "There you are, Popsicle," said Delilah. "We've been looking everywhere for you! They're about to try out a brand new dance. You coming?"

Poppy looked at the strange ensemble in the library. "Er yes, of course. Wouldn't miss it for the world."

But as she left she caught the eye of the curly haired girl. She was trying to communicate something with her eyes. Before Poppy could enquire further, the library door was closed behind her and she was whisked onto the dance floor.

Chapter 22

Poppy woke in a comfortable but unfamiliar bed as the red fingers of dawn teased the bedroom curtains. She reached over to the side table and checked her watch: half past five. She groaned. Had she only had four hours' sleep? It was after one in the morning when Poppy had managed to corner Toby and ask him if she could have a room for the night. It had been a long day at work and, unlike Delilah, who had only woken in time for lunch, she had had an early start at the newspaper office. Toby understood, saying that if he wasn't hosting the party he might just join her. "Golly, not like that! I mean, have an early night, y'know . . ."

Poppy assured him she understood what he had meant and then followed him upstairs.

The band was still playing as Poppy fell asleep – alone – in one of the guest bedrooms.

And now it was dawn. The house was silent and she could easily drift off back to the land of nod . . . but she soon stirred, realising she needed the toilet.

She had not thought to bring a change of clothes, not realising she would be staying over, so she had slept in her undergarments. Not wanting to traipse around the house so inappropriately dressed, she draped her outdoor coat over her as a dressing gown to go down the hall.

The polished wooden floorboards were cool beneath her bare feet as she passed three closed doors. Behind one of them someone was snoring like a bear in hibernation. *He won't be awake for a while,* Poppy chuckled to herself.

The fourth door, however, was slightly ajar, and Poppy couldn't resist a little peek in. Was someone else awake? Where was Delilah? But no, sprawled on his back with one arm draped over a sagging belly was a large middle-aged man – and he was completely naked. Poppy gasped with embarrassment and pulled the door shut to preserve the man's modesty. She quickened her pace and found the bathroom, closing the door behind her before she let out a giggle – only to discover she was not alone.

Sitting in the empty bathtub, with her knees drawn up to her chest, was a young woman who too was only wearing underwear. She looked up when Poppy came in, her face streaked black with charcoal tears streaming from a swollen eye to a split lip.

Poppy ran to her and knelt down beside the tub. "Are you all right?"

She reached out her hand to push the hair from the girl's face: it was dark, curly hair. Poppy recognised the girl from the library.

"Are you all right?" Poppy repeated.

The girl shivered. Poppy took off her coat and covered her.

"What happened?"

The girl looked up at Poppy, her brown eyes dark with devastation. "He hurt me. The man hurt me."

"Which man?" asked Poppy.

The girl shrugged. "Cam-man."

"His name was Cameron? The man's name was Cameron?"

Poppy mentally flicked through the names of people she had met the previous evening. Was there a Cameron among them? She couldn't recall.

The girl shook her head. "No. No. Not Cam-man. Me not know name."

"Not Cameron. All right. What's *your* name?" asked Poppy gently.

The girl looked to the door, fearful. Poppy got up quickly and pushed the bolt. She turned back to the crumpled mess in the bathtub. "You're safe now. What's your name?"

The quivering young woman pulled Poppy's coat more closely around her shoulders. "Mimi Yazierska. I see you on big ship. *Olympic* ship."

"The *Olympic*? You saw me on the *Olympic*?"

"Yes. Me and sister."

The girls at Southampton! "Of course. I thought I'd seen you somewhere before. But how did you get here? Do you know someone? Do you have friends here I can call?"

Mimi shook her head. "No friends. No call."

Poppy was puzzled. How did a Russian girl, who spoke very little English, end up at this party? And dressed to the nines too. The girl she'd seen in Southampton – the one who dragged her sister back off to steerage class – didn't look as if she frequented these sorts of circles. But then again, neither had Poppy up until a year ago . . . Still, there was something different about this. Could she possibly be a *prostitute*?

"You Pow-pee," said Mimi.

"Yes, I'm Poppy and I'm going to help you. Can you identify – can you show me – the man who hurt you? Is he still here?"

Mimi shook her head vigorously. "No."

"What? You can't show me or he isn't here?"

Mimi shook her head again. "No."

Poppy sighed. It was difficult going without a translator. Maybe one of the other girls could help. Or maybe the police. Something like this needed to be reported to the police. She checked her watch – it was quarter to six. It was early, yes, but this was important. She needed to wake Toby to tell him what had happened. Then he could call the police. He would undoubtedly be as shocked as she was to learn that a young woman had been assaulted at the party.

"Look, Mimi, I'm going to get help." She reached down and took hold of the girl's elbow. "I'll take you back to my room. It's just down the hall."

Mimi shook her head vigorously again. "No. Me not go. They make me leave. Me and sister."

"Who will make you leave, Mimi?"

Mimi frowned, her face twisted in concentration as she tried to summon up the long English word. "Im-im-gay-shun."

"Imgayshun? Oh! Immigration!"

And then it dawned on her. She remembered what Rollo had said about Mimi's sister – the simple one – not being allowed into the United States. And yet, here she was. Had Mimi let her sister be sent home and she had remained? Poppy doubted it. So did that mean they were both here? Illegally? Then should she call the police? She didn't want to get the girl into trouble . . . but then again, she *had* been attacked. Oh! She didn't know what to do. *Toby might know. I'll talk to Toby.*

Again she tried coaxing Mimi out of the bath. But the girl still wouldn't budge.

Poppy sighed. She'd have to leave her and come back.

"All right, Mimi," she said, speaking slowly and making hand gestures. "I'm going for help."

"No!" said Mimi, panic in her large brown eyes.

"It's all right. It's all right. No Immigration. No police. My friend . . ." she gestured widely, implying the whole building, "this is his house. He's a doctor. He can help you. Doctor? You know doctor?"

Mimi nodded. "Doctor."

Was that assent? Poppy didn't know, but it was the best she'd got out of the girl so far. "All right. You stay here. I'll be back soon."

Mimi nodded. Poppy smiled reassuringly and left the bathroom, closing the door behind her. She ran down the hall towards the stairs that would take her to the top floor where, Toby had told her, he had his bedroom. But as she did, she caught her reflection in a mirror. *Oh no! I'm just in my briefs!* She turned around and ran back to her room. Inside she wasted no time pulling her pink satin dress over her head – she didn't bother with stockings or shoes – then emerged onto the landing again. Back down the hall and up the stairs, hitching her skirt to her thighs, Poppy was soon on the top floor of The Lodge, wondering which room belonged to Toby.

Dreading walking in on any naked people – asleep or otherwise engaged – Poppy had no choice but to open each of the six doors and peak in.

Behind the first door was a couple – a man and a woman – their limbs draped over one another like rag dolls. Blonde hair splayed across the pillow. Poppy, who did not doubt for a moment that Toby was a gentleman, immediately decided this was not the correct room and closed the door quietly behind her. Fortunately for Poppy the next room revealed only one person – a man – in bed. And the auburn hair on the pillow suggested it was Toby. Poppy tiptoed in and shook his shoulder, whispering: "Toby! Toby! Sorry to wake you. But something's happened. Something terrible."

"W-what? Poppy?" His blue eyes struggled into focus then he leaned up on his forearms. The sheet slipped down to reveal a tanned, muscular torso. Poppy noted it then chastised herself for such inappropriate thoughts when another young woman was in distress.

"I'm sorry," she said and stepped back, giving him space to gather himself, then explained what had happened.

A few minutes later Toby was attired in a dressing gown and slippers, and Poppy was wearing another of his gowns over her scant evening dress. They rushed downstairs and knocked on the bathroom door. No answer.

"Mimi," said Poppy quietly as she pushed open the door. "Don't worry, it's just me – Poppy. And I've brought the doctor . . ." But the bathtub was empty. Mimi was gone – along with Poppy's coat.

Suddenly they heard the roar of a motor car engine. Poppy and Toby ran out of the bathroom and towards the window at the end of the hall. She looked down to the driveway below, just in time to see a barefooted young woman – wearing Poppy's sage green coat – climbing into the front seat of a car. She could also see three other young women crammed into the back seat and a dark-suited man, wearing a Homberg hat, shutting the door behind Mimi and climbing into the driver's seat. Poppy opened the sash window and screamed: "Mimi! Stop! You don't have to go!"

But the motor – a nondescript black Model T Ford – chugged away.

"I'm telling you, Toby, she was there and she was hurt. There was no way she would have willingly left with someone. Not after what he did to her."

Poppy was sitting at the kitchen table, nursing a cup of tea. Toby was sitting opposite her, a cup of strong American coffee in hand.

"I thought she mentioned the name Cameron, but I could be wrong. Was there anyone here last night called Cameron?"

Toby thought for a moment then shook his head. "Not that I recall. But I can check up on that. Discreetly, of course. We don't want to bandy around false accusations here."

"False accusations?"

"Well, if he'd forced her, we would have heard a commotion, surely?"

"Perhaps he threatened her – quietly – with a gun or a knife."

Toby raised an eyebrow but didn't comment.

He thinks I'm being melodramatic, thought Poppy, irked that she was having to justify herself. She desperately wanted to suggest they call the police. But Mimi's comments about not wanting the Immigration Department to find her had given her pause for thought. Instead she said: "And you didn't recognise the driver? He wasn't at the party last night?"

"Not that I recall," said Toby, sipping at his coffee.

Poppy's temper was wearing thin. "Not that you recall! Was he here or not? A crime has been committed!"

Toby slammed down his cup, spilling black liquid onto the polished redwood table top. "We do not *know* that a crime has been committed! For all we know a little bit of hanky panky got out of hand. A lovers' tiff and now they've made up."

It was Poppy's turn to slam down her cup – and then she stood up, her arms akimbo. "Hanky panky? A lovers' tiff? A girl has been raped in your house, Toby, and that's all you've got to say?" Her voice blasted like a foghorn through the silent lodge.

Toby raised his hands placatingly. "Shhh, Poppy, shhh. I know you're upset – and I don't blame you after seeing a young woman in distress like that – but I do think you are jumping to conclusions here."

Poppy was just about to open her mouth to retort when the kitchen door opened and Miles and Delilah shuffled in, yawning. "What's all the racket about?" asked Miles, heading to the stove and pouring coffee for himself and Delilah.

Poppy noted that Delilah was wearing day clothes. Where on earth had she got those?

As if reading her mind Delilah said: "Miles's sister left these here the last time she was on vacation. Miles said she won't mind. And there's more if you'd like to change . . ." Delilah's voice tapered off as she noticed Poppy's face like a thundercloud. "What's wrong, Pops?"

Poppy explained to a visibly shocked Miles and Delilah.

"Good Lord! Raped?"

"Yes! She said a man had hurt her – "

"Did she say a man had hurt her in . . . *that* way?" asked Delilah.

Poppy paused to consider this. "No," she said eventually, "she didn't. But she had a swollen eye and a split lip and she was in her underwear . . ."

"But there was no other evidence – no blood – anywhere else?" asked Toby.

"Well, no, I didn't *examine* her, not like that. There wasn't time. She was hurt and I thought . . . I thought . . ." Poppy stopped and looked at the three other people. "You don't believe me, do you?"

Delilah, Miles and Toby looked at one another sheepishly.

"It's not that we don't believe you, Poppy; it's just that we're trying to get all the facts. Isn't that what you always do?" said Delilah, putting a soothing hand on her friend's shoulder.

Poppy shook her off. She'd expected more from Delilah. More loyalty. The two men she barely knew, but Delilah? What was wrong with her?

Poppy stood up. "If you are not going to pursue this any further, I want to go home. Will you take me please, Miles?"

"Of course. But can it be after lunch? I've got a couple of meetings lined up for Delilah with those producers I was telling her about. They're busy sleeping it off now, so it will be later this morning . . ."

Another brush-off. Poppy could not believe what she was hearing.

She pursed her lips and pulled Toby's gown tighter around her, not caring if Miles and Delilah thought her wearing it implied she and Toby had spent the night together.

"No, it can't wait until after lunch. I need to get back to the city. I have an appointment with Rollo and I have work to do. Is there someone else who can take me? I've heard there is a train out this way somewhere. Can you drop me at the station?"

"I'll take you," said Toby. "But I need to see everyone off first."

His voice was cold. Just like it had been the night at the speakeasy when Poppy had suggested Otto von Riesling was really Alfie Dorchester.

Alfie Dorchester. Poppy was sure he had been here last night. And hadn't Toby said he had arrived with a car-load of girls? Had that been him this morning? No, it couldn't have been; he'd left last night in a Bentley, not a Model T . . . but he could have changed motors. Or asked someone else to pick them up. How much of this did Toby know? First, he claimed ignorance about von Riesling. How could he not know he was coming? Nor who the four girls were in the library? And now he was trying to make excuses for a possible rape . . .

"No, thank you. I'll call a cab and get dropped at the station. May I use your telephone please?"

Toby looked at her curiously. Was that relief on his face? Was he pleased to get rid of her?

But Delilah looked shamefaced. "Oh Poppy, please don't go. If you stick around I'm sure we can sort all of this out. I'll help you get to the bottom of it, I promise. I just need to see these producers first and then I'll – "

Poppy gave a faint smile and patted her friend's hand. "Thank you, Delilah, I appreciate that. But I think perhaps you should stay and do your job and I should go and do mine."

Chapter 23

Kat slapped Mimi across the cheek. "Look what you've done to your face, you stupid girl!" Mimi cowered in front of the dormitory supervisor, clutching and turning the pearl ring on her finger. If she had expected sympathy for the violence she had endured at the hands of her first "client" she was mistaken. Kat, who had accompanied Mimi and two of the other girls to the party, had waited until they were dropped back into the factory compound by the Boss Man's hired driver before she had turned on her charge.

Back at The Lodge she had found the Jewish girl hiding in a bathroom and heard that the "lady from the library" had gone to get help. Kat knew time was of the essence and had grabbed Mimi and dragged her downstairs before the do-gooder could get back. Fortunately the driver was on time; otherwise she would have had to hide Mimi in the stables – something she'd done before with another new girl – until their lift arrived.

She was pathetic, this Jewish slut. What the Boss Man saw in her she had no idea. Now the stupid girl had angered the client and made him hit her. With a face like that she wouldn't be able to work for another week. And there she was snivelling and crying in that ridiculous green coat. She'd left her new clothes in the bedroom. There hadn't been time to get them. That's something else she would have to explain to the Boss Man. And who would get the blame? Not the Jewish tart, but her, Katerina Kruchkow. She only had three months left of her contract and she would be free. Free to follow the film career the Boss Man had said she could easily get. But she had to keep him sweet, or she'd be out on the street and on the run from Immigration like the other wenches who'd served their time, unable to get a proper job, and selling the only thing they actually owned.

Kat threw a towel at Mimi. "Clean yourself up."

The Jewish girl, her shoulders slumped, turned towards the communal bathroom. But before she reached the door the imbecile – the feebleminded sister – came out of the dormitory, rubbing sleep from her eyes.

"Mimi! What wrong, Mimi!" She ran to her sister and threw her arms around her.

"Pathetic!" spat Kat. "You're both pathetic."

It was nearly lunchtime when Poppy finally crossed the threshold at Rollo's place. Back at The Lodge she had to wait for the cab, then be waved off by a guilty-looking Delilah and a polite-but-cool Toby (from whom she'd had to borrow money for the journey). Then there was a nearly three-hour train ride from Ronkonkoma Station to Manhattan, stopping, painfully, at every little platform between the lake and Queens, before eventually chugging into Pennsylvania Station. Then, after asking for further directions, she'd found her way to the 34th Street subway and taken the train uptown to 57th Street with a short, but confusing, connection to Fifth Avenue (after first getting on the wrong train and heading a couple of stops in the wrong direction), until finally emerging at the south end of Central Park and catching a trolley to the Metropolitan Museum of Art. Exhausted, Poppy walked the final block to the Rolandsons' 82nd Street townhouse, by which time all she wanted to do was have a bath and catch up on some sleep. But there was far too much to do.

Mr Morrison, the butler, let her in with a "Good afternoon, ma'am". He looked nearly as exhausted as Poppy. The empty crate of champagne bottles waiting to be taken out to the trash suggested the reason. *Poor Morrison,* thought Poppy, *having a last-minute party thrust on him like that.*

But Rollo, descending the stairs on the stair-lift like a god in a Greek play, looked as bright as a button as he declared: "Welcome home, Miz Denby! I thought you were never going to get here! Get yourself a bite to eat – Morrison, help her, will ya? – then come into the study. I've got lots to tell you!"

Then he alighted from the lift and all but skipped down the hall, whistling "Yanky Doodle Dandy". Despite herself, Poppy smiled. "Good party?" she asked Morrison.

"Mr Rolandson seemed to enjoy himself," came the circumspect reply as the butler helped Poppy out of her borrowed coat.

"Is my aunt in?"

"She isn't, ma'am. She and Miz King are having luncheon at the Algonquin, I believe. Apparently she's been invited as a guest at the Round Table."

"The Round Table?" asked Poppy. "What's that?"

The butler sniffed as he hung up the coat. "Your guess is as good as mine, ma'am."

"Ah," said Poppy. "No doubt we'll find out soon enough."

Half an hour later and Poppy was washed and changed and eating a crab sandwich provided by Morrison. Once she'd finished the last delicious morsel she found her way to the study where Rollo was sitting in a winged leather armchair, smoking a cigar and reading the Saturday edition of *The New York Times*. "Well, that's good to know," he said, indicating that Poppy should take a seat next to him.

"What's that?" she asked, shifting a pile of unshelved books from the nearest chair.

"Australia won't be going to war with us after all."

"Oh," said Poppy. "I didn't know they were planning to."

"Some rags down under thought they might declare war on the United States because of the Anglo–Japanese trade agreement. But apparently not."

"Well, that's a relief," Poppy grinned and settled down on the chair. "Anything else of interest?"

Rollo flicked to page three. "A fur factory has burned down just over the river in Newark. I remember attending the opening of it. Five storeys. $300,000 damage, and hundreds of workers out on the street. Oh, and a dead dog."

"A dead dog?"

"Yes, apparently it raised the alarm but couldn't get out."

Poppy sighed. "That's sad."

"Yes it is," said Rollo, "but what's even more sad are the conditions these people were working under. I'm surprised the place didn't go up in flames earlier. And the blighters were darned lucky they weren't locked in."

"Good heavens! Do they do that?"

"At some of these places, yes. That's why there's so much industrial action at the moment in the garment industry. Like these women in Boston." He pointed to a smaller article further down the page headlined "Women Strikers in Fight".

"Is it happening in New York too?" asked Poppy.

"Oh yes," said Rollo. "The city's health and safety executive is trying to put pressure on the owners to clean up their act; but you know what it's like – better conditions cut into profits . . ."

Poppy knew exactly what it was like. It was one of the things the miners in England were striking against. She wondered for a moment how Ike Garfield was getting on covering it all for the *Globe* and, with a tinge of guilt, how her parents were managing running the soup kitchen up at Ashington Colliery.

"Do you think there might be a nationwide strike here too?" she asked.

Rollo shook his head. "No, it's different here. It's not a national industry. And it mainly employs poor women. And no offence, Miz Denby, but not many people care about them."

Poppy sighed again. She knew Rollo did not share those views of women. But there were too many men – and women – who did. "Besides," he added, "most of them are immigrants, a few of them illegal. And not many people care if they live or die. And if they die, well . . ." he splayed his large hands, "there was no record of them in the first place."

Poppy's ears had pricked at the phrase "illegal immigrants". "Funny you should mention that," she said and went on to tell him everything that had happened at the Spencer lodge.

"Jake, Mary and Jehoshaphat!" declared Rollo. "You telling me that a girl was raped at a US senator's holiday home and his son denied that it ever happened?"

"That's what it looks like, yes."

"What a story!" said Rollo, his eyes twinkling.

Poppy frowned. "Rollo . . ."

He raised his hands. "I know, I know, I'm sorry. It's terrible what's happened to her – and we must try to help her if we can – but I'm not sorry that you might have stumbled onto a cracking news story. Miz Denby, I think your days on the Death Beat and mine in copy tasting might be numbered." He rubbed his hands together.

Poppy folded her hands in her lap. "That's all well and good, Rollo, but I don't really know what happened. I just have my suspicions. And unless I can find the girl and get her to tell me the details, I'm not sure we have a story."

Rollo chewed on his lip. "True, true. We'll need a bit more before we can go to editor Quinn with this. Do you have any ideas how you might follow it up?"

Poppy unfolded her hands and smoothed down her skirt. "I'm thinking of going to the Carter offices on Monday. The girl came over on the same ship as us. Perhaps they can tell me what happened to her when she arrived. If she was turned away – she and her sister – there should be some record of them returning to Southampton. Don't they have to go back on the same ship?"

Rollo nodded. "I think that's how it works, yes. Good thinking, Miz Denby. And I'll see if I can probe some of my old sources on Ellis Island. Back in the day I covered some stories on the White Slavery scare that turned out to be more urban legend than fact, but if I recall there were a few 'unaccounted for' immigrants that did slip through and end up in less than salubrious circumstances."

Poppy made a mental note to find out more about the White Slavery story.

"But as you say, Miz Denby, that will all have to wait until Monday when office hours resume. What we can do now is go look at a body in a mortuary."

Poppy blinked in shock. "I beg your pardon!"

Rollo laughed. "Oh, your face is a peach, Miz Denby, an absolute peach. I've managed to – how do I put this? – *influence* someone down at the city morgue, to let us have a look at old Prince von

Hassler. And . . ." he paused dramatically ". . . I've also managed to get the key to his apartment."

Poppy blinked in double time. "How did you –"

Rollo raised his hands again. "Ask me no questions and I'll tell you no lies." Then he grinned. "But best of all, today we'll be travelling in a cab, m'lady."

"I thought you couldn't afford it," said Poppy.

"I can't," said Rollo, looking like the Cheshire Cat, "but *The New York Times* can. And I'll be slapping them with the bill as soon as this becomes front page news."

Chapter 24

Saturday, 20 April 1921, Midtown East Manhattan

It was the second time in two days that Poppy was visiting Bellevue Hospital. But this time it was not to see Toby at the orthopaedic department, but the official mortuary of the Chief Medical Officer housed at the facility. Rollo, through his sources, had arranged an unofficial viewing of the body of the octogenarian prince, courtesy of an underpaid and financially compliant mortuary assistant.

Behind a pair of half-moon spectacles, the mortician raised an eyebrow at Poppy's presence. He did not, however, query it. Poppy, sadly, was not unfamiliar with dead bodies. At the military hospital she had become all too familiar with the dead and dying. One of her jobs had been to wash the corpses to prepare them for viewing. It was a sad, lonely task, but one she performed with as much dignity as she could muster. It was the least she could do for the brave young men who had given their lives fighting for what they believed in; and the thing she wished she could have done for her brother, Christopher.

But the body lying on the marble slab was nothing like the broken young men, many of them with limbs amputated, that she had ministered to back in 1917. This one was large, flabby and old. Folds of flesh sagged like a serving of tripe, and the extremities were blackened with lividity. Thanks to refrigeration, putrification had not yet set in, but a greeny-grey pallor was beginning to creep up the neck. The face, drained of blood, looked little like the photographs Poppy had seen of the prince in life, although the thick grey moustache remained full and proud. Rollo pointed to a two-inch gash on the prince's forehead. "Was that the cause of death?"

The mortuary assistant hooked his thumbs into his braces under his unbuttoned lab coat. "Yes and no. Yes, in that that was the fatal blow that caused the haemorrhage, but no in that he would not have hit his head like that unless he had fallen."

Well, that's stating the obvious, thought Poppy. She wanted to ask something herself but Rollo had suggested she leave all the questioning to him. He was the one calling in the favour, he was the one with the *New York Times* credentials and, if their presence there was questioned, he would be the one to take the rap. "And," he added, grinning, "some fellas don't like being questioned by a dame."

Poppy scowled but agreed to his request. "So . . ." probed Rollo. "Why did he fall?"

The mortician ran his finger down and across the prince's chest following the line of a recently sutured incision from navel to clavicle. "We thought it might have been his ticker. He was on medication. But while it's not in great shape, the heart was still in working order."

"So . . ." probed Rollo again.

"So . . ." said the mortician, rocking back on his heels.

Get on with it!

The mortician took the prince's head in both hands and rotated it so the back of his head was visible. A square of hair had been shaved to reveal a purply blue swelling. "This," said the mortician, "is what caused him to fall. A powerful blow from behind with a blunt instrument. It could not have been self-inflicted."

"How do you know that?" asked Rollo. "Couldn't he have slipped on the tiles – this was in a bathroom, wasn't it?"

The mortician nodded.

"And then he could have hit the back of his head, then fallen forward."

The mortician shook his head. "No. That's not what happened. If he had fallen with sufficient force to create a contusion with this severity of swelling then he would have continued to fall backwards. If he could have stopped his fall after he hit his head he would not have been falling fast enough to generate this degree of force."

He peered over his half-moon spectacles at Rollo with an expression that almost said "Elementary, dear Watson". Poppy chuckled.

Rollo cleared his throat. "So, you're saying he was murdered."

The mortician shook his head vigorously. "That's not my call,

Rolandson. All I'm saying is that someone hit this man on the back of the head, causing him to fall and then hit his forehead, which caused his skull to fracture, which then led to a haemorrhage with fatal consequences. Whether the initial blow was accidental or intentional, and what the motive was, is beyond the scope of the medical examiner's office. And, if I may say so, that of *The New York Times* . . . if you are even working for them. I'd heard you were canned, Rolandson, then you went to England. Remind me again why you are here?"

Rollo looked at Poppy. "Are you taking notes, Miz Denby?"

She wasn't. Although she had her notepad open and pencil poised there was nothing the man had said that she couldn't remember. However, she recalled what Rollo had once told her during a mentoring session. "Always take notes, Miz Denby. It makes the interviewee think they've said something important."

"Of course, Mr Rolandson," she said. "This is crucial information and I doubt we'd be able to recall it as well as doctor . . . doctor . . ." The mortician straightened up and pulled back his shoulders. He was not a doctor. Only a technician. Rollo had already told her that. Nonetheless he primped with pride.

"Best you leave my name out of it, Miz; we doctors don't like to boast, you know."

"Of course not," said Poppy, making a note. "Sorry, doctor. Could you please spell contusion? These medical words are so far beyond me . . ."

Poppy and Rollo stepped out of the elevator onto the top-most floor of one of the most exclusive addresses on Lexington Avenue. This was the home of Prince Hans von Hassler. Yellow police tape zig-zagged across the doorway warning them to keep out. Rollo looked to left and right in the small vestibule and then inserted a key into the lock. The door opened.

"After you, Miz Denby," he said and indicated with a wave of his hand that she was to crawl under the tape.

"Are you sure this is allowed?" asked Poppy.

Rollo shrugged. "Depends who you ask." Poppy didn't move. "Come on, Poppy, shake a leg. All right, all right. If it makes any difference to you we are not breaking and entering. And I didn't steal the key; it was loaned to me by someone close to the victim. Practically a family member."

Poppy cocked her head to one side. "Practically?"

Rollo grinned. "Practically."

Poppy sighed, shook her head and got down on her knees, crawling under the bottom line of tape and dragging her satchel after her. Rollo followed.

Inside the apartment Poppy gasped. It was nothing like she'd imagined an old man's home to be: fuddy duddy and filled with bric-à-brac. The décor was like something out of a Hollywood celebrity magazine. The centrepiece was a recessed oval marble floor surrounded by polished black teak steps. A Steinway grand piano filled one corner, while floor to ceiling glass doors opened onto a topiarian roof garden.

Rollo let out a long whistle then summed up his opinion in one word: "Swell."

Along the wall behind the piano were photographs of the prince with various Hollywood celebrities, including Charlie Chaplin and Douglas Fairbanks Jnr. There were also photographs of him with leading politicians, including the late Teddy Roosevelt, the new President Warren Harding in his younger days and Senator Theodore Spencer.

"Nothing that appears to have been snapped in the last three years," Rollo noted. "Didn't you say Toby had told you he'd become a bit of a recluse?"

"Yes," said Poppy. "I wonder why."

Rollo shrugged. "Old age?"

"Perhaps," agreed Poppy. "But this apartment doesn't look like it belongs to someone who has given in to his dotage. It looks almost like a bachelor pad."

Rollo grinned. "And how many of those have you seen, Miz Denby?"

Poppy flushed. "You know what I mean."

"Yes," agreed Rollo, "I do." He took one more look around the plush living room then said: "Should we check out the scene of the crime?"

"You mean the bathroom?"

"I do indeed. Over there, I think."

Someone had very helpfully left a white-tape outline of where the body had lain: between the lavatory and the recessed round bathtub with gold taps. Poppy paused to imagine the cadaver she had seen in the mortuary splayed on the tiled floor, its head face down where now there was only a sticky dark red stain. *The poor old man,* she thought. *Did he die instantly? Or did he lie there for a while, lonely and afraid, as his life seeped away?*

"Wish I could have brought a camera," Rollo grumbled. "It was one of the conditions of entry. No photographs. If the *Times* goes with the story they'll have to get a pic from the official police photographer."

"If?" said Poppy.

Rollo grinned. "Sorry, Miz Denby – *when*."

Poppy looked around the bathroom – at the plush towels, the modern shower cubicle with the Bakelite seat. Her aunt had one in her shower in London. Poppy had never used a shower before moving in with her aunt. Only the most well-to-do people could afford them. And Prince von Hassler was certainly that. He was also, by the look of the shower seat, either disabled or frail with age.

She voiced her observation to Rollo. "Perhaps it was just his age that kept him indoors after all."

"Perhaps," offered Rollo. "But I think there's more to it and that's why we're here. I'm hoping –"

Suddenly there was the sound of elevator gears grinding and pinging to a stop. Poppy clutched Rollo's arm. "Someone's here!"

Her eyes flicked around the bathroom, looking for somewhere to hide. Rollo might fit into the laundry basket . . .

Then a key turned in the lock.

Rollo patted her hand. "Don't worry, Miz Denby. It's all arranged. Come on, let's go meet her."

"Her?" mouthed Poppy and followed Rollo back into the living room.

Clambering from her knees to her feet was a negro woman in her sixties wearing a grey mackintosh, black skirt, hat and gloves. She brushed down her skirt as she stood, then closed the door on the web of police tape.

"I see you let yourself in, Mr Rolandson," said the woman.

"I did, thank you, Mrs Lawson. Here's your key." He walked across the room and placed the key on the woman's outstretched palm. She took it and put it into her handbag, snapping the catch shut.

"May I introduce Miz Poppy Denby, my assistant. Miz Denby, this is Mrs Nora Lawson, Prince von Hassler's housekeeper."

Poppy crossed the space between them and reached out her hand. "I'm sorry for your loss, Mrs Lawson."

The older woman looked at Poppy curiously then offered her hand in return. "Good day to you, Miz Denby. He brought you with him from England?"

"Yes he did. We're here for three months."

"Lucky for me I caught him then."

"Caught him?"

"Yes. He's one of the only ones I'd trust. Back in 1910 Mr Rolandson here helped catch a negro man's killer. Do you remember that, sir?"

Rollo looked surprised. "So that's why you agreed to see me."

Mrs Lawson nodded. "Yes siree. You're not like those other white reporters. You look for the truth." By now she had released Poppy's hand and was indicating a cluster of black leather and chrome armchairs. "Your boss here, Miz Denby, did not believe that a negro man had killed himself."

"As he had clearly been beaten to death, it was obvious," said Rollo, heaving himself up onto a chair as Mrs Lawson and Poppy lowered themselves onto a sofa.

"Not so obvious to those who would not see," answered Mrs Lawson, folding her gloved hands in her lap. "And that's what I think might happen here too – that there'll be a cover-up."

"Oh?" said Poppy. "But the medical examiner has already suggested it wasn't self-inflicted. They can't cover it up now."

Mrs Lawson nodded, pursing her lips. "So I hear. But that don't mean the police'll do anything about it. Or at least it won't be high on their list of priorities to do something."

"And why's that?" asked Poppy.

Mrs Lawson looked at Rollo.

"Because, Miz Denby, Mrs Lawson here thinks the police don't want it in the papers. If it's declared a murder it will get onto the front page, not just the obituaries – and certain people don't want that."

"But why wouldn't they want that?" asked Poppy, puzzled. "And who are these 'certain people'?" Poppy's lack of sleep was catching up with her and it was slipping into her tone.

"Because, Miz Denby," answered Rollo, patiently, "Mrs Lawson tells me the prince was a homosexual. And he'd had relationships with a number of high-profile people. People who would not want that sort of thing to be known. People with the power to put pressure on the police to sweep the death of an already old man under the carpet."

"That's right," intoned Mrs Lawson. "Now while I didn't approve of his . . . his *behaviour*, Prince Hans was a goodly man and he don't deserve to die like this and he don't deserve for it to be covered up just so."

Poppy blinked a few times, giving herself time to absorb the new information.

"Righteeo. I see. But isn't it already out there? Haven't the next of kin now been informed it wasn't an accident? Surely they would want justice to be done."

Mrs Lawson gave a snort. "Next of kin? If you mean that good for nothing nephew of his, that's exactly what he wouldn't want."

Bingo! Poppy cleared her throat and tried to keep the excitement out of her voice. "So you've met him? Count von Riesling?"

"Yes, ma'am, and a more slithery snake in the grass I ain't never seen."

If you're talking about Alfie Dorchester, I couldn't agree more.

"So . . . what exactly does this count look like?"

"Tall, dark hair, white . . . Why do you want to know that, Miz? It's got nothing to do with nothing."

"Well, I – "

Rollo interjected. "It might just help us with another story we're working on. I think we might be able to help each other here, Mrs Lawson; that is what you want to do, isn't it?"

The older woman pursed her lips again for a moment and then nodded her assent. "If I can, I will, sir." Then she got up and walked towards a sideboard. She opened a drawer and pulled out a photograph and brought it back to Poppy and Rollo. She held it to her chest.

Oh, turn it round!

"This was taken at Christmas. When Prince Hans thought Otto was here to say he was sorry."

"Sorry for what?" asked Rollo.

Mrs Lawson looked at him gravely then answered: "For blackmailing him for the last three years."

Poppy's heart sank. *Three years? Then it can't possibly be Alfie after all.*

"About him being a homosexual?" probed Rollo.

Mrs Lawson nodded. "Yes – some. But more about who he had . . . well – you know – done *unnatural* things with. Prince Hans did not want to hurt anyone. Not his friends. And definitely not the people he loved. Otto – who lived in Monty . . . Monty . . ."

"Carlo," prompted Poppy.

"Yes, that's right. Monte Carlo. Somewhere in Europe, I think. Well, Otto wrote Prince Hans and said he needed money. He was a gambler and a drinker and a general ne'er do well and he'd lost his family money. So he thought his rich uncle might help him out. But Prince Hans told him to get off his lazy – his lazy . . . Well, ma'am, he told him to get a proper job."

"Good for him," nodded Rollo approvingly.

"That's what I thought too. Until the letters started coming, threatening to tell all unless Prince Hans sent him money. Oh, the poor man! It nearly broke him. Not financially . . ." Mrs Lawson gestured around the apartment. "He had more than enough, but it nearly broke his heart. He hadn't seen his nephew since he was knee high to a grasshopper – and then this."

"And is that when he stopped going out?" asked Poppy.

Mrs Lawson lowered her chin to her chest. After a moment she raised it again and spoke in a small, quiet voice: "It destroyed him, Miz Denby. He became a shadow. A sad, sad shadow. He was always full of life, the prince. He never acted like an old man. Not until that boy started writing him . . ."

"So," probed Rollo. "What happened when Otto arrived? Around Christmas, you say?"

"End of November. Soon after Thanksgiving. Completely out of the blue. The prince didn't even recognise him. It had been years since he'd last seen him – his late sister's son, I think. He'd been sent to school in England." She nodded at Poppy. "Same place you're from, Miz."

Poppy smiled in acknowledgment and waited for the housekeeper to continue.

"Prince Hans said it had ruined his German."

"What did he mean by that?" asked Rollo.

"The way he spoke it, more English than German, I think – with an English accent, y'know? The prince mentioned it – more than once."

Poppy's ears pricked at this. "May we see the photograph please, Mrs Lawson?"

The older woman unfurled her arms, turned the photograph around, and let the two journalists see it.

Poppy gasped. Seated on the very sofa where she was now sitting was a frail old man: a shadow, as Mrs Lawson had said, of the man in the other photographs Poppy had seen. And beside him, sitting tall and erect, was none other than Alfie Dorchester, with his hair dyed black.

"Great Scot!" said Rollo and jumped up, pointing a stubby finger at the photograph. "Is that Otto von Riesling?"

"It is," replied Mrs Lawson. She almost spat the words.

Rollo turned to Poppy, his eyes wide with excitement. "You were right, Poppy! By Jove you were right!"

Mrs Lawson's eyes narrowed. "What you going on about? Right about what?"

Poppy was just about to tell her all about Alfie Dorchester when Rollo put up his hand to silence her. "Excuse me, Poppy, may I?" His tone did not suggest it was a request.

Poppy acquiesced.

"Sorry, Mrs Lawson. I'll explain. Miz Denby and I have met the count before in London, but he had a different name. He might have been involved in something dishonest – we're not really sure . . ."

Not really sure? I'm quite sure!

Rollo gave Poppy a warning look. She held her tongue.

Mrs Lawson twisted her lips in disdain. "Doesn't surprise me, Mr Rolandson. Not an honest bone in that boy's body."

"Well, nothing has been proven, Mrs Lawson. But we'll see what we can do to make sure the police do not sweep the prince's death under the carpet. That we can assure you."

Mrs Lawson smiled thinly, her wrinkled cheeks lifting towards her grief-faded eyes. "Thank you, sir. Is there anything else I can do to help you?"

Rollo nodded. "Yes, there is. Firstly, do you know if the prince left a will?"

"Yes, he did. It's with his lawyer. I can give you his name and address."

"Good, good. And the second thing: do you know where Otto von Riesling lives? I gather it isn't here . . ."

Mrs Lawson shook her head. "No, it isn't. But I'm not sure where it is, exactly. Somewhere near the factory . . ."

"Factory?" asked Poppy.

"Yes. The garment factory. In the Garment District. The prince signed it over to Otto at Christmas – hoping that would be the end of it. But it wasn't. He kept coming back for more money . . ."

Mrs Lawson stopped as tears welled in her eyes. Rollo reached into his pocket and took out a handkerchief.

"Thank you, sir," she sniffed.

After allowing her a few moments to compose herself Rollo probed again. "So the prince signed a factory over to Otto."

Mrs Lawson nodded, clearing her throat. "Yes. At least his share in it. That senator from Long Island owns the other half."

"Senator Spencer?" asked Poppy, remembering something that Toby had said about the prince and his father being in business together.

"That's the one. The lawyer should be able to tell you more. He might also have Otto's address. Hold on a moment."

The housekeeper went to the telephone table, pulled out an address book and wrote down a name and address on the back of one of Prince von Hassler's gold-trimmed calling cards.

She held it out to Rollo, who took it. But she didn't let go. "Promise me you'll find out who killed him, Mr Rolandson."

Rollo looked up at the woman and said gently, "I'll do my very best, ma'am."

Chapter 25

It was approaching five o'clock by the time Rollo and Poppy stepped out of the yellow cab at the 87th Street townhouse. On the drive over they had discussed what they had learned from the mortician and Mrs Lawson, and decided on a plan of action for the next few days. They agreed that they could not start writing articles about a police cover-up until they were sure there really was one. So far they only had Mrs Lawson's suspicion to go on. "I'll be able to see on Monday," Rollo said. "The crime reporter will submit his copy for subbing and I'll find out then which way they're playing it. If it's murder, it'll be in Monday's paper. If not, well . . ."

"Who's on the crime beat for the Lexington Avenue area?" asked Poppy.

Rollo laughed. "A fella called Tony Steele. But he called in sick on Friday. Flu. He'll probably be off most of next week."

"What's so funny about that?" asked Poppy.

"Not funny ha-ha. Funny ironic. You see, your pal Paul Saunders is the first stand-in for anyone who's sick. That's probably where he was on Friday. And why he had the von Hassler file in his desk."

"Not just to torment me then?" asked Poppy as the cab turned left into Park Avenue.

Rollo grinned. "Not just – but I'm sure that was a bonus."

The journalists agreed that nothing could be done now until Monday. The lawyer's office wouldn't be open until then and neither would the Carter Shipping office. Poppy reminded Rollo that she wanted to continue following that story too – she needed to find out if Mimi Yazierska was in the country illegally and, if so, if she could help her in any way without getting the young woman into trouble with the authorities. She wasn't sure whether the two stories were linked, but it did seem odd that Alfie Dorchester was at the party where those foreign girls were possibly being forced to have sex with men. There was also the new revelation that Alfie now co-owned a factory with the Spencers. Exactly how the stories intersected – or if they actually did – would hopefully come to light as she and Rollo continued to dig.

But for now, Poppy had the night off. She yawned as she stepped into the entrance hall and gave Morrison her coat. The butler informed her that her aunt and Miss King were going out to the theatre, that Delilah had telephoned to say she was staying for the rest of the weekend at The Lodge and she'd be back on Monday, and that a telegram had arrived for Miz Denby.

Poppy took it from him and read it out loud to Rollo. As expected, it was from Marjorie Reynolds, about Otto von Riesling in Monaco. "On the case STOP Will need few days to investigate STOP Love to all STOP"

"Well, no new developments there," observed Rollo. "Looks like we've got the night off then. What are your plans?"

Poppy yawned again. "Dinner and then an early night, I think. And you?"

Rollo frowned. "My mother is in town."

"Oh. Will she be coming here?"

Rollo shook his head. "No. She's not staying the night. I'm meeting her at the Astoria for dinner. Then she's going to the theatre with friends." He smiled wryly. "I'm not invited."

Poppy gave him a sympathetic look. He laughed. "It's all right, Miz Denby. I'm a big boy now."

Poppy slept like the dead. She was awakened by a knock on the door and a call of "Poppy darling, are you awake?" and then Aunt Dot wheeled herself into the room. Poppy shuffled up to sitting, wiping the sleep from her eyes.

"Ah, Aunt Dot, sorry I wasn't up when you got in last night," yawned Poppy. "Did you have fun at the theatre? And Morrison said you were invited to the Algonquin Round Table. Rollo told me all about it. He said it's a gathering of the finest literary and political minds in the city – and the wittiest social commentators. Harpo

Marx . . . Noel Coward . . . Dorothy Parker . . . Quite an honour to be asked. Was it fun?"

Poppy readied herself to hear all about Aunt Dot's fabulous day with the intelligentsia of New York City, but surprisingly the older woman just said: "Yes, fun, lots of fun. But I'll tell you about it later. There's something I need to ask you first." Her voice was serious.

Poppy frowned. "Of course. What is it?"

"I was wondering if you might take me to see Elizabeth Dorchester today. Just you and me. Gertrude doesn't know her, and Delilah – well, what with everything that happened with Elizabeth and her mother, it could be a bit awkward. But I really need to see her."

"Of course," said Poppy, pulling a bed coat over her shoulders. "But is a surprise visit wise?"

Dot shook her head. "No, it's not. She might still be . . . fragile – mentally, emotionally. I sent a letter a couple of days ago." Aunt Dot held up an envelope. "She sent a reply yesterday."

"Does she want to see you?"

Dot nodded. "Yes. She has a settlement house over in Chelsea. She's trying to help the immigrant women." Dot smiled. "Typical Elizabeth. After all she's been through, she still wants to help people."

"When is she expecting us?"

"Lunchtime. She said she'd do an English Sunday roast. Yorkshire puddings and all!"

Poppy's tummy grumbled. "Ooooh lovely! All right, no trouble. Do you want me to order a cab?"

"I've already done it. It's coming in two hours."

The yellow cab wound its way through the Garment District – an area to the west of Fifth Avenue that had been zoned for fashion houses and factories. The cab driver told them that businesses had been forced to move from the "better" parts of Manhattan. "City Hall stopped issuing permits. They wanted to keep all the immigrant fashion factories in one place. Your friend doesn't live here though. She's in Chelsea, just south of here, ma'am. We're entering there now. Just the other side of 34th Street."

They drove past the imposing entrance to Penn Station, which

Poppy had passed through the previous day, and then left onto Ninth Avenue.

"Do you think that's why Elizabeth settled here? Because it's got the same name as where you all lived in London?"

Dot smoothed down the collar on her fur coat. "I'm not sure," she said. "It doesn't look quite as comfortable as *our* Chelsea, does it?" Poppy looked out of the window: no, it didn't. It was a bustling semi-industrial area where tenement houses stood cheek-by-jowl with workshops and factories. Market traders sold their wares from barrows and horse-drawn carts jostled for space with motorised delivery vehicles on the pot-holed roads. The cab stopped at a junction as a man in a flat cap, grey shirt and braces manoeuvred a rack of clothes across the road, wheeling it skilfully around the muddy depressions.

"You've got dock workers to the west and garment workers to the north," explained the cab driver. "It's not the best of areas for two ladies like you to visit. Are you sure your friend gave you the right address?"

Aunt Dot opened her reticule and pulled out a silk-covered notebook. She slipped her pince nez onto her nose and read out loud: "Number twelve Chelsea Square. Just off Ninth Avenue. She said it was a 'settlement house.'"

The cab driver snorted. "Well, ma'am, that'll explain it. Your friend a do-gooder by any chance?"

"She certainly is," answered Aunt Dot proudly, either ignoring or not noticing the sarcasm in the cab driver's voice.

"Well, here we are."

The yellow cab pulled up outside a three-storey house that had seen better days. On one side was a boarded-up property and on the other what looked like a warehouse. The front door of number twelve had not seen a lick of paint in years and was patched in places with odd bits of wood and nails. The cabby got out and unstrapped Aunt Dot's wheelchair from the back of the motor while Poppy readied his fare.

"Can you help us up the steps please?" she asked, adding an extra tip.

The cabby doffed his cap with his thumb. "Sure thing, ma'am."

When Aunt Dot was safely in her chair, the cabby and Poppy lifted it together up the six steps while Aunt Dot declared: "Oh, I'm so sorry to put you to all this trouble! I'm such a bother!"

"No bother at all, ma'am," said the cabby, straightening his back and wincing. Poppy smiled her thanks at him, waited for him to retreat, then rapped on the door.

After a few moments it opened to reveal a young girl in her early teens, wearing a blue and white gingham dress, black lace-up shoes and white bobby socks. Her black hair was plaited in two pigtails, tied off with frayed scraps of blue cloth.

"Hello?" she said in thickly accented English. "You Miz Liza's friends?"

"We're here to see Miss Elizabeth Dorchester. Is she in?" said Aunt Dot.

"Miz Liza! Yes! Come in!" The girl turned around and skipped down the hall, calling out, "Oh Miz Liza! Your friends come! They come!" Then at the bottom of the corridor, lined with a threadbare paisley patterned carpet, she turned around and gestured for Poppy and Aunt Dot to come in.

Poppy smiled at the sheer exuberance of the girl and pushed the wheelchair over the threshold, shutting the door behind her. She didn't know whether she should wait where she was, or follow the gay girl into the house. But before she could decide, a familiar figure emerged through a doorway, wiping her hands on a white apron. She had put on weight since the last time Poppy and Dot had seen her, her large physique handling it well. But the same thick auburn hair framed her square face and the same sadness shaded her grey eyes. "Thank you, Helena," she said and pushed a strand of hair behind the giggling girl's ear. Helena bobbed a little curtsey and skipped away.

"Oh Elizabeth!" exclaimed Aunt Dot, her voice thick with unspent tears.

Chapter 26

The knife sliced through the mutton, releasing juices that pooled on the carving plate. Poppy inhaled the aroma of Sunday dinner: roast meat, roast potatoes, Yorkshire pudding, boiled carrots, peas and cauliflower, mint sauce and lashings and lashings of gravy. She shuddered with pleasure. The food she'd eaten this last week in New York had been tasty and tantalisingly new, but nothing could beat good old fashioned home cooking.

"Enough?" asked Elizabeth, layering meat slices on Poppy's plate.

"Yes, thank you," answered Poppy, lying but not wanting to appear greedy.

"And a small glass of wine? It's a lovely cabernet sauvignon from California," she said to Dot. "They might have rivalled the French if given half a chance, but prohibition is killing the industry. Still, let's enjoy it while we can."

Both Dot and Poppy said they would have some.

Finally, Elizabeth sat down and asked Poppy to say grace. Poppy did. And in addition to thanking God for the food, she thanked him for friends, new and old, and for helping Elizabeth in her new life.

When Poppy had finished there were tears in Dot's eyes.

And then the floodgates opened. "Oh Elizabeth, I'm so, so sorry. I know I said it in England, but I mean it – I really, really do. I should have tried harder during those years when you were locked up to visit you. I shouldn't have believed what everyone was saying – that you'd lost your mind. I should have checked for myself. Like Poppy did. And thank God she did! Yes, Grace has suffered because of it, and so have I, but justice has finally been served. And it should have been served long ago. And I'm sorry that it wasn't. And –"

Elizabeth raised her hands to silence Dot. "It's all right, Dorothy.

I forgive you. And I've forgiven Grace. It's taken me a while, but I have. I do sometimes still get angry about it. I've got to be truthful. It still hurts. But, as my priest says, we choose to forgive and keep on forgiving. It's not a one-off thing. So today I forgive you again."

Elizabeth passed a napkin to Dot. "Here, dry your eyes; your food's getting cold."

Poppy sniffed back her own tears as her aunt brought hers under control. "Th-thank you. I can't tell you how much this means to be able to settle things between us. A-are you happy here?"

Elizabeth gestured around the kitchen. "In this house or in New York as a whole?"

"Both. Either."

Elizabeth put a piece of meat in her mouth and chewed slowly and thoughtfully. Dot and Poppy looked at one another across the table. If Elizabeth didn't want to talk, she didn't want to talk. And, she was right, the food was getting cold. Poppy and Dot picked up their cutlery and started their meals. However, after a while, Elizabeth did speak.

"I arrived last August, after my father's trial. I needed to see that he was safely behind bars before I left England."

"And your brother?" probed Poppy.

Elizabeth looked at her sharply. "You know he's on the run, don't you?"

Poppy nodded. "Yes." She wondered whether she should mention that she'd seen him in New York. But no, she didn't want to frighten Elizabeth. And Aunt Dot might just get hysterical. She didn't want to have to deal with that. For now she would keep that bit of information to herself. "Last seen in Monte Carlo, I believe."

Elizabeth's eyes narrowed. "So I've been told."

"Let's not talk about him!" declared Dot. "I want to hear what you've been up to here."

Elizabeth took a sip of her wine, savoured it for a moment, and then swallowed. "Well, prohibition is mad. It's causing more problems than it's solving. It's not stopping the poor from drinking; it's just making them into criminals for doing so. And it's killing people too. There's some foul stuff being brewed in bathtubs."

"Do you see much of it here, in this area?" asked Poppy.

Elizabeth nodded. "Yes. That and every other social ill you can imagine. The conditions some of these people live and work under are appalling."

"All of them?" asked Poppy.

This time Elizabeth shook her head. "No, not all of them, if they are lucky enough to get a decent job. But for that they need to speak English. I'm running classes here. I also have a small library the community can use. It's mainly the girls that come here. Like Helena, the Italian girl you met. I actually employ her now. There are eight children at home and her mother is pregnant again. Her father has tuberculosis and can't work."

"So is that what settlement houses do?" Poppy asked.

Elizabeth continued to eat and then answered at her own pace. "Some settlement houses are run as religious missions, teaching Christianity while helping the poor. Others aren't."

"Who runs them?"

Elizabeth shrugged. "Some of them are under church control. Others are privately set up by people with financial means and a social conscience." Elizabeth smiled coolly. "I inherited money when my mother died. Once I'd been declared legally sane I was able to access it again. I think she'd be happy knowing it was being put to good use."

Lady Maud Dorchester, Elizabeth's mother, had died on the *Titanic*. She had been a friend of Aunt Dot's and the founder member of the Chelsea Six, the suffragette cell that Dot, Elizabeth, Grace and Delilah's mother, Gloria, had belonged to. "She'd be very proud of you, Lizzy," said Dot quietly.

"Thank you, Dot; I hope so. It's a drop in the ocean, but at least I feel that I'm doing something."

"So what else do you do here?" asked Poppy. "Apart from English classes."

Elizabeth poured some more gravy over her roast potatoes before answering. "I help them fill in forms and apply for jobs. I help them understand rent agreements. In some cases I go to court with them if they've got into trouble."

"And do many of them get into trouble?" asked Dot.

Elizabeth grimaced. "The prostitutes do, yes."

"Prostitutes? Oh my! You are in the thick of it here, aren't you?" declared Dot, wringing her plump hands together.

Poppy's ears pricked at the word "prostitute". She thought of the Jewish girl, Mimi. Perhaps Elizabeth might be able to help find her. So Poppy went on to tell the other two women what had happened at The Lodge the previous day, carefully omitting any mention of Alfie from her account.

Dot was horrified. She put down her knife and fork, unable to continue. "Poppy! Why didn't you tell me this before!"

Poppy lowered her eyes, chastened. She knew why she hadn't told Dot – she hadn't wanted to worry her – but perhaps announcing it at a luncheon arranged to reconcile two old friends was not the best way of doing it. "I'm sorry. Rollo knows all about it. He's helping me investigate. So it's not as if I'm out there on my own."

Dot took a series of calming breaths. "And Rollo is a good man to have on your side. I know I shouldn't patronise you. You know I think women should be allowed to do anything men do, but oh, my darling, I worry! If anything were to happen to you . . ."

Elizabeth slammed down her fork. "Good heavens, Dorothy! Have you forgotten what this young woman did back in London? What dangers she faced, single-handedly?"

"Well, it wasn't quite single-handed . . ." Poppy started, but faltered when she saw the fury in Elizabeth's eyes.

Dot cleared her throat. "You're right, Lizzy. I'm sorry, Poppy. I trust you will make wise decisions, as you have always done. But do be careful."

Poppy reached out and patted her aunt's hand. "I will, Aunt Dot. I probably shouldn't have brought it up like this – it's been a bit of an emotional ambush for you – but, well, now that I have I . . . well, I was wondering if Elizabeth could help me." She turned to the older woman, who was pouring herself a second glass of wine. "Can you?"

"In what way?" asked Elizabeth, gesturing with the bottle that a top-up was available. Poppy declined; Dot accepted.

"Well," said Poppy thoughtfully, "I was wondering if you might know of women who are here illegally and working as prostitutes. Perhaps they know where Mimi is."

Elizabeth took a sip of wine and pondered the question. "Most people who live in this community are legal. There isn't a big problem with illegal immigrants in New York – most people are admitted or turned away at Ellis Island. And they're quite efficient about it. But . . . money talks and some slip in. So yes, I do know a few. But I don't think they'd talk to you, Poppy. They don't trust anyone. They're terrified they'll be turned in to Immigration."

Poppy folded her napkin and put it beside her plate. "Do they trust you?"

Elizabeth twirled the stem of her glass between thumb and forefinger. "Some do. I'm working on it."

"Do you think you could make some enquiries for me?"

Elizabeth held Poppy in a fierce stare. "Not so it can get into the newspaper and they'd be exposed, no."

"Of course not, no. I can do it in such a way as to protect their identities. And, if there is no way to do that, I won't write the article at all. I just want to help this girl."

Elizabeth assessed the younger woman with guarded grey eyes. "All right," she nodded, "I'll see what I can do. I'm doing the rounds of the garment factories tomorrow. Again, most of them are legal, but there are one or two places that are not all above board. I've heard rumours of some of them keeping girls locked in."

"That is shocking!" declared Dot.

Poppy thought of Mimi's bruised face. She wondered if she was locked up somewhere now. *Oh please God, help me find her.*

Elizabeth continued: "There's a place I know where a few girls work by day but earn extra at night, if you know what I mean. I'll let you know if I find anything out."

"Thank you," said Poppy. "I appreciate it."

"So do, I Lizzy. I –"

But before Dot could finish her sentence Elizabeth stood up and declared: "Right, who's for bread and butter pudding?"

Both Poppy and Dot said they would love some. Poppy cleared

the table as Elizabeth opened the oven and took out a steaming dish of baked bread, milk, honey and raisins, topped with toasted almonds.

Aunt Dot smiled broadly. "My, my, Lizzy, I never knew you were such a good cook."

Elizabeth winked mischievously, giving Poppy a glimpse for a moment of a younger woman, not worn down by tragedy.

"I have hidden depths, Dorothy. Now, custard or cream?"

"Oooooh, custard please."

"Same for me," said Poppy.

Suddenly there was a knock on the door. Helena's cheeky face popped around. "That man he is here, Miz Liza."

"Which man?"

"The one he come last week. The one sleep the night."

Elizabeth, whose face was usually so impassive, went pale. She jumped up. "Excuse me. I've got to sort this," she said, and ushered Helena out of the room.

"I wonder what that's about?" asked Dot.

"No idea," said Poppy, scooping a spoonful of steaming pudding towards her mouth.

Dot giggled. "The man who 'sleep the night'. Do you think Elizabeth has a beau?"

Poppy looked at her aunt and smiled. "Well, if she does, I hope he brings her some happiness."

Dot raised her glass to Poppy. "I couldn't agree more."

A few minutes later Elizabeth returned, without explanation. Poppy did not feel it would be polite to ask. Dot, who usually didn't worry about such niceties, also held her tongue – much to Poppy's surprise.

The rest of the meal passed uneventfully. After coffee Elizabeth offered to call a cab.

When Dot was safely lifted into the back seat, Elizabeth turned to Poppy. "Thank you for bringing her, Poppy. And I'm glad you came too. I would not have this new life if you hadn't helped me back in London. So I'll do what I can to help this other young woman. I'll contact you at Rollo's as soon as I can."

"Thank you, Elizabeth," said Poppy, and stepped forward to embrace the older woman.

But Elizabeth stepped back, her face impassive, the old barriers once again firmly in place.

Chapter 27

Monday morning – another day in the office. But for the first time since she started work at the paper, Poppy had a spring in her step. She was doing what she loved: following down leads on a story that would hopefully bring the bad fellas to justice and right a fair few wrongs. The only problem was, she wasn't supposed to be doing it.

Fortunately, Paul Saunders had been seconded to the crime department to cover for the reporter who was off sick, so at least she didn't have him leering at her across his typewriter. Poppy shuddered at the thought of it.

Her first job for the day was, as usual, to read the morning edition. The lead was about New York dock workers objecting to a pay cut and threatening to close down the ports in strike action. So, it was happening this side of the Atlantic too . . . Then there was a report from Paris where German representatives of the Weimar Republic had apparently balked at the $32 billion reparation demands of the Allied powers. There was talk too of it leading to unrest and even revolution, once again threatening the peace of Europe. *Dear God, we've just got out of one war; let's not start another.* There was an intriguing story from Chicago about a young woman called Marie Vance who was part of a love triangle. She died suddenly of apparently natural causes but her body was later exhumed and an autopsy revealed she might have been poisoned with nicotine. The coroner in Chicago was urging the police to open a murder inquiry.

However, here in New York there were no further updates on Prince Hans von Hassler. So the coroner's findings had not yet been released into the public domain. Rollo would be checking the copy for the next edition; hopefully it would be in there. They had agreed to meet up at lunchtime to swap notes.

Her next job was to check the crime report to see if there had been any overnight deaths of public figures: none. There was, however, mention of the body of a young woman that had been found in a tenement house in the Garment District. The police were still trying to identify the body, as none of the neighbours seemed to know her name. She had died of "natural causes" – whatever that meant. *The poor girl. Anonymous in life. Anonymous in death.* It was further noted that she was believed to be a prostitute. Poppy doubted it had anything to do with her case but she would ask Elizabeth about it when she next spoke to her.

Poppy spent the next two hours going through the long list of "about-to-turn-seventy" public figures and wrote up three draft obituaries.

At twelve o'clock she closed the file and checked to see if any of the other journalists were watching her. There was only the young telegram operator and an older man who was dictating a telegram to him.

"Anyone mind if I use the telephone?" she asked. "I need to fill in some gaps in an obit."

The journalist waved her away, seemingly annoyed that she had interrupted him. The telegram operator ignored her. She shrugged, taking the non-response as permission, and made her way to the office telephone.

She sat down at the telephone desk with her notebook and pencil, gingerly moving a cup with cigarette butts festering in dregs of coffee onto the windowsill behind her. Then she picked up the earpiece and spoke into the receiver. She lowered her voice so the other journos wouldn't hear what she was saying, but spoke loud enough for the operator to understand her: "Carter Shipping office, please, New York City."

She waited a few moments and listened to the whirrs and clicks of the exchange, before a female voice declared "Connecting" and a male voice answered, "Carter Shipping, how may we help you?"

"Ah, good day. I wonder if you can help me. I travelled recently on the *Olympic* and I am trying to get hold of a fellow passenger. We met briefly and agreed to get together for lunch here in New York. But, well, I seem to have lost her contact details. Might you have them, please?"

"Well," came the reply, "I'm sorry, ma'am, but we don't usually give out our passengers' details. We honour their privacy."

Poppy had prepared herself for this. "I understand, completely, and I'm grateful you take this sort of thing so seriously. However . . ." she allowed her voice to crack a little, ". . . I – I just want to thank this lady for her kindness. You see I was upset about something – the recent passing of my brother – and she was so kind to me. Please, could you make an exception, just this once?"

There was an uncomfortable silence on the other end of the line, followed by: "Well, I'm sorry to hear that, ma'am. I'll see what I can find."

"Oh, thank you!" said Poppy, trying not to sound triumphant. "The name is Mimi Yazierska . . . No, I'm not sure how that is spelt . . . I think it starts with Y-A-Z, but it could also be Y-I-Z. Can you check both? Thank you . . . Oh, and she was travelling with her younger sister . . . No, I don't know the name. But it might help you if there are two Yazierskas together – easier to spot, perhaps?"

The man asked her to wait while he found the correct ship's manifest and muttered to himself as he went through the list.

Poppy imagined him running his finger down the column of handwritten names.

"Aha! I think I've got it, ma'am. There is a Miriam Yazierska – you were right, Y-A-Z – and an Esther Yazierska who embarked at Southampton. Do you think that might be them?"

Miriam . . . Mimi . . . it has to be. "Yes, that sounds like the right lady. Foreign. Russian perhaps . . ."

There was another pause and then: "Ukrainian. From Yalta. But . . ." The man's voice took on a puzzled tone. "She and her sister were travelling steerage class. I'm not sure how you could have met them. Are you sure it's the right name?"

Poppy laughed – hopefully engagingly – and answered, "Oh, I got lost one day. You know how big the ship is. I couldn't find my way back to my cabin and took a wrong turning . . ."

There was silence again and then the sound of a muted conversation. Poppy imagined a hand over the mouthpiece as the clerk spoke to someone else.

Eventually he spoke to her. "May I ask your name please, ma'am?" Poppy's heart sank. Should she give a false name? Despite the little pantomime she'd just engaged in, lying did not come easily to her. "It's Denby, Miss Poppy Denby. You'll see I am on the manifest too."

"Indeed, I see that. I see too that your occupation is listed as 'journalist.'"

Poppy laughed again, trying to keep the tone light. "It is! I'm working here for a few months."

The hand went over the mouthpiece and more mumbles were heard. "I'm sorry, Miz Denby. If this is about Seaman Jones, we have nothing more to say. The port authority has cleared us of all on-board negligence and the immigration authorities have cleared us of all wrongdoing too. Those two women escaped from the island on their own. It had nothing to do with Carter Shipping. As ever, our reputation remains impeccable. My supervisor here tells me that if anything contrary to that appears in your newspaper you will be hearing from our lawyers. Good day."

The line went dead. Poppy stared at the telephone, wide-eyed. *Good heavens! What on earth was all that about?* And then her newshound nose began to twitch. She grabbed the pencil and wrote down, verbatim, as much of the conversation as she could remember. She must show this to Rollo! She circled the words "Seaman Jones", "port authority", "immigration" and "escaped from the island". *Seaman Jones, Seaman Jones.* What had he said the day she visited him in hospital? Something about it not being his fault... that other people were doing it too... *Doing what? Something to do with immigrants escaping from Ellis Island?* But how could Seaman Jones have helped the Yazierska girls escape? He was unconscious when they arrived in port. In fact, hadn't he been taken off the ship the evening before the passengers disembarked? *Yes, that's right... so what did he mean?* And why had the Carter clerk made the connection between Jones and the girls? Or had he? Perhaps they were two separate incidents that he just mentioned at the same time... *Hmm, no, I think there's something else going on here. I need to speak to Seaman Jones... and I need to track down those girls.*

Chapter 28

Poppy filled Rollo in on the conversation with the Carter office as they met to go to lunch. He agreed that there was something fishy going on and that they should investigate further. Then he told her what he had discovered about the von Hassler affair. Paul Saunders had indeed filed a story that morning announcing the news of the prince's death, as well as a pre-written obituary. There was no mention of foul play; just that the elderly aristocrat had slipped in his bathroom. The next of kin, Count Otto von Riesling, was quoted as saying he was deeply saddened by the news of his uncle's death and asked for privacy in order to come to terms with his grief.

"Come to terms with his grief?" blustered Poppy. "He was kicking up his heels at a party only twenty-four hours later!"

"Indeed," observed Rollo. "But the good thing for us is that Saunders is in touch with him. If we can't get contact details from von Hassler's lawyer, I will ask Judson Quinn, as senior editor, to compel him to tell me where von Riesling is."

"Do you think Quinn will do that?"

Rollo nodded, picking up his briefcase and accompanying Poppy to the lift. "I hope that by the time we've spoken to the lawyer this afternoon we'll have enough to take to him. Quinn's a good man and an even better journalist. I know he's been told to keep me in my place and not let me do any – how did he put it? – *career-furthering* work, but he'll see things my way. I'm sure of it."

The lift shuddered to a halt on the ground floor.

"Whoa! Slow down, Miz Denby," Rollo called after her as she all but sprinted out of the contraption.

"Sorry, Rollo." She slowed down and waited for him to catch up with her in the middle of the foyer. Then they picked up some lunch-on-the-go at the nearby bagel shop and ate it en route to the

Midtown office of Barnes and Abramowitz, Prince von Hassler's lawyers.

Rollo had called ahead, saying he had some information pertaining to the estate of the prince. He had told them that the prince's housekeeper, Mrs Lawson, could vouch for him.

"Blasted lawyer called my bluff and said he'd have to get a reference from her first!"

"And did he?"

"Yes. Seems like Mrs L. is mentioned in the will so he had her contact details." He chuckled. "She said I was her adviser!"

Poppy brushed away some crumbs from her lap onto the floor of the subway platform as they sat waiting for the next train. "In what capacity?"

"I'm not sure," said Rollo, "but it seems to have done the trick and we've got an appointment with Barnes at half-past one."

Poppy looked at her watch. "We'll go well over the allocated time for our lunch break."

"Oh, to hell with our allocated time! We're on a story, Miz Denby. And if they fire us, they fire us. We can go freelance – sell the story to the highest bidder!"

Poppy chuckled at Rollo's enthusiasm. He was right. *The New York Times* didn't formally employ them. They could do what they liked. Poppy doubted she would be as brave as to tell them to stick their job, but as long as Rollo was on her side – and she had a job to go back to in London – she was prepared to throw caution to the wind.

"Freelance it is then!" She laughed and clutched at her cloche hat as the train steamed into the station. Then she surged forward with the rest of the passengers and jumped onto the over-full carriage, pulling Rollo up behind her when his short legs struggled to negotiate the high step.

He tipped his bowler hat and grinned up at her. "Much obliged, Miz Denby, much obliged."

Half an hour later and Poppy and Rollo were seated in the waiting room of the teak- and leather-clad offices of Barnes and Abramowitz. The room was lined, floor to ceiling, with weighty tomes of legal interest, and, although it was a mild spring day in New York City, a log fire roared in the grate. The wood smoke mingled with a faint aroma of tobacco and whisky, while the firelight played on the cut-glass surface of a crystal decanter and silver tray. Poppy felt she was in a gentlemen's club.

She knew without Rollo having to tell her that she would be expected to play the role of the pretty young assistant, there merely to take notes and not offer opinions. It was a game she had played before, and one she had frequently managed to turn to her advantage when pompous older men underestimated her intelligence, or let something slip when she innocently asked them to explain something "beyond her female understanding". It was a game Rollo enjoyed immensely.

A young man in a grey pin-striped suit showed them into the office of the senior partner, Mr Barnes. Barnes sat behind a huge desk embossed with green leather and brass studs. A brass reading lamp was on, lightening the gloom but casting shadows across one side of a jowly face. Barnes, a rotund man, looked like something out of a Dickens novel, Poppy thought: out of time and out of place in this most modern of cities. *The offices of an Old World-style lawyer,* thought Poppy. An unsurprising choice, she supposed, for a European aristocrat.

He stood as they entered, appraising them from under a pair of unruly eyebrows. He looked first down at Rollo then up at Poppy, then gave an almost inaudible "hmm". "Mr Rolandson, thank you for coming." He walked around the desk and reached out his hand. Rollo shook it firmly.

"May I introduce my assistant, Miz Denby," said Rollo, gesturing to Poppy.

Barnes turned towards her and gave a curt nod. "Miz Denby."

Poppy nodded back. "Mr Barnes."

"Take a seat," he said and walked back around the desk.

Without being instructed, Poppy took out a notepad and pencil.

Barnes frowned. "Your assistant will be taking notes?" he asked, addressing his question to Rollo. "I thought you were here to give me information, not to take it."

Rollo leaned back in his chair and crossed one leg over the other. "I thought we could, perhaps, *exchange* some information."

Barnes pursed his lips. "Rolandson. Rollo Rolandson. I thought the name was familiar. You used to work for the *Times*, didn't you?"

Rollo nodded. "I did, yes. Left to cover the war. Then bought a paper in London."

Barnes drummed his nails into the green leather desktop. "A bit off your patch, aren't you?"

Rollo inserted his thumbnail under the edge of his middle nail and made a little clicking sound in syncopation with the rhythmic thrum of the lawyer's fingers.

Poppy held her breath.

"I'm back for a few months. Helping Judson Quinn out while Archie Weinstein is away."

Barnes stilled his fingers. "Quinn's a good man."

Rollo silenced his clicking. "The best."

All he has to do is ring the paper and ask to speak to Quinn and we'll be busted, thought Poppy. But she also knew that he was only likely to do that once they'd left and by then they would have the information they needed – or not. Either way, their "freelance" activities would be exposed. Rollo, it seemed, thought it was a risk worth taking.

The lawyer pursed his lips and made a little popping sound with his mouth as he opened a file and perused the contents. Without looking up he said: "Mrs Lawson said you were her representative. Is that correct?"

"It is," said Rollo.

The lawyer jerked up his head and looked directly at Poppy. "Is that correct, Miz Denby?" His tone had turned from curious to interrogative. It reminded Poppy of the barristers she had seen at work in the court cases she'd attended the previous summer.

Poppy's knuckles whitened as she gripped her pencil. But she held his gaze. "It is, Mr Barnes. Mrs Lawson has requested that Mr Rolandson assist her in relation to Prince von Hassler's death."

"Assist in what way?" asked Barnes, still looking at Poppy. Was Rollo going to interject? Should she answer? She flicked her eyes to the right to try to get some clues from her editor.

But none were forthcoming, other than the click, click, click of his nails that had resumed. *He trusts me,* Poppy reminded herself. *He trusts me to say the right thing.*

"Mrs Lawson believes her employer's death will not be properly investigated and that no one will listen to her concerns, as she is a negro woman and he was an elderly homosexual man. She has asked Mr Rolandson to speak on her behalf." She could have added that she was also speaking on behalf of Mrs Lawson, but she did not. Instead she said: "If her suspicions are true – and they come out, either in our newspaper or another – it could delay the reading of the will. So we thought you would be interested in helping us clear up this matter as quickly as possible in order" – her hand was beginning to quiver – "in order to *minimise* any further delays."

Barnes lowered his eyebrows and renewed his drumming. Then he turned his attention to Rollo. "You've rehearsed her well, Rolandson. Sounded almost spontaneous."

Rollo continued clicking. He did not correct Barnes's patronising assumption. Poppy had not expected him to.

"So," Barnes continued, addressing only Rollo, "you know about my client's predilections. No doubt that will soon be all over the papers."

Rollo stopped clicking. "That is not why *we* are here, sir."

Poppy smiled slightly at Rollo's use of the collective pronoun.

Barnes's lips pursed again. "Then let's cut to the chase, Rolandson – why *are* you here?"

Rollo uncrossed his legs and leaned forward. Poppy had seen him do this before. He was about to take control of the interview.

"Well, Mr Barnes, sir, I thought you'd never ask." Then he grinned his biggest Cheshire Cat grin.

Poppy tried not to chuckle.

Barnes did not look amused but clearly his curiosity had got the better of him. He leaned back in his chair and moulded his shoulders into the leather. "Go on."

"Miz Denby, do you have that photograph please?"

Poppy reached into her satchel and took out the picture of Alfie Dorchester and Hans von Hassler, now removed from its frame. Rollo had asked Mrs Lawson for it before they left the penthouse.

Rollo took it from her and passed it over the desk to Barnes. "Do you know this man? The one with your client?"

Barnes took it from the editor, gave it a cursory glance, then passed it back over the desk. "Otto von Riesling. Von Hassler's nephew."

"And heir to his fortune."

Barnes's lips pursed and then he templed his fingers. "Possibly."

"And have you actually met the man?"

"I have. Twice. The first time, before Christmas –"

"To sign over the deeds to the garment factory," blurted Poppy, before she could stop herself.

Barnes's head snapped around to look at her, then he returned his gaze to Rollo.

"And the second was on Friday morning. The police contacted me to tell me of my client's unfortunate accident and asked for details of his next of kin. I telephoned von Riesling myself to tell him and then met him at the mortuary to identify the body."

Rollo nodded. "So you know where to reach him?"

"I do." He closed the file in front of him. "So that is why you have come. To get in touch with von Riesling. I'm afraid I cannot give you his address. Client confidentiality."

Rollo leaned back and resumed his clicking. "But von Riesling is not your client. Von Hassler is. And your first loyalty should surely be to him. To protect his rights and his reputation – even after death. Isn't that what lawyers do?"

Barnes cleared his throat, clearly not enjoying being lectured on the responsibilities of his profession. "It is. Until my duty of care has been dispensed."

"And when will that be?" asked Rollo.

"Once the will has been read and the estate tied up."

It was Rollo's turn to temple his fingers. "And what if that was delayed?"

"Delayed? What might delay it?"

Rollo smiled benignly over his fingertips. "Well, as my assistant has already told you, Mrs Lawson suspects her employer's death might not have been an accident. That surely would delay the reading of the will and the wrapping up of the estate now, wouldn't it?"

Barnes resumed his drumming. "It would. However, it's a moot point."

"Moot, how?"

Barnes opened the file and extracted a document on a letterhead from the coroner's office. "Because this morning I received the official autopsy report and it has been declared an accidental death." He put the report back into the file and closed it again. "Case closed."

Rollo, his fingers still templed, his eyes still on Barnes, said, "Miz Denby. Do you have the notes you took at the mortuary on Saturday?"

Barnes's eyes flicked to Poppy.

"I do, yes."

"Would you be so kind as to read them to Mr Barnes here? I think he might finally be interested in what you have to say."

He was interested. Very interested. And he was more than interested to hear that the man claiming to be Otto von Riesling was an imposter. He told Poppy and Rollo that he had been shown a birth certificate authenticating the count's identity. However, he agreed with the two journalists that this could have been either forged or stolen.

No doubt, thought Poppy, *if it ever came out that he and his firm had been duped, it would do no good for their reputation.*

So she was not surprised when he looked relieved to hear that the British Foreign Office (in the guise of Marjorie Reynolds) was busy tracking down the real Otto von Riesling in Monte Carlo. And he most emphatically agreed that the reading of the will should be delayed until the real Otto von Riesling was found.

He then gave them the address of the man calling himself Otto von Riesling, who lived in a low-rent basement apartment just off Broadway. "No doubt he was hoping to upgrade to Lexington Avenue sooner rather than later," observed Barnes dryly.

Barnes agreed not to call the police for now, concurring with Rollo that the change of the coroner's findings from "unnatural" to "accidental death" was indeed suspicious and they needed to find out who had authorised the cover-up from on high. Barnes said he would do some investigating of his own, as he had been the prince's attorney for nearly twenty years and knew his business affairs inside out. He said he would be able to tie up the case in sufficient red tape to delay the reading of the will for a few more days. He also added that as Mrs Lawson was listed as the second beneficiary of the will, she would need to be further consulted.

"Second beneficiary?" queried Rollo. "So she will inherit too?"

The lawyer shrugged. I cannot give you any details, but suffice to say, Otto von Riesling will get the lion's share unless he dies before the will is read – highly unlikely – or it is proven that he killed his uncle. He cannot then inherit and his share will be transferred to the only other beneficiary, Mrs Lawson. That of course won't happen if the killer is only proven to be someone impersonating the nephew. Frankly, it's a legal nightmare."

"Does Mrs Lawson know any of this? About the nephew not being able to inherit if he's found guilty of killing the prince?" asked Poppy.

"I doubt it. She's a simple woman."

Not that simple, thought Poppy, but refrained from commenting further.

"However," continued Barnes, "if we don't have any further evidence by the end of the week I will not be able to delay further without getting a court order to re-open the inquiry. The funeral is scheduled for Saturday. But getting the court order might alert the people behind the cover-up. And that could be dangerous."

"Dangerous?" asked Poppy, her blue eyes widening.

Barnes took on a paternal air. "Indeed, Miz Denby. Let's not forget that someone has already been killed. And who knows to what lengths the killer might go to keep it quiet? Whether that person was Otto von Riesling – or your Alfie Dorchester – has yet to be determined." Then he nodded sagely at Rollo. "But don't worry, my dear. Mr Rolandson and I will protect you."

Poppy gave an inward sigh.

Chapter 29

Rollo was feeling so buoyant after their meeting with the lawyer that he hailed a cab.

"Another taxi? Feeling flush, are we?" asked Poppy. "Or will our 'freelance' employer be paying for it?"

Rollo grinned and held the door open for her. Inside he instructed the cabby to first take him to the *New York Times* building, then to drop the lady at Bellevue Hospital. He gave Poppy some money to cover the fare. "Ask for a receipt," he reminded her, tapping the side of his nose.

With the divider between the front and back firmly closed, Poppy and Rollo discussed the latest developments in the story and their plans for the rest of the day.

"I know I need to head down to Ellis Island sometime, Poppy, but I think the priority at the moment is the von Hassler story. And I need to cover our backs with Quinn. No doubt Barnes would've been straight on the blower after we left; Quinn will be spitting nails that I've gone behind his back. But I'm sure he'll calm down after I've explained everything to him. He's a newspaperman first and foremost and he'll see this story is dynamite. I'll cover for you too with the Death Beat. So you just do whatever you need to do today and come back to the office tomorrow. Agreed?"

"Agreed," said Poppy.

Rollo was looking at her curiously from under his bowler hat.

"What?" she asked.

"I was just thinking . . . we've got a lot to go on with the von Hassler story. Do you think it's wise to get distracted by a second story right now?"

Poppy took a sharp breath. "Distracted? Rollo, this is not just a *distraction*; it's important. A young woman's life might be in danger.

Or, if not in danger, she might be suffering under duress. The prince is dead, nothing can change that, but I might be able to change something for Mimi. I read a story this morning about a young woman found dead in the Garment District. A prostitute. Apparently natural causes – whatever that means – but it could easily have been Mimi. I don't want to read about her one day in the morning paper knowing I might have done something to prevent it."

Rollo took off his hat and put it on the seat between them, then ran a hand through his hair. "Okey dokey, that's fair and dandy. But promise me you won't drop the ball on the von Hassler story."

"Pinky promise," said Poppy, and hooked her little finger and smiled. "Besides," she added, "I can't help thinking the two stories might be related."

"How's that?" asked Rollo, bracing himself as the cab swerved to avoid a spewing water geyser and a group of children splashing in the impromptu fountain.

Poppy steadied herself before answering. "Well, for a start, Alfie Dorchester has turned up in both stories. He was at The Lodge when I got there on Friday night. Toby told me he arrived with a car-load of girls. It might have been the same girls; it might not. But it's odd, isn't it?"

Rollo agreed that it was but pointed out that it might just have been a coincidence too. When it came down to it, the number of bright young dandies in New York who orbited the top social echelons was not that large. It was almost incestuous, in fact, with the same names and faces turning up at parties and eventually getting jobs on boards of the same companies and the same banks and becoming patrons of the same charities.

Poppy listened intently, then nodded her agreement. "Well, yes, and that's my second point. Alfie – or Otto as he is pretending to be – has just been given shares in the same clothing company as Theo Spencer. And whose picture was on the wall at the prince's penthouse?"

Rollo's eyes widened. "Theo Spencer. Bingo!"

"Yes!" Poppy exclaimed, talking faster and faster. "And there was a picture of Amelia Spencer and the prince at the launch of the Eugenics Society, both in the Death Beat file and in the trophy room at The Lodge. And who was Alfie with the first time we saw him at Chester's Speakeasy?"

"The Spencer boys!"

"Bingo!" said Poppy, in an appalling approximation of a New York accent.

Rollo chuckled, then picked up his hat and placed it firmly on his head. They were just a block away from the *Times* building now. "So do you think the Spencer boys are involved?"

Poppy remembered the first time she'd met them at the swimming pool on the *Olympic;* how charming and urbane they were. Then the kind and compassionate way Toby had dealt with the accident victim, Seaman Jones. And then, at The Lodge, Miles had appeared just as shocked as Delilah to hear about the assault on the young woman – and Delilah, despite her faults, was always a good judge of character. Hadn't Toby said they only knew Otto because of their father's business association with the prince – and they didn't even know where he lived?

She chewed on her lip. "I'm not sure. Probably not. But there is something in the business connection between Theo and the prince . . . and this garment factory. I've asked Elizabeth Dorchester to see if she can find out anything about that. And, of course, I need to pay it – and Alfie – a visit sometime soon."

Rollo raised his hands. "Whoa there, Miz Denby. Just hold your horses for one doggone minute. We know that Alfie Dorchester tried to kill you back in London. And he might have killed old Hans von Hassler too. Promise me you won't pay him a visit without back-up. And I don't mean me," he laughed. "Despite appearances I'm not as fit, young and strong as I look. Let's work on gathering evidence, quietly, and then we'll hand it over to the authorities at the appropriate time. Agreed?"

Poppy let out a frustrated breath. She was itching to confront Alfie Dorchester again. How dare he try to escape justice like this! After all she and her friends had suffered . . . how dare he! Her shoulders slumped and she sank back into the cab upholstery. "All right. Agreed."

The cab pulled up outside the *Times* office just as Paul Saunders was approaching on the sidewalk. Poppy slumped down as far as she could in the seat.

Rollo laughed and opened the door. "Don't worry, Miz Denby; I'll handle him."

Poppy would have loved see and hear what happened next, but she was too scared to raise her head above the parapet.

"Bellevue Hospital, ma'am?" came the query from the cabby.

"Yes please," said Poppy.

The hospital receptionist did not think it would be a problem to let the young English lady see the patient. "The poor man's far from home and you're one of the only people who has been to visit him."

Poppy's curiosity was piqued. "Who were the other visitors?" she asked.

"There was someone from the shipping company and one other person . . ." But before the nurse could finish she was called away to an emergency in one of the wards.

"Just go in and see him," she called over her shoulder as she ran towards the ringing bell.

Seaman Jones looked a lot better than he had the last time Poppy visited. His cheeks had some colour and he was sitting propped up by pillows, reading a copy of the *Saturday Evening Post* magazine. The frame was still over the stump of his amputated right leg, but he otherwise looked comfortable. Poppy gave him the basket of fruit she had bought at the hospital shop and reintroduced herself as the woman who had helped Dr Spencer on the ship. Fortunately for Poppy, Dr Spencer was not around. She was glad of that. First because things were awkward between them after the events at The Lodge, and second because she wanted to speak to Seaman Jones privately.

"Thank you again for helping on the ship, miss, and for visiting me. It gets a bit lonely just lying here on my own. Not even other patients to talk to," said Jones before popping a grape in his mouth. "Oooh, lovely and sweet. Thank you."

"Can't they put you in a general ward?" asked Poppy, picking a grape for herself.

"The company's paying for it. Only the best for their staff. They're a good company. Good to work for."

"But if you'd prefer to be in a ward, surely they wouldn't mind. Have you spoken to Dr Spencer about it?"

Seaman Jones nodded. "I have. And he said he'd see what he could do. He's a good man too," added Jones. "In fact, I can't complain one little bit about my treatment on board the ship or in this hospital. It's been top notch. I haven't got one complaint. Not one – apart from being a bit lonely, but you understand me saying that, miss, don't you? I'm not being ungrateful, I swear."

Poppy assured him that she did not think he was being ungrateful. But she did feel Jones was over-egging it a bit. Was he being sycophantic? Or was he just a working-class man feeling a bit nervous in the presence of a middle-class lady? She remembered how quick the Carter office was to assure her that all was rosy too . . . and that they'd be suing the newspaper if anything else was reported. *Methinks the lady doth protest too much*, thought Poppy.

"Seaman Jones . . ."

"Please, miss, call me Harry."

Poppy smiled. "Harry. Thank you. Harry, the last time I was here – the time you had that turn – you said something I found a little curious. You said that 'other people were doing it'. What did you mean by that?"

Jones stopped chewing his grape, stared at Poppy, then swallowed. It looked as though he was swallowing nails.

"I don't know what you mean, miss. I was ranting and raving. Delirious, like – you know what I mean."

Poppy straightened the bedspread with a sweep of her hand. "Yes, I understand you weren't well, but you did seem to want to say something to me. And I was wondering if you still wanted to. You see, I think it's got something to do with helping people into the United States who would otherwise be turned away. You know, illegal immigrants. Now I could be wrong . . ."

Jones's jaw tightened. "You *are* wrong, miss."

Poppy sighed and leaned back in her chair. *How do I approach this?* Then she noticed a photograph on the bedside table of a young woman.

"Is that your wife, Harry?" She had not seen a wedding band. "Or your sweetheart?"

Harry's jaw relaxed. "No, miss, that's my sister, Betty. She's only fourteen. Looks older, I know. Hopefully she won't be anyone's sweetheart for quite a while yet."

"And quite right too. No young girl should be kissed before she's ready. Which is why I think you can help me." Harry looked at her curiously. "Why I think you *should* help me," she continued.

"Oh, and why's that, miss?"

Poppy took a deep breath and dived in. "Because some girls – or at least one girl I know of – who were on the *Olympic*, are now in trouble. This girl has been physically assaulted – she's been –"

The basket of fruit toppled onto the floor as Seaman Jones flung his arms wide. "I did not assault that girl! I did not force myself on her! I don't know what she's been saying, but it's not true! I didn't do it! You have to believe me, miss! I just wanted to talk to her. To be friendly. And she started screaming and then she pushed me and then – and then –"

"And then you fell into the gears of the machine," Poppy finished for him, everything suddenly slotting into place. Jones started thrashing from side to side. *Oh dear God, is he having a fit?* She stood up and pressed her hands against his shoulders, in the way she had been taught to do at the military hospital, accompanying the gentle pressure with shushing noises. Eventually he calmed. No, he was not having a fit. Poppy let out a sigh of relief.

"It's all right. I believe you. You didn't want to hurt her. But I bet you're scared other people won't believe you, aren't you?"

Jones nodded, trying to hold back tears. "Yes," he choked. "I don't know what she'll say when she gets back to England. Who she'll tell. She'll want her money back for a start . . . or at least her sister will . . . and I bet she'll tell her sister. I bet she will!"

He started shaking. Poppy continued to console him until eventually he stilled.

Just then an orderly arrived with a tea trolley. Jones looked panicked, wondering perhaps if Poppy was about to tell on him.

But instead she gave him a reassuring smile and said: "Would you like a cup of tea, Harry? I know I need one. Then perhaps we can have a little chat."

Chapter 30

Poppy never underestimated the restorative power of a cuppa.

After a few sips of the sweet brew Jones was visibly calmer and she was finally able to coax the story out of him, after swearing she would do everything she could to try to keep him out of trouble.

Jones, it seemed, helped register the third-class passengers on the ship's manifest when they first embarked in Southampton. The shipping company had an agreement with the United States government, for which it received a substantial payment, to weed out potential undesirables at the port of origin. All manifest clerks were given a list of things to look out for that would be likely to prevent a passenger's admission to the United States, including obvious physical and mental illness or disability. However, some of the clerks occasionally overlooked potential problems and fast-tracked the passenger through. The passenger paid a little extra "assurance fee" so that they would indeed be able to get through Ellis Island.

Poppy was shocked. "But surely you'd know they would be turned away? That they'd have paid all that money for the ticket – and your added fee – only to be sent back when they got here. It might have been all the money they had!" exclaimed Poppy, thinking of the poor third-class passengers she'd seen shuffling up the gangplank in Southampton.

She was glad to see Jones looked cowed. *And so he should.* However, berating him now would not help her get the whole story out of him, so she took a deep breath and calmed down.

Jones waited for her to speak, anxiety written all over his face. "However," said Poppy, "I'm sure you did not intend to do any harm. Perhaps you had not really thought through the consequences properly. You probably didn't know what would happen to them . . ."

"Exactly!" said Jones, visibly relaxing. "We didn't know. Besides, it's hard to tell what the Immigration will do this side. We're not trained like they are. We're not doctors or anything. How's we to know if they're fit or not?" He looked at Poppy, pleading for understanding.

She nodded, trying to look as sympathetic as she could. "Of course, of course. An impossible situation they put you in. It really wasn't fair. So," she said, putting down her cup and saucer, "you took a fee from a young woman called Miriam Yazierska for her sister Esther, who may or may not have been feebleminded."

Jones nodded. "That's right. May or may not. I wasn't sure. I could have sent her away then and there, but that wouldn't be fair. I thought they deserved a chance to convince the Americans they were fit to enter. So I let them through."

"For a fee," said Poppy sharply, before she could stop herself.

"Yes, for a fee," said Jones and lowered his head.

At least he has the decency to look ashamed, thought Poppy, before pasting the sympathetic smile back on her face.

"Go on, Harry, tell me the rest. What happened on the ship?"

The rest of the tale went pretty much as Poppy suspected it would. Jones had come across one of the sisters – the feebleminded one – and asked if she wanted to see the engine room. "Because she seemed to be interested in how things moved," he explained.

"Of course," said Poppy, trying very hard to keep the sarcasm out of her voice. "Why else would you be alone with a young woman in an engine room?"

Jones skirted very quickly over the events leading up to him falling into the gears, saying only that the girl "misunderstood something"; that she "got upset" and in the confusion he fell – or perhaps was pushed – into one of the machines. After that he remembered nothing until he woke up here at Bellevue Hospital in New York where the staff were "lovely people" and where he had "no complaints whatsoever".

Poppy took the now finished tea cup from Jones and put it down beside her own.

"Did you not think of laying a charge against the young woman? If she pushed you into the machine? You could have died!"

Jones lowered his eyes. "I could have, yes, but – well – I didn't want to get her into trouble."

Poppy smirked. "That was good of you."

Before Poppy could say anything further, a nurse came in to change the dressing. Jones looked at the young reporter beseechingly. "What are you going to do now, miss?"

Poppy buttoned her coat and straightened her hat. "I'm going to try to find them, Seaman Jones, and then I'm going to help them. But beyond that . . ." She paused as the nurse pulled back the covers to reveal the bandaged, bloody stump. "I think, perhaps, you've suffered enough."

Jones looked as if he was about to cry.

"Are you all right, Harry?" asked the nurse.

He sniffed. "Yes, nurse, I am. Thanks to Miss Denby, I am."

Poppy left Seaman Jones's room not quite knowing what she was going to do with the information he had given her. She genuinely did believe he had suffered enough, but on the other hand, if she didn't speak up and expose the corruption of the manifest clerk and his colleagues, other poor people might suffer more. She would have to mull it over for a while. She needed to find a way to stop the injustice without getting Jones into more trouble. As a handicapped man, stripped of his livelihood, with no wife to help him, he would need all the support he could get from his employer. But if she named and shamed him, he would be cut loose without any means.

She was pondering this moral dilemma when a voice cut through her thoughts. "Poppy? What are you doing here?"

Poppy turned to see the white-coated figure of Toby Spencer holding a clip chart. He signed something with a flourish and passed it to a nurse. Poppy waited for him to finish, although for a split second she had thought of slipping away while he was distracted.

"I've just been to visit Seaman Jones. He's looking a lot better than the last time I saw him. Would you say he's on the mend?"

Toby looked over her shoulder to Seaman Jones's room. "Yes, I would say so. He'll need a lot of therapy to help him get back to health, but he looks like he's over the worst of it. With amputations it's either blood loss or infection that people die of. But he seems to be through that now."

Poppy nodded. She wondered if Toby knew about how the

accident had happened. Or the shipping company. She was curious to find out what story Jones had told, but didn't want to mention the Yazierska girls to him. She needed to think it all through first. "Terrible accident," she said instead.

"Yes," said Toby. "It happens too often though. I've seen it in factories as well. Sometimes it's the worker's fault for not being careful enough – which is what I think happened here with Jones – but sometimes it's the employers to blame for making people work long shifts or not having the right safety precautions in place."

He chuckled and Poppy noticed the fine wrinkle lines around his blue eyes.

"What's so funny?" asked Poppy as he held her in his gaze.

"Nothing, nothing," said Toby. "Just that I'm sounding like your socialist friends. My folks would have a cadenza if they heard me talking like that."

"Oh?" said Poppy. "I thought your parents were in favour of workers' rights."

He shook his head. "They're in favour of a woman's right to vote – the right sort of woman – but, like many business people, they're scared of the power of the unions."

He put his hands on his hips and appraised Poppy. "You really are a remarkable young woman, Poppy Denby. I don't know any other girls I can talk politics with and know they'll understand."

Then you don't know the right sort of "girls", thought Poppy, but kept her opinion to herself.

Toby was looking at her earnestly. "I was just due for a break. Would you care to join me? I'm sure I could rustle up a pot of coffee – or tea if you prefer."

As Poppy had just had a cup, she was going to decline, but she realised Toby was offering more than a beverage. Nothing in his demeanour suggested he was still angry with her about events at The Lodge. Her heart softened. "Yes, that would be lovely, thank you."

He escorted her to the staff canteen and ordered a pot of tea and some muffins.

"I thought you Americans only drank coffee," observed Poppy. "Rollo drinks gallons of the stuff."

Toby chuckled as he placed the tea strainer over Poppy's cup and poured. "We drink both. The Boston Tea Party didn't totally eradicate the brew. Lemon or milk?"

"Milk please," said Poppy. Suddenly she had a flashback to the first time she and Daniel had shared a pot in a tea room in Windsor. She blinked twice to rid herself of the memory, then to change the hair colour of the man in front of her from brown to auburn, and his eyes from grey to blue.

Toby offered her the milk jug. Their fingers brushed against one another. For a moment he did not retract. Neither did she. "Look, Poppy, I want to apologise for the way I behaved on Saturday. You were perfectly within your rights to question what was going on with that poor girl. And after you left, I did a bit of investigating myself – speaking to some of the guests who were still there and telephoning some of the others. It turns out four – how can I put this tastefully? – four *professional* girls were indeed brought to the house. They had been ordered . . ."

Poppy raised her eyebrows.

"Yes, I know it's an unpleasant word, but I don't know how else to put it . . . They were *requested* by the film producers Miles had invited over. They asked him to – er – provide some ladies for them while they were there. Seems like that's what they do in Hollywood."

He opened his hands in apology. "I'm sorry, Poppy. You should never have had to see that. I've asked Miles to ensure it never happens again."

Poppy put down her teaspoon on her saucer and looked at Toby. "One of the girls was assaulted, Toby. Surely a criminal charge should be laid. Did you find out which of the men did it?"

Toby shrugged. "I didn't, I'm sorry. And none of them – nor anyone else at the party – was called Cameron, first name or surname. I'm afraid unless the girl herself lays a charge – and positively identifies the man in question – I don't think there's much we can do."

Poppy tapped a finger on the edge of the saucer, making a tinkling sound. "Well, for a start we can ask Miles where he 'ordered' the girls from and then get him to call again and ask for Mimi."

"Mimi?" asked Toby, his head cocking to one side.

"Yes, Mimi. She told me her name." She decided not to mention the surname just yet.

"Could just be a stage name," observed Toby.

Poppy nodded. "It could. But we could ask to see the girl who calls herself Mimi. And then describe her. Curly black bobbed hair. Probably Jewish. Ukrainian . . ."

"Ukrainian? How do you know that?"

Poppy shrugged. "The accent."

"That's very specific," Toby observed. "Most people would just have said Russian."

Poppy shrugged again. "I have a good ear for accents." She picked up her cup and took a sip of the tea, looking at Toby over the brim and hoping he had bought her explanation for how she knew Mimi was from the Ukraine. She didn't want him to know she'd been doing investigations of her own. She needed him to think he was in control of this. Helping her. Making up for his failings on Saturday. "So," she said, "do you think you can ask Miles to follow it up?" She held her breath. This would be a test for Toby. If he agreed, she could dismiss the nagging doubts that he was somehow involved in all this. And that would be an immense relief. But if he didn't . . .

"Yes, I can do that," smiled Toby and took another sip of his tea.

Ten minutes later Toby was called away to see a patient. He had asked Poppy if he could take her out to dinner on Wednesday night. She had readily agreed. Her heart was warm and there was a spring in her step as she left the hospital. She said goodbye to the receptionist, who smiled at her knowingly and waved. "Oh, Miz Denby," the woman said as an afterthought. "Sorry I was called away earlier. You asked who else had visited Seaman Jones. It was Mrs Amelia Spencer, Dr Spencer's mother. She came on Saturday, I think. She said she wanted to see the man her son had saved. She's a lovely lady, so gracious. Have you met her?"

Poppy absorbed the information, tucking it away for future reference. "Yes, I have," she said. "And I agree; she's very gracious. Very gracious indeed."

Chapter 31

Poppy was swimming in the sea at Whitley Bay. Her brother was with her. The waves lifted them up and down, their legs kicking frantically under the water to keep them afloat. Their mother called to them from the shore: "Be careful! Don't go too far out!" and their father waved to them, a pease pudding and ham sandwich in hand. It was getting dark and a light swept over them in a wide arc: it was coming from St Mary's lighthouse.

Suddenly her brother cried out and disappeared under the waves. Poppy waited for him to pop back up or to grab her ankle and pull her down, pretending he was a shark. She waited. And she waited. The light from St Mary's was sweeping from left to right faster and faster. She looked to shore but could no longer see her parents. She thought she could still hear her mother's voice, distantly calling: "Come back, Poppy; come back!" But she couldn't leave without her brother. So she dived under the water to find him.

As her eyes adjusted to the murk, she saw him below her, face down, his arms and legs splayed like a tortoise in his red-and-white striped bathers. His blond hair was spread out like a halo. She dived down further and grabbed his collar and pulled him up. His body rotated until he faced her, his eyes and mouth wide and lifeless.

The light above her was getting brighter. She dragged her brother towards it but as she burst through the surface she lost her grip and he drifted away from her, back below the waves. She flipped herself over to dive again but then someone grabbed her shoulders and pulled her upwards. She fought, she screamed, then she stared into the face of Daniel, who was mouthing, "I love you!"

She calmed and sank into his arms, feeling the warmth of his embrace. Then she was being lifted onto the beach and laid out on the warm sand. Her body ached for him. She raised herself towards him and opened her mouth to receive his kiss – but it wasn't Daniel; it was Toby.

A surge of guilt shot through her but her desire was too strong. She closed her eyes and gave herself to Toby's lips, until she felt something running down her chin and onto her neck. She touched it and brought her fingers to her lips to taste. Blood. Her mouth was filling, gagging; she pulled away from Toby, pushing with all her might. She threw her head back to scream, and blood gushed out like a water geyser. Children were playing around her, jumping in and out of the bloody fountain; and in their midst was Alfie Dorchester, like the Pied Piper, playing a tune on a champagne flute, a Victoria Cross hanging around his neck.

And the children became soldiers; and the soldiers became corpses with amputated legs; and each of them had the face of her brother.

Someone was filming it on a hand-wound camera and she was in a cinema, watching. In the seats next to her were young women, immigrant girls, while the Statue of Liberty walked across the screen, turned to the audience and screamed.

"Poppy, Poppy, wake up! You're having a dream."

Poppy, her nightgown drenched in sweat, opened her eyes to see the pale, worried face of Delilah. She blinked a few times to test that she was really awake. She was. Her heart was still racing, the images of the old recurring dream of Whitley Bay still fresh in her mind, overlaid by new images that she could not quite grasp. She closed her eyes and scrunched up her face, trying to give them conscious form, but as sleep fell from her, so did the dream.

"I'm sorry – did I wake you? I was dreaming. It was Whitley Bay again, and . . ."

Delilah passed Poppy a glass of water and waited for her to drink. "I thought you'd stopped having that dream."

Poppy sipped at the water, swilling it around her mouth and allowing it to trickle down her throat, erasing the taste of blood.

"It's been awhile," said Poppy and put the glass on the side table. She sat up, propping the pillows behind her. Delilah was fully dressed, her fur coat unbuttoned, revealing a silver and black sequined ensemble beneath.

"You just getting in?" asked Poppy, peering through the gloom to try to see the clock. It was one o'clock in the morning. Delilah chuckled. "I am. I would have just gone to bed and seen you in the morning but I heard you crying in your sleep. Thought I'd come in and see if you were all right." Delilah stared intently at her friend. "You are all right, aren't you?"

Poppy reached over to the bedpost and unhooked her bed jacket. "I am, yes, thanks."

Delilah shrugged out of her coat and laid it on the bed beside her.

"Listen, Poppy, I want to say sorry for what happened on Saturday. I should have come home with you. You were upset. I shouldn't have let you leave on your own."

Poppy smiled. "That's all right; no harm done . . . to me, anyway."

Delilah bit her lip. "Did you find out any more? About the girl? Toby told me he'd made some enquiries and couldn't find her."

Poppy pulled the cashmere bed jacket over her shoulders. "When did he tell you that? Because I spoke to him earlier today" – she looked at the clock – "earlier yesterday, and he said he would investigate further. He said he would ask Miles."

Delilah's brown eyes widened. "What could Miles possibly know about it?"

Poppy cleared her throat. She didn't want to suggest Miles was involved in any way – not without evidence and certainly not while Delilah and he seemed to be starting out on a relationship – so she considered for a moment how best to phrase her answer. "It seems . . . it seems that Miles invited the girls there as companions for some of the other guests – the film producers."

"The producers! Oh my! You mean they were there in a – a – *professional* capacity? The girls were prostitutes? The ones in the library?"

"It seems that way, yes."

Delilah flicked her fringe away from her eyes and sighed. "It happens. Unfortunately. I wouldn't have known, though, by looking at them. They were very well turned out."

Poppy considered how well turned out Mimi had looked the

next morning in the bathtub. "Yes, well, not everything is as it first appears."

Delilah picked a bit of fluff off her fur coat and flicked it onto the floor. "We mustn't judge though, Poppy. If that's how those girls make a living, then that's their business. In some parts of the world it's perfectly legal."

"It is," Poppy agreed, "as long as they did genuinely choose to do it."

Delilah's eyes narrowed. "What do you mean? Do you have any proof that they weren't there by choice? Did you speak to them? Did they tell you that?"

"Well, no," Poppy admitted, "but the girl I found in the bathroom told me one of the men had hurt her."

Delilah nodded thoughtfully. "Yes, you said." Then she shook her head. "It makes me so mad! Did she say which one it was? I met the four of them the next day and they all seemed like perfect gentlemen."

Poppy raised an eyebrow. "On their best behaviour, were they?"

"Oh yes," said Delilah. "They were kind and patient, and not one of them suggested I do something . . . improper in front of the camera."

"They had cameras?"

"Just one. Miles had it. They did some test shots of me. They all agreed I'd be perfect for the role." Delilah's face lit up, all thoughts of the bruised girl in the bathtub seemingly left behind. "So they've invited me to Hollywood for a proper screen test. Hollywood! Can you believe it?"

Poppy's brows furrowed. "Which film company did you say they were from?"

"Black Horse Productions. Miles works for them too. His Uncle Theo is a major shareholder."

"Oh?" said Poppy, her ears pricking at the mention of Senator Spencer's name. "I didn't know Theo was in the film business."

"He's not really. Not any more. Apparently he dipped his toe in five or six years ago. Bought the company. Turns out he didn't have much of a talent for it, though. But that's how Miles got his start. He went to California with Uncle Theo and had a go. Turns out he *has* got talent for it. You've seen *Baby and the Bluebird*, haven't you?"

Poppy nodded. She and Daniel had seen it together at the Electric Cinema in Chelsea.

"Well, that was one of his! Amazing! I never realised when I first saw it. And now he's asked me to try out for one of his films."

Outside, in the New York sky, a cloud that had covered the moon shifted, and silver light filtered through the crack in Poppy's bedroom curtains. It lit up Delilah's face like a spotlight: her doe eyes, her rosebud mouth, her long elegant neck, her sleek, black bobbed hair... oh yes, Delilah would be perfect for Hollywood.

But then a shadow fell across her visage. "But now you're telling me Miles might be involved in hurting this girl."

Poppy shook her head firmly. "Oh no! That's not what I'm saying at all. I'm just saying that he was the one who telephoned to ask for the girls to come. I'm sure he had nothing to do with what actually happened. So, I was hoping he could tell me who he telephoned so I can speak to them to find out if Mimi – that's the girl I met – is all right. And if it turns out she is, and she did go there of her own free will, then that will be the end of it – assuming she doesn't want to lay charges, of course. And from what I've heard about how prostitutes operate, she might very well not. But if she does..."

Delilah looked near to tears. Poppy took her hand. "Oh Delilah. I'm sure it won't get Miles into trouble. He just made a phone call. He was probably asked to. Perhaps he didn't think he had a choice – if they were his employers in the company."

Delilah nodded vigorously. "They were. They are. So you – you don't think Miles has done anything wrong, then?"

Poppy inhaled and then let out a long, slow breath. How was she to phrase this? "Well, I wouldn't go *that* far. However... while I don't think people should encourage that sort of thing, as you say, it does happen. It's up to you whether you think Miles's involvement is something you can condone. It's not my business, Delilah."

Delilah squeezed Poppy's hand so tightly it was beginning to hurt. She had a strong grip for a slightly built woman. "Oh Poppy, I don't know. If all he did was make a phone call... and as you say, he might not have felt he could say no... Tell me, what would you do if it was Daniel?"

Poppy felt her stomach churn at the mention of her former beau. A sudden flash of an image of the two of them on a beach came to mind. Was that her dream? She shook her head to bring her thoughts back to Delilah and the here and now. "Well, if it was Daniel – before we'd called it off, of course, because now it wouldn't be any of my business – I think I would have confronted him and told him that that behaviour was totally unacceptable to me. Even if a girl hadn't been hurt." Poppy shook her head. "But it's not Daniel, and it's not me. This is a decision you have to make for yourself, Delilah."

Delilah's shoulders slumped. "I know. And I'll have to decide soon. We're leaving for California on Friday. I'll have to speak to him about it before then. I don't think I can go with him until we've had it out."

Poppy patted Delilah's knee with her spare hand. "I think that's wise, Delilah, very wise."

Chapter 32

The next morning, Poppy was summoned to Judson Quinn's office. On her way she passed Paul Saunders, seated at a spare desk in the news department. Her attempt at a polite greeting was met with a glare. Rollo was already waiting for her in the editor's office, and the two old friends were chewing the cud over a pot of strong coffee. Poppy declined Quinn's offer of a drink.

"Take a seat, Miz Denby, take a seat," said Quinn, returning to his own. "Rollo has filled me in on the latest developments." He chuckled. "It hasn't taken you long to get your feet under the desk now, has it?"

Poppy lowered her eyes. "I'm sorry, Mr Quinn. I know it's distracting me from my job on the Death Beat . . ."

"Nonsense!" said Quinn, and toasted her with his coffee cup. "You're a newshound, not a secretary. I'd be more upset if you'd let this pass. And besides, it was through doing your job on the Death Beat that you picked up on this von Hassler story. Good work, Miz Denby. Very good work."

Rollo beamed from ear to ear like a proud parent. "So, Judson, where are we going to go from here?"

The editor sipped at his coffee, looking thoughtful, then pushed his wire-rimmed glasses further up his nose. "I think the first thing I need to do is find out if Saunders has actually covered this up or he's just printed the statement from the coroner's office and taken it at face value." He grimaced. "Either outcome's not good. Either he's taking back-handers or he's just incompetent."

Poppy pursed her lips. "Or he's just new on the job and still finding his feet?"

Quinn ran his finger over his moustache to wipe off the coffee droplets. "Very true, Miz Denby; you shame me with your fair-mindedness. I'll reserve judgement on Saunders until I've got more facts to hand. But," he picked up his pen, dipped it in the inkwell and made a note, "that's going to be my first port of call." He winked at Rollo. "I've got a few favours I can call in at the department – and higher up."

Rollo put down his cup, cradled his head in his hands and leaned back in his chair. "Higher up?"

Quinn blotted the ink and put his pen back in its holder. "City Hall . . ."

Rollo unmeshed his fingers and leaned forward. "City Hall? The mayor's office? You don't think . . ."

Quinn shrugged. "I'm not sure yet. As Miz Denby has already said, we shouldn't jump to conclusions." He tapped his nose. "But there's a scent. There's definitely a scent."

Rollo nodded. "Well, let me know what you find out. I think I'm going to follow up with the mortuary assistant. He and I both know the initial report said it wasn't an accident. And he took my money without blinking an eyelid. I think he's got some explaining to do. Miz Denby, may I have your notes from that interview please?"

"Yes, of course," said Poppy, and passed Rollo her notebook. But then she remembered the notes she'd made after her conversation with the Carter office. She needed them to follow up the Mimi story. "Is there any way you can copy the notes and then give them back to me? There's stuff in that notebook I might need. And I'd rather not tear out those pages."

Rollo thought for a moment and said, "Maybe I can have the notes photographed. That way the morgue guy can see it written in your hand – which will remind him there's two people's word against his." He nodded assertively. "Yes, that's what I'll do." He tapped the outside of the leather-bound book. "I'll get it back to you in two shakes of a lamb's tail, Poppy."

Quinn nodded his agreement. "Good, good. What's your next move, Miz Denby?"

Poppy thought about it for a moment. "I think I'll visit the Carter office. And, if you don't mind, Rollo, I need you to call your contact on Ellis Island."

Quinn frowned. "What's this about?"

Poppy looked up. "The illegal immigrant prostitute story."

Quinn turned to Rollo. "You never told me about this."

Rollo gave Poppy a disapproving glance. "That's because I thought we'd agreed we would give the von Hassler story priority for now."

Poppy shrugged apologetically. "I think we can do both. I don't think there's much more I can do on the von Hassler story until we hear from Marjorie. You and Mr Quinn have leads to follow, but I'm twiddling my thumbs for now. So I thought I'd do some work on the other story. And as I've said, I think they're connected anyway . . ."

"Whoa! Will someone tell me what's going on here?" Quinn looked from the young reporter to the middle-aged hack.

"Sorry, Judson," said Rollo, and proceeded to fill the editor in.

Five minutes later he concluded with: "And Poppy here thinks there might be a connection between the two stories because Alfie Dorchester has turned up in both of them, and von Hassler and the Spencers have shares in the same factory. Does that about sum it up, Poppy?"

She nodded. "It does, yes, although some further information has come to light since I last saw you, Rollo, which I think might justify me giving it a bit more priority." She then went on to tell the men about her conversation with Seaman Jones and the revelation that there might be some kind of organised scam going on involving Carter officials and the US Immigration Service. She also told them the details of her conversation with Toby Spencer about his cousin ordering prostitutes for his producer colleagues, and that she was trying to get information on where they came from.

Quinn leaned back in his chair and let out a long whistle. "This one's a keeper, Rollo, definitely a keeper. Miz Denby, if you ever decide to move to New York permanently, I can guarantee you a job here."

Rollo grinned. "Back off, Judson." Then he turned to Poppy. "My first thought, Poppy, is that we should do this story in tandem with Ike Garfield back in London. That's where the corruption seems to start. What do you think, Judson?"

Quinn nodded. "Yes, I think you're right. Can you speak to Ike without Archie Weinstein at the *Globe* finding out, though? He and I need to sort out our problems when he gets back, but I don't want him getting the idea I'm siding with you over him."

"What exactly has he got over you, Jud?" asked Rollo.

"This and that. Nothing I can't handle." Quinn nodded briefly towards Poppy. "But now I want to hear what Miz Denby has planned."

"May I borrow my notebook for a moment, Rollo?" she asked.

He passed it to her. She paged through it, then stopped, her finger tapping on a particular note.

"I don't think we can go much further on this until we confirm that the girls – Mimi and her sister – are indeed illegal immigrants. Otherwise it's just a story about a prostitute that got slapped about by one of her clients at a party of toffs. And unfortunately, that's not much of a story."

Both Quinn and Rollo nodded in agreement.

"So, can one of you call your source at Ellis Island and get them to check the records? If the Yazierska girls are here legally, then its newsworthiness diminishes."

Quinn grinned at Rollo. "Oh Rollo, hats off to you – and Miz Denby, of course. I wish half my cub reporters were as astute as this little lady."

Poppy cringed inwardly at the phrase "little lady" but let it pass. *Rome wasn't built in a day . . .*

Quinn picked up his pen and asked: "How do you spell that name again. Y-A – or is it E . . ."

Poppy repeated the spelling she had received from the Carter clerk. Quinn wrote it down, circled it, then opened his contacts book. He flicked through until he found the number, then picked up the telephone and asked to be put through to Ellis Island. When connected, he asked to speak to Immigration Inspector Jim Brown.

"Jim, hello. Judson Quinn here . . . yes, yes, they're well, thanks . . . Ha! Third grandchild already? I've just got the one . . . That's right, Edward's married now . . . I know, just seems like yesterday, doesn't it . . . Jim, listen, I need a favour . . ."

Quinn proceeded to ask Brown to check the processing records for Friday 12 April from the *Olympic*, which had arrived in port the night before. He spelled out the sisters' names. Then he put his hand over the mouthpiece and said to Rollo and Poppy: "He's checking. How about another cup of coffee while we wait?"

Poppy knew without being told that as the most junior member of staff there – and, whether she liked it or not, because she was a woman – she was expected to make the brew. She did so, checking with Quinn exactly how he liked it. As she busied herself Rollo and Quinn chatted about "Edward", whom Rollo said he hadn't seen since the boy was in college. Then, laughing, he confirmed that yes, he was still a bachelor and no, that's exactly the way he liked it.

No mention of Yasmin Reece-Lansdale, thought Poppy. She kept mum. It wasn't her place to tell.

As Poppy served the coffee Quinn was alerted to a voice on the telephone. "Righto, Jim. Thanks." Then he looked directly at Poppy. "So, just to confirm, an Esther Yazierska was denied entrance to the United States on the grounds of being feebleminded, but her sister, Miriam, was admitted . . . Yes, yes, thanks, Jim, got it. But Miriam decided to return with her sister, is that right? . . . Okey dokey, and when was that?" He picked up his pen and made a note. "On the *Olympic*'s return journey, Saturday the 20th . . . Right, right, and are you sure they were on board . . . Of course, sorry, Jim, not your department. Thanks for your help . . ." Quinn frowned, nodding. "Yes, of course we can discuss highlighting some good news stories in return. Tell you what, I'll get someone to call and set up an appointment. I'll send one of my best fellas down . . . No trouble, Jim, always happy to help the US Immigration Service."

Quinn said his goodbyes, promised to pass on his regards to Edward and put down the phone. He placed a hand on either side of his notebook and leaned forward: "Well, you heard it, Miz Denby. Your Miriam Yazierska went back to Blighty last Saturday."

Poppy templed her fingers. "Funny that, as I saw her the very same day in a bathtub on Long Island."

Rollo nodded. "Yes. Very funny. Definitely follow up with Carter. But wait until I've telegraphed Ike first though; then we can co-ordinate our efforts. When will you hear from Toby about Miles and the prostitutes?"

Poppy shrugged. "I'm having dinner with him tomorrow night. I'll ask then."

Rollo gave her a quizzical look, but didn't comment further. *He's thinking about Daniel,* she thought and quickly changed the subject. "In the meantime I think I'll drop by Elizabeth Dorchester's house to see if she's made any progress asking around the girls in the Garment District."

"Good idea," said Quinn. He leaned on the desk and stood up, hunching slightly to the left.

"Right, you two, good work. Rollo, you off to the morgue?"

"I am," confirmed Rollo, also standing up. "After I've photographed and processed the pages from Miz Denby's notebook."

"And I'll go and see Elizabeth Dorchester," said Poppy, gathering her things.

"While I get onto the cops, then City Hall if needs be. Hopefully I'll have an answer on who put a lid on the von Hassler investigation by the end of the day. Go to it, troops!" laughed Quinn, his eyes alight with journalistic passion. Poppy smiled. *He's enjoying this.*

Chapter 33

Poppy waited at her desk for Rollo to return her notebook. While she did, she pondered the conversation she'd had with Delilah in the middle of the night. What was it that had caught her attention? That Theo Spencer owned a film production company? Why was that important? She couldn't quite put her finger on it. Something to do with her dream . . . She closed her eyes and tried to remember . . . an image of a cinema . . . the Statue of Liberty . . . No, nothing more concrete than that. But there was something – something Mimi had said . . . *Cameron! That's it! She said "Cam-man" when I asked her if she knew who'd hurt her. Perhaps it wasn't Cameron the girl was saying; perhaps it was cameraman. A man with a camera . . . Miles!* A wave of nausea passed over her. *Oh Delilah!*

She waited for the nausea to pass and then, although still feeling a little shaky, walked over to the communal telephone and put through a call to Rollo's house. Morrison answered. "The Rolandson residence, good morning."

Poppy asked the butler if Delilah was in. Apparently she was. He would just go and get her, but before he did, he was glad Miz Denby had rung. A telegram had arrived for her.

A telegram! Marjorie! "Thank you, Morrison, I've been waiting for that. Would you mind awfully opening it and reading it please?"

Morrison said he would. There was a sound of paper tearing then the clearing of a throat.

"Hello Poppy STOP Found von Riesling at Hotel du Paris MC STOP Down at heel STOP Sold name title and birth certificate for gambling debt STOP Thinks it was joke STOP Person who paid him Alfie Dorchester STOP Do be careful STOP Call if more help needed STOP Marjorie STOP".

Poppy's stomach churned again. *Proof! We finally have proof!*

"Miz Denby, are you still there? Is there anything else you need me to do or should I fetch Miz Marconi?"

"Er, sorry, thank you, Morrison. Yes, please call Miss Marconi."

Poppy waited while Morrison went to fetch Delilah. She could imagine him pacing his way down the hall and up the stairs. Morrison never hurried.

But Poppy's mind was racing. *So Otto sold his title to Alfie. And Alfie's using it to impersonate him. Doubt Otto knows that! Marjorie said he thought it was a joke. Perhaps he'd been too drunk to realise. I'd better let the lawyer know. What was his name? Barnes, that's right. Suppose he could contact the real Otto and let him know about his uncle's death – and that he's finally inherited a fortune. There was an address in the telegram, wasn't there? Hotel du something . . . du Paris, that's right. Wonder if Barnes will get the court order now to re-open the coroner's investigation . . . and if he does, might that scupper Rollo and Quinn's story? Hmmm, maybe I should hold out on telling him . . . I'll let Rollo decide . . .*

"Poppy? – ahhhh, sorry – is that you?" It was Delilah stifling a yawn. Poppy looked at her watch: half past ten. It was practically the crack of dawn for Delilah.

"Delilah, sorry to wake you. But I need to ask you something. Something about Miles."

"Ahhhh. What about him? I haven't had a chance to speak to him since last night. I will though, I promise."

"No, no, it's not that. I just wanted to ask you – you said Miles had a camera."

"Uh-huh."

"Did he use it at all on Friday night?"

"Er – let me think. No, I don't think so."

"Are you sure?"

"Yes. The first time I saw it was on Saturday morning."

Poppy absorbed this, trying to see where the pieces of the puzzle might fit. "And – well, I'm sorry to be so indelicate about it, Dee, but . . . did you spend the whole night with Miles? In the – er – in the same – erm –"

Delilah giggled. "In the same bed? Yes, Poppy, we spent the night in the same bed."

"The whole night? He didn't leave you and go elsewhere?"

"I should jolly well hope not! No, he was with me all night."

Poppy could feel herself blush. "Oh, all right. That's good."

"Why do you ask?"

Should she tell Delilah that she had thought for a moment that her new beau might have filmed and then assaulted Mimi? No, she'd better not.

"I'm just eliminating him from the inquiry, that's all. Listen, Dee, can you remember the names of the producers who were there? The ones from – what was it? – Black Horse."

Delilah said she could – or at least the first names of most of them. They were Howard Parker – he was the famous one, apparently – someone called Frank, another called Bob and a fourth the others referred to as Chucky Boy. Poppy wrote them down.

"All right. Thanks, Delilah. Sorry to get you up. You going back to bed now?"

Delilah yawned again. "No, I said I'd take Dot for an audition. Don't know if she's told you yet but the radio station has been in touch; said they loved us both and want us to do another show. Dot is beside herself."

Poppy smiled. "I bet she is. Tell her good luck from me, please, and I'll hear all about it tonight. Where does that leave you though? Will you not go to California if you get it?"

Delilah sighed. Poppy could imagine her in her white satin dressing gown, draped across the Chippendale chair that sat next to the telephone table in the hall. "I don't know, Pops. I've still got to speak to Miles."

She sounded downhearted. "Oh Delilah, I'm sorry. I didn't mean to confuse you. Look, let's have a girls' night out tonight. Maybe we can go to Chester's."

Delilah perked up immediately at the mention of the speakeasy. "Oh yes, Poppy, let's! Shall I meet you after work?"

Poppy looked up and saw Rollo enter the office. He held her notebook aloft.

"Yes, I'll ring you to arrange a time. All right, I'll speak to you later. I've got to get back to work. Good luck at the audition!"

Poppy and Delilah said their goodbyes and Poppy put down the telephone.

"What was all that about?" asked Rollo, taking a seat at Poppy's desk. Poppy picked up her notes on the film producers and joined him. They were the only two people in the office so she felt free to talk.

"Hold on . . . I'll tell you in a minute. Just got to write something down . . ." She wrote down as much as she could remember of the telegram that Morrison had read out and then made a note "confirm with original" beside it. She put down the pencil and said: "There." She passed it to Rollo.

He read it, twice, then looked up at Poppy, a huge grin on his face. "Bingo!"

"That's the gist of it, yes," Poppy grinned back. "So I was thinking we should probably let the lawyer know. What do you think?"

Rollo scratched his scalp. "Yes, yes we should. But we need to be careful how we time this. If the lawyer gets a court order to re-open the coroner's inquiry that might block – or at least obfuscate – our investigation. We need a bit more time to sniff around before the suspects are alerted that we're on to them."

Poppy nodded. "Yes, that's what I thought too. So what should we do?"

Rollo took out his own notebook and pencil and tapped on the cover. "For now I think we stick to the plan we discussed with Quinn. But let's be very careful how we go about it. I'll head over to the mortuary. There was a traffic accident this morning. Some poor schmuck was run down by a taxi on the corner of Fifth Avenue and 34th Street – again – and traffic safety folk are calling for some kind of light system to be installed. As if the city is just made of money! I'll use that as an excuse to chat to our mortician friend. I'll let it be known here that that's what I'm covering – and that Quinn has authorised it.

"Meantime, you go see Elizabeth Dorchester. There's no reason why you shouldn't. She's a friend of the family etcetera etcetera. I'll let it be known around here that Quinn has authorised you to do a couple of feature articles. The first one will be on settlement houses." He hooked his thumbs into his braces and leaned back in his chair. "Perfectly plausible."

Poppy never ceased to admire how Rollo could think on his feet. He didn't seem to go through all of the agonising and ruminating that she did. Or maybe he did, but hid it well. Perhaps one day she too might do the same . . .

She nodded slowly. "Yes. Good plan. I'll head over there now." She started gathering her things, packing them into her satchel.

Rollo stood up and stretched. "And I'll head across to Bellevue Hospital as soon as the photographs of your notes are developed. I wonder . . ." He paused. "Let's meet up later." He looked around. "But not here." He tapped his nose and winked. "Walls have ears."

Poppy agreed. "Where then?"

Rollo wrote down an address. "Here. It's a diner near the lawyer's office. We can swap notes, assess where we are and then decide whether or not to tell Barnes about Marjorie's telegram. I'll swing by home on the way there and pick it up from Morrison."

"Sounds like a good idea," agreed Poppy. "What time?"

Rollo looked at his watch. It was approaching eleven o'clock. "Say two o'clock for a late lunch?"

Poppy nodded. "It's a date."

Now that Poppy was officially on the job, she could have taken a taxi. But she could not bring herself to spend so much money. Besides, it was one thing for Rollo Rolandson, former star reporter of *The New York Times*, war correspondent and now senior editor of a London newspaper, to justify travelling in style; she was a mere cub reporter who, until this morning, had been writing obituaries. No, she would use public transport to get to Elizabeth's house in Chelsea; more specifically, a bus that first wove its way through the Garment District.

The vehicle turned left and right through the maze of narrow streets – slowing down for horse-drawn carts and belting out its horn for idling traffic to get out of its way. On either side Poppy watched as row after row of tenement houses, warehouses and workshops went by. A group of young women sitting on a step caught her eye, their hair up in scarves, their dresses covered by aprons. They were eating bread and butter and sharing a cigarette – might Mimi and her sister be among them?

Poppy realised she hadn't told Rollo the latest information about the prostitute story. She would do so when she met him later for lunch. She wanted to do some more research on the film producers and Black Horse Productions. She wondered if the *Times* had a Jazz File on any of them. Or perhaps there might be some information at the New York City Library. She would ask Rollo to suggest a way forward.

Something else she had been meaning to do, but hadn't because of all the excitement around Marjorie's telegram, was to have a good jaw-wag about potential suspects for the murder. Of course, Alfie Dorchester topped the list, but as she'd learned from her previous two big stories, the most obvious suspect was not always the correct suspect . . . Nonetheless, she felt she and Rollo had not done the same degree of thinking-through as they normally did. Up until today they were having to sneak around to do their investigations, whereas in London they both had free rein to do whatever they liked.

So, Poppy, think it through. Top of list: Alfie Dorchester. Now what about motive, means and opportunity?

Poppy took out her notebook and scribbled some notes.

#1 ALFIE DORCHESTER

***Motive**: To inherit fake uncle's fortune. But wouldn't he have inherited anyway when old man died? Why now? Might have wanted to speed it up. Or maybe uncle discovered he was imposter. Killed him to keep his secret. All the new connections he's making in NYC would be lost. But . . . wouldn't death turn spotlight on nephew? Not as killer. Heir. Unwanted attention might expose fraud – exactly what's happened! So would killing uncle be best thing for him? No, if thought out properly. Spur of the moment? To keep him quiet? Or Alfie just too thick to think it through?*

Poppy drew a little smiley face beside the last note and chuckled to herself.

> ***Means***: *Don't know. Murder weapon uncertain. Any blunt object? Easy to find in apartment. If police found something with blood on it would they be able to say it was just an accident? Surely not. Much harder to sweep under carpet. So . . . did killer take murder weapon away with him?*
>
> ***Opportunity***: *Did Alfie have key to "uncle's" apartment? Check with Mrs Lawson. Or did old man let him in? No sign of forced entry. Where was Alfie on Thursday night? Does he have alibi? How can we find out? Did doorman/concierge of Lexington Avenue apartment building see anyone go up? Has anyone asked? Police might have . . . NB interview doorman! NB2 get time of death from coroner's report – lawyer has copy.*

Poppy paused and looked out of the window to check the bus's progress. It was just passing Penn Station. She wasn't sure where to get off. "Excuse me," she asked another passenger. "Where do I get off for Chelsea Square?"

"Three more stops," was the answer. She thanked the man then hurriedly made some more notes before she lost her train of thought.

> *#2 THE REAL OTTO VON RIESLING*
>
> ***Motive***: *To inherit fortune. To pay off gambling debts. Already shown he is nasty piece of work by sending blackmail letters to uncle over last three years. That couldn't have been Alfie. Had to have been real Otto. But . . . sold title. But . . . didn't seem to think it was serious. Still very slim . . .*
>
> ***Means***: *Same as for Alfie.*

***Opportunity**: Hard if in Europe . . . unless . . . hired hitman? Hmmm.*

#3 MRS NORA LAWSON, HOUSEKEEPER

***Motive**: Didn't lawyer say Mrs L. would inherit if nephew didn't? Dies, gets sent to prison for murder? He can't inherit fortune if proven he's offed his uncle. Might be motive for Mrs L. to kill prince and frame nephew. Strange how she was pointing fingers at him before case had been officially declared accident or murder . . .*

Poppy thought for a moment of the quiet black woman, apparently stricken with grief. But, Poppy had to admit, at the time she'd thought the woman's dominant emotion was anger, not grief. *Why?*

She wrote a final note under motive: *unlikely but not impossible.*

***Means**: Same as others – or could have cleaned up and put it back in its place if from apartment.*

***Opportunity**: Better than anyone! Again, must speak to doorman.*

The bus was just pulling away from stop number two. She wrote a final quick note.

#4 ANY OF THE PRINCE'S FORMER/CURRENT LOVERS

***Motive**: Was he threatening to expose someone? Sodomy illegal. Scandal could ruin careers. Who were his lovers? How can we get list? Mrs Lawson? Lawyer?*

"Here's your stop, miz," said the helpful passenger. Poppy thanked him and rang the bell.

Chapter 34

Poppy stood at Elizabeth's front door, trying to resist the temptation to slip her thumbnail under a sliver of peeling paint and rip it off the timber. After a few moments the door opened to reveal the bright and bouncy Helena, jumping from foot to foot as if she needed to use the lavatory. "Mees Poppy!" The girl leapt forward and threw her arms around Poppy. Poppy, laughing, gave the young Italian a hearty squeeze in return.

"Hello, Helena! Is Miss Dorchester here? Miss Liza?"

Helena pulled away and skipped down the hall. "Yes, yes, come!"

Poppy followed, shutting the front door behind her. Helena led her down the hall and past a couple of open doors. Through one Poppy saw four young people – two teenage boys and two girls – poring over books and newspapers in what appeared to be a small library. Through the other door three women were packing baskets of "essentials": toothpaste, soap, underwear and female sanitary products, while a toddler played on the floor. *Settlement house business*, thought Poppy. *I definitely want to do a feature on this after these other stories go to press.*

Soon they were in the kitchen where she, Aunt Dot and Elizabeth had shared a Sunday roast a few days earlier, and then through the back door. They stepped into an enclosed yard with a gate at the back leading, Poppy assumed, to a rear alley.

"There she is!" said Helena, then scampered back into the house before Poppy had a chance to thank her.

A clothesline was strung from the corner of the house to the back wall, and standing in the middle of the yard, her sleeves rolled up to reveal strong forearms, was Elizabeth. She was hanging up washing that had just been put through a laundry mangle. *It's funny seeing the daughter of an English lord looking like an East End washerwoman*, thought Poppy. *And to think it's all voluntary. Remarkable woman.*

Elizabeth dried her hands on her apron and pushed a long strand of auburn hair behind her ear. "Poppy, hello. I didn't know you were coming today."

Poppy smiled. "Yes, sorry, I would have called but I didn't know your telephone number – or even if you have one."

"We don't," said Elizabeth. "I use the one at the post office. But let me finish hanging this out then I'll put the kettle on."

"I'll help you," said Poppy and bent over and picked out a cotton shirt-waist dress.

Elizabeth passed her two wooden dolly pegs.

As the women worked in tandem, Poppy asked Elizabeth if she had made any progress tracking down the illegal immigrant prostitutes.

"I have actually. I was going to try to ring you this afternoon. But now you've saved me the trouble – and the nickel."

Poppy smiled at the aristocratic woman's penny-pinching. "So?" she asked, picking out a pair of cotton bloomers that had been patched more than once.

"Magriet Fashions. The corner of 36th and Ninth. It's got a legitimate workforce, but my source tells me there's a loft workroom kept separate from the rest. It's run by illegals who live in a dormitory on the premises. Apparently a handful of the girls are sometimes let out to do other business. My source says they're dressed up to the nines and are picked up and dropped off at funny hours."

Poppy absorbed the information. "Yes, it sounds suspicious, doesn't it? Have you been into this Magriet Fashions?"

Elizabeth shook her head. "No. I've tried before, but the guards won't let anyone in. Everything's behind lock and key."

"But you've spoken to some of the girls?"

"Some of the legals, yes, but very reluctantly. I only got one of them to talk because she's the cousin of young Helena and she appreciates what I've done to help the family. But she told me if anyone found out she'd talked she'd be out of a job. So, Miss Lady Journalist, I need your word you will not allow that to happen. Nothing must come back to me or the workers. Can you do that?"

Poppy nodded. "I can. Thank you."

There were two tea towels left at the bottom of the basket. Elizabeth gave one to Poppy and hung the other one up herself. "Good. Then let's have a cup of tea before you go." She gave the peg bag to Poppy, picked up the empty basket and turned towards the house. But as she did someone stepped out of the kitchen and into the yard.

"Oh Lizzy! Just thought I'd drop in to tell you . . . dear God! Poppy Denby!"

Poppy dropped the peg bag, the wooden dollies scattering across the paving. "You!" she screamed, her voice ricocheting off the brickwork like a Gatling gun. There, standing in the doorway of his sister's kitchen, was none other than Viscount Alfie Dorchester.

"Poppy, calm down." Elizabeth clutched Poppy's shoulder.

Poppy shrugged her off. "You knew? You knew he was here?"

"Yes. But it's not what you think. Let's have a cup of tea and we can talk about it."

Alfie stood nervously on the doorstep. "Maybe I should go, Lizzy."

"Go where?" screamed Poppy. "To your dead uncle's apartment? To plot how you can wangle the old man out of more money? Or perhaps you want to figure out how you can continue to avoid facing justice in England for your disgusting crimes?"

"Now that's enough, Poppy," said Elizabeth, standing, hands on hips, between the hysterical Englishwoman and her brother.

"You're absolutely right it's enough!" screamed Poppy, her hands on hips a mirror image of Elizabeth's. "I cannot believe you are defending him! After all he's done to you! After all he's done to me! Just what is going on here?"

Elizabeth lowered her eyes and then raised them again. "I know. I, more than anyone, have reason to hate him – so surely that must mean something that I've given him the time of day. Please, Poppy, let me put the kettle on; listen to what he's got to say. He's just as shocked as you are at old von Hassler's murder. And he even has some information that could help you with the prostitutes at the garment factory. Please, Poppy, listen to him. It's all I ask."

Poppy felt as if she was going to faint. There was Alfie, his blond hair dyed black, standing on the kitchen step like Mephistopheles. And his sister – the woman he had tortured for years and years and years – was defending him. There was only one answer: she had lost her mind. There had been signs of it back in London – which Poppy had refused to accept – but it was true: Elizabeth Dorchester was certifiably insane.

She spun around and pinned Elizabeth in her gaze. "I trusted you!" Then she ran to the back gate and heaved it open. Without looking back, Poppy Denby fled into the back alley, leaving a massacre of pegs scattered in her wake.

Chapter 35

Poppy's hands were shaking as she spooned sugar into her tea, spilling more on the tablecloth of the diner than into her brew. Rollo took the spoon from her and scooped more sugar into her cup and stirred it. Then he brushed the spilled sugar into a napkin and folded it, placing it on the side of the table. "I'm sorry, Rollo," Poppy whispered, her voice thick with tears.

"That's all right," said the editor, "you've had a huge shock."

Poppy nodded and, still trembling, brought the cup to her lips.

"Now, should I order for us both?"

"I'm not hungry."

Rollo looked at his protégé with sympathy. "I'll order a steak and pickle sandwich for you then, and if you don't eat it, I'll ask the waitress to wrap it up in a doggy bag."

Poppy nodded.

Rollo called over the waitress and gave the order of two steak sandwiches and salad on the side.

"So," he said, "let me get this straight. Elizabeth actually knew that Alfie was here in New York and has been covering for him?"

She nodded again. Words were beyond her for now.

"And he – and she – seemed to know something about the murder of von Hassler. Confirming, perhaps, that it is murder and not just an accident. Alfie, of course, claiming he didn't do it. Hmmm . . . not sure what to do with that for now. We need to wait and hear what information Quinn comes up with about who put the lid on this thing. If we tell the police what we know before we have that intel to hand, it could just get swept under the carpet again. I'll check in on him after the meeting with the lawyer."

Poppy looked up, more alert than she'd been for a while. "So we're going to the lawyer then?"

Rollo nodded. "I think so, yes. The one thing we haven't followed up on yet – and I think he can help us with this – is to find out who all the owners of the garment factory are. What did you say the name was? Magriet Fashions?"

"Yes," said Poppy and summoned up a weak smile for the waitress as she arrived with the sandwiches. The woman smiled back, looking relieved that the distraught young woman was finally pulling herself together.

"Thanks," said Rollo, and picked up his knife to cut the sandwich in half. He gestured with the blade, offering to do the same for Poppy.

"Yes please." The tea was beginning to work its magic. Poppy thought she might be able to manage some food after all. Rollo smiled approvingly as she picked up the sandwich and took a small bite.

"I think you're right about these two stories being linked," Rollo continued. "It's too much of a coincidence that Alfie is involved in both. Did I hear you right? Elizabeth said Alfie knows something about the prostitutes too?"

Poppy nodded, unable to speak this time because her mouth was full of a juicy piece of steak.

Rollo held his sandwich in both hands, ready to take a bite. "Then we definitely need to find out more about the ownership structure of the place. Who else is involved? Who knows what's going on there? Is it just the Spencers? Do they know what's actually happening at their own factory, or are they owners in name only? That wouldn't surprise me. Theo is busy with his senatorial work – it takes up the bulk of his time now. As far as I know, he's become very hands-off with his various business interests in recent years. So who has he put in charge in his absence? And do they know about the prostitution ring and/or the murder? Or is it, after all, just Alfie who connects the two stories on his own? We won't know until we do a bit more digging."

Rollo took a large bite and started to chew.

Digging, yes: that's exactly what they needed to do. Poppy put down her sandwich, wiped her hands on her napkin and reached into her satchel to retrieve her notebook. "Not that I don't think Alfie is the prime suspect in this, Rollo, but I've been wondering whether or not we've adequately considered other scenarios. I don't want to be blinded by my personal prejudice in all this." She opened the notebook to the pages she'd written on the bus, brainstorming the motive, means and opportunity of various suspects in the von Hassler murder.

Rollo put down his sandwich and picked up the book. He perused the notes, grunting approvingly and tapping various phrases with his fingernail. He looked up at Poppy, smiling, a bit of pickle stuck in his front teeth.

"Excellent work, Miz Denby. I couldn't have done better myself."

Poppy felt a small quiver of pride. "Thank you, Rollo; that means a lot to me."

Rollo's finger tapped the note relating to the doorman knowing who went up or down in the prince's building. "This is just around the corner. We can swing by there before we go and see Barnes. Shouldn't take us more than a few minutes."

Poppy nodded her agreement before taking a much larger bite of her sandwich.

Rollo grinned. "I see you've got your appetite back."

237 Lexington Avenue, a ten-storey apartment building, was one of the most swish addresses in New York. Rollo listed a who's who of Manhattan elite in the short walk over there, all of whom either lived permanently at the address or kept an apartment there for when they were in town. One of the names caught Poppy's attention: Howard Parker.

"The film producer?" asked Poppy. "From Black Horse Productions?"

"Yes," agreed Rollo as the two journalists negotiated a gap in the traffic to cross the road and approach the entrance of the building. "Have you heard of him?"

Poppy said she had only just heard the name that morning, and went on to tell Rollo what Delilah had told her about the producers.

Rollo stopped a few paces out of earshot from a doorman. "How very interesting."

"And he lives here?" asked Poppy.

"Not all year round, no. He's one of the fellas who keep a place here for when they're in town. Like most film people these days he splits his time between the east and west coast. And you say he was at the party? Did you see him?"

Poppy tried to picture the four men she had seen in the library. "I think so, but I'm not sure which one he was. There were three younger men, and one older – my guess would be that was him. He seemed to be in charge." Poppy described the man with mutton-chop sideburns.

Rollo grunted. "Sounds like it might be him. I'll show you a photograph of him when we get back to the office and you can identify him properly. Hmmm, very interesting – very interesting indeed. Let's see what the doorman has to say, shall we?"

Poppy and Rollo approached the man who was wearing a top hat, tails and full livery.

"Good day to you, my good man," said the editor in the poshest accent Poppy had ever heard. She stifled a smile. "I do believe there may be an apartment available in this building after that most unfortunate accident. The penthouse?"

The doorman raised his hat in greeting. "Good day, sir. I don't know if it is available yet. Or whether it will be. I believe the prince's nephew might be taking it over. It's still early days."

Rollo nodded sympathetically. "Of course, yes, a dreadful business. Very upsetting for everyone involved."

The doorman nodded, his face sinking into an appropriately concerned expression. "Yes, it was."

"Was it you who found the body?" asked Poppy. "I've never met anyone who found a dead body before . . ." Poppy allowed her blue eyes to widen into what she hoped looked like unbridled admiration.

The doorman visibly straightened, proud of his small role in an important story.

"Forgive my niece; she's new in town and thinks America is exactly like they show in the movies." Rollo winked at her.

Poppy took the hint. "Oh yes! The movies! I heard that Howard Parker lives on this street somewhere. Is that true?"

The doorman smiled indulgently at the eager young English girl.

"Oh yes. And in this very building! We have a lot of famous people who live here, miz. If your uncle does manage to get the penthouse, you'll be in the very best company."

Poppy's mouth opened in awe. "Oh uncle, did you hear that? Howard Parker lives here! Was he here the night the prince died?"

The doorman said that he was. And that Mr Parker was just as shocked as everyone else.

"A terrible business," Rollo agreed, then tipped the doorman handsomely. The man doffed his hat before turning his attention to a car pulling up. Poppy carried on playing the part of the wide-eyed innocent as a well-heeled couple emerged from the vehicle. "Oh uncle, look! Is that Douglas Fairbanks and Mary Pickford? Oh, do get us that apartment!"

Rollo chuckled before leading his "niece" away.

Mr Barnes ushered them into his office as soon as his assistant told him they were there. He opened a silver cigarette holder and offered it to his guests. Poppy declined; Rollo accepted, leaning in to allow the lawyer to light it.

Then Rollo laid Marjorie's telegram on the green leather desk. Barnes picked it up, read it and drew on his cigarette. He held the smoke in his mouth for a while, then slowly exhaled. "Thank you for this. It's the evidence I need. The question is, when do I alert the police that he's about? Because I must do that. He's a fugitive from justice, you understand. British justice, to be fair, but it's just a matter of time until a request for an arrest warrant is brought by the Brits. And . . ." he re-checked the telegram, "if I'm not mistaken, this 'Marjorie' is Marjorie Reynolds of the British Home Office." He tapped his ash into the onyx ash tray, looking at Rollo over the desk.

"It is," Rollo conceded.

"Hmmm," said Barnes. "Yes, I can use this. I will need to get a court order to re-open the coroner's investigation into von Hassler's death though. Any further word on who put a lid on it?"

Rollo shook his head. "I went to visit the mortuary again, to speak to the fella who initially told me the prince had not died of natural causes. But he has suddenly, and unexpectedly, taken leave. His colleagues don't know when he'll be back. Very suspicious. However, Judson Quinn is looking into it via his contacts too. He thinks he'll have something by the end of the day."

"Good," said Barnes, rolling his cigarette between thumb and forefinger. "However, Alfie Dorchester is another kettle of fish. The moment I alert the police, he will be a wanted man. Not in the von Hassler case necessarily, that's still up in the air, but the fact that he has been impersonating Otto von Riesling and seeking to benefit financially from it. That's fraud and potentially blackmail – before we even add murder to the charge sheet. And as far as I can tell, alerting Alfie that we're on to him might not be what you want at this stage of the investigation. Am I correct?"

Rollo drew on his own cigarette and exhaled. "You are; however, developments this morning might make that a moot point."

"Oh?" said Barnes, tapping another tip of ash into the tray.

"Yes," said Rollo and went on to explain how Poppy had come across Alfie only a few hours earlier at his sister's house in Chelsea.

Barnes leaned back in his chair, blowing a plume of smoke into the air. "So, he's probably on the run anyway. He no doubt thinks Miz Denby here would waste no time going to the police. Is that right, Miz Denby?"

"Yes and no," said Poppy. "I haven't been to the police. I'm not sure yet if that is the best thing. I do want him to face justice, but I'm aware that timing in this is important – particularly because we don't yet know if the New York police are to be trusted on this."

Barnes leaned forward and tapped some more ash into the tray. He smiled. "Congratulations, Rolandson; you've trained her well."

Of course not one word of this was directed at her. Yes, Rollo had "trained her" – in newsgathering technique – but she was not an automaton.

Rollo put his cigarette in the tray. "I'm afraid, Mr Barnes, Miz Denby has a mind of her own. And one I greatly respect. If we were to go to the police about this, I would like to have her opinion, and to consider it carefully. Poppy, what do you think?"

Poppy was silent for a moment. Eventually she spoke. "The cat's out of the bag, I think. If Alfie wants to run, he will have done so.

The moment I left he would have thought his time was limited. If he had any sense he'd have packed a bag and been on the first train out of here." She looked at her watch. "Three hours later, I think he'll already have gone. Alerting the police will only get Elizabeth into trouble. On the other hand, if she has been harbouring a fugitive..." Poppy put her palms together and twiddled her fingers.

"So what to do..." Rollo crushed out the stub of his cigarette and exhaled. "As you say, Poppy, I think the cat's out of the bag with Alfie. So Barnes, if you can alert the authorities regarding an arrest warrant, they might still be able to catch him. The details can be worked out later. Regarding the cover-up of the von Hassler murder, if you can give me until the end of the day, I can see what Quinn can add to this."

Barnes nodded. "I can do that. Is there anything else?"

Poppy and Rollo looked at each other and shared a knowing glance. "Actually, yes," said Rollo. "You arranged for the transfer of deeds from Hans von Hassler to his – supposed – nephew, Otto von Riesling, relating to Magriet Fashions. Is that correct?"

Barnes templed his fingers. "It is. Up until today I had no legal reason to doubt Otto von Riesling was who he claimed to be. He produced a birth certificate, his uncle vouched for him..."

Rollo raised his hands. "We are not apportioning blame here. Perfectly understandable. I accept that. However... what we'd like to know is who else has shares in Magriet Fashions. Was it only Hans von Hassler and Theo Spencer, or is there someone else?"

Barnes popped his lips against his fingertips. "Hmmm. I'm assuming here you already know something."

"And you'd be right," said Rollo.

Fibber, thought Poppy. *We don't know anything for sure.*

"Well," said Barnes. "Then I'm sure it comes as no surprise to you that the third shareholder in Magriet Fashions is the film producer Howard Parker."

Rollo nodded sagely. "No, Mr Barnes, thank you. That comes as no surprise at all."

Chapter 36

Back at *The New York Times*, Poppy and Rollo went straight to Judson Quinn's office. As they arrived, a red-faced Paul Saunders was just leaving. He made no effort to avoid a collision and rammed into Poppy with his shoulder. Poppy staggered but retained her balance.

"Steady on, Saunders!" called Rollo.

"Leave him; it's all right. I believe Mr Quinn has had a few words with him."

"You're right." Judson Quinn appeared in the doorway. He looked pale and tired. Poppy noticed his left arm drooping more than usual. "Come in, come in."

"So . . ." said Rollo, cocking his head back towards the door. "Has Saunders got his marching orders?"

Quinn shook his head wearily. "No, just a dressing down. There's no evidence that he was aware of the cover-up; just lazy journalism."

Poppy nodded. Yes, that was fair. She didn't like the man much, but he didn't deserve to lose his job if he wasn't guilty of a cover-up. "So did you find out who was responsible?"

Quinn closed his eyes and rubbed his temples. Poppy and Rollo waited. He opened them and met Poppy's concerned gaze with a wan smile. "My contacts in the NYPD – that's the police, Miz Denby – said word had come from above. They had not actually found any evidence of foul play, so were not really covering anything up – that's their excuse anyway – but they were told to wrap up the case as quickly as possible. In other words, not to look too carefully in case they did find anything. The actual cover-up, it seems, was directed at the coroner's office."

"Yes," agreed Rollo, and told Quinn that the mortician was now "on leave".

"You have the notes, though," probed Quinn, "about the first autopsy report? A judge will no doubt want to see them."

"Agreed. I've given the von Hassler lawyer copies of the photographs I took of Poppy's originals. He'll use them in his application to have the case re-opened. Poppy and I may also have to swear affidavits, but we'll cross that bridge when we come to it."

Quinn frowned. "Don't do it without one of our legal boys being there. Remember Barnes is not your lawyer and does not have your – or the paper's – best interests at heart."

Rollo agreed and asked Quinn to arrange a meeting with the legal team. Quinn said he would.

"So . . ." pressed Rollo, "if the police are clear, but the coroner is dirty, who gave the order from above? The police chief or the chief medical officer?"

"Neither," said Quinn, pushing his spectacles back onto the bridge of his nose. "Apparently it was political."

"City Hall? Why?"

Quinn shook his head. "Higher. I don't have any corroborating evidence yet, but my sources tell me that influence was applied from a senator's office."

"Senator Spencer?" asked Poppy, her mind racing, trying to piece it all together.

Quinn raised his one good hand. "I wasn't given a name. So that, for now, is just a guess."

"A very educated guess," observed Rollo. "But what would his motivation be, if it was him? Why would Theo Spencer want to stop an investigation into von Hassler's death?"

Poppy was flicking through her notebook, looking for the interview with the housekeeper, Nora Lawson. "Mrs Lawson said she thought there was going to be a cover-up because von Hassler was a homosexual and certain people would not want their association with him to be known."

"You think Theo Spencer might be a pansy?" Rollo grinned. "Oh, my mother would just love that!"

Quinn laughed but then added the caution: "We have no proof that he is . . . homosexual – or for that matter involved in this in any way. And for something as inflammatory as that, we would need cast-iron evidence."

"Agreed," said Rollo.

Poppy chewed her lip. "You know, at the time I thought the whole thing very strange. Mrs Lawson was crying foul before anything had happened. How did she know this would be the case? I think she might know more than she's telling us. And, let's not forget, she has a motive for ensuring Alfie Dorchester – or who she thought was Otto von Riesling – goes down for murder."

"Oh, and what's that?" asked Rollo.

"If you recall, Barnes told us she was the secondary beneficiary of the will. If von Riesling was prohibited from inheriting because of his involvement in his uncle's death, she would get it all."

"Great Scot!" declared Quinn. "That's a motive if ever I've heard one."

"And means, and opportunity . . ." added Poppy.

Rollo twiddled his thumbs together. "She certainly does appear suspect, doesn't she? Either she killed the prince herself or knows for certain that Alfie did . . . but how would she know? Was she there? Did she see him? Did Alfie visit his uncle that day? Or did anyone else? These are probably questions we should have asked when we first met her. But we were distracted by other concerns . . . Water under the bridge . . . Another visit to Mrs L. is definitely needed. Righto . . ."

Rollo started gathering his things then stopped, raising his index finger as something occurred to him. "Another thing I've been thinking about is the murder weapon. Either the killer brought it with him or something in the apartment was used. Who better than the housekeeper to know if something was missing or had been moved? Apart from the police activity in the bathroom, everything else appeared ship-shape. Would you agree, Poppy?"

Poppy nodded. "Yes. It was a very tidy apartment. She probably would know if something was missing." She grimaced. "You would think the police would have checked already, though, wouldn't you?"

Quinn agreed. "Yes, but as we've already established, they were not particularly looking for any evidence of foul play. I agree, though, another meeting with the housekeeper is essential – before the police get to her," observed Quinn. "So it will have to be tonight, if possible. Once Barnes gets the court order invoked to re-open the case things will move very quickly. No doubt they'll work double-time to make up for their failings. And as soon as they do, the story's fair game for every paper in town."

Quinn looked at his pocket watch and grunted. "So, lady and gent, I want some articles written up by you two before you leave today. Yes, you need to speak to the housekeeper again – and I'll ring Barnes and let him know what I found out about the cover-up – but we need something on the newsstands in the morning. You can write up a couple of pieces then meet up with Mrs L. Agreed?"

"Agreed," said Poppy and Rollo in unison. Poppy looked at her watch too. It was five o'clock. She was supposed to be going out with Delilah after work. It would have to wait.

Rollo reached for the telephone. "I'll set something up with Mrs Lawson. I'll tell her we've got some information for her. We'll arrange to meet at von Hassler's penthouse. I also want to see if I can get a glimpse at the visitor book – if there is one in the lobby – or else speak to that doorman again."

Mention of the doorman reminded Poppy of something. "And perhaps we can see if Howard Parker is in too. He's also connected with this somehow."

"And how's that?" asked Quinn.

Poppy told him. Quinn nodded, more wearily than ever. "Good, good, but we probably need to prioritise. Do Mrs L. first and then, perhaps tomorrow, follow up on the Parker and factory lead. I know you think the prostitution story and this one are linked, and they probably are, but murder trumps prostitution in the news game, so I want you to focus on von Hassler first. Can you do that, Miz Denby?"

"I can," said Poppy, but her mind was already going over ways she could have her cake and eat it. "Rollo," she said, "if Mr Quinn is finished with us, I'll join you in your office in a few minutes to write up a couple of articles. I just need to telephone Delilah and cancel our date for tonight. Is that all right?"

Both Quinn and Rollo said it was.

* * *

Two hours later, Poppy and Rollo had written two articles between them: a "prince's death might have been murder" article, speculating that the case into the aristocrat's death might be re-opened, according to sources in the coroner's office; then a biography of von Hassler, taken primarily from the Death Beat file, but supplemented with information from the general Jazz Files.

Poppy took the opportunity to get the files of Theodore Spencer and Howard Parker too. There was nothing in either file to suggest homosexual leanings. Spencer was a respected senator, happily married for thirty-five years. Parker, on the other hand, had been a playboy in his younger days and a notorious womaniser in his middle years.

One thing did catch her eye though – a photograph of Parker, von Hassler, Miles, Theo and Amelia Spencer at a film premier in 1918. The fleshy-faced producer was indeed the man she had seen in the library at The Lodge. Attached to the photograph was an article about Black Horse Productions being the second business venture the three older men had entered into together. The first was a fashion business. The senator was quoted as saying: "Prince von Hassler and I are more shadow investors in both companies. I'm far too busy serving the good people of Suffolk County, Long Island, in the Senate. And Prince Hans here has many other business concerns to attend to. So our good friend Howard Parker ensures the day-to-day running of things at both concerns. And a splendid job he does of it too."

Parker was then asked how he managed to divide his time between Black Horse on the west coast and Magriet Fashions on the east. He answered: "My future is in film. I devote most of my time to that. But it's a new industry and I need to ensure our other business does well enough to keep the funds flowing. I have appointed a top-notch manager here in New York, and I make sure I drop in every time I'm in town. Don't worry, folks – you'll be seeing plenty of new films from us!"

He then went on to talk up Miles Spencer and what a fine young director he was. One to watch. A talent to be reckoned with . . .

Poppy looked carefully at the photograph of the five people. Which, if any of them, was involved in all this? And how did Alfie fit into it all? What was it that Elizabeth was trying to tell her this morning? Now that she'd calmed down, she felt she should visit the former suffragette again to hear what she had to say for herself. She would do it tomorrow. And then perhaps try to see if she could get into the factory too . . .

But this evening she had other plans, which she had already cleared with Rollo, although not Quinn. Both she and Rollo agreed he hadn't been looking well and it was best she not add any further pressure to him by telling him what she intended. So Poppy and Rollo filed their stories and rode down to the foyer in the lift. It was seven o'clock. And there, waiting for them, was Delilah. She was dressed to the nines – in full flapper regalia – carrying a small suitcase and a parcel with a Macy's department store logo on the wrapping. She smiled widely as Poppy and Rollo stepped out of the lift.

"I thought you'd never get here! Here . . ." She passed the suitcase and parcel to Poppy. "I've got what you asked for."

"Thanks," said Poppy. "Rollo, would you mind waiting a few minutes while I get changed?"

"Not at all," he grinned. "I can't wait to see what you two gals have cooked up."

Chapter 37

The doorman at 237 Lexington Avenue stepped forward and opened the door of the yellow taxi cab as it pulled up at the kerb. Out stepped two young women: one with black bobbed hair wearing a silver and black-fringed flapper dress and boa, and the second, a red-head wearing a red shift dress embroidered with cobalt blue beads. And with them, to the doorman's surprise, was the dwarfish gentleman he had met earlier that afternoon. The doorman raised his top hat in greeting. "Good evening, sir, ladies. Welcome to Lexington Towers. How may I help you?"

The dwarf greeted him with: "Good to see you again, dear man," and then went on to explain that he had arranged a viewing of the penthouse with the prince's lawyer and that the former housekeeper had been enlisted to let him in and show him round.

"That was quick, sir," the doorman observed.

"A property like this will be snapped up in no time. So after I spoke to you earlier I contacted the prince's lawyer – he's an old school friend, you know."

The doorman nodded sagely. So many of these toffs knew each other from the old days – or claimed to. It was no skin off his nose, as long as he got a good tip . . .

As if reading his mind the dwarf discreetly produced a clip of dollar bills.

The doorman, with a sleight of hand that would have been admired in the circus, slipped them into his pocket and bowed his head. "Of course, sir. Right this way, sir."

The girls followed, giggling. "Isn't your young English niece with you this evening? She seemed very set on seeing the penthouse herself, sir."

The dwarfish gentleman said that she was, but he wanted to

surprise her with it and didn't want her to be disappointed if the sale fell through. "You know how weepy these young girls can get," he observed.

The doorman said that he did, although, he thought, looking at the two good-time girls, young enough to be the little fella's daughters, that not much weeping would be done tonight. But it wasn't for him to judge. He'd seen far worse going in and out of Lexington Towers over the years. Not least to Howard Parker's apartment, which attracted an endless stream of hopeful young actresses, most of whom never made it from the white sheets to the silver screen. So, he was not the least bit surprised when the dark-haired girl, speaking with a hint of an Italian accent, announced that she and her friend would be stopping by to visit Mr Parker while their uncle – how many nieces could one man have? – viewed the penthouse.

"Is Mr Parker in?" asked the uncle.

A slight raise of an eyebrow under the grey top hat elicited another dollar bill which disappeared as deftly as the first lot. "I believe he is, sir," came the reply.

Poppy and Delilah stepped out of the lift on the floor below the penthouse, and agreed to meet Rollo in the foyer in half an hour. If they were not there he was to ask the concierge to accompany him up to Parker's apartment to tell the young ladies that their ride was leaving. Delilah had already got the concierge to ring up to ask the producer if he was available to receive visitors: Miss Delilah Marconi and her Scottish friend, Miss Flora McDonald.

Coming from Northumberland, Scottish was the only other accent Poppy could successfully imitate. So Flora McDonald, aspiring film actress, was who she became. She had got the idea earlier in the afternoon when she and Rollo had done the impromptu play acting and thought it might be a good way in to see Parker. She was encouraged that the doorman had not recognised her in her glad rags and red wig. She hoped the film producer would not do so either. He had only seen her briefly in the library at The Lodge, and there she had been blonde and wearing a pale pink calf-length gown.

Delilah and Poppy held hands as they approached Parker's door.

"Ready?" asked Poppy, her face suddenly serious.

"Ready," said Delilah, then took a deep breath and knocked on the door.

A few moments later the door opened to reveal a large man – well over six feet tall – with mutton-chop sideburns and slicked-back greying hair. He was wearing a dark green velvet smoking jacket with black trim and was chomping on a fat cigar. He unplugged the cigar from his mouth, opened his arms wide and boomed: "Delilah! Honey! What a dandy surprise!"

He moved in and kissed Delilah on each cheek in the way Poppy had seen French people do in Paris.

"Howard! Thanks for seeing me at such short notice. My friend and I – may I introduce Miss Flora McDonald from Scotland – were just heading down to Chester's and thought we'd pop in."

Parker appraised Poppy with apparent approval. Then he bowed slightly and took her hand, kissing the back of it with tobacco-stained lips. Poppy felt the skin on the back of her neck crawl. "Och aye, a wee Highland lass. A Rose of Scotland och aye the noo," Parker intoned in a caricature of a Scottish accent.

"Pleased to meet you, Mr Parker," Poppy said with a soft Border burr.

"And where are you from in Scotland?" asked Parker, his head cocking to the side to catch her words more clearly.

"Coldstream. Just over the border," said Poppy, naming the nearest Scottish town to where she used to live in Northumberland.

"Well, Miz McDonald, I don't know if Delilah has told you, but we're thinking of filming *Lorna Doone*. We don't need your accent in a silent movie, but with your looks, a Highland lassy like you might just fit the bill."

Poppy did not bother telling him that Coldstream was almost as far from the Highlands as you could possibly get in Scotland without being in England. Instead she put on her wide-eyed look and said with a charming burr: "Och Mr Parker, that would be grand!"

Parker chuckled and put the cigar back into his mouth.

Then he stepped aside and ushered the young women in.

The room was as garishly decorated as Poppy had imagined it

would be. Turkish carpets adorned the walls and floors, while thick red velvet curtains with gold brocade trim obscured the windows. It was like a set from the film *The Sheik* – just with colour added, thought Poppy – complete with ottoman loungers and brass incense holders. Poppy hoped that was as far as the comparison would go, and tried not to shudder when she thought of the abducted English woman and the predatory Arab prince. There was not a chance in Hades that Poppy would be wooed in the same way Lady Diana Mayo had been.

Poppy had already briefed Delilah on Parker's possible connection to the prostitute ring. Delilah, in turn, had told Poppy that she had spoken to Miles, who had told her that Parker had given him the telephone number for someone called Slick. She had no idea who Slick was, but Miles said that he seemed to know Parker and the type of girls who would fit the bill. For Poppy, that was all the confirmation she needed. She had Slick's number and was going to ask Rollo or Quinn to call in the morning to set up some kind of sting. They would say they were calling on behalf of Parker and "order" a girl who would meet the description of Mimi. That was as far as Poppy had thought it through. No doubt Quinn and Rollo would have their tuppence-worth to add, but she was confident that it was a possible way forward. Then why were they here tonight?

Poppy wasn't really sure what she expected to get out of Parker. She certainly didn't want to alert him to the fact that the authorities might be on to him – and they weren't just yet, anyway. Quinn and Rollo were focused on the von Hassler murder, which so far had not yielded any links to Parker other than he lived in the same building. But surely that was a link? That and the fact that they had shared business interests.

Actually, that's what she thought she might try to explore. And it was too good an opportunity to miss with Rollo currently upstairs with Mrs Lawson. If nothing came of it, so be it. She would just follow through with the Slick lead tomorrow.

Parker invited them to sit, offering them a choice of port or sherry from a well-stocked drinks cabinet. Delilah asked for port; Flora said she might just have a wee sherry.

Parker poured the drinks – with a whisky for himself – and seated himself very close to Delilah on an ottoman. Delilah did not pull away.

"Well, Delilah, did you drop by for business or pleasure?" His eyes ranged up and down her silk-stockinged legs as he spoke.

"A little bit of both," giggled Delilah. "But mainly business. I don't know if Miles has told you, but he asked me to go to California with him on Friday to have a proper screen test at your Hollywood studio."

"He did," said Parker and took a large mouthful of whisky. He swilled it around in his mouth, savouring it, before swallowing. "Me and the boys were very impressed with your performance at The Lodge. We want to show you off to the rest of the team at the studio and try to match you with a leading man."

"What film do you have in mind for Delilah?" asked Flora.

"*The Lady of the Lake*," answered Parker. "Not the Walter Scott one." He raised his glass to Flora. "You see, I'm well versed with the literature of your homeland, Miz McDonald. But no, we have our very own version here in the United States. At Lake Ronkonkoma, in fact."

"Yes!" said Delilah. "Miles told me all about it. An Indian squaw, in the days of the early settlers, falls in love with a white man. But their families try to keep them apart. It's a Romeo and Juliet story. The young man dies and then the squaw drowns herself in grief. But then, so the legend has it, every year her ghost lures a young man, between the ages of eighteen and thirty-eight, into the lake. Apparently it's a fact that every year a man of this age really does drown in the lake. Creepy, huh?"

"Very creepy," agreed Poppy.

"And we think Delilah, with her dark colouring, will be perfect to play the squaw. We'll film the outdoor shots at the lake and the rest in our sound studio out in Hollywood."

"It does sound like a good opportunity for you, Delilah," said Poppy, really meaning it. She felt sorry for her friend – and more than a bit worried for her. What would happen to the film if Parker – and perhaps even Miles – was found to be mixed up in something involving illegal immigrants and prostitution? It had been Delilah's dream for so long. Poppy could tell that Delilah was thinking something similar. Behind her fixed smile, Poppy could see worry in her friend's eyes.

"So," said Poppy in her Flora accent. "How is this film going to be financed?"

Parker looked at her curiously. "That's a queer question to ask. Don't worry your pretty little head about it, Miz McDonald; it's none of your concern."

"Sorry," said Flora, thinking on her feet. "My father is a banker from Edinburgh so finance is in the family. And he's always on the look-out for a new investment. Might you need a new investor?"

"Why do you ask that?"

"Oh," said Poppy, as nonchalantly as possible. "I just read an article, that's all, about you and the other investors in Black Horse Productions..."

Parker's eyes narrowed.

"It was in the newspaper, if you recall..."

He nodded. "Yes it was. I wouldn't have put you down as a reader of the financial papers, Miz McDonald."

"Oh, I'm not really!" Flora exclaimed, adding a fake little giggle. "Only now and then. Besides, I think it was in the entertainment section anyway... It said you and Miles's uncle owned a factory that helped finance the films. And now that your other partner, that prince what's his name, has died, there might be room for another investor. My father pointed it out to me; he said it might be a good opportunity for him..." she added.

"I think I should meet your father," said Parker, putting down his now empty whisky tumbler. "He sounds like a man with a good eye for an investment. Is he here in New York?"

"No, but he will be. He'll be coming over the next time the *Olympic* is in port. I came ahead of him to see if I could get to meet you first."

Parker took another cigar from a wooden box on the coffee table, snipped off the end and lit it. "You came all this way to see me?"

"I did, sir," said Flora and gave what Poppy hoped was a shy but charming smile.

"Yes," chipped in Delilah, always ready to improvise. "Mr McD asked if I would mind introducing Flora to you first; then he hopes to meet you when he arrives. He was delayed, you see, banking problems back home..."

Parker sucked on his cigar. He nodded. "It's a difficult time for banks at the moment . . . You've finished your drink, Delilah. Do you want another? Then you can tell me what's concerning you about coming to Hollywood with Miles. He's a good boy. You'll be safe in his hands."

An opportunity to change tack? pondered Poppy. Delilah must have been thinking the same thing. "Yes, please, to the top-up." She passed her glass to Parker, who then gestured to Poppy.

"I'm fine, thank you."

Parker got up and went back to the drinks cabinet. Delilah spoke to his back. "Well, yes, that's just it. I've been hearing stories of some girls who – well – get sucked into things, if you know what I mean. Get lured to the bright lights. I'm sure it will be all right – Miles is a brick – but my father, and my Uncle Elmo . . . you've heard of my great uncle, haven't you? Guglielmo Marconi, the radio pioneer . . ."

Parker's back straightened but he didn't turn around.

Another potential investor? wondered Poppy.

"So," continued Delilah, "they've both warned me about young girls getting into trouble. Being lured by the bright lights . . . young foreign girls, and . . ."

Parker laughed and turned around. In his hand was not another glass of port but a revolver. "Oh Delilah, Delilah, Delilah. And now you've overplayed the scene. Not quite as good an actress as I thought you were."

Delilah's hand went to her throat. "What on earth are you talking about? And put that gun away, please! It's not very funny."

"It's not meant to be funny," said Parker. "Although your attempts at entrapment are." He pointed the gun at Poppy. "You, Miz Denby, sit beside your friend."

Poppy swallowed hard. So he knew. The game was up. They should never have come here tonight. They should have just followed up in the morning as they had planned to do. Parker was right. They had overplayed the scene. She got up and sat beside Delilah on the ottoman. Delilah clutched her hand. Poppy checked her watch. Half an hour had passed. There should be a knock on the door any minute . . .

Parker smirked. "If you're expecting that dwarf to save you, you'll be very disappointed. He's not even half the man he thinks he is." He laughed, cruelly, at his own joke.

Delilah gasped.

"Yes, sweet cheeks, I know that Rolandson is upstairs now speaking to Mrs Lawson."

Poppy's face must have shown a reaction to that because he said: "Not such a hot-shot reporter then, after all. Or you would have found out that I'd been paying that negro woman all this time. When Rolandson called her to arrange a meeting she told me straight away. I was planning on going up and dealing with him myself. But then you arrived . . . That was a surprise . . ."

Dear God, what should we do now? In all the detective novels she'd read this was usually the time the sleuth managed to get the killer to confess everything – in long and meandering detail – before somehow managing to turn the tables on him. But Poppy's throat was too dry to say anything. She swallowed hard again.

"He – he'll be here in a moment," said Delilah. "With the c-concierge. It's all been arranged."

Parker laughed again and gestured for the two women to get up. "The best laid plans of mice and little men will suddenly come to nought. Stand up. We're going for a ride."

Poppy and Delilah stood, still holding hands. They were both shaking.

"Turn around and walk to the door. And don't try any funny business."

The telephone suddenly rang. *It's the concierge!* thought Poppy. Parker smiled coldly and held the gun steady as he answered.

Should we try and run?

The door was bolted shut from the inside. It would take too long; it would . . .

"Hello? . . . Yes, Slick, I'm coming down now . . . No, around the back, the trade elevator. Meet me at the bottom. And oh, Slick, shift things around a bit. We've got another two passengers tonight."

Chapter 38

Mimi Yazierska had finished her quota of zips for the day and packed up her machine. She was looking forward to a good night's rest. The swelling on her lip and eye had finally gone down and her ribs – which the Poppy lady hadn't seen – ached a little less. Hopefully she'd be able to sleep the night without stabbing pain. The other girls in the workshop had looked and lowered their eyes. No one, except sweet Estie, had bothered to ask her what had happened. And with Estie, of course, she had tried to sugar-coat the story. She said she'd fallen in her high heels and hit her face. But Estie had shaken her head and asked: "Man hurt you? Man hurt Estie."

Mimi's temper flared. "What man hurt you, Estie? Here? Was it Slick?"

Estie shook her head. "Man on boat. Big boat."

Her sister's stomach churned. "What man, Estie? What did he do?"

Estie was doodling with a pencil and paper, drawing childish stick figures. One of them, Mimi noticed, was lying on the ground with a crooked leg. She pointed to the figure. "Is that you, Estie? Is that what the man did to you? Did he knock you down? Did he hurt you?"

Estie shook her head again, then took the pencil in her fist and scribbled aggressively over the figure, completely obliterating it.

"Man kiss Estie. Estie not like. Man pull Estie's hair." She clutched and tugged her long black plait to demonstrate. "Estie push man. Man fell. Big machine."

Estie looked up at her sister, worry on her face. "Estie do bad thing? Soldiers take Estie away?"

The sailor who lost his leg... The third-class passengers had heard about it. They'd seen the stretcher being loaded into the ambulance on the dock. They'd been told it was an accident. But it wasn't! What if the man survived? What if the man told the authorities what had happened? What if they tried to track Estie down – back in Southampton? Then discovered she wasn't there . . . that neither of them was . . . Would they be hunted down? Would Immigration find them?

Mimi looked around at the other weary young women making their way back to the dormitory after their shift. She had two more years of this. Was she safe here? As long as Immigration didn't know about them, then yes . . . but what if they tracked them to here? And was here such a safe place anyway? Not with what had happened to her on Saturday, it wasn't.

However, it was a price she was prepared to pay. To protect Estie. She knew her dream of being reunited with Anatoly was over. She had come to the realisation that her fiancé, in all probability, was dead. And if he wasn't, how on earth were they ever to reunite? The address she had wasn't a home; it was a newspaper office. Anatoly wouldn't live at a newspaper. Had he known that when he had given it to her? Had he just been stringing her along? She touched the pearl on her engagement ring and bit her lip. Oh, she had been a fool to believe it for so long. Estie was looking at her, her head cocked to one side. Mimi reached out and stroked her hair. She would be a fool no longer. There was still hope for them. They were in America. And eventually – please God – they would be free to live their own lives.

"Estie," she said. "Promise me you will never tell anyone about the man on the ship. Can you do that?"

Estie was drawing again, this time something that looked like a flower. "Uh-huh," she said.

Mimi sighed. That was the best she'd get for now.

Mimi took off her apron and put it in the small bedside cupboard. Then she straightened up and said: "It's time for food, Estie. Let's go."

But as she helped her sister get ready to go to the dining hall, the blonde, scowling figure of Kat stalked towards them. "The Boss Man's called. He wants to see you. And her." She jerked a thumb towards Estie. "Slick will take you."

"But we haven't eaten," said Mimi. "And why does he want to see Estie?"

Kat slapped her. Mimi took a step back. But Estie launched herself at the supervisor like a rabid dog, her nails clawing at the older girl's face. "Get her off me!" screamed Kat.

Mimi grabbed her sister by the shoulders and heaved her back. Kat's face was scratched and bloodied. *That'll teach you,* thought Mimi, just managing to keep the smirk off her face.

"Take some bread with you, then meet Slick in his office," said Kat, backing off and eyeing Estie warily.

Mimi did not know what to do. She hoped – she really hoped – that the Boss Man wanting to see Estie did not mean that she too would be put to work servicing men. Mimi could not – would not – allow that. But what choice did they have? Mimi looked at her sister and imagined her fighting off the sailor on the boat. It would not end well for any man who tried to have his way with her. Estie would not be as compliant as her older sister. And then what would happen? Would the man get even more violent? Might he *really* hurt Estie? She'd have to talk to the Boss Man. To make him see sense. Slick was just obeying orders; he'd be no good to talk to. But she must convince the Boss Man to leave her sister alone, for all of their sakes.

Poppy and Delilah stepped out of the service entrance to Lexington Towers. Poppy's eyes flitted from left to right. They were in an alleyway. Bins and skips were lined up at the rear of a number of apartment buildings, and about a block away, the rear entrance of Bloomingdale's department store. If this was daytime she might have expected to see delivery vans and refuse collectors driving up and down the alley, but it was nearly eight o'clock on a Tuesday night. The flashing lights at the end of the alley from the traffic on 59th Street might as well have been on the moon.

Howard Parker was close behind them, hiding a gun under the draped coat on his arm. Poppy could hear his breathing – tense but steady. The smell of whisky suggested he'd had enough to give him Dutch courage but not that he'd be dropping off into a drunken stupor any time soon. Now was not the time to run. Poppy prayed, fervently, that she and Delilah would be given a chance to do so soon – either that or they would be able to alert someone to help them.

What's happened to Rollo? Poppy was desperately worried for her editor. Was he still upstairs with Mrs Lawson? Had the woman somehow incapacitated him? If she was, in fact, the killer of Prince von Hassler, she was more than capable of hurting Rollo. But Rollo was strong – short but not puny. In a physical tussle he would probably hold his own against the older woman. But what if she took him unawares? Hit him from behind, as she had the prince? Or if she too had a gun like Parker?

Suddenly the lights of a motor vehicle flashed at the end of the alley. *Someone's coming! This is our chance!*

Poppy held her breath, waiting for the vehicle to approach. She would run at the motor, waving her arms, then it would stop. Surely a young woman in distress would cause the driver to stop. And Parker would not shoot, would he? Not with a witness . . .

"Don't try anything," growled Parker. "I will not hesitate to shoot."

Should I still try? Should I . . .

The car was a few feet away and beginning to slow; then it pulled to a stop in front of them. Poppy heard the handbrake being pulled up and saw the window open. She prepared her face to communicate fear, hoping the person would see she and Delilah were in distress.

"Evening, sir," said the driver with a flick of a finger to the brim of his hat.

Poppy mouthed the word "help".

The man in the motor grinned, revealing blackened teeth.

She heard Parker chuckle behind her. Her heart sank.

"Evening, Slick. Are the other two under control?"

"Aye aye, sir," said the driver, opening the door. Poppy caught a glimpse of crumpled bodies on the back seat. "Chloroformed as you said. They shouldn't be waking up for a while."

"What have you done? Who's that in there?" asked Delilah. "Listen, Howard, I think this has gone too far. I don't know what you're trying to do, but you won't get away with it. You won't be able to . . ."

Delilah yelped. Poppy looked down to see the barrel of Parker's gun jab into her friend's ribs.

"You got any of that chloroform left, Slick?"

Chapter 39

Poppy was swimming in the sea at Whitley Bay. Her brother was with her. The waves lifted them up and down, their legs kicking frantically under the water to keep them afloat. Their mother called to them from the shore: "Be careful! Don't go too far out!" and their father waved to them, a pease pudding and ham sandwich in hand. It was getting dark and a light swept over them in a wide arc: it was coming from St Mary's lighthouse.

Suddenly her brother cried out and disappeared under the waves. Poppy waited for him to pop back up or to grab her ankle and pull her down, pretending he was a shark. She waited. And she waited. The light from St Mary's was sweeping from left to right faster and faster. She looked to shore but could no longer see her parents. She thought she could still hear her mother's voice, distantly calling: "Come back, Poppy; come back!"

No, it wasn't her name she could hear; it was another's. Delilah's . . . and the voice was male: "Again Delilah, again!" The light from the lighthouse flashed once more.

Poppy closed her eyes against the glare then opened them again. She was not on a beach. She was not in the sea. She was on a stone floor in some kind of shack. The wall planks were higgledy-piggledy, with gaps in between through which bright, artificial light seeped.

Poppy shook her head to clear it. Was she awake? Yes. The pain in her arms was real. She shifted to move them, then felt something pull against her wrists. She peered through the gloom and saw that her hands were tethered with a rope, and the rope was tied to a metal ring on the wall of the shack. Where was she?

"No, Delilah! Not like that!"

Delilah? Poppy thrashed her head from left to right, looking for her friend. But she was alone. Alone in what looked like a boat shed. Yes, that's what it was: the lap of water against wood and stone, the dank smell of soaked timber, the roughness of hessian under her bare, cold shoulders; and in the corner, a pile of oars and a rusty anchor. But there was no boat.

"For God's sake, Delilah. I thought you were an actress!"

That sounds like Parker. What's he doing with Delilah? Poppy tried to peek through the cracks in the walls, but all she could see was the glaring light. *What is that? Where's that light coming from?*

"I-I-can't, Howard. I-I'm too scared. P-please. Please stop this!"

Poppy pulled at her bonds. They didn't give. She looked around, trying to see if there was something she could use to cut through the rope. Nothing obvious . . . She manoeuvred herself up onto her knees, then shuffled over to the wall. She poked the wood around the metal ring. It was soft and rotting in places. She started picking at the timber, clawing it away. If she could undermine the wood around the bolts . . .

After a couple of minutes her nails were cracked and her fingers raw. She needed some kind of tool . . . What could she use? A pile of shells! Some kind of oyster shells, just within reach. Poppy picked one up and started scraping at the wood as Delilah's crying and Parker's shouting got louder and louder . . .

And then . . . yes! The bolts began to shift and twist, the wood splintered, and with a heave, Poppy pulled the ring free of the wall.

Her wrists were still tied, but at least she was free to move around. She picked up the ring and shimmied her way around the shed until she came to the entrance. She feared that it would be bolted or padlocked shut. It wasn't. *Thank God.*

Poppy pushed open the door, freezing as the hinges creaked. But Parker, still berating Delilah for whatever it was she was failing to do, was making too much noise to hear. With the door open not much more than half a foot, Poppy slipped through.

Yes, she had been in a boat house. She was now standing on a slipway, and a few yards below her was the blackened water of what appeared to be a lake. A lake? Poppy looked around her. Around the lake and on either side of the boat house were spruce and maple trees in early spring bloom. This place was familiar. Poppy sniffed the air: yes, she'd smelled that smell very recently.

"This is your last chance, Delilah – do it or I'll shoot you!"

Delilah! Poppy ran to the corner of the shed and peered around. There was the source of light; and there were Parker and Delilah. Delilah was standing, ankle deep in water, wearing what appeared to be an Indian squaw's dress and head gear, her shoulders shuddering as she wept. On the shore, behind three film studio lights and camera, was Parker. Sitting to his left in a director's chair, one leg draped over the arm, was Slick . . . holding a gun. Beyond Delilah, on the lake, a boat bobbed up and down. The boat from the shed, Poppy assumed.

"Now Delilah, let's try that again. Peer to left and right. Look all around, desperate. You are calling for your lover! He doesn't come. Then in despair you walk, slowly, into the lake."

He's mad! Totally mad! He's filming a movie at gunpoint!

Poppy thought for a moment of running up behind Parker, swinging the heavy iron ring and whacking him on the head. Or perhaps she should attack Slick first. He had the gun. If there was only one of them, Poppy thought, she might have a chance, but with two . . . She turned away from the lake and looked up the hill. Yes, it was just as she thought. They were at Lake Ronkonkoma, just below the Spencer holiday lodge. Through the trees she could see the lights of The Lodge blazing. *If Slick and Parker are both here, maybe I could slip up to The Lodge and call the police . . . Yes! I'll use the telephone in the library!*

She turned back to the perverse film set behind her. Delilah was ham acting the role of the lovelorn squaw. Parker seemed to be happy for now. But how far would he take it? Up to the drowning?

There was no time to waste. Poppy ran as quickly and quietly as she could, with her hands tied and holding a metal ring, up to the house.

Mimi had been in this room before. It was a library, smaller than the one where she'd first met Anatoly . . . *Oh my love, if only I could turn back time and stay in that library with you forever . . .* This was the library in the house she had been taken to a few days earlier. The place where she had first seen the Boss Man and his friends. The place she had seen that Poppy lady. This time, though, she was not with Kat and the other two girls, but Estie. Estie was still sleeping beside her; Slick must have given her an extra dose of that foul-smelling potion to subdue her when she attacked him.

Mimi had woken up about fifteen minutes ago. She already knew where she was and she already knew that only a few feet away was a telephone – the same telephone the Poppy lady had used. But she knew too there was no chance she would be able to use it, as seated between her and the telephone was someone she'd never met before – someone who had made it clear that if she tried to run, or scream, or do anything the woman did not like, she, or her sister, would be shot.

The woman sat quietly with the gun on her lap, staring into the flames of a fire in the grate. The pine cones popped and sizzled, and under any other circumstances it might have been described as a cheerful blaze.

But the woman scowled, her brows furrowed, deep in thought.

Poppy, breathless, climbed the steps onto the front porch of The Lodge. She was about to burst in, when suddenly it occurred to her that the house might not be unoccupied. Why hadn't she thought of that before? Perhaps Slick and Parker were not acting alone . . . She fell to her haunches and shuffled along the porch and hid herself, as best she could, behind some pot plants. She needed to think a moment, but not too long . . . She didn't know how long poor Delilah had. Who could be in the house? Any of the Spencers. Toby had told her it belonged to the extended family. Cousins had been mentioned . . . But who would let Parker set up a makeshift film set on their private beach – a command performance at gunpoint? Or didn't they know? Surely they would see the lights . . . and the motor car . . . two motor cars! Slick's and another one. There was definitely someone here. Miles? It wasn't his fancy sports car. Toby? To be honest, she didn't know what he drove. Mr and Mrs Spencer? Other family members . . .

Time's running out! Nonetheless she didn't want to barge in through the front door – not if whoever was inside was in cahoots with Parker. The lights were only shining on the ground floor, so the chances were that whoever was in the house was downstairs. She got up on her knees and peered into the nearest window – the trophy room: a small lamp in the corner but otherwise it seemed unoccupied. She crawled along, looking in each window. Some curtains were drawn, some not. Then she came to what, from what she could recall of the layout of the house, was probably the library. She edged up, clutching the metal ring, and . . . bingo! There were three people in the room. Two on a sofa and one in an armchair. Poppy could not see the person in the armchair very well; their back was to the window. But on the sofa was a very frightened-looking Mimi Yazierska and beside her the sleeping form of another young woman, most probably her sister, Estie. Mimi looked towards the window. Her eyes caught Poppy's; her eyebrows rose in surprise. Then her eyes flicked towards the person in the armchair. Poppy still could not see, but from Mimi's expression the person was likely a captor, not a captive. *What should I do now?*

Suddenly, there was the roar of an engine and the blaze of car lights. Poppy crouched down again. *Who's coming now?*

Down on the drive a car pulled up and three people jumped out of the vehicle: Rollo Rolandson, Elizabeth Dorchester and . . . Poppy's stomach lurched . . . Alfie Dorchester. Suddenly, a human shadow was cast further along the porch, suggesting someone was standing at a window, in front of a light. The movement caught Rollo's eye and he looked towards the library. Poppy tried to get his attention, but he was looking at the lit window, not the shadowy porch. And then the shadow moved away.

"Rollo!" called Poppy in a stage whisper.

"Hold on, Poppy, I'm coming!" hissed the editor in reply. He ran as fast as he could up to the front porch. Meanwhile, screams from the beach suggested all was not well with Delilah. Poppy was just about to run back to help her when Elizabeth and Alfie turned and ran in the direction of the cries for help. Elizabeth was carrying a tyre iron. She wasn't sure why Alfie was there, but she had no doubt Elizabeth would do her best to save Delilah. Poppy turned her attention back to Rollo, hoping to intercept him. But it was too late. He had run past without seeing her and was already in the house. She ran through the front door and across the foyer, just in time to see Rollo push open the library door.

"Where are you, Poppy?" he asked. And then he stopped in his tracks.

"Rollo Rolandson," came a woman's voice. "Why can't you keep out of other people's business?"

Poppy recognised the patrician tones of Amelia Spencer. She edged forward, trying to alert Rollo that she was there, but not wanting to be seen by Amelia. If the woman didn't know she was on the loose she might still be able to use the element of surprise to her advantage.

"Rollo!" Poppy whispered, as close to him as she dared. He tensed. Had he heard her? "Don't turn around. I'm here. I'm fine. Does she have a gun? Nod if she does."

Rollo nodded.

"Then keep her talking."

And Rollo did, giving Poppy time to think of what to do next.

"It's hard to keep my nose out of your business, Amelia, when you insist on getting involved in so many newsworthy stories. Oh, and by the way, the police are on their way."

The police are on their way! Or is he bluffing?

Poppy wondered what was happening down at the lake. She cocked her ear to hear. The screaming had stopped. Was that a good thing?

Back in the library, Rollo and Amelia continued their conversation. Poppy tried to imagine what the woman was doing. What were the Yazierska girls doing? Where exactly were they positioned? Could they overpower Amelia if necessary?

"Why don't you put the gun down, Amelia, and let those girls go? They've done nothing to you."

There was silence for a moment, then Amelia's reply. Her voice was devoid of any emotion, almost matter-of-fact. "They haven't. But now they know too much."

"What about?" asked Rollo.

Amelia laughed mirthlessly. "Are you trying to trap me into a confession?"

"Do you have one to make?"

Mrs Spencer's voice puffed with derision. "Of course not. I am just having a quiet night at the lake. I needed to get away for a few days."

"A quiet night in, holding two young women hostage, or didn't you know they were going to be here? Did you arrange to meet Parker? Did he bring them here?" asked Rollo.

"Parker?" There was a slight edge to Amelia's voice.

"Yes, the police should be arresting him" – there was a pause and Poppy imagined Rollo looking at his watch – "about now." *Oh, if only that were true!* She must think of something. What could she do?

"We know that you murdered von Hassler, Amelia; his housekeeper has told us everything."

There was silence for a moment. Poppy could imagine Mrs Parker weighing up the damning evidence provided by Mrs Lawson. It was a difficult accusation to sidestep.

A slight note of concern slipped into Amelia's voice. "That woman has got it all wrong. It wasn't murder. And I'm sure I can convince the police of that. Who will they believe: a negro woman or me? I didn't mean to *kill* him, you know, but he wouldn't stop telling filthy lies about my husband. I hit him – yes – but I didn't mean to kill him. I'm sure the judge will understand that. A respectable woman like me."

And then, finally, Poppy knew what she had to do. She headed as quietly as she could back to the door.

"How did Parker get involved?" asked Rollo.

"I'm not being interviewed here for a *New York Times* exclusive, Rolandson. Get in here. You, girl – tie him up."

Poppy heard something indecipherable; half in Russian, half in English. Then, as she exited the house and made her way back along the porch, she could hear no more. She could, however, hear shouts – and shots! – from the lake. *Dear God! Delilah!* She turned, tempted for a moment to go and help her friend, but then pulled herself up. *I'm too far away to help her now. But I can still help Rollo . . .*

At the library window Poppy peeked in. Amelia Spencer was standing in the middle of the floor, her back to the window. Her gun was trained on Rollo and Mimi as the Jewish girl fumbled to tie a scarf around Rollo's wrists.

Now! Poppy swung the iron ring with all her might. The window smashed. Amelia turned and cowered as glass cascaded around her; then Mimi and Rollo jumped on her from behind. The other girl, who had just woken up, piled in too. Amidst screams and flailing limbs, Rollo crawled out of the scrum holding the gun. He pointed it in the air and fired. The three wrestling women froze. Rollo looked up at the window and grinned. "Good work, Miz Denby."

Poppy left Rollo to deal with Amelia and the two girls and ran towards the lake. *I hope I'm not too late!*

She stumbled and fell onto the gravel drive, the stones tearing her silk stockings and gouging her flesh. *Damn this ring!* But she dragged herself back up and continued to run – over the road and towards the maples and the lake beyond. Then, as she breached the tree-line she was met by the bloodied faces of Howard Parker and his sidekick Slick, whose nose was splayed across his face.

"All under control here, Poppy," said Elizabeth Dorchester, with Slick's gun trained on the two men, the only indication of her part in the scuffle an angry welt on her left cheek.

But Poppy continued to run. "Delilah!"

"She's all right!" called back Elizabeth.

As Poppy stumbled onto the shoreline, she saw that she was. A wet, bedraggled, but very much alive Delilah was in the arms of an equally wet Alfie Dorchester, standing knee deep in the lake. He waded the rest of the way to shore and laid the quivering actress on the beach. Poppy fell to her knees beside her friend. "Delilah! Are you all right?"

"I-I am. Th-thanks to Al-Alfie. He s-saved my life, Poppy!"

Poppy looked up and into the blue eyes of the man who had once tried to kill her. "Why?" was all she could say.

Alfie ran his hand across his face, wiping away the lake water. "I'm not a killer, Poppy. I never meant to hurt you in London. I just wanted to scare you. I drove the car at you – yes – but I didn't mean to hit you. If I had, I would have just left you there in the street. But I didn't. I took you to hospital. I saved your life."

Poppy felt a blaze of anger. But she suppressed it. He was lying, she was sure of it, but he had saved Delilah.

"You don't have to thank me."

"You're right, I won't," Poppy growled.

"I've done some terrible things – I know that – but I couldn't say no to my father. I'm a coward – I admit it."

Poppy could hear the sound of police sirens getting closer. "You deserve to be in prison," she spat.

Alfie lowered his eyes. "Perhaps. Goodbye, Poppy. Goodbye, Delilah. And good luck."

And with that, Alfie Dorchester, also known as Otto von Riesling, ran off into the night.

Chapter 40

Thursday, 25 April 1921

The front-page article of *The New York Times*:

SENATOR'S WIFE & FILM PRODUCER CHARGED WITH MURDER

By Judson Quinn

NEW YORK – Amelia Spencer, wife of Senator Theodore Spencer of Long Island, has been charged with the murder of millionaire Prince Hans von Hassler in his Lexington Avenue penthouse.

Hollywood producer Howard Parker (60), best known for *Baby and the Bluebird*, has been charged as an accessory to the murder in which the prince (83) was struck on the back of the head.

In a sensational sting, orchestrated by undercover NYT reporters Rollo Rolandson and Poppy Denby – in which Miss Denby and her friend the actress Delilah Marconi's lives were at risk – Mrs Spencer (55) admitted to killing the prince to "keep him quiet" about her husband's love life.

Sources in the NYPD have told the *Times* that she allegedly then went on to use her husband's senatorial credentials to put pressure on the coroner's office to declare the death accidental. Police are currently investigating those allegations.

Howard Parker, who lives in the apartment below

the prince, allegedly found out about the suspicious circumstances surrounding the death via the prince's housekeeper, a Mrs Nora Lawson (68), who had worked for von Hassler for twenty years.

Investigations by this newspaper have revealed that he then examined the visitor book in the lobby of Lexington Towers, a luxury apartment complex in the heart of Manhattan, and discovered that Mrs Spencer visited the prince on the night of his death.

Further investigations have revealed Parker, Senator Spencer and von Hassler were partners in the film company Black Horse Productions, which was financed by means of profit from a factory in the New York Garment District, Magriet Fashions.

A parallel investigation by this newspaper has uncovered that Magriet Fashions was using illegal immigrants as slave labor and, in some cases, forced prostitution.

Evidence of this has been passed to the Department of Immigration, which has assured the *Times* that in return for their co-operation in exposing the trafficking ring – which is believed to have trans-Atlantic connections – the fifteen women who were imprisoned there will be granted leave to remain in the United States.

Prince von Hassler's attorney, Richard Barnes, has told the *Times* he has passed evidence over to the police that Howard Parker was attempting to frame the prince's nephew and heir, Count Otto von Riesling, for his uncle's murder.

Mr Barnes suggests this was in order to remove von Riesling from the board of Magriet Fashions. Von Riesling and his uncle had allegedly been concerned about the use of slave labor in the factory.

Mrs Nora Lawson, the housekeeper, confessed to the *Times* that she had taken a bribe from Parker to implicate von Riesling. She said she had agreed because "I didn't like the boy and he has made Prince Hans's life a misery".

It is alleged that von Riesling had been blackmailing his uncle for the last three years about his involvement in homosexual activities.

However, in a bizarre twist, it can be revealed that the *Times*, in a joint investigation with the British Secret Service, has discovered that the real Otto von Riesling is in fact in Monte Carlo and that a British aristocrat, Viscount Alfie Dorchester, had been impersonating him in New York.

Dorchester, a disgraced war hero who has been stripped of his fraudulently obtained Victoria Cross, is already wanted for attempted murder in London, and is a fugitive from justice.

This newspaper can now reveal that the woman he tried to kill in England is none other than our very own reporter, Poppy Denby, who is currently on loan to us from the London *Daily Globe*.

However, in circumstances that are still unclear, Dorchester, with the help of his sister Elizabeth, helped save the life of Miss Delilah Marconi in the sting that brought Amelia Spencer and Howard Parker to justice at the Spencers' luxury holiday lodge on Lake Ronkonkoma.

Dorchester is again on the run and we may never know his true motivation until he is caught. If anyone recognizes Dorchester (aka von Riesling) from the photograph below, please report it to the police immediately.

Three months later:

13 July 1921, Southampton

Poppy, Delilah, Rollo, Aunt Dot and Miss King waited for the gangplank from the *Olympic* to be lowered at Southampton harbour. It was a glorious summer's day and Poppy felt hot in her new green coat, bought to replace the one she had given to Mimi Yazierska three months earlier.

Poppy smiled as she thought of the last time she had seen Mimi and Estie. It was at Elizabeth's settlement house. The former suffragette had offered to take the two girls in until their status with the Immigration Department and the various court cases involving the Spencers and Parker were finalised. Although Estie spoke no English, the bubbly Helena soon befriended her and the girls were now inseparable.

Mimi was given the job of managing the small library. Her English was improving every day, and with money received from the von Hassler estate for suffering endured in one of the prince's businesses, she intended to go to college and fulfil her dream of becoming a teacher.

Poppy had got very little more information from Elizabeth about her brother. The older woman had become guarded and just said: "Let sleeping dogs lie, Poppy." It galled Poppy to do so, but she agreed – for now. She also agreed not to mention to the police that Elizabeth had given refuge to Alfie. Whatever her thoughts about the suffragette's gullibility regarding her dastardly brother, Poppy recognised that Elizabeth was doing a wonderful job with the settlement house and she had, after all, saved Delilah's life.

Poppy finally found out what had happened at the beach. Delilah, it seemed, had weights tied to her ankles and was about to be dropped from the boat by Slick, while Parker filmed from the shore. He was so busy preparing to capture the dying moments of the Lady of the Lake that he didn't hear Elizabeth and Alfie sneak up behind him. There was a scuffle which was swiftly brought to an end when Elizabeth retrieved the gun from the director's chair.

Alfie swam out and dealt with Slick, who, without his weapon, was no match for the younger man, but in the process Slick and Delilah fell overboard. Slick swam back to shore where he was greeted by Elizabeth at gunpoint, while Alfie dived in and saved Delilah from drowning. And it was all captured on film! The police, who arrived shortly afterwards, confiscated the reel for evidence.

But that was as far as Delilah's film career went. Although he had been cleared of any involvement in von Hassler's murder or the shenanigans at the garment factory, Delilah could not bring herself to go to Hollywood with Miles. They parted as friends, and

Poppy would not be the least surprised if something came of the relationship – and the film career – in the future.

Instead, for the next three months, Delilah worked with Aunt Dot on a series of radio dramas.. Poppy smiled down at her aunt, resplendent in her fuchsia travelling coat and hat. The ageing actress and former suffragette had come alive in New York as she was given a chance to re-launch her career. She was returning to London as an up-and-coming radio star – and, Poppy chuckled, London had better watch out!

Behind her the quiet, dependable figure of Miss King was always present to serve her employer's needs. But her days were numbered. On the cruise home she had informed Aunt Dot that she had been offered a post as a companion in the south of France and she would be serving her notice when they got home. Aunt Dot said she would write her an excellent reference and wished her well.

Aunt Dot had a few months still to find a replacement, but, thought Poppy, if the information from Yasmin Reece-Lansdale was anything to go by, she need not worry. Yasmin, Rollo's sweetheart and now Aunt Dot's solicitor, had hope that Grace Wilson – Dot's dearest friend – might soon be released on parole. So all would again be well in Aunt Dot's world.

"Happy to be home, Poppy?" asked Rollo.

Poppy looked down at her editor and grinned. "Oh yes; it's been a long three months. An exciting three months, but my word, am I looking forward to a few quiet gallery openings!"

Rollo laughed. "And I'm looking forward to kicking that shyster Archie Weinstein out of my office!"

Poppy chuckled. The day before they had left New York Rollo received a telegram from senior reporter Ike Garfield which read: "Greetings Rollo STOP Re your request to get intel from ad dept STOP Weinstein swore them to secrecy STOP But a couple of beers loosened tongues STOP Happy to report Weinstein failed to double ad revenue STOP Welcome back chief STOP."

So, having won the bet with his former colleague, Rollo was returning to London once again the sole proprietor of *The Daily Globe*. He was relishing getting back to work – the old Rollo was back!

However, Poppy noticed, there was something different about him. He appeared more at peace with himself and the world. He had spent the last three months being reconciled with his mother while she did everything she could to distance herself from the disgraced Amelia Spencer. She even resigned from the board of the Eugenics Society and allowed Rollo to accompany her to various social engagements, where she introduced him as "my son the journalist who exposed that dreadful Spencer woman".

Rollo had done more than simply "expose that dreadful Spencer woman", Poppy thought. If he and the Dorchesters hadn't arrived when they did, Delilah would have been dead and she, Mimi and Estie . . . Well, she wasn't sure what would have happened, but she doubted she could have saved the girls on her own.

On the drive back to New York, once statements had been given to the police, and Slick, Parker and Amelia had been carted off, Rollo told Poppy, Delilah and Elizabeth what had happened with Mrs Lawson.

He had met her at the apartment, as arranged, but the woman had seemed distracted and kept looking at her watch. She had been evasive, too, when questioned, and Rollo soon suspected something was wrong. Rollo decided to put some pressure on her and informed her that he knew she was the second beneficiary to the will and that the police might consider that motivation for murder. She almost fainted when she heard that, and, when recovered, blurted out her innocence and pointed the finger squarely at Amelia Spencer. The housekeeper told him that Mr Parker downstairs had discovered Mrs Spencer was the real killer but had paid her to keep quiet about it and help him, instead, frame the nephew, Otto von Riesling.

After hearing all that Rollo had rushed downstairs to ask the concierge to accompany him to Parker's apartment. But it was too late. By the time they got there, Parker, Delilah and Poppy had gone.

Fearing the worst, Rollo was not sure what to do at first. Then he remembered what Poppy had told him about Elizabeth saying Alfie knew something about the murder. So he called a cab and went over to Elizabeth's house to press her further.

When Elizabeth heard Poppy and Delilah might be in danger she told Rollo her brother was still hiding out, waiting to leave the next morning on a train. She took Rollo to him; then, after hearing what was at stake and being begged to help by his sister, Alfie took them to the factory where he said they could find Parker's assistant, a fella called Slick. But at the factory, which, as a shareholder "Otto von Riesling" was able to gain entry to, they were told Slick had left with a couple of girls. When pressed, and threatened with being turned over to Immigration, one of the other girls – a blonde Russian called Kat – told them Slick had taken two of the girls to see "the Boss Man" out at the lake.

Rollo telephoned Quinn from the factory and asked him to use his contacts to get the police out to Ronkonkoma. Quinn said he would, but it might take a while as the NYPD would have to ask the Suffolk County PD for help. But Rollo wasn't prepared to wait it out. Instead, he commandeered a motor car and Alfie drove him and Elizabeth out to the lake, arriving there shortly before midnight and – as if it were the plot of a detective novel – they got there just in time to help Poppy and save Delilah.

Phew! It was exhausting just thinking about it. *Yes,* thought Poppy, *a few quiet gallery openings are just what I need. I've had enough complications in my life for a while – professionally and personally.*

Poppy sighed as she thought of Toby. Needless to say she did not manage to get to the dinner date with the young doctor. And although in the subsequent three months he was cleared of any involvement in his mother's crimes, any spark of romance that might have been between them was well and truly quenched. She saw him, occasionally, with his father, accompanying Amelia to court, but they never had another conversation. *Oh well, perhaps it's for the best.*

Now that she was back in London she would see Daniel every day at work. She had no idea how she would cope with that. She fingered the red enamel poppy brooch he had given her for her birthday. She had started wearing it about a month ago. Delilah noticed and asked her if that meant things were back on again. Poppy said she wasn't sure. Too much water might have gone under the bridge. She was still angry with him for not being prepared to support her in her career, and although, she admitted, she still loved him, there could be no future for them unless his views in that regard had changed.

Might they have changed? Poppy simply did not know.

The gangplank was finally down. Poppy and her friends descended with the rest of the first-class passengers and at the bottom were greeted by the smiling face of Ike Garfield.

"Rollo! Poppy!" Then he tipped his hat to the rest of the party. "Welcome home, ladies. As per your request, Miss Denby, I arranged to get the yellow Rolls out of storage. My, what a lovely vehicle! There'll be room for you three ladies and your luggage." Then he turned to Poppy and Rollo. "I've made other arrangements for you two."

"What's that?" asked Rollo.

But Ike didn't have to answer. Strolling through the crowd with car keys in hand was Daniel. "He's brought the Model T," Ike explained.

"Not much room in there," observed Rollo. "Surely you can squeeze another one into the Rolls, Ike."

Ike grinned. "We'll give it a go, chief."

Delilah and Aunt Dot giggled.

They're setting us up! thought Poppy. But she didn't care. And neither, it seemed, did Daniel. He barely looked at the rest of the party and homed in on the young blonde woman in the middle.

"Welcome back, Poppy," he said, his grey eyes full of love.

Poppy felt her heart melt.

"Thank you, Daniel. It's very good to be home."

Acknowledgments

Murder on Lexington Avenue was first published as *The Death Beat* in 2017 by the team at Lion Fiction. I remain indebted to the guiding hand of Jessica Gladwell in the development of this book. I am, however, delighted that Poppy Denby is being given a new lease of life under Embla Books and I am very grateful to the whole team – particularly, Martina Arzu and Emma Wilson (I hope you will one day grow to love my maps, Emma).

Writing a Poppy Denby book requires months of research. I am always surprised at how generous people are in supporting me, freely, with their expertise. An enormous debt of gratitude goes to Professor Vincent Cannato, Associate Professor in history at the University of Massachusetts, Boston, for his insight into immigration to the USA in the 1920s. I would also like to thank Professor Richard Hand, of the University of East Anglia, for his knowledge of American radio drama. Thanks too, to Keith Jewitt for introducing me to the feminist icon Annette Kellerman. In addition, the publicity departments at *The New York Times* and the Lyric Theatre, New York, have been very responsive to my queries.

A special word of thanks goes to a group of friends (now scattered around the world) whom I've known since we all studied at Rhodes University, South Africa, too many years ago now to count. Thanks to Louis Brandt, now a solicitor in England, who advised me about early twentieth-century divorce law; and Michael Carklin, now the principal lecturer in drama at the University of South Wales, who introduced me to Professor Hand, an expert in early radio. Also, to Michelle Shaw, a freelance journalist who now lives in Canada, for sending me a wonderful book on the Roaring '20s in America.

And finally, thanks to my agent Sara Keane and to my wonderful family for their unwavering love and patience.

Characters

Fictional Characters (in order of appearance)

London

Poppy Denby – arts and entertainment editor at *The Daily Globe*, London. Our heroine.
Mavis Bradshaw – receptionist for *The Daily Globe*.
Vicky Thompson – assistant to *The Daily Globe* archivist.
Rollo Rolandson – owner and managing editor of *The Daily Globe*. A native New Yorker.
Daniel Rokeby – photographer at *The Daily Globe*. Poppy's beau.
Ike Garfield – senior journalist at *The Daily Globe*.
Ivan Molanov – archivist at *The Daily Globe*.
Archie Weinstein – one of two associate editors for *The New York Times*, currently in London trying to buy an interest in a British newspaper.
Delilah Marconi – Poppy's best friend. Actress, singer, flapper and Bright Young Thing.
Dot Denby / Aunt Dot – Poppy's aunt. Former West End leading lady and suffragette. Now in a wheelchair.
Gertrude King – Aunt Dot's companion.
Alfie Dorchester – Disgraced aristocrat, wanted for attempted murder, on the run from police.
Marjorie Reynolds – British Member of Parliament, minister of state for the Home Office, secretly works for the Secret Service (psst: don't tell anyone).

The Ship / New York

Captain Gilbert Williams – Captain of the *Olympic* cruise liner. Admirer of Dot Denby.

Estie / Esther Yazierska – Jewish Ukrainian refugee with a learning disability.

Mimi / Miriam Yazierska – older sister of Estie. Former maid to White Russsian aristocrats.

Anatoly Pushtov – White Russian aristocrat.

Dr Toby Spencer – orthopaedic surgeon at Bellevue Hospital, Manhattan. Son of US senator from Long Island.

Miles Spencer – cousin of Toby Spencer. Film director.

Senator Theodore Spencer – US senator from Long Island. Friend of Rollo Rolandson's family.

Amelia Spencer – wife of Theodore Spencer. New York socialite and philanthropist.

Seaman Jones – third-class steward on the *Olympic.*

Judson Quinn – associate editor at *The New York Times,* holding the fort when Weinstein is in London, and editor in chief Charles R. Miller (real historical character) is out of town.

Paul Saunders – journalist at *The New York Times.* Cousin of Lionel Saunders, former arts and entertainment editor at the *Globe.*

Chester Wainwright – owner of Chester's Speakeasy, Greenwich Village, Manhattan.

Count Otto von Riesling – expat playboy from Liechtenstein. Heir to fortune.

Prince Hans von Hassler – millionaire businessman, philanthropist, member of the New York Eugenics Society, formerly of Liechtenstein. Uncle of Otto.

Kat – Ukrainian immigrant. Workshop supervisor, Magriet Fashions.

Slick – manager at Magriet Fashions.

Helena – fourteen-year-old Italian immigrant, housemaid at Chelsea settlement house.

Elizabeth Dorchester – sister of Alfie Dorchester, daughter of British lord, former suffragette, friend of Dot Denby, owner of Chelsea settlement house.

Mrs Lawson – housekeeper of Prince Hans von Hassler.
Mr Barnes – lawyer of Prince Hans von Hassler.
Morrison – butler for the Rolandson family in Manhattan.
Howard Parker – film producer.

Historical Characters (cameo appearances)

Rudolph Valentino – Italian American silent moving picture actor and heart-throb. Star of *The Sheik* (1921).

Annette Kellerman – champion Australian swimmer and swimsuit designer. Star of synchronised swimming-themed moving pictures. First woman to appear naked on film (*A Daughter of the Gods*, 1916). First woman to be arrested for wearing an "indecent" one-piece bathing suit (Boston, USA, 1907).

Dorothy L. Sayers – Christian apologist, playwright and mystery novelist, whose first novel, *Whose Body?*, was published in New York in 1923. Literary heroine of the author.

Dr Carl G. Jung – Swiss psychiatrist and one of the fathers of psychotherapy. His ground-breaking article "Personality Types" was published in New York in 1921.

Theda Bara – American silent moving picture actress, best known for her starring role in *Cleopatra* (1917).

The World of Poppy Denby
A Historical Note

Mimi Yazierska, the young Jewish immigrant, first appeared when I was writing the second book in the *Poppy Denby Investigates* series, *Murder at the Old Vic Theatre.* Mimi was originally a maid in the house of the wealthy Moscow family who feature in book 2. However, I struggled to weave her story into the already complex narrative, so I decided to leave her out. Fortunately for her – and her newly created sister – she was given another chance in *Murder on Lexington Avenue.*

I was interested in contrasting the experiences of rich and poor refugees and how the privilege of wealth and social connections can make the journey to safety far easier for one group than another. At the time of writing that book – and this – I was assailed with images of refugees fleeing the modern-day civil war in Syria. The wealthiest are able to buy air tickets out, the less well off, a spot in an inflatable raft, and the very poorest have to stay where they are or flee on foot and be housed in refugee camps.

I have an emotional connection to immigrants and immigration because my parents immigrated to South Africa when I was ten – and life was not easy as an "outsider". I now live in England, and here it is my South African husband who is an immigrant.

Those readers who have read *Murder at the Old Vic Theatre* will know that the early 1920s, like today, was a period of mass migration, when people from the war-torn countries of Eastern Europe and the Russian Empire tried to find a safe place to call home. And then, like now, countries on the receiving end of migration, like Britain and the USA, held public debates on how many more people they could or should receive. I was fascinated to read about the American Immigration Restriction Act of 1921. In that act quotas were put on immigrants from different countries, with some countries of origin considered less desirable than others. I'm sure I don't have to point out the parallels with what is happening now. In addition, fuelled by the popular theory of eugenics, which aimed to "purify" the bloodline of the population, there were other restrictions (pre-dating the 1921 act). People with physical illness or disability, mental health issues (which were frequently confused with a simple lack of education), communist sympathies or morally questionable behaviour were regularly denied entry to the United States.

Since conceiving the character of Rollo Rolandson as a New York expat I knew that at some stage he was going to take his protégé to visit his home town. As a young journalism student in the late 1980s I was fed on a steady diet of *New York Times* articles as examples of excellent reportage and design. So for me the *Times* had always held an exalted position. Oh, what I would have done to work on that newspaper! But my life has taken me in another direction. Poppy, however, still had a chance – and I gave it to her!

So we have Poppy and her friends travelling to New York first class and Mimi and Estie in steerage. Both have problems getting into America, but both eventually succeed. And of course, because this is a Poppy Denby mystery, their paths inevitably cross.

As mentioned in my acknowledgments I am deeply indebted to Professor Vincent Cannato of the University of Massachusetts, Boston. Professor Cannato's book, *American Passage: The history of Ellis Island*, was invaluable in my research, and he was gracious enough to personally respond to various queries. He very kindly helped me decipher an original 1921 ship's manifest, which I used in the scene with Aunt Dot being interviewed by the immigration official. I would, however, like to point out that the people-smuggling storyline in *Murder on Lexington Avenue* is entirely fictional. While no doubt some illegal immigrants did slip through, on the whole Ellis Island ran a tight ship. This is a story of what might have happened to two illegals if they had managed to get through the back door.

My re-creation of life on the *Olympic* was helpfully aided by some wonderful original film footage from 1922, which readers can find on my Poppy Denby website, www.poppydenby.com, under "locations". Poppy and Delilah's dresses were based on originals in the Victoria and Albert Museum fashion archive.

As always in the Poppy Denby books, I have tried to include as much historical fact as I can, without overshadowing the fictional tale. The news stories you read of in *Murder on Lexington Avenue*, apart from the main story with Poppy and her friends, are all original articles from the 1921 archive. The *New York Times* publicity department was very helpful in this regard and pointed me in the direction of additional resources.

The radio broadcast of *The Wolf* is also based on fact. Both the Lyric Theatre in New York and radio drama expert, Professor Richard Hand of the University of East Anglia, were very helpful in helping me track down original material. There is some debate as to whether the first radio drama broadcast was in 1921 or 1922. In 1921 there was a broadcast of an audio track of the Broadway stage play *Perfect Fool*, but the first play that was especially recorded as a radio play was *The Wolf* in 1922, an adaptation by Edward Smith of the Eugene Walter stage play of the same name (which was first staged at the Lyric Theatre, New York, in 1908). So I have taken some creative licence and merged these two broadcasts. Needless to say, Aunt Dot and Delilah were not part of the original cast.

Another piece of creative licence is linked to Chester's Speakeasy. In my research I discovered that the famous Chumley's Speakeasy was originally housed at 86 Bedford Street, Greenwich Village, which is where the term "doing an 86" came from. However, Chumley's, owned by Leland Chumley, only opened in 1926. So I decided to create a fictional speakeasy, Chester's, at the same address and brought the use of the term "86" forward. In addition, although the Rudolph Valentino film *The Sheik* was released in 1921, it didn't receive its London premiere until 1922. So Poppy and her friends got to see it early. Apart from these, I'm unaware of any other conscious historical discrepancies, and I hope you have enjoyed reading Poppy's latest adventure as much as I did writing it.

About the Author

Fiona Veitch Smith is a lover of Golden Age mysteries and historical fiction and has been shortlisted for the CWA Historical Dagger. She has worked as a journalist, a university lecturer and a communications manager, and mentors new novelists. She grew up in Northumberland, then spent her teens and twenties in South Africa. She now lives in Newcastle upon Tyne.

Visit http://www.poppydenby.com/ for more information about the author, and about the world of Poppy Denby.

Visit http://www.claravalemysteries.com/ for information about the world of Miss Clara Vale.

About Embla Books

Embla Books is a digital-first publisher of standout commercial adult fiction. Passionate about storytelling, the team at Embla publish books that will make you 'laugh, love, look over your shoulder and lose sleep'. Launched by Bonnier Books UK in 2021, the imprint is named after the first woman from the creation myth in Norse mythology, who was carved by the gods from a tree trunk found on the seashore – an image of the kind of creative work and crafting that writers do, and a symbol of how stories shape our lives.

Find out about some of our other books and stay in touch:

X, Facebook, Instagram: @emblabooks
Newsletter: https://bit.ly/emblanewsletter